INTRODUCING
KATIE MAGUIRE

KATIE MAGUIRE was one of seven sisters born
to a police Inspector in Cork, but the only
sister who decided to follow her father
into An Garda Síochána.

With her bright green eyes and short red
hair, she looks like an Irish pixie, but she is
no soft touch. To the dismay of some of her
male subordinates, she rose quickly through
the ranks, gaining a reputation for catching
Cork's killers, often at great personal cost.

Katie spent seven years in a turbulent
marriage in which she bore, and lost, a son –
an event that continues to haunt her. Despite
facing turmoil at home and prejudice at
work, she is one of the most fearless
detectives in Ireland.

Graham Masterton was a bestselling horror writer who has now turned his talent to crime writing. He lived in Cork for five years, an experience that inspired the Katie Maguire series. Visit katiemaguire.co.uk

ALSO BY GRAHAM MASTERTON

Ghost Virus

THE KATIE MAGUIRE SERIES

White Bones

Broken Angels

Red Light

Taken for Dead

Blood Sisters

Buried

Living Death

Dead Girls Dancing

Dead Men Whistling

Begging to Die

The Last Drop of Blood

THE BEATRICE SCARLET SERIES

Scarlet Widow

The Coven

GRAHAM
MASTERTON

THE LAST
DROP
OF
BLOOD

HEAD
of ZEUS

First published in the UK in 2020 by Head of Zeus Ltd

9 7 5 3 1 2 4 6 8

A catalogue record for this book is available from
the British Library.

ISBN (HB): 9781789544114
ISBN (XTPB): 9781789544121
ISBN (E): 9781789544107

Typeset by Divaddict Publishing Solutions Ltd

Printed and bound in Great Britain by
CPI Group (UK) Ltd, Croydon CRO 4YY

Head of Zeus Ltd
First Floor East
5–8 Hardwick Street
London EC1R 4RG

WWW.HEADOFZEUS.COM

'Is minic Cuma aingeal ar an Diabhal féin.'

'There's often the look of an angel on the Devil himself.'

IRISH PROVERB

The two gardaí were still struggling to pull the drunken traveller out of The Bridle's front door when they heard a *boom!* in the distance, like a bomb going off.

Garda Micky Phelan looked around and said, 'What in the name of Jesus was that?'

'Take your filthy crubeens off me, will you?' the traveller blurted at him. 'I'll report you for racial discrimification, you see if I don't.'

'Shut your bake, you're totally mouldy,' Garda Neasa O'Connor snapped at him. 'You know full well that you're barred from The Bridle. And the bang of benjy off of you, I swear – it's enough to make a maggot gag.'

Patrick the barman came out of the doorway, wiping his hands on his apron. 'Holy Mother of God, that was one hell of a wallop, wasn't it? What do you think it was?'

'No idea at all,' said Garda Phelan. 'It was way too loud for a crow banger.'

'You're right. It sounded to me like it came from those new houses – the ones over there at Sean-áit Feirme. Let's hope it wasn't a gas main blew up. They had a ball of trouble there with gas leaks only a couple of months ago. Bord Gáis was around there every other day.'

'For feck's sake, will you let go of me,' the traveller demanded. He must have been somewhere in his mid-fifties, with wild grey hair like a bramble patch and a face so crimson with drink that it was almost purple. He was wearing a tan leather jerkin and a soiled check shirt with his belly hanging out. The front of his baggy green corduroy trousers was dark with urine.

'We'll let you go, boy, as soon as we're sure that you're well on your way.'

'Okay, okay. My truck's over there, see, next to them rubbish bins.'

'If you think we're going to let you drive you must be Fecky the Ninth. Off you go. It's only a couple of kilometres down to your halting site. If you don't fall into too many ditches you should be able to get there before it starts pouring.'

Between them, Garda Phelan and Garda O'Connor managed to heave the traveller across the car park like a sackful of rotten potatoes. Once they had reached the pavement they released their grip on his arms and he stood in front of them for a few moments, swaying.

'Curse a God on you altogether, both of you,' he slurred, and let out a ripping two-tone burp. 'My cat's curse on you, too. I hope the Devil uses your spines for a ladder.'

With that, he went shuffling off down the Ballyhooly Road, occasionally stumbling, and at one point stopping and holding on to a telephone pole to steady himself.

'Maybe we should have given him a lift,' said Garda O'Connor.

'What, and have the back seat soaked in Pavee piss? No thanks.'

The traveller had just disappeared around the bend in the road when they heard another boom, not as loud as the first, but still enough to make them frown at each other and then turn around. About half a kilometre away, somewhere along the Ballincollie Road, a column of thick black smoke was piling up into the pale grey afternoon sky.

'That's no gas main,' said Garda Phelan. 'I don't know what the feck that is but we need to go and check it out so.'

The barman was still standing in the doorway as they hurried past him. He raised his hand and said, 'Thanks a million! Come along and have a scoop when you're off-duty! It's on the house!'

The two officers climbed into their squad car, slammed the doors, and sped out of The Bridle's car park with a squitter of tyres. They turned down Ballincollie Road, a narrow hedge-lined boreen that ran south-westwards towards Dublin Pike. As they passed the new housing estate at Sean-áit Feirme with its red-brick detached houses, they could see now that the smoke was rising from somewhere further down the road. There was scarcely any wind, and so the smoke was towering up above them, higher and higher like some mythical ogre.

About three hundred metres past Sean-áit Feirme they came around a curve and saw a burning car by the side of the road. It was blazing so fiercely that it had set the hedge alight, too, so that the blackthorn and hazel bushes were lit up with thousands of crackling orange sparks. The car was white, but already its roof and the upper part of its bodywork had been blackened by the fire. All its windows had shattered and inside it was an inferno, so it was impossible to see if there was anybody inside it.

A tractor had been parked about fifty metres away, blocking the road, and a farmer in a tweed cap and a black donkey jacket was standing close to it, holding a bucket and looking hopeless.

Garda Phelan pulled their squad car into the verge and both he and Garda O'Connor jumped out. Garda O'Connor opened the boot and lifted out their fire extinguisher, and as they walked quickly towards the burning car, Garda Phelan called the fire station at Ballyvolane and Garda headquarters at Anglesea Street, breathlessly giving them the car's location and its registration number.

The heat was so ferocious that they were still ten metres away from the flames when their faces began to feel scorched. They slowed down and stopped, and even backed away a little. All around the car, the asphalt road surface was bubbling up, and above its roof the air was rippling like a desert mirage.

Garda Phelan took the fire extinguisher from Garda O'Connor and started to spray dry powder towards the fire, waving it up and down over the top of the car. The flames subsided a little, but as soon as the extinguisher was empty they leapt up again, and now the car's tyres were blazing, too.

The farmer came bustling up to join them. His boots made a wobbling sound as he walked, and he shielded his face with his arm as he passed close to the car.

'Ah, Jesus. I never saw nothing like it. I tried chucking dirt over it, but it was like pissing in the wind, do you know what I mean?'

'Did you see it go up?' asked Garda Phelan.

'I didn't, no. I was on my way up to that field yonder to pick up some bales of hay and that's when I heard it. *Badoom!* like. I drove back down the hill as fast as I could but by that time it was raging away already. I could see that there was a feller sitting behind the wheel but he was flames all over and I couldn't get nearly close enough to pull him out of there. I just pray to God that he didn't suffer too much.'

The farmer crossed himself and shook his head. In the distance – over the snapping and popping of the burning car – they could hear a siren. Ballyvolane fire station was only five minutes away, and there was always an engine there on standby, twenty-four hours a day. At least one more engine would probably be sent up from Cork city centre.

By the time the fire engine appeared, with its blue lights flashing, the flames had begun to die down, although the tyres were still smouldering and smoke was billowing out of the passenger compartment even thicker than before. Garda O'Connor tugged at Garda Phelan's sleeve and said, 'Look, Micky. You can just about see the driver. Mother of God, he's burned to a cinder.'

'Could be a she, like.'

'Not in a car like this. I doubt it. It's a Jaguar XJ6, isn't it, an old one? That's probably why we heard two explosions. It has the twin petrol tanks, one in each wing.'

'Okay, if you say so. You know a whole lot more about cars than I do, Neasa, but then my da didn't run a garage like yours did.'

Three firefighters had started spraying the car with copious streams of white foam, which rolled in puffballs across the road and clung to the hedges on either side. Noel Hogan, the station officer, strode over to Garda Phelan and Garda O'Connor, chunky and broken-nosed like a middleweight boxer and brusque as ever, with no time at all for 'what's the story?' or 'how're ye going on?'

'Totally gutted,' he said. 'Any notion how it happened?'

'Not a clue, Noel. Neasa and me were busy at The Bridle, slinging out this langered knacker who'd gawked all over the shop and then had the gall to call out for another pint of Murphy's. We *heard* it, though. One fecking great bang, and then another, but the second one not so loud. Neasa here reckons it has two fuel tanks, this car, and so maybe one went up after the other. Hard to say for sure, looking at the state of it now.'

The farmer came forward again, his hand raised like a boy in school. 'There's something I didn't tell you. When I heard the first *badoom*, like, there was another car stopped right in front of this one. It went shooting off straight away, though, so I didn't get much of a look at it.'

'What type of car? Any idea?'

'No, I couldn't tell you. It was a fair old size, though, do you know what I mean? One of your VSUs I'd say. Silver, or grey. But I couldn't say what make or nothing like that. Maybe a Toyota, or a Range Rover – something like one of them.'

'And which direction did it go in?'

'That way... down towards Ferncarrig.'

Two of the firefighters approached them now. One of them took off his helmet and tucked it under his arm.

'There's only the one occupant, sir,' he told Station Officer Hogan. 'Still strapped in his seat belt. If he had any ID on him I'd say it's been thoroughly incinerated, along with him.'

'Well, I've already called in the reg number, so we may find out who he is in a minute or two,' said Garda Phelan. 'I'll be after calling in a description of that other vehicle, too – the SUV. It could be that somebody spotted it going through Ferncarrig, especially if it was speeding along real quick. You never know.'

The five of them walked towards the blackened wreckage of the Jaguar, although Garda Phelan turned around to the farmer and said, 'If you don't mind staying back, sir. I'll be taking a statement from you later so.'

'I've seen burned bodies before,' the farmer protested. 'My cousin worked at the Rocky Island crematorium.'

Despite saying that, he held back as Garda Phelan, Garda O'Connor and Station Officer Hogan approached the car.

Both of its rear wings had been blown upward in tatters, so that it looked as if a monstrous crow had landed on it.

'You were spot on about them two petrol tanks, Neasa,' said Garda Phelan.

A stooped figure was sitting in the driver's seat, charred completely black. From its apparent height, it was more likely than not to be a man. He was wearing an epaulette of foam on each shoulder and a foam wig on top of his head, which was gradually dripping down on each side, where his ears had been. He was still wearing steel-rimmed spectacles, although the heat had melted the plastic lenses so that they were drooping down from the bottom of the frames like teardrops.

For almost half a minute, none of the officers spoke. Then Station Officer Hogan turned to the firefighters and said, 'Give it all a while to cool off, like. Then haul the sheet over it. It looks like rain's on the way.'

Garda Phelan's phone rang. He walked away to answer it, one finger in his ear to drown out the roaring noise of the fire engine.

'Okay, yes, I have you,' he said. Then, 'You're not codding me, are you? Jesus. Okay. Well, we can't say for sure if it's him, the state he's in. Totally, yes. Clonakilty black pudding isn't in it. No, not yet. But okay, that's grand altogether. Thanks a million, Josh.'

He came back to join Garda O'Connor and Station Officer Hogan.

'It's a Jaguar XJ6 all right, V12, first registered in 1992 to Mr Sean Buttivant. Ownership was transferred in 1998 to Mr Garrett Quinn, and the car hasn't been re-registered since then to anybody else.'

'Not *the* Garrett Quinn?' said Garda O'Connor. She looked back at the blackened corpse sitting behind the

Jaguar's steering wheel with an expression of both horror and disbelief.

'That's your man. The Honourable Mr Justice Garrett Quinn, of the Central Criminal Court, may he rest in peace. Always supposing that's him, of course.'

'Well – he has the wig, like,' said Station Officer Hogan, just before the lump of foam finally slid off the top of the corpse's head and into his lap.

2

Katie and Kyna were passing Rathcormac on the main M8 road back to Cork city when drops of rain started to measle their windscreen.

'At least it held off for the burial,' said Kyna.

Katie didn't answer. She was still feeling that she had dreamed the funeral they had attended at Caherelly Graveyard in Limerick. She had loved Conor so much that it had been impossible for her to think it had really been him inside the pale oak coffin that had been lowered into the ground right in front of her feet. Him – or what had been left of him after he had blown himself up.

Over a hundred mourners had come to the service, including Conor's former wife, Clodagh, although Clodagh had been dressed in grey rather than black, with a white lily in her lapel, as if to show she wasn't altogether sorry that he was dead.

Most of the mourners had been relatives or friends from the ISPCA or people whose stray or stolen dogs Conor had found during his career as a dog detective. Katie had thought it was sadly appropriate that he was being buried not far from the grave of Dolores O'Riordan, the singer from the Cranberries. Her 'Dreams' had been one of Conor's favourite songs: *The person falling here is me.*

The rain fell harder and harder, so that Katie had to switch the windscreen wipers to beat backwards and forwards as fast as they would go. There was hardly any other traffic on the road, and they drove for several kilometres without seeing any other cars at all, which increased Katie's feeling of desolation.

Kyna must have sensed how she was feeling, because she reached across and gave her thigh a gentle squeeze.

Katie's phone played *Mo Ghille Mear*, my gallant hero, which she had first used as her ringtone when she and Conor had started living together. She saw that it was a call from Detective Patrick O'Donovan, so she passed her phone over to Kyna.

'Patrick? This is DS Ní Nuallán. Herself is driving at the moment.'

She listened, and then she said to Katie, 'He's apologizing for ringing you, because he knows you've been to Conor's funeral. But he says there's something you need to know urgent-like. Like, *pure* urgent-like.'

'Go on, then, if it's that urgent. What is it?'

Kyna listened again, frowning, and then she said, 'Holy Saint Rita.'

'Come on, tell me,' said Katie. 'Don't keep me in suspense.'

Kyna raised her hand to indicate that she was still listening. 'Where? Okay. And the two of them are still there, O'Connor and Phelan? All right, Patrick. I have you. We'll see you there so. Well, yes – I'll have to ask her, of course.'

'Ask her what?' said Katie, as Kyna handed her phone back.

'Gardaí O'Connor and Phelan have just attended a car that was on fire on the road between White's Cross and Dublin Pike. The fire brigade have put it out, but the driver's still inside it. He was burned to death.'

'Was there anybody else in the car, apart from him?'

'Not so far as we know. There's a witness, apparently, and if anybody else had escaped from the car before it blew up he would have seen them. He saw another vehicle, though, an SUV, which drove off quick as soon as the car caught fire.'

'Is Patrick going up to White's Cross himself?'

'Yes, with Sean Begley and Padragain Scanlan. And of course Bill Phinner's sending up a forensic team, too.'

'So what's so desperately urgent?'

'Well, it depends on who the driver is. He's too badly burned to make an identification on the spot, like. But the car's an old Jaguar that's registered to Mr Justice Garrett Quinn.'

'*What?*'

'That's what he said. Mr Justice Garrett Quinn.'

'How can that be? Justice Quinn's supposed to be in court this afternoon. He's due to be handing down the sentence to Donal Hagerty.'

'If that's him in the car there's no chance of that.'

'Mother of God,' said Katie. 'Where did you say this car was? White's Cross?'

'That's right. On the Ballincollie Road, not far from The Bridle.'

'Ring Patrick back. Tell him to get in touch with the court office manager and find out if Justice Quinn has showed up yet.'

'He's already done that, ma'am. There's no sign of him yet, although the sentencing isn't due till three.'

'Right. Let's go and take a look at this car. If we turn off at Killalough Cross it isn't too far.'

Katie put her foot down and they began to speed at more than 100 kph into the lashing rain. Kyna sat silent for a moment, but then she said, 'Are you sure you want to do this? Sean can take care of it, no problem at all. And you've just laid Conor to rest.'

'I know. But it'll give me something to take my mind off it. And besides, I've known Justice Quinn since before I was promoted. If it *is* him – it'll be a tragedy. He's kind, and he's fair, and he's the handsomest judge I've ever known.'

Kyna said nothing, but sat with her hands in her lap as they turned off at Killalough Cross and drove down the winding roads that would take them to the scene of the burned-out car.

They arrived at the same time as Assistant Chief Fire Officer Matthew Whalen, and parked right behind his red Ford Ranger. As they were climbing out of their car into the rain, a second fire engine came down the boreen, its blue lights flashing, although it was obvious now that it wouldn't be needed. The burned-out car had been draped over with a large grey tarpaulin and the first-responding firefighters were standing around it, shuffling their feet, dripping wet and subdued.

Katie lifted her shiny black raincoat out of the back seat. It had a pointed hood and Conor had always told her that it made her look like one of the witches of Islandmagee. Kyna's yellow anorak had a hood, too, with a furry surround. They caught up with Matthew Whalen, and as they did so, Garda Phelan and Garda O'Connor got out of their car, where they had been sheltering, and Station Officer Hogan came over, too.

'So, what's the story?' asked Katie.

'It looks like both petrol tanks went up, one after the other,' said Station Officer Hogan. 'We'll have to see what the fire investigation fellows have to say about it, of course, and your technical experts. As a general rule, though, almost all spontaneous vehicle fires start in the engine compartment, not the petrol tank.'

'Meaning that you don't think this was spontaneous?'

'Like I say, we'll have to wait for Cumann Imscrúdaitheorí Dóitéan to check it out. But I'd bet money that this fire was started deliberate-like.'

'Detective O'Donovan said that a witness saw another vehicle here, just before it blew up.'

'That's right, ma'am,' said Garda O'Connor. 'That farmer standing over there by his tractor. A grey or silver SUV, that's what he said it was. We're going to be showing him pictures of various vehicles to see if he can narrow it down a bit.'

'O'Donovan also told me that this car's registered to Justice Garrett Quinn. Have you been able to tell if it's him who was driving?'

'We haven't been able to identify the driver for sure. We didn't want to touch him before the technical experts, do you know what I mean. There's an iPhone lying on the floor in front of the passenger seat, but its screen is all shattered, like, and again we didn't want to touch it in case we messed up any forensics.'

Katie turned back to Station Officer Hogan. 'I'd like to take a look at the driver.'

'He's a bit on the burnt side, ma'am, as you can imagine.'

'I've seen worse.'

'Okay, then,' said Station Officer Hogan. 'Lads – can you be after lifting up that tarp so that DS Maguire can take a sconce at the body?'

Two of the firefighters raised the wet tarpaulin and folded it noisily over the roof of the burned-out car. Katie approached it, walking stiffly, and then stood looking for almost half a minute at the carbonized figure sitting behind the steering wheel. His skin had been burned away, so that his muscles were exposed and ruptured, all bobbly and black, as if he had been roughly sculpted out of lumps of coal. His eye sockets were empty and his brown teeth were bared in a wolfish snarl.

The interior of the car was skeletal. All that remained of the seats was their metal framework and the shiny walnut fascias had been blistered and charred. Katie noticed that the driver's right hand was still resting on the steering wheel, almost casually.

She stepped right up close to the driver's door. She had already seen what she had been dreading she would see, but she wanted to make absolutely sure. There was no question about it. The carbonized man was Justice Garrett Quinn. She crossed herself and whispered, 'Please, Lord, grant him eternal rest.' Then she turned away, tugging her hood down low so that Station Officer Hogan and the rest of the firefighters wouldn't see that her eyelashes were crowded with tears.

Kyna came up to her. 'Are you all right, ma'am?'

'Yes, thank you, Kyna. Grand altogether.'

'You're not, though.'

'Why are you always so perceptive? No, I'm not.'

They walked back to their car together. They had almost reached it when two more cars arrived, as well as a white Transit van from the Technical Bureau. Detective Sergeant Sean Begley and Detective Padragain Scanlan climbed out of the first car, while Detective O'Donovan climbed out of the second.

'How's it going, ma'am?' asked Detective Sergeant Begley. He was wearing a camel-coloured duffel coat that was far too tight for him because he had regained almost all the weight he had lost before Christmas, and a flat brown tweed cap that resembled a large cowpat. Detective Scanlan was looking tired but as pretty as ever. She had grown her blonde hair longer and pinned it back in a tight French pleat.

'It's Justice Quinn all right,' said Katie. 'He's been burned beyond any facial identification, but I recognize the ring that he's wearing.'

'Really?' said Detective Sergeant Begley.

'It's a claddagh band, Sean. White and yellow gold. There's only one exactly like it, and it's his.'

Matthew Whalen had come up to join them. Katie said, 'I've just been telling DS Begley that there's no doubt at all. Our victim is Justice Quinn. He's wearing a claddagh band that I know he never takes off, and it's unique.'

'Holy Saint Joseph,' said Detective O'Donovan. 'I'm fierce surprised it didn't melt, like, you know what I mean?'

Matthew Whalen shook his head. 'If it's gold, it wouldn't have done. Gold doesn't melt below one thousand and sixty-four degrees Celsius – not your eighteen-carat gold, any road. The hottest temperature that we've ever recorded in a burning test vehicle is nine hundred degrees.'

'Don't tell me they persuaded some gombeen to sit inside a burning car holding a thermometer,' said Detective Sergeant Begley, but Kyna immediately gave him a look that told him this wasn't the time to make jokes. Katie had turned her head away so that she could wipe her eyes with the back of her hand, and both Detective O'Donovan and Detective Scanlan had clearly realized from her tone of voice that she was distressed.

She wasn't about to tell them why she had been able to identify Justice Quinn's ring – not yet, anyway, and even then she wouldn't tell them the whole story. Briefly, a long time ago, shortly after she had been promoted to inspector, she and Garrett Quinn had been close. That claddagh band meant what all claddagh bands are meant to signify, an affection and a friendship that will last as long as life.

3

Thomas O'Flynn was sitting in the back bar of The Weavers with his latest girlfriend and three of his henchmen when Billy Hagerty came in to tell him that his brother's sentencing hearing had been postponed.

'So why's that, then?'

'I haven't a baldy. I asked them at the court but they wouldn't tell me. They said it may be a couple of days now before they tell him how long he's going down for, do you know.'

'That's a fecking pain in the arse. I was told that it was all going to be over by this afternoon, for definite.'

The Weavers was a small run-down pub on a steep corner of Gerald Griffin Street in Blackpool, on the north side of Cork city, with dark oak-panelled dados and faded photographs of 1960s' hurling heroes clustered on the walls. A peat fire was sullenly smoking in the corner, with a damp mustard-coloured water spaniel lying in front of it.

Thomas O'Flynn was the smartest man in there. He was wearing a shiny grey three-piece suit from Gentleman's Quarters, with a high-collared white shirt and a black-and-white St Nick's GAA tie. His face, though, was the kind of face that might suddenly appear out of nowhere in a nightmare. Underneath a thinning blond comb-over he was white as chalk, with sharp triangular cheekbones, a long, pointed nose and a narrow jaw that almost seemed to go on for ever until it was suddenly squared off at the end. His eyes were so small and squinched that it looked almost as if he didn't have eyes at all, although he had tangled blond eyebrows, which rose and fell as he talked, especially when he was angry, or threatening, so that he didn't need his eyes to convey how he felt.

Billy Hagerty pulled out a chair and sat down on the opposite side of the table. He was a short, bulky man with a shaved head and he looked even bulkier in his bronze puffer jacket.

'I tell you – they should've given Donal a fecking medal for offing that Micky Riordan, not fecking charged him.'

'Oh, yeah?'

'I mean, Christ on a bicycle, he was only doing what the cops should've done, donkey's years ago. When Jimmy the Nixer and Aodghan got shot and dumped in the river, did the cops lift Micky Riordan then? They must've known for sure who'd done it, but they didn't even haul him in and ask him what he'd had for breakfast.'

'Fair play to you, Billy,' said Thomas, lowering his eyebrows. 'But your Donal overstepped the mark by way too far when he did for Micky's missus and his two little wains as well. If he'd taken out Micky alone – well, maybe the razzers might have looked on him a sight more lenient, like, or even turned a blind eye.'

'It was self-defence, like. He didn't do it for choicer.'

'Oh, yeah. Self-defence against a nine-year-old girl and a lad of six, and their mammy, and Donal with nothing at all to protect himself but a couple of fully loaded Glocks.'

'He was worried they'd be witnesses, Thomas, and he was pure sorry about it afterwards. He even went to confession.'

'Well, I suppose that might have done some good, because it's a miracle that the razzers never connected him to me. And any road it's too late now. They can't be unkilled, and I've done as much as I can to make the judges go easy on him. We'll just have to wait and see now what kind of a sentence they come up with.'

'Hey, Tommy – I'll tell you what *you* can give *me*,' put in Thomas O'Flynn's girlfriend, in a throaty voice.

'Not in here, Muireann. Not in front of the lads, like. You'll be giving them all heart attacks.'

'Oh, get out of here, Tommy. I didn't mean that. I'd like another Bertha's Revenge, that's all, but with a rake more ice this time.'

Muireann was at least fifteen years younger than him, with a jet-black fringe and crimson plumped-up collagen lips and false eyelashes like two straggly blackbirds, although one of her eyelashes was starting to flap loose. She was wearing a tight red woollen dress, short and low-cut, and a Celtic moon pendant was abseiling deep into her cleavage. Thomas had bumped into her about two months ago in the Zombie Lounge and taken her back to his house that night for several hours of strenuous but silent sex, punctuated only by grunts. Since then she had stayed with him and followed him almost everywhere. He didn't even know where she lived, and he didn't actually care.

'Haven't you had enough?' Thomas asked her. 'What's that, your fourth? Next thing I know you'll be decorating my keks again.'

'Come on, Tommy. Don't be so tight. I've such a throat on me today, I don't know why.'

Thomas looked across at Billy Hagerty. 'Are you having one, boy?'

'A Vitamin G will do me, thanks.'

Thomas nodded to one of his three henchmen, who had been sitting close together and arguing among themselves about which horses to back in the bumper races at Leopardstown this weekend. They could have been mistaken for triplets, these three, because they were all wearing black leather jackets and they all had floppy long-top hair shaved up at the sides, and beards, and snake tattoos wriggling out from under their collars.

'Same all round, Darragh,' said Thomas. 'And a pint of plain for Billy.'

The young man was on his way to the bar when his phone rang. He answered it while he indicated to Lenny the barman by pointing his finger that he wanted refills all round and a pint of Guinness.

Suddenly, in a stage whisper, he said, 'You *wha*'? Stop the lights, boy! Serious? Holy feckin' Mary!'

He held out his phone to Thomas. 'It's Willie. He's just heard it on the radio, like. Judge Quinn's dead. He's been killed in a car accident.'

'You're *codding* me,' said Thomas, but he raised his hand to show that he wouldn't take the phone. He never carried a phone, not even a burner or a stealth phone, because he was convinced that the Gardaí could still track his whereabouts and listen in to his calls. His philosophy was that if they didn't know where he was and they didn't know what he'd been talking about, they couldn't lift him and they couldn't prove what he was planning to do next.

'Yeah, no. I'll tell him,' said Darragh. 'See you later, boy. Okay.'

'When did this happen?' asked Thomas.

'This morning sometime, that's what Willie said. Somewhere up by Dublin Pike. There was no other cars involved. The cops are looking for a grey or a silver SUV, though, because whoever was driving that might have been a witness.'

'No other cars involved?' said Thomas. His long, thin jaw slowly rotated as he began to grind his teeth. He took several deep breaths and his eyes seemed to disappear altogether. Everybody else at the table leaned away from him, almost as if they were worried that he might physically explode and spatter them all.

'*No other cars involved?* I'll fecking murder that eejit O'Malley! I'll fecking strangulate him myself and throw him off the Shakey Bridge. I can't believe it! I cannot fecking *believe* it! After all the fecking trouble I took, Billy! All that fecking wheedling and needling! And there's Quinn due to hand down your brother's sentence this afternoon!'

'Maybe it *was* just an accident, Tommy,' said Muireann. 'You know, like what Darragh said.'

'Be whist, will you, you stupid slag. It was fecking O'Malley, it must have been. What was Quinn doing up at Dublin Pike when he lives in Tivoli? "Have a last word," that's what I told O'Malley. "Give him a final reminder." But polite, like. *Polite.*'

Thomas sat simmering while everybody else at the table finished their drinks in quick, uncomfortable gulps.

After a few minutes Thomas swallowed the last dregs of his Murphy's, and his Paddy's chaser, banging both glasses down on the table so hard that everybody jumped, and stood up.

'Right, lads,' he said, 'we're up to Farranree to have a word with O'Malley. I want to know exactly what kind of an "accident" it was that Quinn was killed in. The razzers could well be after coming around looking for us before too long, asking awkward questions, do you know? And how can you say that you don't know nothing about something unless you know what that something is that you don't know nothing about – am I right?'

Billy was zipping up his puffer jacket, and blinked. 'You're right,' he agreed. Then, 'Do you want to say that again?'

'Just get going, Billy. I'll have Darragh ring you later when we've found out a bit more.'

'See you later, men!' called out Lenny the barman as they made their way to the pub's front door. Thomas lifted his hand but didn't answer.

Billy was the first to step into the street. It was pelting now, and the rainwater was running in rib-like patterns down the middle of Gerald Griffin Street and gushing out of the blocked-up shores. The clouds were so low that they looked as if they were being ripped apart on the TV aerials like ragged grey sheets. A truck loaded with scaffolding was grinding slowly down the hill, and at the same time a bronze Honda Accord was coming up the hill towards The Weavers, with its headlights full on.

The Honda slowed down as it approached the corner of Cathedral Walk. As it came level with the pub door, its rear nearside window was lowered, and there were two suppressed gunshots, like loud sneezes, followed by a third. Billy danced a little jig and then tumbled sideways on to the pavement, ending up flat on his back with his arms spread wide. Thomas had been following him out of the door but he threw himself backwards, colliding with Muireann, and then he dived to the floor, knocking over the umbrella stand.

Darragh pushed Muireann to one side and leapt out of the door, yanking a pistol out of his black leather jacket. He pointed it up the hill, but it was too late now. The Honda was already turning the corner into Cathedral Road, its red brake lights flaring for an instant before it disappeared.

Darragh turned around. Billy was still lying on his back on the pavement and dark red blood was streaming from his head and down the hill. Thomas peered out of the pub door and when he saw that the Honda had gone he stepped outside.

'Muireann, stay there, girl,' he told her. 'You don't want to be seeing none of this.'

Thomas and his henchmen gathered around Billy, looking down at him in silence as if they were distant relatives who had just arrived at a wake. One shot had hit him in the right side of his mouth, so that his jawbone was hanging to one side, with all his teeth in it, most of them filled with silver amalgam. A second shot had hit him about three centimetres above the left eye. The entry wound was nothing more than a neat circle, but the hollow-point bullet had burst inside his head and cracked open the back of his skull. His custard-coloured brains were slowly sliding on to the paving stones, mingled with blood.

The third shot had punctured the front of his puffer jacket, slightly to the right, so that it had probably penetrated his liver.

Lenny the barman appeared in the doorway. 'I've rung the guards, like. I told them that we'll be needing an ambulance, too.' He peered over at Billy and said, 'Jesus. Is he dead?'

'Of course not,' said Thomas. 'He's having a bit of a snooze, that's all. What the feck does it look like?'

'What do we do now, boss?' asked Milo, the second of his henchmen, anxiously gnawing at his thumbnail. On the opposite pavement, a small crowd of curious onlookers was gathering, but none of them ventured across the road because they could quite plainly see that Billy was beyond any mortal assistance.

'We wait here until the razzers arrive, and when the razzers arrive and ask us what we saw we tell them the truth. We saw nothing and we know nothing. We don't even know who this is, who's been shot.'

'I know who he is,' said Milo. 'He's Billy Hagerty.'

'Did he ever show you his birth certificate?'

'Well – no, of course not.'

'So how do you know that it's really him?'

'I don't.'

'So that's what you tell the razzers. You don't know who he is. End of story.'

Milo was about to say something else when he saw the expression on Thomas's face, and this time Thomas's eyes were about as wide open as he had ever seen them, like the heads of two steel nails.

'No, you're right, boss. I don't know who he is at all. In fact I never even saw him before, even when we had a scoop together in The Constellation last Friday.'

'God, give me strength,' said Thomas, and took a deep breath. He couldn't hear sirens, but flashing blue lights were being reflected from the shop windows all along Gerald Griffin Street, as two Garda squad cars came speeding down towards them.

4

Katie had intended to drive straight home to Cobh after Conor's funeral, so that she could take her Irish setter, Barney, and her red-and-white setter, Foltchain, out for a walk up to the tennis club. Conor had always made such a fuss of them, and whenever she arrived back at Carrig View alone it was clear that they wondered where he was, but how could she explain his death to two dogs?

After what had happened to Garrett Quinn, though, there was no question that both she and Kyna would have to return to Garda headquarters. Before she had left Ballincollie Road, she had already put in a call to the Anglesea Street control room and told Sergeant Murphy to check his CCTV screens to see if he could trace how Garrett's car had ended up at White's Cross. To reach the courthouse, he should have been driving directly down to the city centre from his home in Tivoli by way of the Lower Glanmire Road, which ran westwards along the north bank of the River Lee. White's Cross was more than six kilometres due north.

Katie had also spoken briefly with the Garda press officer, Mathew McElvey, telling him to arrange a media conference at 5:15, well in time for RTÉ to feature a report about Garrett on the *Six One News*. A newsflash that he had been fatally injured had already been given out on Cork FM, but she intended to announce only that he had been involved in a traffic incident, and that a Garda investigation was ongoing. She was not going to say that he had been cremated as he sat inside his car.

She parked in her usual place behind the Garda station, but before they went inside she said to Kyna, 'I think we need to pay a visit to Stephen Herlihy first. I'd like to know when they're going to reschedule Donal Hagerty's committal hearing. Apart from giving him my condolences.'

They crossed over to the new criminal courthouse. The administrative offices were facing the street, in renovated red-brick buildings from the Model School of 1864, with a sixty-foot campanile, in which the older pupils used to be taken up to look at the stars. A squarish modern limestone block had been erected behind these buildings to house the courtrooms and the custodial suite and the judges' accommodation. Inside the pale wood-panelled interior, still smelling of fresh varnish and echoing with footsteps, they found Stephen Herlihy, the court office manager, standing in the corridor talking to two of his clerks.

'DS Maguire,' he greeted her in his baritone voice. 'I've been expecting you so.'

He was a large man, barrel-chested in his sober black suit, with wiry grey hair. He reminded Katie of Robert Mitchum – big and slow-spoken and very masculine – and yet she knew that he had reason to be guarded. In the short time that she and Garrett Quinn had been close, she had learned a lot about the workings of the court, and who owed favours to whom, and why.

'We're not five minutes back from White's Cross,' said Katie, clasping Stephen Herlihy's large right hand between both of hers. 'It was a fierce shock, I can tell you, Stephen. The scene itself was bad enough anyway, but it put my heart crossways when I realized who it was. I just came over to offer you my sympathy. This is Detective Sergeant Ní Nuallán, by the way.'

Stephen Herlihy nodded at Kyna and then he said, 'What happened exactly? Was it a crash?'

'We don't know for sure yet. So far as we know, there was no other vehicle involved, but of course we're still waiting for Bill Phinner to tell us for definite.'

'It's a tragedy. A desperate, desperate tragedy. And such a brilliant career ahead of him. I reckon he could have been a Supreme Court justice one day, or even Chief Justice.'

'He was the kindest judge I've ever known,' put in one of the clerks. 'He never forgot to thank me at the end of every hearing, and he had flowers sent to me on my birthday.'

Katie said, 'I know it's kind of previous, Stephen, but I need to ask you what arrangements you'll be making for Donal Hagerty's sentencing. We're holding a media conference in a couple of hours' time, and the press will be wanting to know. Let's face it, it's been the most publicized trial of the year, easy.'

'Well, of course Mr Justice Quinn had been presiding jointly over the Hagerty trial with Ms Justice O'Rafferty, on account of it being so serious. But I've already had a conversation with Mr Justice Kelly and he assures me that it will be perfectly legal and proper for Ms Justice O'Rafferty to hand down the sentence by herself. She told me that she and Mr Justice Quinn had already agreed on a prison term, and what length it should be, and she has emails and notes to prove it, so there won't be any necessity for a retrial.'

'So when will he be sentenced now?'

'After Mr Justice Quinn's funeral, whenever that is. We want to show some respect.'

'That's kind of problematical. He still has to be given a forensic post-mortem.'

'You're not certain how he died?'

'It's a matter of routine, that's all. I'll let you know of course when we've had the results. In the meantime, though, I'll tell you what you can do for me. Can you prepare me a list of all the trials that Justice Quinn conducted over – say – the past two years. Also a list of those defendants he convicted, and what fines or sentences he gave them.'

'Of course, yes. It's all in the court records.'

They were still talking when Justice O'Rafferty herself came walking along the corridor, wearing a long black belted trench coat and carrying a briefcase. She was about the same height as Katie, and in looks they could almost have been sisters, but she was chestnut-haired, not red like Katie, and she wore no make-up. As she came up to them, Katie could see by the puffiness of her eyes that she had probably been crying.

'Detective Superintendent Maguire, how are you?' she said.

'Shaken, Your Honour, like I'm sure you are – and like everybody else who knew Garrett.'

'His wife's been told? Orla?'

'She should have been, yes. As soon as he was identified I asked Superintendent Pearse to send officers around to his home address to tell her.'

'I tried twice to ring her myself, but she didn't pick up,' said Stephen Herlihy. 'I imagine she knew by then.'

'I suppose that's one blessing. At least she didn't have to hear about it on the news.'

Katie said, 'Do you have a couple of minutes to spare, Your Honour? There's one or two quick questions I'd like to ask you.'

Justice O'Rafferty glanced at Stephen Herlihy and then shrugged. 'Okay. But I'm meeting a friend at four at The Bookshelf, so I can't be too long.'

'Use my office,' said Stephen Herlihy.

Katie and Kyna and Justice O'Rafferty went into the court manager's office and sat down. Looking down on them was a benignly smiling portrait of The Honourable Mr Justice William O'Brien FitzGerald, a Corkman who had been Chief Justice of Ireland for only a year before his premature and unexpected death. Katie couldn't help thinking that Garrett hadn't even lived as long as him.

'So – what do you want to know?' asked Justice O'Rafferty. She kept looking around the office as if she were expecting to catch sight of something she had accidentally left there, like an umbrella, or a book, or a Brown Thomas shopping bag.

'You've been close to Justice Quinn for over four months now, during the course of the Hagerty trial. Did he ever give you any indication that he was concerned about his safety?'

'His safety? In what sense?'

'In the sense that the O'Flynn gang might have warned him that there would be a price to pay if he found Donal Hagerty guilty?'

'If they did warn him, he never said a word to me about it. I mean – as you know yourself – the O'Flynns would regularly come to court and sit in the public gallery and give us the evil eye. But no evidence was ever presented that Hagerty was a member of their gang, or that they had commissioned him to kill Michael Riordan.'

'If they hadn't, why were they taking such an interest?'

'I wouldn't know. And I certainly wasn't about to ask them.'

'They didn't approach *you*, then?'

'No.'

'All the same, Your Honour, don't you seriously suspect that the O'Flynns might have been behind it?' asked Kyna.

'Like, the O'Flynns and the Riordans have been feuding with each other since before Father Mathew gave up drinking. The last body count was thirteen – six O'Flynns and now seven Riordans, counting Michael.'

Justice O'Rafferty shrugged. 'Of course it's highly likely that they had a hand in it somewhere, even if they only supplied Hagerty with the murder weapon. But I can only make judgements on the evidence that's presented to me. Hagerty said word for word the same thing in court that he told you when you questioned him after his arrest. He shot Michael Riordan because Michael Riordan had cheated him over a seventeen-thousand-euro consignment of cocaine and cannabis.'

'What did Justice Quinn think about it?'

'Garrett? So far as he was concerned, there was no question about it at all. He was totally convinced that the O'Flynns had hired Hagerty. But unless Hagerty ratted on them, there was no way that anybody could prove it. *You* couldn't get him to admit it, could you – and in court the prosecution couldn't get him to admit it, either, even though they tried, God knows. Garrett said that it would have been a death sentence for Hagerty if he had. He said he wouldn't have lasted five minutes in prison before one of O'Flynn's cronies got to him with a razor blade or a sharpened toothbrush.'

'When exactly did Garrett say that?'

Justice O'Rafferty suddenly looked flustered, and blushed. 'He said it – I don't know. He said it over lunch, I think. I don't see what that has to do with it.'

'No, well. Fair play to you, Your Honour. I'm just interested. You and Justice Quinn must have discussed the trial, like, exhaustively between you. It would be helpful to know what he thought about it.'

'Yes, we discussed it in very great detail. For hours, in fact. Especially the killing of Saoirse Riordan and the two young Riordan children.'

'What did Garrett have to say about that? You don't mind me calling him "Garrett"? It sounds like you became good friends, as well as fellow judges.'

'Well, we did, yes,' said Justice O'Rafferty. She paused for a moment, and then, softly, she repeated, 'Yes.'

Kyna waited, saying nothing. Eventually Justice O'Rafferty looked up and said, 'He said that at least Saoirse would never know what it was like to lose a husband and the children would never know what it was like to lose a father.'

'What do you think he meant by that?' asked Katie.

'I don't know. I don't think he meant anything by it, to be honest with you. I think he was just – musing.'

There was a long silence between them. Although she had said that she needed to go to The Bookshelf to meet her friend, Justice O'Rafferty made no move to leave, but sat with her fingertips pressed lightly to her lips, as if she had forgotten that she was here, in the court manager's office, and was thinking about another place, and another time. Eventually, Katie said, 'We'll let you go then, Your Honour. We'll be in touch if we have any more questions. And of course we'll let you know the results of Garrett's post-mortem.'

Justice O'Rafferty gave a quick, bleak smile and stood up. She left the office without saying another word. After she had left, Katie said to Kyna, 'That was ruthless.'

'She couldn't have made it more obvious, though, could she? She loved him.'

'The poor woman's in shock, Kyna. She hasn't even had the time to start grieving yet.'

Kyna gave Katie a look that was part sympathetic but part acute, as if she were thinking, *Justice O'Rafferty isn't the only one, is she?*

Almost as soon as she had hung up her coat in her office, Chief Superintendent Brendan O'Kane rapped at her open door. Katie didn't turn around to acknowledge him, or say anything, but sat down at her desk and picked up the messages that her PA, Moirin, had left for her.

'Could I have a word with you, Katie?'

'Could I stop you?' she asked him, without looking up.

'It's a fierce shock about Justice Quinn, isn't it?' he said, slowly approaching her desk, but stopping before he came too close. 'Sean Begley told me that it was you who identified him.'

'It was, yes. He was wearing a claddagh band, which I'd seen him wearing in court. It was pure unusual, so that's how I knew.'

'Oh. Well, that was a stroke of good luck. Or bad luck, really, considering what happened to him. But at least you knew who he was. So what's the strategy?'

Katie still didn't raise her eyes to look at him. 'We're running through the CCTV to see if we can work out why he headed north instead of driving directly here to the courthouse. Cailin Walsh went along with the officers who broke the news to his wife, and she asked her what he might have been doing up there, but his wife had no idea at all.'

She paused, frowning at the paper that she had just picked up, and then she said, 'As soon as the technical experts have finished up at White's Cross, they'll be taking his remains to CUH for a post-mortem. I'll be after getting in touch

31

with Mary Kelley in a minute to see if she's free to do that. What's left of his car will be hauled off to Midleton for a full forensic examination. There was a witness who saw another vehicle at the scene when his car caught fire, a local farmer. He's been shown pictures of various SUVs and he thinks it might have been a Range Rover or a Land Cruiser. We'll be putting out an appeal for anybody else who might have noticed it.'

'Sean said it didn't look like an accident.'

'No, it didn't.'

'Do you have any possible suspects in mind? The O'Flynns would seem the most likely, don't you think?'

'The O'Flynns had a motive, admittedly, what with Donal Hagerty about to be sentenced. But Justice Quinn has sent down scores of criminals in his time on the bench. Hundreds, even. Any single one of them could have been harbouring enough of a grudge to want to get their revenge on him.'

'Yes, I suppose you're right. Do you know, once I had a sledgehammer thrown through my living-room window by some scuzzy drug-dealer that I'd arrested five years previous.' He was silent for a while, but looking at her intently. 'All right, Katie,' he said, at last. 'Keep me posted, won't you, if there's any developments?'

'I will of course.'

Katie continued to leaf through her messages, occasionally jotting down a note, and still she didn't raise her eyes.

Brendan glanced over his shoulder to make sure that Moirin couldn't hear him, even though her office door was open. Then he said, in a very low voice, 'Erm... about the other thing.'

Katie put down her pen and looked up at him. He could never stop looking handsome, with that dark wavy hair and those hawklike features and mischievous eyes, but what she had once found so amusing and attractive about him she now found shallow and insincere. She couldn't even stand the smell of his Boss aftershave.

'Have you... had any more thoughts about it?' he asked her.

'No, to be honest with you.'

'So you won't be taking it any further?'

'I don't know. I'm not sure I've even been able to come to terms with it yet.'

'Katie... I admit that I made a mistake. I misread the signs that you gave me.'

'What signs did I give you? I was totally wrecked. I wasn't even conscious, for the love of God.'

'But, you know – considering the past between us – you can scarcely blame me for thinking that you would have wanted it as much as I did.'

'Brendan, that was fourteen years ago, and in between times I've been married, and widowed, and lost a man that I dearly, dearly loved. Jesus – it wasn't four hours ago that I was throwing a handful of soil on to his coffin. And you want me to sit here now and think about that sordid thing you did to me and give you absolution?'

Brendan stood staring back at her, his hands by his sides, biting his lip. He looked more like a chastened schoolboy than a chief superintendent.

'Yes, okay, then, let's leave it for now,' he told her. 'But I hope that you'll find it in your heart to put it behind you and see it for what it was. An honest and genuine misunderstanding.'

On any other day, at any other time, Katie would have rocketed up out of her chair and given Brendan a blistering retort. Today, though, and now, she was grieving too deeply for Conor, and still numb from having seen Garrett sitting burned to a cinder in his Jaguar.

'I'll be discussing what to do with my solicitor first,' she said, almost as if she were talking to herself. 'Then I'll decide if I want to report it to the Ombudsman.'

'The Ombudsman? Oh, come on. You wouldn't do that, surely? It's just a personal matter between us, nothing to do with the GSOC.'

Katie was about to answer him when her phone rang. It was Superintendent Michael Pearse.

'Kathleen? We had a 112 call fifteen minutes ago from The Weavers, on Gerald Griffin Street. The barman reported a shooting and a fellow down. Killed stone dead, he was. Hickey and O'Dea were up at Fair Hill so they responded within only a couple of minutes, like. You're not going to believe this.'

'Go on, try me.'

'The victim is Billy Hagerty, Donal Hagerty's brother. They clear blew out his brains so he didn't stand a hope in hell.'

'Mother of God, Michael. Are you serious?'

'Oh, believe me, it gets even more complimicated than that. There were two eyewitnesses to the actual shooting, and you'd never guess in a million years who they were – Thomas O'Flynn and Muireann Nic Riada. Three of O'Flynn's heavies were there, too.'

'Thomas O'Flynn was there? And Muireann?' Katie covered her phone with her hand and said to Brendan, 'Billy Hagerty's been shot dead. And one of the people who saw it happen was Thomas O'Flynn.'

'Holy Jesus. The Riordans, it must have been,' said Brendan. 'The court had to put off Donal Hagerty's sentencing hearing, didn't they? I'll bet the Riordans decided to hand out some vigilante justice of their own.'

'Michael – did O'Flynn see who the shooter was?' Katie asked him.

'No. Well, at least he said that he didn't. But Muireann told O'Dea on the quiet that the shots were fired from a brownish Honda saloon. Just as they were leaving the pub, it slowed down and a fellow in the back seat fired three times. She said he had a scarf over his face so she couldn't identify him, and the Honda shot off so quick that she couldn't get the number. She couldn't tell O'Dea any more than that because – well, you know.'

'Sure, I have you. Thanks, Michael. Do we know where O'Flynn is now?'

'We've closed The Weavers of course and cordoned it off for now, but Muireann texted to say that he's gone down to Eugene's Lounge in Shandon Street and four more of his hard chaws have come to join him. He's probably holding a council of war.'

'Okay. I'll send Robert Fitzpatrick and Ronan Caffrey up to Eugene's right away to have a bit of a chat with him. Robert's known the O'Flynns for ever, Thomas and all the rest of the gang. I think he went to school with Aodhan O'Flynn.' She paused, and then she said, 'I imagine the media are on to this already.'

'They will be, yes. I've just had Mathew on the other line. But you're holding a press conference in about twenty minutes, aren't you?'

'Search me what I'm going to be saying to them, Michael. I mean, Jesus. This has been the darkest afternoon since the last eclipse of the sun.'

Katie laid her phone down. Brendan was still standing

there, watching her. She didn't try to read his expression because she didn't want to know what he was thinking and she wasn't interested in anything that he was going to say. On the evening she had been told that Conor had killed himself she had drunk far too much vodka. Brendan had driven her home to Carrig View, and after she had passed out, he had climbed on top of her, pulled down her thong and penetrated her. Gently, not violently, like a lover rather than a rapist, but it still amounted to rape. It was no excuse that they had been lovers for a few months while they were training at Garda college in Templemore. In any case, that relationship had finished abruptly when she had caught him cheating on her with her room-mate.

'Katie—' he began, but she picked up her phone again and stabbed out the number for Detective Inspector Robert Fitzpatrick.

When he answered, she said, 'Robert? Have you heard about Billy Hagerty being hit? You have? And you've heard that one of the witnesses was your old pal Thomas O'Flynn? I know, unbelievable. You couldn't make it up, like, could you? No. So how do you fancy a scoop with him, up at Eugene's?'

Brendan waited for a few moments while Katie was talking to Detective Inspector Fitzpatrick, but then he quietly turned around and left her office, raising his hand as he walked out of the door like Lieutenant Columbo, as if to say, *Do your worst, Katie – do your worst.*

5

The rain clouds had cleared away now, but it was growing dark, so Roisin was pushing Ita's go-car as fast as she could along the path beside the river. She hadn't wanted to come out, but Ita had been sick twice, and had a temperature, and so she had taken her along to the Dundanion Medical Centre in Blackrock. The doctor had given Ita a dose of phenobarbitone and now she was sleeping.

Roisin felt exhausted. Ita had woken up five or six times in the night, crying, and she had been grizzling all day, but Roisin had still had to go to Buckley's Dry Cleaners to pick up the latest bundle of dresses and jeans that she had to alter. When she had been expecting Ita, she had given up her job as a ground hostess for Ryanair. Now she survived on the money she made from sewing, her child benefit and her one-parent family payment.

She had celebrated her twenty-first birthday last week at the Pronto café, on her own. Her father and mother hadn't spoken to her since she had told them that she was going to have a baby – neither had her two brothers. Her boyfriend, Colm, had disappeared without trace as soon as her pregnancy test had proved positive. She didn't look twenty-one: more like sixteen. She was small and skinny with long dark-brown hair that was bundled up untidily under her beret. In her green woollen coat, she could have been a foundling or a schoolgirl on the hop.

She had almost reached Church Avenue when she saw old Peadar Ó Dálaigh walking towards her with his straggly white wheaten terrier, Póg. Peadar lived in the bungalow opposite hers in Sunnyside. His hair was as white and straggly as Póg's, and he was wearing a crumpled raincoat with sloping shoulders that made him look as if he had been clumsily wrapped up in brown paper. He even had knotted sisal string for a belt.

He stopped and whistled to Póg to stop, too.

'Roisin, how're ye going on, girl? I don't never normally see you out this time of the day.'

'Ita's been poorly, like, Peadar. I had to take her to the doctor.'

Peadar bent over and looked down at Ita, fast asleep with her thumb in her mouth. 'Every time I see her, d'ye know, I think of my little Sinéad. She was only two-and-a-half years old, Sinéad, when she passed away. It would be her forty-third birthday on Thursday next if the pneumonia hadn't taken her.'

'I expect God had a reason for wanting her back in Heaven,' said Roisin.

'Well, maybe you're right. But I wish He could've allowed us to enjoy her company a little longer than He did and given us the chance to show her how much we adored her. I still have her dolly at home, d'ye know, sitting on the back of my settee, smiling away like she thinks that little Sinéad will be trotting into the room one day to pick her up again and give her a cuddle.'

Roisin didn't know how to answer that. She laid her hand on Peadar's shoulder and gave him a rueful smile, but just as she did a chilly wind blew across the river, so that its silver-grey surface rippled, and the few remaining leaves in the trees along The Marina rustled anxiously.

'I'll have to be taking Ita back in the warm now, Peadar,'

she told him. 'Why don't you come over for a mug of scaldy tomorrow morning and we can have a bit of a chat, like?'

'That would be grand, Roisin. I'd like that. I don't think I've spoken to no one at all since Monday. Well, only to say "what's the craic?" to Dermot in the Menloe Stores.'

Póg let out a sharp impatient yip and Peadar limped off after him. Roisin gave a shiver and carried on pushing Ita's stroller along the path. The wind was gusting even harder now, and the river was slapping repeatedly against the steps where people sometimes tied up their boats.

She didn't see or hear the tall, thin man in the loose grey tracksuit who came running from the corner of Church Avenue towards her. Even if she had, she wouldn't have paid him much attention. Joggers were common along The Marina, along with dog walkers and anglers, although there wasn't much to catch in the Lee apart from grey mullet, and they'd been feeding off the sewer outlets.

As he came nearer, the man started to run faster. By the time he was less than ten metres away from her, he was running at full pelt. It was only when he had almost reached her that she heard the pattering sound of his footsteps and caught sight of him out of the corner of her eye.

With both of his hands extended straight in front of him, he slammed into Roisin's shoulder and into the handle of Ita's stroller, too. Roisin was so startled that she didn't cry out. Both she and the go-car were pitched sideways into the river and the next thing she knew she was gasping and floundering in freezing water and the go-car was sinking fast.

'Oh God, help me!' she screamed. 'I can't swim, somebody help me!'

She thrashed at the surface of the water, trying desperately to reach the go-car. She could see that Ita's pink-and-blue blanket was quickly becoming sodden, so that it was not only dragging the go-car downwards but tilting the handles forwards, beyond her grasp. Ita must still be sleeping, because she made no sound at all.

'*Help me! Help me!*' screamed Roisin again. '*My baby's going to drown! Help me!*'

She was kicking her legs and flailing her arms, but her coat was quickly becoming heavier and she kept swallowing mouthfuls of filthy cold water. She tried to scream again but all she could manage was a gargling splutter.

She went right under the water, and even though she kept her mouth tightly closed and tried to hold her breath, the shock of going under made her sniff, and she felt a nostrilful of water drop painfully into her lungs.

She kicked even more frantically, and surfaced, and when she lifted up her head and blinked the water out of her eyes, she saw to her horror that only one handle of Ita's go-car was still visible. She tried to strike out towards it, but she had almost no strength left, and her coat was weighing her down.

It was then, though, that she heard a hoarse voice shout out, 'Hold on, Roisin! Hold on, love! I'm coming for ye! Hold on!'

She turned her head and saw that Peadar was standing on the steps, and that he had stripped off his old brown raincoat and was tugging off his rushers.

'Keep on paddling there, girl! Keep on paddling!' he shouted. He balanced his way awkwardly down to the slippery bottom step with his arms held out wide. Then – after a moment's hesitation – he flopped himself into the water, chest first. Póg immediately came running across the grass and jumped into the water after him.

'Póg! Ye feckin' eejit! Get back out!' Peadar shouted at him. But Póg kept on bobbing up and down after him, and there was nothing Peadar could do. He came swimming towards Roisin, and even though he was old, and still wearing a thick cable-knit sweater, he swam with a strong, even breaststroke. He kept his head held high above the water, his white hair tangled and wet.

'Ita!' gasped Roisin. 'You have to save Ita!'

Peadar said nothing, but swam with four or five strokes towards the go-car's handle. He took hold of it, and then began to swim back towards the steps, tugging the submerged stroller after him.

Before she saw him reach the steps, Roisin went under again. Again she tried to hold her breath, pedalling her legs and flapping her arms up and down like a rain-soaked fledgling trying to fly, but this time the weight of her coat was too much for her, and she was numb with cold, and the water pulled her relentlessly down as if it were refusing to give her another chance to survive.

Her feet touched the riverbed, and her knees sagged. She made one last effort to kick herself upward, but her lungs felt as if they were going to burst apart and she took in a huge swallow of water. The pain in her chest was so intense that she let out a high-pitched bubbly scream and took in even more water. She had never imagined that drowning would hurt so much.

She sank slowly into the mud, which rose around her in billowing black clouds. As she fell back, her beret was lifted off and her long brunette hair spread out in a fan. Póg came floating down, too, his white fur barely visible in the gloom, and he settled down beside her, as if to keep her company in death.

6

Katie and Kyna were about to enter the conference room to give their media briefing when Detective Inspector Mulliken called out, 'DS Maguire! Ma'am!' and came hurrying along the corridor towards her.

'What's the story, Tony?' she asked him. 'I have the hungry wolves in there, waiting to be fed.'

'Francis O'Rourke has just called me. The Lee Pusher's been at it again.'

'You're not serious. Who is it this time?'

'A young woman and her wain in a buggy this time. The wain's been rescued but the young woman's missing presumed drowned. We don't yet have a name for her.'

'Oh, God help us. Where was this?'

'Along The Marina, about halfway between the park and the rowing club. That's the second time now he's pushed somebody in from there, and that makes it seven he's pushed in altogether.'

'Who rescued the wain?'

'Some auld wan about eighty. They've taken both him and the wain to the Mercy. The paramedics said they were haunted to be alive, the both of them.'

'What about the young woman?'

'There's no sign of her yet but we've contacted the Search and Rescue to see if they can find her body and recover it. If they can't manage it we'll call the Navy.'

'Any other witnesses?'

'None, so far as I know. Superintendent Pearse has sent

Sergeant O'Farrell out there, along with half a dozen uniforms, and he's informed Bill Phinner.'

Katie turned to Kyna and said, 'Jesus. As if this day couldn't have turned out any worse.'

'Caffrey and O'Sullivan are both free. Well, free-ish. I can send them out. And I can send Cullen to the Mercy to see if the auld wan's in any kind of condition to tell us what he saw.'

'Okay, Tony, grand. It's a fierce pity Markey's still convalescing from that knock on the head. He has a bit of an obsession about catching the Pusher.'

'I think we all have. But it's like trying to hunt down a ghost. From all the descriptions we've been given, he even *looks* like a fecking ghost.'

Katie could hear that the conversation from inside the conference room was growing louder, and that the reporters were growing impatient. 'Listen...' she said. 'I have to go in now and throw some scraps to the wolves, but I shouldn't be more than ten minutes – if that. Come up and see me afterwards because I definitely think we need to revise our strategy for nailing this header. It seems like he picks on his victims totally at random, so maybe we need to talk to some psychiatrists about what his motive might be, and what kind of a mental condition he might be suffering from, do you know? Or maybe he's simply doing it for the fun of it.'

'Okay, ma'am. I'll see you after so.'

Katie and Kyna walked into the conference room and sat down at a long table facing the assembled media. Mathew McElvey was there already and he passed Katie a notepad and a pen. Even before she had time to look around and see who was there, the dazzling TV lights were switched on, and behind the glare she could just make out Fionnuala Sweeney from RTÉ *Six One News*. Dan Keane from the *Examiner* was sitting next to her, and she could also see Rionach Barr from the *Echo*, Johnny Bryan from Cork FM, Douglas Kelly, who was a stringer for the *Irish Times*, and a big-bellied fellow with thick-rimmed glasses from the *Irish Sun*, whose name she had forgotten because he turned up only for the more lurid and spectacular stories. All she knew was that he was always blunt to the point of rudeness and she didn't like him at all.

'Good afternoon to all of you,' she said. 'I'm pure sorry to have to confirm what you already know – that His Honour Mr Justice Garrett Quinn was fatally injured in his car earlier today on the Ballincollie Road at White's Cross. We are still investigating the cause of the incident, but Justice Quinn's car was set alight and it was completely burned out before the fire brigade were able to get the blaze under control.'

Dan Keane lifted his pen and said, 'Good afternoon to you, too, DS Maguire. I'm interested to note that you said "set alight" rather than "caught alight" and that you used the word "incident" instead of "accident". Does this mean that Justice Quinn's car didn't catch fire because of a traffic collision or a mechanical failure or something of that kind?'

'We're still investigating how the fire started, Dan. I'm expecting reports from our forensic experts and from Cumann Imscrúdaitheorí Dóitéan within the next few days. Of course we'll let you know as soon as we can confirm exactly what happened. For the time being, though, I'm simply being cautious and trying not to give you any statements that might be misleading.'

'Was any other car involved in this incident? Or lorry? Or bus? Or bicycle? Or combine harvester? Did he crash into a tree, or a telegraph pole?'

'As far as we can tell at the moment, there was no collision with any other vehicle and he didn't hit a tree or any other roadside object.'

'Was any other person injured?'

'No.'

'What about witnesses?'

'Only one so far, Dan, a local farmer, but he only saw Justice Quinn's car when it was already on fire. He didn't see what the cause of it was.'

'What was the nature of Justice Quinn's injuries?' asked the reporter from the *Irish Sun*.

Katie said, 'I'm sorry, I've forgotten your name.'

'Owen. Owen Dineen. You might remember I covered that story about those cops in Cork who were taking a slice from the profits of five different brothels.'

'Yes, Owen. I remember the story well. And *you* – by sight anyway. As for the nature of Justice Quinn's injuries, he was fierce badly burned, as you can probably imagine. Whether his burns were the primary cause of his death, we have yet to determine. His remains have been sent to CUH for a full post-mortem by the assistant state pathologist.'

'He was due to pass sentence on Donal Hagerty today, was he not? Is there any indication that his death might in any way be connected to that?'

'No. Not that I'm currently aware of.'

'But Donal Hagerty's younger brother Billy was shot and killed this afternoon, was he not?'

'That's correct. I was about to get to that. Billy Hagerty was shot outside The Weavers pub in Blackpool this afternoon and died instantly.'

'Any idea at all who was responsible?'

'There were several witnesses to the shooting but so far we haven't been able to identify any suspects and no arrests have been made. All we have so far is that the shots were fired from the back seat of a bronze Honda saloon.'

'I'm told that one of the witnesses was Thomas O'Flynn, am I right?'

'You are, yes.'

'And Billy Hagerty is or *was* an active member of the O'Flynn gang, am I right about that?'

'Billy and Thomas knew each other, for sure, but if Billy ever took part in any of the O'Flynns' criminal activities, we have no evidence of it.'

'Donal Hagerty not only murdered Michael Riordan, but he also murdered Michael Riordan's wife and his two young kiddies – shot and killed all four of them in cold blood, while the kiddies were sitting in front of the telly watching *Paw Patrol*. The O'Flynns and the Riordans have been at each other's throats for decades and you know that as well as I do, DS Maguire. And you're trying to tell us here today that none of these deaths are in any way connected?'

'No, Owen, I'm not. All I'm telling you is that we can't yet prove that they are – not beyond any reasonable doubt.'

'But, come here, the feud between the O'Flynns and the Riordans here in Cork, it's becoming as bad as the Hutches and the Kinahans in Dublin. *Worse*, in many ways, because it's not so much of a territorial war over drugs, it's more because they plain hate each other, and they've hated each other for so long they can't even remember why.'

'I know that, Owen.'

'I know you know it. But what are you *doing* about it, that's the issue? A criminal court justice has been burned to death. The streets of Cork are running with blood. But what are you all doing here in Anglesea Street? Sitting on your hands waiting for evidence, that's what you're doing.'

Katie glanced at Mathew, who pulled a non-committal face, as if to say, *Typical Irish Sun reporter, deliberately stirring it.* Then she turned back to Owen Dineen and said, 'I don't know if that merits any kind of an answer, Owen, to be honest with you. Are you trying to suggest that crime in the city is now out of control?'

'Those are your words, DS Maguire.'

'Well, listen. In the past eighteen months I've set up a dedicated new team to work with the Regional Drugs Unit to investigate and break up the illegal trade in drugs and opioids. I've also assigned over fifteen detectives to gather intelligence on the various criminal gangs who operate in and around the city – and I'm not only talking about the Riordans and the O'Flynns, but the Romanian begging gangs and the Nigerian sex-trafficking gangs and the shoplifting gangs and the travellers conning elderly ladies out of thousands for repairing their roofs when they don't need repairing. I don't think you could call that "sitting on our hands", not by any stretch of the *Sun*'s imagination.'

'All the same, DS Maguire, the latest crime figures don't paint such a rosy picture, do they?' said Owen Dineen. 'Cork's touted as the safest city in the country, but last year it had more killings per capita than Dublin or Limerick. Burglaries were up by thirty-four per cent, sex crimes by two per cent, and so many cars were stolen that if they'd all been driven up the M8 at once there would have been a solid traffic jam from here to Fermoy.'

'Sure, like – there has been an increase in some offences, I'd agree with you,' Katie retorted. 'But there was also a corresponding increase in successful convictions – especially for murder and manslaughter and domestic abuse. We've seized over three-quarters of a million euros' worth of drugs in the first six weeks of this year alone. We've also confiscated a record number of guns and explosives. On top of that, we've closed down four brothels and deported ninety-four illegal immigrants.'

Just then, Mathew McElvey reached out for Katie's pad and wrote on it *Lee Pusher??* before sliding it back. Katie glanced down at it but gave him an almost imperceptible shake of her head. If none of the reporters in the conference room had heard about the Lee Pusher's latest victim yet, she wasn't going to tell them. It could wait until tomorrow morning's TV news and tomorrow evening's papers.

Up until today, the media had almost always been supportive of Katie's efforts to cut down on violent crime in Cork city. It helped that she was a woman, and red-haired, and attractive, and that she had so recently been bereaved. She was a regular favourite on Cork FM and the *Today with Maura and Daithi* show. But here at today's conference she could sense that they were beginning to ask themselves if she was losing her grip. The ruthless murder of Michael Riordan and his family had already seen questions raised in the media about Cork's criminal gangs attacking each other and getting away with it.

'Maybe there's one last thing you can comment on, Detective Superintendent,' said Owen Dineen. 'They used to call Limerick "Stab City", did they not, and some people still do today. But I've been hearing in some of the local bars that Cork is now being referred to as "Ducks Town". If you haven't heard that yourself, it doesn't refer to the ducks on Cork Lough. It means that there's been so many shootings in Cork that whenever anybody slams a door or a car backfires, everybody ducks down.'

'I have heard that, Owen, sure. We don't live in some kind

of ivory tower here in Anglesea Street. But it's only a bad joke as far as I'm concerned and I've nothing to say about it. Cork is still the safest city in Ireland. I just want to close this briefing by saying that we have the most highly trained officers investigating both the tragic death of His Honour Mr Justice Garrett Quinn and the shooting of Billy Hagerty, and I'm confident that we'll be able to make arrests very soon. Thank you.'

Katie stood up, but before she could turn to leave, Fionnuala Sweeney called out, 'DS Maguire – before you go! Is it true that you were friends with Justice Quinn?'

'I've known him for a number of years, of course, and we've worked together on more criminal cases than I could count. Naturally this was done on a friendly basis. It wouldn't have been very professional if we'd been snapping at each other all the time, now would it?'

'But were you ever friends outside the courtroom?'

'I'm not sure what you're getting at, Fionnuala.'

'I'm simply asking if you were close, like. If you ever had a relationship that didn't involve the law.'

'Who gave you that idea?'

'I can't tell you who, but it was a pure reliable source, I can assure you of that.'

'Well, whoever it was, I've no comment to make.'

'So can I assume that's a "yes"?'

'You can assume whatever you like. I'm saying nothing.'

'I'm told you identified Justice Quinn's body by a claddagh band that he was wearing.'

'Fionnuala – how can I make this any plainer? I've nothing further to say. Justice Quinn's death is under investigation and you'll be informed of any developments when we have them.'

'How was it that you could identify this one particular band, ma'am? Thousands of people wear claddagh bands, don't they, and they're all basically the same – two hands with a crowned heart in between them.'

'Like I've told you, I've known Justice Quinn for a good number of years, and I'm not the least observant woman in Ireland.'

'Did you buy it for him, this band?'

Katie didn't answer that, but gave Kyna a pat on the shoulder to tell her to move, and together they walked out of the conference room. The TV lights were switched off behind her, but she could still hear the sudden babble of conversation as the reporters surrounded Fionnuala Sweeney, asking her to tell them more about Justice Quinn's claddagh band.

Katie and Kyna went up to Katie's office. It was dark outside now, and hundreds of sparkling raindrops were clinging to the windows. Katie sat down at her desk, picked up a blue folder that had been left there for her, and then put it down without opening it.

'Did you?' asked Kyna gently.

'Did I what? Did I buy it for him?'

She stood up and walked to the window, and her ghostly reflection walked through the raindrops towards her, until they stood face-to-face. In Moirin's office, the phone started ringing, although Moirin was no longer there to answer it.

'Yes,' she said. 'I bought it for him. He bought one for me, too, although I never wore it.'

'Was there a reason for that?'

'What – for not wearing it? Yes. And I pray to God that those nosy reporters never find out what it was.'

7

Detective Inspector Robert Fitzpatrick and Detective Ronan Caffrey walked into Eugene's just as Thomas O'Flynn and his gang were finishing their drinks and standing up to leave.

'Well, if it isn't Robbie the Razzer,' said Thomas. 'I was wondering if you'd be sniffing around sooner or later.'

'How's she cutting, Tommy?' asked Detective Inspector Fitzpatrick. He said it in his usual tone of voice, which was expressionless, just as his face was expressionless, too. He never needed to be openly threatening, though. He had tousled grey hair, which made him look older than his fifty-four years, but he was built like a rugby prop, with an S-shaped broken nose.

'I'm in good form, boy, thanks for asking,' said Thomas.

'You don't mind if me and Detective Caffrey ask you a question or two?'

'So long as you don't ask me where I get my green diesel from. That's a joke.'

'Oh, stop. I'm in stitches.'

Thomas turned around and gestured to his gang to sit down. Eugene's was a long narrow lounge with an L-shaped bar at one end, with stools clustered around it, but Thomas and his henchmen had been lined up shoulder to shoulder along the red padded seats that ran along the right-hand wall, as if they were sitting in a doctor's waiting room. Muireann had been sitting next to Thomas, and Darragh and Milo were still there, as well as four leather-jacketed young men with tattoos and bad teeth. Detective Inspector Fitzpatrick recognized three of them. They had all served several short prison terms in Rathmore Road for robbery or drug possession or threatening behaviour, or all three. They stared back at him with open hostility.

'If you're here to ask me about Billy Hagerty getting himself shot, I saw nothing,' said Thomas.

'I've spoken already to Garda O'Dea so I know what you say you saw and what you say you didn't see. What I want to ask you is if you know of any reason why anybody would want to take down Billy Hagerty, and if you have any notion who it might have been?'

Thomas lowered his eyebrows and slowly shook his head. 'I haven't a clue, boy. He was a pleasant enough fellow, Billy. All right, he could get fierce shouty sometimes when he was motherless, but then who doesn't?'

'Why did he come to see you? Was it because of Donal's sentencing being postponed?'

'We talked about that of course. But he didn't come to see me special. He only came into The Weavers for a quick scoop, like, that's all.'

'What about Justice Quinn? Did you talk about him at all?'

'Sure, like. But it was all over the news, wasn't it? And it was an accident, wasn't it? Accidents can happen to anyone, can't they? Even to judges.'

'Let's go back to Billy Hagerty being shot – do you think that could have been a case of mistaken identity? What I'm saying is – do you think that the shooter might actually have been after you?'

'Up the yard, boy, why would anybody want to shoot me?'

'You really want me to answer that?' asked Detective Inspector Fitzpatrick, his voice flat and his face completely deadpan.

'Oh, come on,' said Thomas. 'I might have a bit of a reputation, do you know what I mean, but most of it's invented by them fecking Riordans. These days, I tell you, Bishop Buckley himself can't hold a candle to me for saintly behaviour.'

'Okay, Tommy. But this is only what you might call a preliminary chat. We'll be investigating further and whoever shot Billy Hagerty we'll nail him for certain, you can lay money on that, and then we'll see for sure who he thought he was aiming at.'

'Fair whack. Good luck to you, boy, that's all I can say.'

Thomas stayed seated until Detective Inspector Fitzpatrick and Detective Caffrey had walked out of Eugene's, drumming his fingers on the table. After a few moments he sent Darragh to go out into the street to make sure that they had driven away. Once Darragh came back and gave him the thumbs up, he said, 'Right, lads. Time to call on Eamonn O'Malley. Muireann – you go back to the house, girl. Ring Sorley at Comet Taxis, he'll take you.'

'But I want to come with you, Tommy.'

'You can't. And you'll do what I fecking tell you, that's what.'

Outside Eugene's, the seven men gathered in a circle to light up cigarettes. Then they crossed the street and walked up the slope to Cattle Market Avenue where their two cars were parked, Thomas's white Audi and his gang's black Toyota Land Cruiser. A wet rain was falling and the roads were shiny. The men barely spoke to each other as they climbed into their cars. Whenever they went out on a mission like this, they took on a frame of mind like a vengeful posse making their way to the OK Corral. They even walked with a cowboy swagger.

They drove up Fair Hill and turned into Liam Healy Road, a narrow side street of three-bedroomed terraced houses. Some of the houses were proudly painted in reds and salmon pinks, with decorative front doors and fancy net curtains, but towards the end of the street most of them were run-down and shabby with grimy pebble-dash and battered vans parked outside. Eamonn O'Malley's house was one of the shabby ones, with a silver Honda CR-V in its paved front yard.

The gang parked and climbed out of their cars. Thomas waited on the pavement with his coat collar turned up and hands in his pockets while Milo and one of the other men went to Eamonn O'Malley's front door and rang the bell. They could see that there was somebody at home because the sagging yellow curtains didn't quite meet in the middle and behind them a television screen was flickering.

At first there was no response so Milo rang the bell again, three times. One of the curtains was drawn aside and a woman peered out. The curtain fell back again, and a few seconds later the light was switched on in the hallway and the front door was opened.

The woman was about forty, with dark puffy circles under her eyes and dyed black hair and cheap dangly earrings. She was wearing only a long mustard-coloured fisherman's jumper and a pair of fluffy slippers. She looked frightened.

'What is it?' she said, in the hoarse voice of a heavy smoker. 'What d'ye want?'

'See that fellow standing there behind me, girl?' said Milo, turning around and pointing to Thomas. 'That there is Thomas O'Flynn and he's after having a word with Eamonn.'

The woman saw Thomas standing in the rain, unmoving, with the collar of his raincoat turned up. He was wearing his soft brown trilby so his face was in shadow.

'Eamonn's off away,' said the woman. She stepped back and tried to close the door but Milo immediately stuck his foot in it. Now Thomas came up to the front steps and stood looking at her.

'I told you, Eamonn's off away,' the woman repeated. 'He's visiting his sister in Waterford.'

'If he's off away in Waterford, how come his motor's still here?' Thomas asked her.

'He took the train, like.'

Thomas lifted his trilby, flicked the rain off it, and then carefully replaced it. 'I don't believe you,' he said. 'I reckon he's inside there now hiding in the press or under the bed and he just doesn't want to see me. That's what I reckon.'

'I told you. He's not here.'

'You can carry on telling me that until the cows give cheese, but I still won't believe you. Go back in there and tell your man to come out or else we'll be coming in to get him. He has ten seconds, tell him.'

The woman hesitated, but then without another word she disappeared. Thomas said to Milo, 'Visiting his sister in Waterford... what kind of a fecking gom does she think I am? I've met his sister and she runs an online knocking shop down in Grafton Street. Great fat ganky she is, too. Mountainy isn't the word. I'll tell you how fat she is, when she was standing on the corner by the GPO a guard came over and told her to break it up.'

He wiped his nose with the back of his hand and then he shouted out, 'Eight – nine – ten! Your time's up, Eamonn! We're coming in so!'

Immediately the door opened wider and there was Eamonn O'Malley. His face was round and smooth and strangely doll-like, with protuberant blue eyes and greasy black scraped-back hair. He was wearing a white open-necked shirt and navy-blue suit trousers held up by red braces, although his feet were bare, with bunions.

'Well,' said Thomas, 'that was a fierce quick sprint back from Waterford. You should be in the Guinness Book of Records. How's your sister keeping?'

'For Christ's sake, Tommy, I'm beat out, like,' Eamonn told him. 'I have the holy mother of all hangovers and I was only trying to have a couple of hours' kip.' He nodded towards Milo and Darragh and the other four men. 'What's the craic? What do you want to see me for? And why've you fetched all these fellers with you?'

'What do you think I want to see you for? Did I not pay you to have a quiet word in Judge Quinn's ear, and warn him what could happen if he didn't go easy on Donal?'

Eamonn O'Malley looked back at him guardedly. 'I did, like. That's exactly what I did. I waited for him in the car park yesterday outside the court, and when he came out about four o'clock after yesterday's sessions I went up to him and asked him pure polite-like how he was going on. You said to be pure polite-like, didn't you?'

'So what did he say?'

'He said he was grand altogether but he had to go. I stopped him, though, before he got into his car. I said that if he gave Donal too long a sentence or if he ordered him sent up to Portlaoise – well, it might not be the brainiest thing that he had ever done. If he did, he might need to be double wide for the rest of his life.'

'Well, that was pure subtle. What did he say to that?'

'He said if that's a threat, like, I'm going to call for the guards and have you arrested. So I said it's not a threat, Your Honour, it's just a word to the wise. I said you'll remember what happened to Judge Donnelly two years ago after he gave Dermot and Francis Finnegan ten years apiece for manslaughter. His house got burned down to the ground and his poor daughter died of the smoke inhalation when she was trapped in her bedroom.'

'Serious? You said that to him?'

'Oh, not just that. I told him that Donal has a whole crowd of pals in Croppy Boy, and all those pals happen to know where you live in Tivoli Park, Your Honour, so you wouldn't be wanting anything like that to happen to *your* house and *your* family, now would you?'

'I'll bet he took that well.'

'Are you codding me? He told me I must be langered and to get the feck out of the garden, not in them exact words. He said he was going to hand down the sentence that Donal deserved for murder and I could threaten him as much as I liked, it wouldn't make a scrap of difference. He said he wasn't afraid of me or nobody. Then he was out the gap.'

'Mother of God, Eamonn. Why didn't you tell me this as soon as you'd spoken to him?'

'I rang you at home, Tommy, but nobody answered and you don't have a moby. I was heading over to The Weavers to tell you but I bumped into some old amigos of mine from the Fairfield Tavern and I thought a couple of cold ones wouldn't hurt before I came over to see you. The trouble was it turned out to be Ger Barrett's memorial sing-song and I ended up totally scuttered.'

'You're lying to me, boy. Now fecking tell me the truth. Where were you this morning?'

'I told you, Tommy. Flat out in me scratcher slowly dying.'

'Nowhere near White's Cross, then?'

'What would I be doing up at White's Cross?'

'Maybe you were showing Judge Quinn that he shouldn't have told you to go off and flah your granma, or whatever it was he *really* said to you.'

'What?'

'How should I know? Maybe you were planning on coming back to me and boasting that you'd sorted Donal Hagerty's sentencing, because there'd be no judge now who would have the balls to send Donal to the slammer for more than a couple of years in case they ended up cremated like Judge Quinn.'

'I have no fecking idea what you're talking about, Tommy, I swear it. Judge Quinn? Cremated?'

'Don't act the innocent with me, boy. You remember what you did when I asked you to sort out Felim Macabe. Give him a couple of clatters, I told you, didn't I, so that he'd quit hobbling my spiggy. That's all it would have needed, a couple of clatters. But what did you do? Shot him in the belly and then torched his mobile home to hide the evidence. You were stone lucky the razzers never cottoned on that it was you.'

'Come on, Tommy – what happened to Felim, that was an accident. I was only waving the shotgun at him to put the fear of God in him. Waving it, that's all, like! I didn't even know it was loaded.'

'So when you topped Judge Quinn, that was an accident, too, was it? How did it happen, Eamonn? Did you accidentally wave your shotgun at him, too? Or did you accidentally stab him? Or did you straighten his tie for him and accidentally strangle him because you tied up the knot too tight?'

'Tommy – I swear on my nuts that wasn't me. I didn't even know he was dead.'

Thomas pointed to the gaping curtains in Eamonn O'Malley's living room. 'Oh, no? You have the telly on and you didn't even know he was dead? You are the worst liar I ever met. Now are you going to tell me the truth or do we have to beat it out of you?'

'Tommy, please.'

But Thomas beckoned to Milo and Darragh and two of the other men and they immediately came striding up towards the open front door. Eamonn O'Malley tried to scramble back into his hallway, but he tripped on the welcome mat and fell backwards, knocking his head against the skirting board. The four men bent down, seized his arms and legs, and hoisted him up, so that they could carry him bodily out on to the pavement. The other men stood further along the road, smoking and keeping watch for the Garda or for any inquisitive neighbours who might venture out to see what all the noise was about.

Thomas went over to the rain-beaded Land Cruiser and opened the passenger door. Milo and Darragh and the two other men dragged Eamonn across to it and positioned his head in between the open door and the door pillar. Eamonn struggled and kicked and twisted, trying to wrench his wrists and his ankles free, but the men's grip was relentless.

'I never did it, Tommy!' he panted. 'I never touched a single hair on Judge Quinn's head! I promise you that in front of God and Mary and Joseph and all the angels!'

'If *you* didn't do it, then who the feck did? There's nobody else had any reason to kill him, except you. Thought I'd pay you more, did you, if you topped him? Thought I'd clap you on the back and say "dowchaboy!", is that it? But you know what's going to happen now? The razzers are going to be sniffing around twice as nosy and if they find even a twinchy scrap of evidence that it was me who sent Donal Hagerty to sort out Michael Riordan, then I'll be in even deeper shite than he is. I'll be up to my fecking neck in it, you gack.'

'I never did it! I'll kiss the Bible for you!'

'You can kiss my arse and call me Katty Barry. I still won't believe you.'

With that, he slammed the Land Cruiser's door on Eamonn's head, hard. Eamonn let out a high-pitched squeal, like a pig being stunned by a captive bolt gun, and his whole body jolted. Even Darragh sucked in his breath.

Thomas opened the door again. Eamonn's right ear was bloody and swollen, and from the angle of his chin it looked as though his jaw been knocked out of alignment.

'Come on, Eamonn. What's the real story? You followed him up to White's Cross and then you stopped him, one way or another, and then what? How did you top him, Eamonn?'

'I never,' Eamonn whispered.

'Just like it wasn't you who torched Judge Donnelly's house, I suppose?'

'That wasn't only me. That was me and Patsy Brady and the Finnegans' dad. I only carried – I only carried the petrol. Christ, Tommy, what have you done to my head? It feels like it's split down the middle.'

'All I want is the truth, Eamonn. If you come clean and say that you topped Judge Quinn off of your own bat, and that it wasn't me who put you up to it, then that'll be an end to it.'

A runnel of blood slid out of the side of Eamonn's mouth and dripped on to his shirt collar. 'It wasn't me, Tommy,' he bubbled, almost inaudibly.

Thomas slammed the Land Cruiser's door on his head a second time, and this time much harder. Eamonn let out an *ooofff!* of breath but that was all.

Thomas opened the door again and shouted at him, 'The truth, Eamonn, that's all I'm asking you for! Tell me the fecking truth!' But even though Eamonn's bulging blue eyes were still open, he looked concussed, and he didn't answer.

'Tell – me – the – fecking – *truth*!' Thomas screamed, slamming the door again and again on Eamonn's head to emphasize every word. The third slam brought a sharp cracking noise, and the four slams that followed it a crunching sound, and when at last Thomas flung the door wide open in disgust and stepped away, he could see that he had smashed Eamonn's skull. His face was no longer round but a lopsided ellipse and blood was streaming out of his nostrils. His right eye was closed but his left eye had burst out of its socket and was staring at his cheek, as if in surprise.

Milo and Darragh and the other two men dropped Eamonn on to the wet pavement.

'It could be that he *was* telling the truth, like, Tommy, and that it wasn't him that did it,' Darragh suggested, in a cautious tone of voice. He had seen Thomas mete out his car door punishment once before, in the week before Christmas. His victim that time had suffered permanent brain damage, even though it had turned out that his punishment had been completely unjustified. Once Thomas lost his temper, justification went out of the window. It was justification enough that his victim had riled him by not doing exactly what Thomas had told him to do.

'Of course he fecking did it,' Thomas snapped back. 'And if he *didn't* do it, he deserved what he got anyway. Two hundred and fifty yoyos I paid him to put the fear of God into Judge Quinn and did he? He did in my gonkapouch. Judge Quinn told him to go and stick his fear of God where the sun doesn't shine. I mean, Jesus – I could have gone down to the courts myself and heard him tell me that for nothing.'

'What are we going to do with him?' asked Milo, cautiously prodding Eamonn's lifeless shoulder with his shoe. 'Sling him in the river, like?'

'There's just one thing I have to do first,' said Thomas. Still sniffing and twitching with temper, he went back to the front door of Eamonn O'Malley's house and knocked at it with his knuckles. After a few moments the kitchen door at the end of the hallway was opened just a crack and the woman stared out like a terrified squirrel.

'Come here to me, love!' Thomas called out to her. 'Eamonn's off away to see his sister in Waterford and it's likely that he won't be back for a while. And when I say a while, I mean a fierce long while. Like, for ever.'

'What have you done to him? You haven't hurt him at all, have you?'

'Never you mind about that. But let me tell you this: if anybody comes looking for him, or asking questions about him, you haven't seen him and you haven't seen any of us. Do you have me? You'll sore regret it if you say that you have, I can promise you that.'

He didn't even wait for the woman to answer, but returned to the Land Cruiser. Milo and one of the other men were heaving Eamonn's body into the luggage space, his arms and his legs flopping, while Darragh and the other two men were standing around and shuffling from side to side to shield them from view.

'Well?' asked Milo.

Thomas looked up and down the road, and then he said, 'No. I don't want to dump him in the river. The tide could well take him out, do you know, but then again it might fetch him back in again, or he might end up floating around in circles in the Tivoli dock. And his head's all broke in half, so the razzers are going to cop on straight away that he didn't die accidental-like.'

'So?'

'So I have an idea to make it look as if he *did* die accidental-like, and we won't have too far to go, either. Come on, let's make tracks. The sooner we get this over and done with, the sooner we can go back to Eugene's. I suddenly have a desperate thirst on me. Milo – would you be after having a spare bifter on you, boy?'

8

By midnight, Katie was exhausted, both physically and emotionally. Her back was aching and her brain felt as if it were stuffed full of fibreglass loft insulation.

Half an hour ago she had been told that the body of the young woman who had been drowned by the Lee Pusher had been brought up from the riverbed by two divers from the Cork Search and Rescue team. The young woman had been identified by neighbours as Roisin Carroll, aged twenty-one from Sunnyside, Blackrock. Her seven-month-old daughter, Ita, was being treated at the Mercy, and was expected to make a full recovery. Katie knew from several drowning accidents in the Lee that very young children can hold their breath under water much longer than adults.

Peadar Ó Dálaigh had been able to speak briefly to Detective Daley Cullen. He had told him that he had seen 'a skinny streak of a fellow in grey' running away from The Marina after Roisin had been pushed into the river, but he was unable to give him a more detailed description than that. 'I was too worried about saving Roisin and her babby. I only wish to God that I could have saved Roisin, and my poor little Póg, too.'

Gardaí were still trying to find more witnesses to the shooting of Billy Hagerty outside The Weavers, although they had so far had no luck at all. They had also appealed for anybody who had seen a grey or silver SUV being driven at speed through Dublin Pike at about 11:15 that morning to come forward. The bodies of Billy Hagerty and Mr Justice

Garrett Quinn had both been taken to the mortuary at Cork University Hospital to await forensic examination and post-mortems by Assistant State Pathologist Mary Kelley.

As she eased herself stiffly up from her desk, Katie realized that she had scarcely thought about Conor since his funeral this morning. Although it had taken three different tragedies to preoccupy her, she was relieved in a way. The pain of watching Conor's coffin being lowered into his grave had been almost unbearable, especially since she had known how mutilated his body was inside it. It had taken all of her strength not to sink down on to her knees into the wet graveyard grass and scream at the top of her voice in grief and bereavement. She had been so sure that she had found happiness at last with Conor, and she had even joked with him about how they would spend the time together when she eventually retired from An Garda Síochána.

'We'll take ourselves off to Ballymaloe cookery school and learn to be professional chefs,' he had told her, and even now she could still hear his voice. 'You've not tasted my beef hand pie yet, have you? I swear to God you won't want even the doonchiest nibble of anybody else's – not after you've tasted mine. It's *neamh i do lámh* – Heaven in your hand.'

But before Conor had died he had never found the time to bake his beef hand pie for her, so now she would never know what it might have tasted like. That was only the smallest part of the emptiness she felt, yet the memory of him saying that filled her eyes with tears. For the short time that she and Conor had been together she *had* held Heaven in her hand, but now it had slipped for ever out of her fingers.

She was buttoning up her raincoat when Kyna came into her office. Kyna already had her furry yellow anorak on, ready to leave.

'You're off home now?' she asked Katie. 'You need to, ma'am, and I mean it. You've had one desperate day altogether and you're only human.'

'Any updates from Superintendent Pearse?'

'No, nothing at all. I mean, Jesus. There's a shooting right out in the street in broad daylight and nobody saw it. You'd think the whole population of Blackpool needed guide dogs.'

'I'll go and see Orla Quinn tomorrow morning to give her my condolences. The poor woman must be devastated. Twenty-one years they were married, I think it was, and they have three children, two of them twins.'

As they walked along the corridor together, towards the lift, Kyna said, 'Does Orla know about you and Garrett?'

Katie pulled a face to show that she had no idea. The lift door opened and Kyna followed her in.

'Would you care for some company, just for tonight?' Kyna asked her. 'I hate to think of you being alone in that house after everything you've been through today. Sure like, I know you have Barney and Foltchain, but they don't have much in the way of conversation, do they?'

Katie took a deep breath, and then nodded. If the lift hadn't been fitted with CCTV, she would have put her arms around Kyna and held her tight.

They drove to Cobh through the dark and the rain. Both of them were too tired to talk much, so Katie played songs by The Japanese House, very quietly. *Oh, you seemed so happy...*

She felt a *tocht* in her throat and wondered if the day would ever come when every song she heard would no longer remind her of Conor.

They parked outside Katie's house in Carrig View, overlooking the Lee estuary. Barney and Foltchain were waiting for them in the hallway when they went inside, circling excitedly around and around so that they almost tripped them up. But Barney, like most Irish red setters, could be thoughtful, too, and once he had calmed down he stood still and looked up at Katie as if he were asking why Conor didn't come home any more. All Katie could do was tug affectionately at his ears, and then ruffle Foltchain's fluffy ears, too.

'How about a nightcap?' she asked Kyna, as they went into the living room.

'I'll have a glass of that Redbreast if you have any left. One of them at bedtime and I can sleep like I'm dead and buried. Oh God, Katie, I didn't mean that. I just meant—'

'You're allowed to say "dead and buried", sweetheart,' said Katie. 'We can't avoid it, can we, in our job? And nothing can hurt me more than I'm hurting already. A couple of words can't make things any worse.'

She held out her arms and Kyna came up to her and they embraced each other and stroked each other's hair and kissed. They both had tears rolling down their cheeks, for their different reasons – Katie because she had lost Conor and Kyna because she couldn't bear to see Katie in such pain.

Both Barney and Foltchain came up to them, too, and stood next to them, and Barney whined thinly in the back of his throat.

Katie let the dogs out into the back garden and then she poured Kyna a Redbreast whiskey and a Smirnoff vodka for herself. They sat on the couch together, not saying much, but sharing that look that they had shared together almost from the moment that Kyna had first arrived at Anglesea

Street. Katie had learned long ago that some people love each other just because they do, no explanations or analysis necessary.

'That Lee Pusher, though,' said Kyna. 'I'd be fascinated to find out what's been motivating him.'

'Maybe he's lost somebody himself through drowning in the river, and he doesn't see why anybody else should be lucky enough not to drown, too. You remember that farm worker in Coolatubrid who pushed two of his fellow workers under a combine harvester because his own son had been killed that way.'

'God, yes I do,' said Kyna, and gave an exaggerated shiver.

It was still raining softly outside, and so it wasn't long before Barney and Foltchain were scratching at the kitchen door to be let back in again. Katie and Kyna finished their drinks and went into Katie's bedroom. Katie took a short lemon-coloured nightdress out of her wardrobe for Kyna and laid it on the bed, and then she said, 'You have your shower first. I have a few emails to catch up with.'

She sat on the side of the bed with her laptop. She had messages from Bill Phinner about the tests that his forensic experts would be carrying out tomorrow on Justice Quinn. They would be using computer tomography to see if there were any bodily fluids still in liquid form that they could use to test for toxins. Most importantly, they would be trying to determine if there was another obvious cause of death than heat-related lesions, especially 'metallic foreign bodies of ballistic origin', which is what Bill always called bullets.

She also had texts from Mary Kelley, the pathologist, telling her that she might be an hour or two late starting her post-mortems in the morning because one of her fillings had fallen out; and an email from Mathew McElvey, the Garda press officer. He had sent her a JPEG of the front page of an early edition of the *Irish Sun*, with the comment, 'Let me know how you want to respond to this – MM.'

Katie enlarged the JPEG and sat staring at it in disbelief. Dominating the front page was an unflattering picture of herself, taken at the media conference. She had both hands raised as if she were surrendering, and her mouth was pulled down. The huge headline read TOP CORK COP FLOPS, by Owen Dineen, and the story underneath began, 'After a leading judge was burned to death in suspicious circumstances, a petty criminal was shot dead in the street, and the maniacal Lee Pusher claimed his seventh victim – ALL IN ONE DAY – Cork's most senior detective has had to admit that "crime in the city is now beyond our control".

'Detective Superintendent Kathleen Maguire also confessed that since she had been appointed top cop the number of serious offences such as murder, drug-dealing, sexual assault and random stabbings has ROCKETED.'

'*Kyna*,' said Katie, and Kyna must have caught the shock in her voice because she came out of the bathroom naked, still drying herself with her towel.

Katie turned her laptop around so that Kyna could see the screen.

'I can't believe it. I never said that crime in the city was beyond our control. I asked him if that was what he was trying to suggest. And I never said that offences had "rocketed". That is a complete and utter fabrication. Talk about false news.'

'Oh sweet Jesus,' said Kyna. 'This is absolutely desperate. It really looks like he's got it in for you, this Owen Dineen. What are you going to do?'

'I don't know. I really don't know. I'll have to talk to

Mathew about it, and our lawyers, too. They need to print a correction, and an apology too.'

She read more of the news report, shaking her head. Then she pressed her hand against her mouth and her eyes filled up with tears again.

Kyna dropped her towel and knelt down on the floor beside her, shushing her and stroking her hair. 'Come on, it's only a nasty fat newspaper reporter being bitchy, for the sake of his story. It'll all be forgotten in a day's time.'

Katie wiped her eyes and nodded. 'You're right. I shouldn't let it get to me. I've always been allergic to that Owen Dineen whenever he's showed up and I think he knows it.'

Kyna hugged her and gave her reassuring little kisses again and again, and then gave her a long, deeply felt kiss, sliding her tongue into her mouth and at the same time cupping her right breast through her sweater.

At that moment, in the kitchen, both Barney and Foltchain started barking, and Katie could hear them scrabbling frantically at the back door. She sat up straight, and Kyna got to her feet, picking up her towel.

'What's got into those two?' asked Kyna.

'Something in the garden. Or somebody. There's been some red foxes around lately. I think they have an earth up by the rugby club somewhere.'

Katie stood up and went over to the window. She hadn't yet drawn the curtains and the light from the bedroom was shining out into the garden. She shielded her eyes with her hand to cut out the reflection of her own face, and it was then that she saw something moving on the left-hand side of the garden, by the rotary clothes line. Both Barney and Foltchain were barking hysterically by now, and she could hear them jumping up and down.

She saw something moving again, and she thought the grey waterproof sheet that she used to cover her bicycle might have blown loose and was flapping in the wind. But why would that set the two dogs off barking? She hesitated for a moment before she drew the curtains, and when she did she saw a man in a grey hoodie appear out of the shadows behind the clothes line and head quickly towards the garden's side gate.

'Intruder!' Katie gasped. Kyna stepped back out of her way as she ran out of the bedroom, along the hallway and pulled open the front door. She ran around the side of the house, into the rain, just as the man in the grey hoodie was coming out of the garden gate.

'Stop!' she shouted at him. 'You're under arrest!'

The man came blundering towards her and collided with her next to her two dustbins, which both tipped over. He pushed her back against the wall of the house, but she hit him hard on the side of his neck with a nippon kempo blow that sent him staggering sideways, and then she kicked him in the groin. He grunted and doubled over, and as he did his mobile phone dropped out of his pocket and clattered on to the path.

'I said, you're under arrest!' Katie panted. 'Kyna! My gun's in the top drawer, in the nursery! Fetch it for me, can you?'

The man was scrabbling on his hands and knees on the path, trying to reach his phone, but Katie kicked him again, in the shoulder, so that he fell over on to his back. She tried to seize his arm but he rolled over, twice, and then clambered on to his feet. She went after him again, but he turned and lolloped away, and by the time she had reached the pavement outside her house, he had vanished. He had probably jumped into a neighbour's front garden, because not even an Olympic athlete could have run that fast, but there was no way of telling which garden he might have jumped into. She waited a few seconds, still panting, and then she saw the red tail lights of a car, about a hundred metres up the road. It sped away and disappeared around the bend in the road by Summer Point.

Kyna came out wearing Katie's brushed-cotton bathrobe and holding out her revolver.

'Never mind,' said Katie. 'He's gone. But I gave him a good kicking where it hurts, so I suppose that's some consolation. And he left this behind.'

Katie tugged the sleeve of her sweater down to cover her fingers and then she bent over and picked up the man's mobile phone. The screen was cracked but apart from that it looked undamaged.

'What are you going to do now?' Kyna asked her.

'Now? Nothing. I could ring Cobh station but what would be the point? I'd only be wasting time and money. I didn't get much of a look at the fellow and I didn't get a sconce of his number plate – even if that *was* him I saw driving off.'

She pressed the 'on' button on his phone but all that came up on the screen was 'try again'.

'What I *can* do is take this phone in to Bill Phinner in the morning and see if he can crack it open for us. Then at least we'll know who the fellow was and maybe we'll find out what he was after.'

They went back into the house. Barney and Foltchain had calmed down now, but all the same Katie went into the kitchen and gave them each a fondle to show them that everything was fine and the intruder had been chased away.

'I wonder what he *was* after,' said Kyna. 'Even a total eejit can see that you have CCTV and a burglar alarm – and if he knew who you were, he must have realized that you were probably going to be armed. And what do you have in your garden that's worth hobbling?'

'My bike, that's all. And that's about a hundred years old with a flange bar, to put it crudely.'

Katie undressed. She went into the bathroom to take a shower and when she came back she put on her stripy pyjamas and climbed into bed. It was 1:47 a.m. Kyna was waiting for her and gave her a smile.

'I doubt I'll be able to sleep,' Katie told her. 'I'm aching for the rest, though, I can tell you.'

They switched off their bedside lamps and then they turned towards each other and held each other close. Katie closed her eyes and felt that nothing could be more soothing than Kyna's steady breathing against her neck.

'I love you, Katie Maguire,' Kyna whispered.

'I love you, too, Kyna Ní Nuallán,' Katie replied.

She was quite sure that she would stay awake all night, but while she was thinking about Owen Dineen's story in the *Irish Sun* and how she was going to reply to it, she dropped off into a deep and seamless sleep, and when she opened her eyes again the sun was shining behind the curtains, and Kyna was still breathing softly against her neck.

9

'Have you seen the paper?' asked Barry Riordan, with his mouth full, as Gavin and Feargal came into the kitchen. He was sitting eating scrambled eggs with a fork in his right hand and a lighted cigarette in his left.

'Sure, like,' said Gavin, taking the *Racing Post* out of his coat pocket and holding it up. 'That fecking Emerald City fell over again. I swear to God that horse has three legs shorter than the other.'

'I don't mean *that* paper, you bulb.' Barry jerked his head towards the folded-up copy of the *Irish Sun* lying on the table next to a wet collapsible umbrella and a six-pack of Satzenbrau.

Feargal picked up the paper and read the headline, moving his lips. Then he passed it to Gavin. 'I don't have me specs on me.'

'You didn't have your fecking specs on you when you shot Billy Hagerty, either, did you, boy?' said Barry. 'You could have seen that Tommy O'Flynn was right behind him.'

'I told you, Barry. Billy was first out the door and I didn't have the time to fooster around waiting for your man.'

'Well, okay, like I said to you yesterday, I'm not that vexed about it. Billy Hagerty was a fecking waste of space no matter which way you looked at him, and it was him I wanted out the way first. I bet when he was born the midwife smacked his ma.'

'Any road, from what it says here, we don't be having too much to sweat about,' said Gavin, dropping the paper back on the table. 'It sounds like the cops in Cork couldn't find their own mebs if they was wearing see-through grundies.'

'They have a woman in charge of them, don't they, the cops, so what do you expect?' said Barry, blowing out a long stream of smoke before he forked up some more scrambled eggs. 'Me – I wouldn't put a woman in charge of lifting up the toilet seats so that the men could take a piss.'

'Sure like, but what are we going to do about Tommy O'Flynn?' asked Gavin. 'The longer we leave it, the longer he's going to believe that he's got away with whacking your Michael and that we don't have the guts to pay him back.'

'It wasn't only my Michael, Gavin. It was Saoirse and Fiona and little Éann. I want Tommy all right, by *Christ* I want Tommy because it was Tommy who paid Donal Hagerty to shoot Michael and nobody can tell me different. And it's not only Tommy I'm gunning for. I want to take down the rest of his shitehawks, like that Milo Milligan. *But* – what do you know, Lenny from The Weavers rang me this morning and told me that it's Maddie O'Flynn's twenty-first birthday on Saturday and that the O'Flynn family are after holding a party. He said that they'll be catering for three dozen of them, at least.'

'So? You're not planning on taking her a present, are you?'

'You might say so, in a kind of a way. I've been thinking, right, about an eye for an eye, and why not? Michael was one thing. Michael did what he did and he was wide to what could happen to him if he crossed the O'Flynns. But Saoirse and Fiona and little Éann never did a scrap of harm to nobody, did they, they never hurt a fecking fly, yet that made no odds. Them fecking O'Flynns still took them down.'

'Holy Joseph, Barry. You're not thinking what I think you're thinking.'

'Give them O'Flynns a couple of hours at that party and they'll all be half-fluthered, won't they? They'll all be singing and dancing and they'll have the music playing so loud that it'll take them a while to catch on to what's hitting them. If there's four or five of us we can be in and out of there before you can say *bás gasta agus ceann éasca.**

'One of us in the front bar, one in the back, one in the upstairs lounge and two outside keeping sketch for the law.'

Feargal whistled. 'It's going to take some fierce planning, though, Barry. We'll be needing two motors at least, and we'll have to work out where we're going to park them and where we're going to drive them off to afterwards. And what shooters we're going to take, and how much ammo.'

'Wouldn't it be simpler to get Molly to leave a bomb in the bean-jacks?' Gavin suggested.

'That would be the simplest, I'll give you that,' said Barry, with his mouth full, but smoke still leaking out of his nostrils. 'But then we couldn't be one hundred per cent certain that we'd be taking out Tommy and the rest of his gang, could we? Like – what if they went outside for a blimmer two seconds before the bomb went off? And then there's Lenny and them two barmaids of his. We wouldn't want to be hurting them at all, would we, especially that Gráinne.'

'Gráinne? Oh, *Gráinne* – that blonde beour you mean, the one with the massive diddies. No, I guess you're right. A bomb would be kind of indiscriminated, wouldn't it? And if we set off a bomb, the law might fetch in the counter-terrorism boys, and those CTI fellers, they know what they're doing all right, even if the local pigs don't know their arse from a bowl of drisheen.'

---

* *a quick death and an easy one*

'Go and have a word with Nocky,' said Barry. 'See if he can soilk us three motors, but not from around here. Maybe Mallow or Fermoy. And he'll be wanting new number plates for both of them. Feargal – you go round to see Johnny Meaney about the guns. I reckon the AR-15s will be our best bet.'

'To be fair, Barry, do you think this might be overdoing it, like?' said Feargal.

'Overdoing it? What do you mean, overdoing it?'

'I mean the shades are going to be down on us like a ton of shite, aren't they? Come here, now, we've already whacked Billy Hagerty, and Donal Hagerty will probably be going down for life. Isn't that enough for the moment? We can always pick off Tommy sometime soon when he's least expecting it, and if we do that the cops will probably send us a thank-you letter and a bunch of roses. But what you're talking about here, like, there's no two ways about it – it's a fecking massacre.'

Barry stared at Feargal as if he had just spat into his eggs. 'I'll tell you what, boy, go to the cemetery and ask Saoirse and Fiona and little Éann if this is overdoing it. I've had it up to here with the fecking O'Flynns. If we don't stamp all of them out now, they're going to be picking us off one by one until there's none of us left. When was the last time you felt safe, even doing Pana on a Saturday afternoon, with the crowds of shoppers all around you?'

'Well, okay. But I still think it's taking a sledgehammer to crack an egg.'

'*Nut*,' said Barry.

'Call me what you like, but I can only see this ending in grief, I truly can, and I'm no fortune teller.'

'Feargal, do what I fecking tell you to do, will you, boy?

And this time, don't forget your glasses. Any harm comes to that Gráinne and I won't be quick to forgive you.'

'Who's Gráinne?' said Barry's wife, Megan, coming into the kitchen with a washing basket under her arm.

'Mind your own fecking business,' said Barry. 'Gavin – Feargal – I'll catch you after at The Cotton Ball.'

Megan went through to the alcove where the washing machine and the tumble dryer were installed and started to sort through the dirty clothes in her basket. She was a tall, thin woman, with long black hair tied back in a ponytail. She had a slightly Spanish look about her, with large dark eyes and pouting lips, and when she was younger she had been pretty enough to model for three of the fashion shows held by Brown Thomas, the Cork department store. But five years of marriage to Barry Riordan had taken their toll on her. She had aubergine-purple circles under her eyes, and bruises on her left cheek and on her wrists, and underneath her jeans she had bruises on her thighs and on her buttocks too.

Gavin and Feargal left without even acknowledging that she had come into the room. They knew that if they gave her a friendly 'howya', Barry might get it into his head that they were trying to come on to her, or that she was coming on to them, and beat her for it.

In Barry's world, reality was the way that Barry saw it, and if anybody dared to see it differently, they would almost always suffer for it, one way or another.

'Them eggs was like fecking cement,' he said, pushing his plate away. 'And they was cold, too. Maybe one day before I go to meet my Maker you're going to find out how to fecking cook.'

'I'm sorry,' said Megan, cramming sheets and pillowcases into the washing machine. She had learned long ago not to retort that he always dawdled over his food and smoked while he was eating it, so it was bound to go cold, and scrambled eggs were bound to solidify.

Barry scraped back his chair and stood up. He was short, at least seven centimetres shorter than Megan, with a large head that was handsome but had a Neanderthal look about it, with deep-set eyes and a heavy jaw. His brown hair was combed forward in a point over the middle of his forehead to hide where it was receding, and he was unshaven. His tight black sweater emphasized his beer-keg chest, and his sleeves were tugged up to expose his hairy forearms.

He stood unnervingly close behind her, so close that she could smell the tobacco on his breath.

'You was listening at the door, wasn't you? How many fecking times have I told you not to listen at the door if you know what's good for you?'

'I wasn't listening, darling. I was upstairs changing the bed.'

'Then how come you asked me who Gráinne was?'

'I heard you say it just when I walked in. And like you said, it's none of my business. I was curious, that's all.'

Barry seized her upper arm and pulled her around to face him. He glared up at her for a few intense seconds and then he reached up, took hold of both of her ears, and twisted them hard. Megan gasped, and bit her lip.

'Don't fecking listen to what's none of your fecking business, do you have me?'

Megan nodded, with tears in her eyes. She half-lifted her hands to her ears, but then resisted the temptation in case he realized how much he had hurt her, and relished it.

'Right,' he said. 'I'm going out to lay a cable and then I'm off to The Cotton Ball.'

'Do you want me to come with you?'

'Why in the name of God would I want you to come with me? Don't I get enough of you cnawvshawling here at home?'

'Well, sometimes you want me to come with you. But if you don't today, that's grand. Shelagh's invited me around to see her new baby.'

'You never fecking told me that. When did you start making plans to go out without telling me? And you never told me that Shelagh had calfed.'

Megan was about to say, *I did, I told you last week but you were too scuttered to remember*, but all she said was, 'I'm sorry. I must have forgot.'

Barry slowly licked his lips as if he were trying to remember something, but then he reached into the back pocket of his brown corduroy trousers and took out a thick folded wad of euros. He pulled off two €50 notes and held them out.

'Here… give Shelagh this for the baby. Tell her to buy it something to wear or something like that. And when I say it's for the baby, she's not to spend it on Baby Powers.' By that he meant the miniature bottles of Powers whiskey that young women put in their handbags for an evening out at the Zombie Lounge. 'What is it, a boy or a girl?'

'Girl.'

'Jesus. Just what we need around Mayfield. Another scanger.'

10

Katie had only just sat down at her desk the next morning when her phone rang. It was Chief Superintendent Brendan O'Kane's personal assistant, Bridie.

'Could you come along to Chief Superintendent O'Kane's office, please, ma'am. He'd like a word.'

He's seen the Sun, thought Katie. *Well, there's nothing I can do about that now. If I could go back in time to yesterday and persuade the Lee Pusher to shove Owen Dineen off Patrick's Bridge, I would, but I can't.*

'Can you tell him I'm up the walls at the moment, Bridie? I can come to see him in a half-hour or so.'

She had memos on her desk from Assistant Chief Fire Officer Matthew Whalen and from the head of the Technical Bureau, Bill Phinner, as well as a thick report on opioid smuggling, which she had been expecting from the Customs National Drugs Team. Not only did she have those to attend to, but Moirin was coming in with a mug of latte and a plateful of shamrock shortbread biscuits. Katie and Kyna had woken up later than they had intended and there had been no time at home for a cup of coffee or any breakfast.

But Bridie said, 'I think he wants to see you now, ma'am. And Assistant Commissioner Magorian is here, too.'

'Frank Magorian? Very well, then, tell them I'll be there directly. Moirin – if anybody wants me, I'll be tied up for a while with Chief Superintendent O'Kane.'

'Aren't you taking your coffee with you?'

'I think not. I have a feeling that this is going to be a bit too serious for sipping coffee.'

Moirin couldn't pretend that she knew nothing about the story in the *Irish Sun*. From the looks that Katie had been given that morning when she walked into the station, she'd been able to tell that the paper had been seen by almost everybody.

She walked along the corridor to Brendan's office. After she had knocked, she saw Kyna coming out of the lift. She pointed at Brendan's door to indicate that she had to go in, and Kyna pressed her fingers to her lips as if to say, *Oh Jesus*. Brendan called out, 'Come!' and in she went.

Brendan was sitting at his desk, while Assistant Commissioner Frank Magorian was standing by the window. He was tall, Frank Magorian, at least six foot three, with grey wings to his slicked-back hair and a large face that was still yellowy-suntanned from his last holiday in Gran Canaria. Katie always thought that he looked exactly his age, which was fifty-three, but that he must have always looked fifty-three, even when he was a schoolboy, and he would probably go on looking fifty-three until he took his last breath,

A copy of the *Irish Sun* was lying on Brendan's desk. TOP CORK COP FLOPS, and that picture of Katie with her arms raised, as if in surrender.

Frank Magorian cleared his throat. 'How are you going on, Kathleen?' he asked her. He sounded as if he had a cold.

'I'm grand altogether, thank you, sir. If you're asking if I'm at all thrown by what's in the *Sun* this morning, then I'm not.'

'Mathew McElvey's warned me that there's worse to come,' said Brendan. 'He's had RTÉ on to him requesting a television interview with you, as well as the *Times* and the *Independent* and every radio station between here and the border.'

'It's a fierce serious matter this, Kathleen,' said Frank Magorian. 'And it's not as if we haven't had enough bad press to cope with lately – what with all the whistle-blowers accusing us of cronyism and sexism and fiddling the crime figures.'

'I'm aware of that, sir. I can totally understand how those three incidents yesterday might have given the appearance that crime in Cork is out of control, coming as they did in the space of less than twelve hours. You can't blame the press for working it up into a sensational story. They're out to sell papers, after all. But the reality is that incidents like this are vanishingly rare, and I can assure you that we're well on top of them.'

Frank Magorian took the newspaper off Brendan's desk and held it up, as if he were holding up an incriminating document in a court of law. 'It's suggested in this story that the death of Justice Quinn and the killing of Billy Hagerty are somehow connected. After all, Justice Quinn was about to pass sentence yesterday on Billy Hagerty's brother Donal, was he not? Do you think there's any truth in this? It seems likely.'

'It's far too early to say, sir. We have yet to conduct a post-mortem on Justice Quinn so we can't say with any certainty if his death was an accident or homicide. And we still have no idea what he was doing up at White's Cross when he was supposed to be at the courthouse across the way here in Anglesea Street.'

'But what about Billy Hagerty?'

'Again, we still have no leads on who might have shot him, or why. He was associated with the O'Flynn gang, although he wasn't an active member as far as we know, but there could have been any number of reasons for somebody wanting him dead.'

'And your Lee Pusher?'

'Again, no leads yet. But Dr Ailbe Power has agreed to come down tomorrow afternoon from Trinity College Department of Neuroscience in Dublin, and she's a specialist in aberrant behaviour. I'm sure that if we understand his motivation more clearly, we'll have a much better chance of identifying who he is. As I say, sir, we're on top of all of these incidents, but they can't be solved in ninety minutes, like they are on TV. This is real life, not an episode of *Columbo*.'

'Is that what you're going to say to the media? I'm not sure that's going to answer all the questions that are being raised about your general grip on things, Kathleen. I admit that your arrest and conviction rates have risen, but at the same time crime of all kinds is on the up – especially drug-dealing and people-trafficking and phone fraud.'

'I'm saying nothing to the media,' Katie told him. 'If I did, I would have to tell them what a struggle it is to keep on top of investigating crime in Cork when I've suffered so many reductions in my budget. Every day I have to make choices about how many detectives I can assign to criminal counter-intelligence, and which forensic tests we can afford – or *not* afford, in many cases. You're expecting instant results, sir, but you know full well that I've had to cut back drastically on overtime, and for instance a rapid DNA test can easily cost two hundred euros more than the regular test.'

'Come here, Kathleen, I've been fighting tooth and nail against the cuts in your finance,' said Brendan. 'But it's not all about money. Our professional competence as police officers is being openly criticized here, and I don't like to say it but your personal reputation is being called into question, too. You need to give the media *some* response.'

'My response to the media will be my results,' Katie retorted. 'I'll have some comments to make as soon as we have some positive forensic evidence, or make some arrests. Up until then, it's no comment.'

'Brendan – you'll have to think of some titbit to throw to the press,' said Frank Magorian. 'We can't possibly tell them that we have nothing to say. Not after yesterday's shambles.'

Brendan looked at Katie in a way she had never seen him look at her before. It was a chilled, calculating stare, as if he were thinking *You thought you had me cornered, did you – you wait until you see what I can do to you.*

'Are you positive you want to stick with "no comment"?' he asked her. 'I mean, can I quote you?'

'Do whatever you judge to be best, sir,' said Katie. 'You're the chief super, after all.'

Frank Magorian pulled out a handkerchief and blew his nose loudly. Then he said, 'You know that the media are likely to ask if it was wise of us to promote a female officer to detective superintendent, don't you, Kathleen? I'll be pure surprised if they don't ask us whether we put political correctness before professional judgement. And how do you think we can answer that?'

She found Bill Phinner in her office, talking to Moirin.

'I was just coming down to the lab to see you, Bill.'

'I've saved you the trip, ma'am.' He handed her a green plastic folder. 'That's our initial report on Justice Quinn's car. We're still going over it with a nit comb, of course, and I shouldn't think we'll have a full report until the middle of next week at the earliest. But at least we've found out what caused it to combust.'

Katie went over to her desk and sat down. She was trying to keep calm but inside she was still trembling with anger inside over the way that Assistant Commissioner Frank Magorian had spoken to her. She had always assumed that he was a strong supporter of her promotion, but now that he was under pressure from the media and presumably from Garda headquarters at Phoenix Park, she was sure that he would think nothing of hanging her out to dry. Her late father always used to tell her that when it came to the crunch, An Garda Síochána was all tight-knit boys together; and not only boys but stonecutters. He had been forced to retire himself as an inspector after a freemason had pulled the rug out from under him.

Bill said, 'The Jaguar's keys were taken out of the ignition and used to open the two locking petrol caps. Then it's likely that fuses of some type were inserted into both fuel tanks and lit. They could have been blasting safety fuses or they might have been nothing more than lengths of cloth soaked in petrol.'

'If the keys were taken out of the ignition, then Justice Quinn was probably dead or unconscious before the car blew up,' said Katie. 'When I saw him, he was still holding on to the steering wheel with one hand, almost casual-like. If somebody had tried to take out the keys while he was still alive, they would have had to open the door or break the window and then there's no question he would have struggled with them.'

'Sure, like. There's no doubt at all that this was homicide, whether he was deceased before the car blew up or not. I've sent Aoife Shaugnessy and Stephen O'Leary over to CUH to help Dr Kelley with the post-mortem. Aoife's our new ballistics expert, and she's brilliant. She has only to take a quick sconce at the bullet hole in somebody's head and she can tell you the calibre of the bullet and what kind of a gun it was shot from and whether the shooter likes milk in his tea.'

'All right, Bill, thanks,' said Katie. 'We'll just have to wait and see now. But there's something you can do for me.'

She opened her desk drawer and took out the phone that had been dropped by last night's intruder, wrapped in a clear plastic freezer bag.

'Just after midnight I caught some gowl prowling around my back garden. I gave him a few kicks where it hurt and chased him away, but he left this behind. I'm wondering if that IT whizz of yours might be able to unlock it and find out who the fellow was.'

'He didn't hurt you at all?'

'No, and he took nothing – not that I have anything in my garden worth taking – and he caused no damage. All I want to know is who he is and what he might have been doing there at that time of night.'

'Okay,' said Bill, taking the phone. 'If anybody can open this for you, our man Conall the Phonecracker can.'

He left, and as he left, Moirin came in with a fresh mug of latte.

'Are you all right, ma'am?' she asked her. 'I hope you don't mind me saying this, but when you came back from that meeting just now anybody would have thought that you'd swallowed a mouthful of wazzies.'

'I'll be grand, Moirin. Nothing to get upset about. Not too much, anyway. Sometimes you can find out quite unexpected who your friends are, and other times quite unexpected you can find out who your friends *aren't*. It's not worth weeping over.'

★★★

Katie asked Moirin to ring Orla, Justice Quinn's widow, to see if she could arrange to meet her and offer her condolences. At the same time, Katie wanted to find out discreetly if Justice Quinn had received any unusual phone calls or threats that he hadn't reported to the Garda, or if they had seen any suspicious characters lurking around their house in Tivoli Park in the past few days.

Moirin came off the phone to say, 'She's in town at the moment, but she can meet you at Isaacs in half an hour, if that's okay.'

'That's perfect. I have to pop into Neville's anyway and get a new battery for my watch. Do you know, Paul bought it for me seven years ago when I was promoted to inspector, and this is the first time it's stopped.' She looked down at it, and said, 'I hope that's not an omen.'

'Oh, come on, ma'am, you know what they say about the papers. Today's news, tomorrow's cat litter.'

As she was buttoning up her coat, Detective Inspector Robert Fitzpatrick knocked at her door. He was accompanied by Detective Caffrey.

'Off out, ma'am? Won't keep you, but we've made some progress with the Billy Hagerty murder. A Honda Accord LX was found only an hour ago burned out behind a derelict barn in Bottlehill. It was Kona Coffee Metallic – that's the official Honda name for that colour – and it matches the few descriptions we were given of the car that Billy Hagerty was shot from.'

'Lord help us, not another burned-out car.'

'*This* car, luckily, was only partially burned out. I'd say that the rain started to pelt down soon after it was set alight, and put it out. We may be able to lift some fingerprints off the steering wheel and the door handles, and the officer who found it says he saw a spent cartridge case lying on the floor in the back.'

'That's brilliant news,' said Katie. 'Don't you just love it when criminals are that careless? You'd think that after all the crime shows they've seen on the telly they would have the brains by now to clean up thoroughly after themselves. Look at that Denny McCarthy. We're still no near to finding out who killed *him*, are we, after nearly a year? Shot in his own house, sitting in his own bath, with both barrels of a twelve-bore shotgun, and whoever shot him didn't leave a single microscopic speck of evidence.'

'It didn't help that nobody could think who would want to kill him, though, did it? Everybody said that Denny was the friendliest fellow you could ever meet. Even his ex-wife.'

'Well, keep at it, Robert,' said Katie. 'The chief super thinks the Riordans were most likely responsible for Billy Hagerty getting shot, and I'm reluctant to say it but I tend to agree with him. What worries me is that the O'Flynns could well decide to get their revenge, and soon. I'm only hoping that Muireann will be able to tip us off early if there's any hint of them planning a payback. I've had more than enough of this tit-for-tat killing. They're worse than kids in a playground, do you know what I mean?'

Detective Inspector Fitzpatrick's phone pinged. After he had frowned at it, he said, 'O'Sullivan's traced the Honda. It was stolen five days ago from the car park up at the airport.'

'Five days ago? Now that could be interesting. Five days ago the Riordans wouldn't have known that Justice Quinn was going to be killed and that Donal Hagerty's sentencing hearing would have to be postponed. So apart from him being Donal's brother, why would they have targeted Billy Hagerty? Of course he might have given them another reason that we haven't heard about, but it wouldn't surprise me at all if it was Thomas O'Flynn they were after, and Billy Hagerty just happened to be standing in the way.'

'Still and all,' said Detective Inspector Fitzpatrick, 'I'm sure you wouldn't exactly be sobbing into your coffee if they *had* hit Thomas O'Flynn.'

'Robert – I don't want anybody killing anybody in Cork, whether they're out-and-out scumbags or whether they're pure as the driven cocaine. I don't want to see myself on the front page of the *Sun* ever again, and I mean *ever* – except if I'm appointed commissioner.'

11

When Katie walked into Isaacs restaurant on MacCurtain Street, Orla Quinn was already waiting for her in the back alcove, half-hidden behind the bare brick walls. Katie had met her only two or three times, at legal functions, and the last time had been at the opening of the new courthouse. She looked white and gaunt, almost like a crack addict, and she was wearing a black suit, with a black three-stranded choker around her neck, made of jet.

She stood up when Katie came in, and Katie embraced her. Underneath her black suit jacket Katie could feel her ribs.

'Oh, Orla,' she said. 'What a tragedy.'

They sat down and a waitress came over, but all Orla wanted was a bottle of sparkling Ballygowan water. Katie asked for a latte, even though she had already drunk more coffee this morning than she usually did, and it was beginning to make her feel jumpy.

'Do you have anybody staying with you for now, to keep you company?' she asked Orla.

'Our daughter's with me – Davina. She drove down yesterday afternoon from Kilkenny and she came along with me this morning to see the solicitor. She's taken herself off to buy herself a new spring jumper while you and I are having a chat. Our two sons will be coming down from Dublin this afternoon so. Jamie and Joyce.'

Orla sat there for a while, looking towards the restaurant door as if she were half-expecting somebody she knew to walk in. She had hooded hazel eyes and a sharp straight nose and her light brown hair was braided into a tight coronet. When Katie had first met her she had been beautiful in a slender, mythical way, like one of the women in a Pre-Raphaelite painting, but her looks had become harder since then.

Katie was about to ask her about her sons, but Orla said, 'Those two officers of yours who came to break the news to me – they were so kind and sympathetic. They told me that Garrett would be taken to the hospital, for a post-mortem. Do you know how long that's going to take?'

'It's impossible to say for sure, Orla. But I know that Dr Kelley has already made a start. She's the Assistant State Pathologist. We've also sent two forensic experts to assist her.'

'Forensic experts? Why? Does that mean you think that Garrett's death might not have been an accident?'

'I never jump to conclusions before I've seen the evidence. But considering the circumstances, do you know, I have to keep an open mind. Do you have any idea why he might have gone up to White's Cross, instead of driving straight to the courthouse?'

Orla gave Katie an almost imperceptible shake of her head, still staring at the door.

'I've no idea at all. We have friends who live in Castletownroche, and sometimes we go above to visit them, but we always use the main roads. In any case I can't think why Garrett would have been driving up to see them by himself, on a day when he was supposed to be in court.'

Now she took her eyes away from the door and looked at Katie directly.

'You saw him yourself, didn't you? You saw him in his car?'

'I did, yes.'

'What did he look like? Did he look like he was at peace?'

Katie was about to say *His car was totally gutted, Orla, it said so on the news*, but then she realized that Orla would never have seen the incinerated occupants of any burned-out vehicles, and probably imagined that Garrett had simply died of smoke inhalation. She wouldn't have realized that his car had been reduced to nothing but a blackened skeleton and that he himself had been charred beyond recognition, head to toe, except for his claddagh band. By the time the press photographers and cameramen had reached White's Cross, his Jaguar had already been sheeted over with a tarpaulin and loaded on to the back of a rescue lorry, ready to be driven to Midleton.

'Yes,' she said. 'He looked peaceful enough.'

'That's something, then.'

There was another long pause between them. Orla lowered her eyes now and she repeatedly moved the salt shaker and the pepper mill backwards and forwards as if she were playing a thoughtful game of chess. Katie could tell that she had something she wanted to say, but was having difficulty working out how to say it.

'Where will you have him interred?' she asked her.

'In St Mary's, in Clon. That's where he came from originally, Clon, and he still has family there. But then you knew that already.'

'Yes, I did of course. I've known Garrett ever since I was first stationed at Anglesea Street.'

Orla moved the salt and pepper until they were side by side. Checkmate.

'And you were lovers?' she said.

'Orla, that was a long time ago now. It didn't last for long and as far as I'm concerned it's over and forgotten. All I'm interested in now is finding out how Garrett died, and if his death *wasn't* accidental, then who could have killed him, and why.'

'He told me about you and him, the night that you finished. He went to confession, too, that Sunday.'

'Well, he loved you and he didn't love me, so he must have felt guilty about it.'

'You weren't the only one, you know. There were others. I could write you a list, and I'd bet you know some of them, or even most of them.'

'He's dead, Orla. He might have strayed a few times but he stayed with you, didn't he, and there's no point in raking up the things he did wrong, not now. God will already be judging him for those. Let's just concentrate on tracking down the person or persons who murdered him, if anybody did.'

Orla poured herself some fizzy water. 'I should have divorced him, shouldn't I, years ago? But I could never think of it, Katie. I couldn't bear to think of us living apart. I loved him so much. I adored him.'

'Tell me – in the past few weeks, did he receive any threats that you know about?'

'Threats? Oh, he often had threats. Almost every time he sent anybody down, or handed them a fine, he'd have trolls on Twitter telling him that they were going to cut his throat or smash his head in with a hurly or put a bomb under his car. He never took them seriously, though, and they never scared him, not at all. He said they were proof that he was doing a good job.'

'How about stalkers? Did he have anybody suspicious following him around lately?'

Orla thought for a few seconds and then shook her head. 'If he was being followed, he never said anything about it to me.'

'How about prowlers, around your house?'

'No. No prowlers. Although now you come to mention it, I did see a strange Range Rover parked up our street a couple of times, early in the week. I don't know what it was doing there because it didn't belong to any of our neighbours. It was there on Monday morning and then again on Tuesday afternoon.'

'A Range Rover?'

'I think it was a Range Rover. That kind of a big car, anyway. It was only about thirty metres away, on the opposite side of the street.'

'What colour was it?'

'Sort of silvery-grey.'

'Could you see if there was anybody in it?'

'I couldn't, no. There was too much reflection on the windscreen.'

'You didn't happen to see anybody getting in or out of it?'

'No. It didn't stay for long. I first noticed it on the Monday morning when I went out the front door to check if we'd any post. Maybe five minutes after that I took Garrett a cup of tea in his study and when I looked out the Range Rover had gone. On the Tuesday afternoon I saw it out of the upstairs bedroom window, but I'd say it could only have been there for ten or fifteen minutes. I didn't really pay it too much attention. Like, I had no reason to.'

'What times of day are you talking about exactly? There's no CCTV on Tivoli Park or Lover's Walk, but we could check to see if a silver Range Rover drove past Silver Springs round about then, or maybe if it went in the other direction, through St Luke's Cross. It would have had to go one way or the other.'

'I'm not sure. I'd say it was there about elevenish on the Monday, and about half past three on Tuesday afternoon, maybe a little later.'

'Thanks a million, Orla. That could be pure helpful, if only to eliminate somebody who wasn't involved.'

They sat in silence again while Orla turned her attention back to the restaurant door and Katie unenthusiastically sipped at her coffee.

After a while, Orla said, 'I suppose you'll be wanting to come to Garrett's funeral.'

'I'd like to pay him my last respects, Orla. We were close, yes, but most of our relationship was strictly professional. It really depends if you want me there.'

'I don't see why not. Like you said, it's all in the past now, and there's no reason to go on picking at old sores.'

'I'll let you know, anyway, as soon as we can release him for burial.'

'Strange, isn't it? He started the week planning our holidays this year. Sicily, that's where he wanted us to go, renting a villa. But he could have saved himself the trouble, couldn't he, if he'd known that by Wednesday he'd be dead and gone.'

'Orla...' said Katie, and she reached across the table to take hold of her hand. At that moment, though, Orla stood up and waved.

'There's Davina, my daughter. Holy Mary, look at all the bags she's carrying! She must have bought up the whole of Fran and Jane.'

Orla's daughter appeared, struggling with five large carrier bags. She was wearing a pink beanie and a red overcoat, although she had a black armband around her left sleeve. Katie had last seen Davina when she had visited the courthouse in Washington Street, more than five years ago, when she was still at school, and she was shocked to see how much she had grown up to look like Garrett. She could almost have been his twin sister. She had inherited his shiny mahogany-brown hair, his blue, wide-apart eyes and his strongly defined cheekbones. Most of all she carried that knowing, slightly amused smile that Katie had first found so attractive about him, as if he had been privy to some intimate secret about her.

'How are you going on, Davina?' she asked her, standing up. 'I'm so deeply sorry about your dad. I can't tell you how much he's going to be missed by everybody at Anglesea Street.'

'Thanks,' said Davina. 'I can't even believe it myself yet. I've been shopping just to take my mind off it.'

Katie laid her hand on Orla's shoulder. Davina's likeness to Garrett had upset her more than she could have imagined.

'I'd best be off now, Orla. It's been grand to chat to you, and thanks for being so understanding. Like I say, I'll be in touch about the funeral arrangements as soon as I can. And thanks a million for that bit of information about the Range Rover. Maybe it'll turn out to be nothing at all, but you never know.'

She left Isaacs and walked along MacCurtain Street to where she had parked her car, opposite the Everyman Theatre. She wasn't even halfway there before she felt tears running down her cheeks, and she couldn't stop herself from letting out a loud croaking sob, almost like Foltchain barking, so that passers-by turned and stared at her.

She sat in her car and tugged out a tissue to wipe her eyes. After she had done that, she checked in the rear-view mirror to make sure her mascara wasn't too blotchy. *Who am I grieving for? Garrett, or Conor? Or am I only grieving for myself?*

She could vividly picture Garrett turning towards her in bed, leaning on his elbow and giving her that enigmatic smile of his. 'I think I'll have to find myself a new shadow,' he had told her. 'This one keeps nagging me to get dressed and leave you, but I want to stay.'

'Who's in charge?' she had asked him. 'You or your shadow?'

'Neither of us. One of us can't live without the other. I can't send my shadow home to Orla on its own.'

When she thought about that, her eyes filled with tears again, so she started the engine and pulled away from the kerb, right in front of a 205 bus, which blasted its horn at her.

12

As soon as Katie walked back into her office, Moirin said, 'Mathew McElvey just rang. He's had a rake of calls from the media and he's asking that you ring him back.'

'Thanks, Moirin. Any other messages?'

'Only an invitation from the Saturday Book Club for you to give them a talk at the Central Library next week – "the life of a female detective". It's their crime novel month, so they told me. I think they need to know quite urgently.'

'Oh, Jesus. All right. I'll have a think about it. As if I didn't have enough on my plate with real crime, let alone imaginary crime.'

She hadn't even taken off her coat before her phone pinged. It was a text message from Dr Mary Kelley. 'Preliminary X-rays of Justice Quinn's body show no foreign objects e.g. bullets. 98 pc 4th-degree burns but no other obvious physical trauma (penetrative stab wounds etc). Skull intact. No broken/fractured bones. Sufficient bodily fluids retrieved for CT scanning – awaiting results.'

Katie sat down and read the text again. If Garrett hadn't been shot or stabbed, then how had he been killed? Further tests might reveal that he had been unconscious before his car was set alight. Maybe he had simply been told at gunpoint to stay in the driver's seat.

But why in the name of God had he driven up to White's Cross, in the middle of nowhere? It was unlikely that he had been heading for Castletownroche because his car was facing south-westwards, in the opposite direction. And who was driving the grey or silver SUV that the farmer had seen speeding away? Could it have been that silvery-grey Range Rover that Orla had spotted parked outside their house in Tivoli Park?

Detective Sergeant Begley appeared in her open door and coughed to get her attention. Detective Scanlan was close behind him.

'Sean, come on in. What's the story?'

'Stephen Herlihy at the courthouse has given us all the information on Justice Quinn's trials that you asked him for. He's made a list of every case that he conducted over the past two years, either by himself or sitting with another justice. He's also attached the two separate lists that you wanted – every defendant that Justice Quinn found guilty, and every defendant that he fined or jailed, or both.'

Katie quickly shuffled through the lists and said, 'Mother of God. There's a fair few here all right.'

'One hundred and twelve, to be exact. Padragain and me will be combing through them to see if there's any possible suspects who might have had cause to look for revenge. I hate to say it, but I know almost all of the scummers that Justice Quinn has sent down – and their scummy families, too. But, you know, most of them are too thick to send a kid to piss through your letter box, never mind set up a hit like this one.'

'I still have a gut feeling that the O'Flynns were behind this,' said Detective Scanlan. 'I mean, how much of a coincidence was it that Justice Quinn was killed on the very morning before he was due to pass sentence on Donal Hagerty? The O'Flynns have tried intimidating judges and jurors more than once before, haven't they? And at least three or four of the O'Flynn gang were sitting in the public gallery almost every single day of Hagerty's trial, giving the jury the evil eye. You know – if you dare to find him guilty we'll happily rip your lungs out for you, given half a chance.'

'You have to admit that they're cute hoors, though, the O'Flynns,' said Detective Sergeant Begley. 'They always pay some poor *amadán* to do their dirty deeds for them. We're ninety-nine per cent certain that they paid Donal Hagerty to shoot Michael Riordan, but there's never a hope in hell of proving it. You might as well try to prove that it was Sonny O'Neill who shot Michael Collins back in 1922, even though everybody in the whole of Ireland knows damn well that it was him.'

Katie was still looking through the list of Justice Quinn's convictions when Detective Inspector Fitzpatrick and Detective Caffrey came in, accompanied by Bill Phinner. Bill was wearing a baggy green sweater and baggy brown corduroy trousers and his usual funereal expression. Katie thought: *Jesus, you look exactly how I feel.*

'How's the form, ma'am?' asked Detective Inspector Patrick. 'We've just had a report from the technical experts at Midleton. They've completed their preliminary examination of the Honda that we believe was used in the Billy Hagerty shooting, and so we thought we'd give you an update.'

'Okay, grand. What's the story, Bill?'

'Nothing much, I'm sorry to say. There's no fingerprints on the door handles or the steering wheel except for those of the owner and his family. They're not yet back from Gran Canaria but their next-door neighbour has a key to their house in Douglas and they gave us permission to go in and take samples. They're cutting their holliers short and flying back to Cork this afternoon.'

'Nothing on the floors or the seats?'

'The carpets and the upholstery were all badly fire-damaged. They had them vinyl seat covers and those were totally shrivelled up, so there was no hope of retrieving any fibres or DNA from them. There's that cartridge case, of course. It's a 9x19mm Parabellum round, which had traces of SR4756, which is a load that scores highly for its firepower. But again – no prints on it.'

'So the shooters weren't as careless as we'd hoped.'

'No, ma'am. In my opinion, this wasn't some random killing – not like some header throwing a rabie because Billy Hagerty called his old doll a moose, nothing like that. Whoever did it has definitely carried out killings like this one more than once before. Sure, like, they weren't as professional as some of the gang hits we've seen. But unless one of them's a sneaky snake, I reckon we're going to find it fierce difficult to find out who pulled the trigger.'

'What do you think, Robert? It seems even less likely to me that it was Billy Hagerty that they were after. It's interesting that they carried it out in broad daylight. A gang shooting like this, usually they go round to the victim's home, don't they? – either at the crack of dawn or late at night, when there's less chance of any witnesses being around.'

'Like you said before, ma'am, the Honda was stolen before anybody knew that Justice Quinn was going to be killed and that Donal Hagerty's sentencing hearing would have to be delayed. I suppose it's possible that the Riordans were looking for Billy Hagerty to pay a blood price for what his brother had done. But if it *was* the Riordans who set up the shooting, we know of course that they've been after nailing Thomas O'Flynn for years now. Maybe they thought it was too risky, trying to hit him at home. His house in Farranree has more cameras around it than the RTÉ news studio. Whereas Billy, he lives in a one-bedroom basement flat on Wellington Road without even a burglar alarm. Or *lived*, rather. Anybody could have knocked at his door and shot him at any time. Why take the risk of shooting him in the street?'

Detective Caffrey said, 'Unfortunately, there's no CCTV coverage on Gerald Griffin Street opposite The Weavers, so we don't have any footage of the shooting itself. We're still checking, though, to see if the Honda was picked up on CCTV leaving the airport car park on the day that it was taken, or anywhere after the shooting between Blackpool and Bottlehill, and if anybody identifiable was filmed getting in or getting out of it.'

'Fair play,' said Katie. 'I'll let you get back to it, then.'

Everybody else left her office, but Detective Inspector Fitzpatrick came up to her desk and stood looking down at her.

'Robert?' she said. His expression was always unreadable, and sometimes she wondered if he had any emotions at all.

'You'll forgive me for asking you a personal question, ma'am, but how are you bearing up? I know you've been through a fierce difficult time lately, and that story in the papers couldn't have helped.'

'That's pure thoughtful of you, Robert, thank you. I'm taking it day by day, do you know the kind of way? Or hour by hour, rather. Or even minute by minute. But concentrating on these cases, that's helping to keep my mind off any of the things that I'd rather not be thinking about.'

'I want you to know that if you need any support, ma'am – anybody to stand up for you and say that you're doing a grand job in spite of your budget restrictions and a chief superintendent who seems determined to throw up as many obstructions in front of you as possible – then I'm here for you.'

'That means a great deal to me, Robert. I appreciate it.'

Detective Inspector Fitzpatrick paused, and for a moment Katie thought he was about to go. But then he said, in the flattest, most expressionless voice, 'I lost somebody dear to me once myself. I know how hard and painful it is, trying to understand why it happened. But you can never really understand, in the end, because nobody can tell you why people you love should die before their time. You just have to learn to live with it. Day by day, like you are. Hour by hour. Minute by minute.'

With that, he walked out of her office. As soon as he had gone, Moirin came in and said, 'Sorry to bother you, ma'am. Have you thought about that talk yet? "The life of a female detective"? They've been on the phone again.'

'I think you'll have to make my excuses, Moirin. Tell them that I'm right up the walls at the moment, juggling with too many cases. The truth is, if I told them what the life of a female detective is really like, they'd all end up in floods of tears.'

Katie started to read the report that she had been sent by the Customs National Drugs Team. Apart from a single smuggler who had been caught off the coast at Ballycroneen in a rubber life raft packed with sixty bales of cocaine, there had been a forty per cent increase in the past six months in OxyContin and other opioids seized by customs at Rosslare and Ringaskiddy. Addiction to painkillers was already becoming a serious problem in Cork, since they were being openly sold in pubs and nightclubs. Seven people had already died this year in Cork city from opioid overdoses.

Her phone rang. It was Dr Kelley, ringing her from the morgue at CUH.

'How are you, Kathleen? I thought I'd let you know that Roisin Carroll's parents are coming here at four o'clock to make a formal identification before she's sent off to Keohane's, the funeral directors. They're also going to visit their granddaughter on Ladybird Ward. First time they've ever seen her, so I'm told. Maybe you'd care to have a word with them and tell them how your investigation into the Lee Pusher is coming along. You could reassure them that their daughter didn't die in vain, something like that.'

Katie checked the time on the gold Piaget watch that Conor had given her. 'Okay, fine, Dr Kelley, thanks. I'll come over directly. How's it going with Justice Quinn?'

'The forensic experts are still analysing the bodily fluids, but it's likely they'll have some results later today. I've just finished the post-mortem on Billy Hagerty too. That turned out to be interesting.'

'Interesting in what way?'

'I'll show you when you get here, that's easier than trying to explain it over the phone.'

Katie shrugged on the black Max Mara wraparound overcoat that had cost her almost a week's salary. It was chilly and damp outside but at least it wasn't pelting.

She told Moirin to ring Mathew McElvey and arrange a meeting with him when she came back from the hospital. On her drive into the city this morning she had begun to come up with some ideas for retaliating against Owen Dineen and his COP FLOPS front page. She had checked the most up-to-date crime statistics from the Central Statistics Office and she could prove that while drug offences in Cork city were still higher than in rural areas, burglary and assault cases had dropped dramatically.

She had also remembered a feature Owen Dineen had written three or four years ago in which he had criticized the promotion of women in An Garda Síochána as 'skirting the issue of rising crime'. So she could accuse him of misogyny as well as getting his figures wrong, and in these #MeToo days that was more serious than blasphemy.

To begin with, she had intended to maintain a dignified silence about the CORK COP FLOPS story, but the more she had churned it over in her mind, the angrier she had become. It didn't help that it had come out at a time when she was grieving, and she felt like screaming at the whole world for tearing away from her so many people that she had loved.

She was walking along the corridor when Chief Superintendent O'Kane smartly opened his office door, as if he had been listening out for her.

'Katie,' he said. 'You're not in a rush, are you? I'd like a word if I could.'

'Well, I'm on my way to CUH. It's that poor girl who was drowned by the Lee Pusher. Her ma and her da are coming in to identify her so.'

'This won't take long.'

She followed him into his office and he closed the door behind her. Then he came and stood very close in front of her and looked down at her for a while without saying anything. He lifted his left hand as if he were going to stroke her hair, but then he lowered it again.

'I was really hoping that what happened... we could put it behind us.'

'You mean you don't want me to complain to the Ombudsman.'

'Well, naturally I don't want you to. Especially since I was only trying to show you that I still have feelings for you. Fierce strong feelings. I've tried to be professional about it, but you're a stunningly attractive woman, Katie. I have to confess that ever since I've been appointed here to Anglesea Street I've dreamed about you again and again, and every time I've woken with a big búdán up on me.'

Katie turned away. 'I don't want to hear any smutty talk like that from you, Brendan. All I can say is that I've not yet decided what action I'll be taking about what happened. As you know full well, I've had other more important and more distressing matters on my mind. Now, I have to go, or I'll be late.'

She started to walk towards the door, but Brendan snatched her coat's wide sleeve and turned her around. She had seen that look on other men's faces, too, when she had defied them. *Who do you think you are? You're a woman! How dare you speak to me like that?*

'Katie, come here, will you? I'm trying to tell you that I want us to get back together again, at least as friends. Hopefully much more than friends.'

'We're both senior officers in the same Garda station, Brendan. Any kind of relationship is out of the question. Apart from that, I don't *want* to get back together with you, not even as friends, not in a million years. You weren't trying to show you still had feelings for me that night. I was unconscious and you raped me. And the reason you're saying that you want us to get back together is so that I don't report you for raping me. You're not only a slimeball, you're an obvious slimeball.'

Brendan slapped her across the left cheek, hard. Katie staggered back, unable to believe what he had just done.

'That was always the trouble with you!' he shouted at her. 'Always so high and mighty! Flirting around like a scrubber and then turning up your nose if any feller showed an interest in you!'

He pulled loose the belt of her wraparound coat, seized the lapels and flung them wide apart, as if he were throwing open a pair of double doors. Katie swung her arm and hit him on the side of the neck, just below the ear, and then tried to thrust up her knee in between his legs, but he pushed her and kept on pushing her until he forced her up against the arm of his office couch and she fell over backwards.

She tried to swing herself off the couch but Brendan climbed on top of her, pressing one knee down on to her thigh and pinning down her shoulder. With his free hand he pulled up her skirt, yanking it seven or eight centimetres at a time until it was up round her hips, and then he dragged her black tights halfway down her thighs. All the time she was struggling and twisting and hitting him as hard as she could with nippon kempo blows, but in that position, squashed down on to the couch, it was impossible to give them all the force she wanted to.

'Brendan, what in the – *name* of Jesus—' she gasped. But Brendan seemed to be possessed. His eyes were unfocused. His teeth were clenched so that his breath was seething in and out between them, and every muscle in his body felt as if it had tightened up into knots. She might as well have tried hitting a wooden statue.

'*Brendan!*' she screamed. '*Brendan! Stop it! No, Brendan! Stop it!*'

But Brendan snapped her thong to one side, and then he tugged down the zip of his dark uniform trousers. He reached inside and twisted out his penis, which was already so stiff that it was curved upward, and his foreskin was pulled back over his damson-purple glans.

'*Brendan! For the love of God Almighty, Brendan! No!*'

Katie lashed wildly at his face. Twice he managed to jerk his head out of her reach, but as he bent forward to push his penis up into her, she clawed at his eyes and his nose and his cheeks, digging in her fingernails as deeply as she could. He let out a scream that sounded more like a woman than a man, violently shaking his head from side to side to get free of her. As he did so he ejaculated, spattering his semen on to Katie's thighs and on to the couch.

With all her strength, Katie hit him again and again, and then heaved herself up and pushed him off her. He sprawled back, and then climbed unsteadily on to his knees, one hand cupping his face. He had bloody scratches on his eyelids and his cheeks and the side of his chin, and his left eye was already closing up, and crimson. His shrivelling penis was still hanging out of his fly.

'I'm sorry, Katie,' he croaked. 'I don't know what got into me there. I'm so sorry.'

'No, you're not,' said Katie. Her heart was thumping painfully and she was breathing hard. 'If you thought I might forgive you, Brendan – Mother of God, you've blown any chance of that now. Blown it sky-high.'

Brendan said nothing, but lowered his head, dabbing at his face with his fingertips. Katie took a tissue out of her pocket and wiped her thigh, wrinkling up her nose in disgust.

'Evidence,' she said, holding up the tissue before she tucked it back into its plastic wrapper. 'In case you ever deny it.'

She pulled up her tights and straightened her skirt, and then, still shaking, she took out her phone and took photographs of Brendan kneeling on the floor, nursing his bloody cheeks.

'What are you going to do?' he asked her.

'Go back to my office and wash off any trace of you. Then – I don't know. But I can swear to you, Brendan, you won't get away with this. This is you finished.'

He stayed where he was as she walked to his office door. She was so dizzy and disorientated that she stumbled and almost fell over before she reached it, but she managed to steady herself. When she reached the door, she found that when he had closed it behind her, he had locked it. She turned the key, opened it and went out, and after she had stepped out into the corridor, she slammed it with a bang behind her.

Detective Sergeant Begley was passing, and he gave her a startled look, as if to say *Jesus, what was all that about?* But when he saw the expression on Katie's face he simply gave her a nod, and an uneasy little grin, and left it at that.

13

Katie was tempted to plead that she was suffering from a migraine and drive home. She could take Barney and Foltchain for a long walk along by the harbour, so that the salty sea breeze could fluff away her anger and her total disgust – not only for Brendan, but for herself.

What really clawed at the inside of her mind was that she had held back on reporting Brendan for raping her when he had driven her back home on the night that Conor had died. She could understand now that his motive had only partly been sexual. His overwhelming need had been to show her that he was dominant, and that he could have her whenever he wanted her, whether he found her attractive or not – just like he had today. He was supposed to be commanding this Garda station and he couldn't tolerate having a woman working for him who was cleverer and stronger than he was. It was crucial for his masculinity to crush her.

'You're back quick, ma'am,' said Moirin, when she returned to her office.

'Left my phone in the toilet,' she lied, trying to smile. 'I'll forget my head next.'

She went into her toilet and stared at herself in the mirror over the washbasin, as if she were trying to remember who she was. She looked strangely composed, not like a woman who was smashed up inside with rage and self-recrimination.

She rolled off her tights and dropped them into the pedal bin. Thank God she always carried at least one spare pair in her purse. She washed herself, rubbing the inside of her thigh until it was scarlet, and after that she tidied herself up, trying to breathe calmly and evenly while she did so. Her hairdresser, Ruari, had cut her dark red hair into a short, sharply pointed bob, and so it needed only a few strokes of the brush to straighten it. Fixing her make-up took only a moment, too. She always wore a trace of mascara when she was working, because her eyelashes were so fair, and foundation, and a hint of blusher, but no more than that.

'I'll see you in about an hour so – maybe a little more,' she told Moirin, as she left for the second time.

'Are you *sure* that everything's all right, ma'am?' Moirin asked her. She could have sworn that Moirin was psychic.

'I'm grand, thanks, Moirin. Just trying to keep too many balls in the air, that's all.' Then she thought: *Jesus, that would be funny if it weren't so sick.*

She walked briskly past Brendan's office, wondering what she would say if he were to suddenly step out, but his door remained closed. *Nursing his scratches and his ego, I expect, and wondering what to do next, like I am.*

As she drove to Wilton, she turned on the radio in her car to Cork's 96FM, loud, so that Billie Eilish's song 'Bury A Friend' drowned out both her anger about Brendan and her grieving for Conor. *Today... I am thinking about the things that are deadly.*

When she turned into the hospital car park, she was surprised to see Dr Kelley standing outside smoking a cigarette, especially since the hospital grounds were a no-smoking zone. She thought that Dr Kelley had put on weight again, too, so that she looked like one of those Russian matryoshka dolls, with one doll inside another.

Katie climbed out of her car and walked across to her, putting on a disapproving expression.

'I didn't know you smoked.'

'I don't. Well, I didn't. I gave it up three years ago. But my father passed last week and he was always my guiding light, do you know? And I felt like a cigarette, that's all. Something to keep me company. Something to smell like my da.'

She took a deep drag and then she flicked the butt away into the street.

'When somebody you love dies, you think, Holy Mary, we're all going to die anyway, so what's the use of worrying about it? All this stuff about exercise and cutting down your drinking and not eating meat. Those three poor souls we have lying in the morgue there right now, they could have been swimming forty lengths a day and eating broccoli until it came out their ears. None of it kept them living any longer, did it?'

Katie took hold of her hand. 'I'm so sorry about your father, Mary. I think I met him once. He used to be head of cardiology at the Mercy, didn't he?'

'That's right. And he died of a myocardial infarction, would you believe, on his seventy-eighth birthday. How ironic is that? One minute he was sitting at the piano singing "The Rising of the Moon". The very next minute he was taken away from us.'

Dr Kelley led Katie into the morgue.

'Roisin Carroll's parents rang me to say that they were running late, but they should be here by 4.30. It'll give us some time to have a good look at Justice Quinn, anyway, and Billy Hagerty.'

'You said there was something interesting about Billy Hagerty.'

'I did, yes, and that was probably the understatement of the century.'

The morgue was as chilly as ever, with washed-out rays of sunlight falling from its clerestory windows, like fine net curtains. Despite the fierce air conditioning and the tang of antiseptic, there was still a faintly rotten odour of dead bodies.

'That's Justice Quinn over there,' said Dr Kelley, pointing to a trolley by the opposite wall with a pale green sheet draped over it. 'And here's your man.'

Billy Hagerty was still lying on the stainless-steel autopsy table – although he, too, was covered by a pale green sheet, stained on one side by a moth-like pattern of dried blood, which resembled a Rorschach test.

'We've wheeled Roisin Carroll off to the visitors' observation room, ready for her parents to see her. I combed her hair myself, the young angel. She looks like she's fast asleep, not passed away.'

'It was tragic, her being drowned like that,' said Katie. 'Absolutely pointless, too. We have a psychologist coming down from Trinity College later today to see if we can come up with any reason why this header might be pushing people at random into the river.'

'Pity your man here's dead. Now *he* could have had a few interesting things to talk to your psychologist about, and no mistake. Denis!'

Dr Kelley's skinny young assistant came in from the sluice room at the back of the morgue, his white lab coat hanging around him as if he had just landed by parachute.

'Would you—?' Dr Kelley asked him, gesturing that he should lift the sheet off Billy Hagerty's body. Denis dragged it off and clumsily folded it up.

Katie approached the autopsy table and stared down at Billy Hagerty's naked body in disbelief. His head was still misshapen from the two bullets that had burst inside it, although Dr Kelley had done her best to reassemble his face, so that at least he was recognizable. There was another entry wound about three centimetres below his ribcage, on the right-hand side.

It wasn't the bullet wounds, though, that riveted Katie's attention. It was the two diagonal scars, one on either side of his chest, and the deep puckered scar over his left hip. Most of all it was his genitals: his penis was erect, but bent downwards and sideways against his thigh, and his scrotum was nothing more than an empty bag of smooth skin, not wrinkled as she would have expected a scrotum to be.

She looked across at Dr Kelley and Dr Kelley nodded.

'Yes. Billy Hagerty's a man, but he's a transgender man. He used to be a woman. He's had a bilateral mastectomy and his chest has been reshaped to give it more masculine contours. That's what we usually call "top surgery". From the scars on the lower pectoralis muscle, I would guess that he used to have quite large breasts.'

Katie said, 'I've heard of this, of course, but never seen it in the flesh. It's amazing.'

'You can see by the scar here across the lower stomach that he's had a hysterectomy – his uterus taken out. He's probably had a BSO, too, a bilateral salpingo-oophorectomy, which means that both ovaries and fallopian tubes have been removed. This we call "bottom surgery".'

'And his genitals? How was that done?'

'His penis was formed out of this tissue graft from his hip. There's a prosthetic inside it with an outer coating of silicone and interlocking plastic joints. All he had to do to get an erection was bend it upwards by hand. He's had the simplest and the cheapest prosthetic. You can get more expensive ones, which are pumped up with reservoirs of saline water inside the scrotum, although those don't tend to last so long and quite often they can go wrong and have to be taken out again.'

'It's so hard to believe that he was once a woman. I mean, he's so masculine-looking. He has stubble on his chin.'

'Well, that's the testosterone. His urethra was rerouted through his new penis so that he could urinate standing up like any other man. You can see that his outer vaginal lips, his labia majora, they've been joined together to form his scrotum. Usually he would have been given prosthetic testicles, but this obviously hasn't been done yet. Maybe he wasn't ready for them.'

Katie stood looking at Billy Hagerty's body for over a minute, saying nothing. Eventually, she said, 'I don't know whether this puts a whole new complexion on this shooting or not. Where do you think this surgery would have been done?'

'Oh, in the UK, almost certainly. In Ireland there isn't enough demand for gender reassignment surgery to set up a specialist treatment centre. There's a scheme run by the Health Service Executive for sex-change treatment abroad. I think on average it costs something over thirty thousand euros for each operation… a bit more for female-to-male than the other way about. To put it blunt-like, it's less expensive to cut off a penis than it is to make a new one.'

'So it's likely that the HSE paid for it?'

'I would say so. He wasn't the kind of fellow who could afford surgery like this out of his own pocket, was he?'

'In that case, we should be able to access his records and find out when he had this done, and who he was before he decided to become Billy. I'll go and talk to his brother, too – Donal.'

'Oh... the one who murdered Michael Riordan and his family. I don't envy you that.'

'You'd be surprised. I interviewed him when he was first arrested, and he's the mildest fellow you could ever hope to meet. A druggie, but not an aggressive druggie, more of a spaced-out druggie. It was hard to believe that he had shot a defenceless woman and two young children.'

Dr Kelley beckoned to Denis to bring over the sheet and cover up Billy Hagerty's body.

'I'll be sending you my full post-mortem by the end of the day,' she told Katie. 'Obviously the cause of death was gunshot wounds to the head, but there's some subsidiary results, too. His blood-alcohol level was on the high side, a hundred and ten milligrams, and there were traces of cocaine in his urine, although not enough to suggest that he was a chronic user. And of course his system was awash with androgenic hormones.'

They left the autopsy table and crossed over to Justice Quinn's body. Denis lifted off the sheet for them, and there he was, a man made of black charcoal. Dr Kelley had split open his chest to carry out her post-mortem, and unlike most of the cadavers that she examined, she hadn't been able to stitch him up again, so Katie could see his barbecued ribs. His right foot had broken off while he was being lifted from the burned-out shell of his car, and it was lying on the trolley next to him, still wearing its charred black shoe.

'I was told you first identified him by a band that he was wearing.'

'A claddagh band. I see you've removed it.'

'Along with his wedding ring, yes. His finger came off with it, but don't tell his wife.'

'We were friends once, me and Justice Quinn. I gave him that band myself.'

'You can have it back once I've finished with it here.'

'You can send it over 'if you want but I'll give it to his wife, or else she'll be wondering what happened to it. She never knew where it came from and I wouldn't want her to find out now.'

'Well, of course I formally identified him with a DNA test, so we don't have to mention the band.'

Katie found it hard to believe that the body lying in front of her was the man that she had once loved. He had no face, and so he had no more personality than a crash-test dummy painted matt black.

'Was it possible for you to tell if he was alive or dead when he was burned?'

'That was the main thing I was going to tell you. His trachea and his lungs were badly scorched, so the likelihood is that he was still alive when the car was set alight, and that he took in at least one breath before the fire killed him. As I told you, we managed to extract a reasonable amount of bodily fluids, and your forensic experts should be able to tell us if he was under the influence of any drug, or drunk.'

'Drunk? At that time of the morning? He was supposed to be driving to court.'

'It has been known, Kathleen. You know that as well as I do.'

They went through to the visitors' observation room. It was a small, plain room with two windows. One window looked out over the back fences of Laburnum Park. Through the other they could see into the room next door, where Roisin Carroll's body was lying on a table, with a white sheet drawn up to her neck. Her face was gently lit and her hair was brushed and shining. Her hands were laid one across the other, as if she were resting, or sleeping.

The room smelled pungently of new nylon carpet, and there was only one piece of furniture, an upright chair in case any visiting relative might suddenly feel faint. Katie and Dr Kelley went up to the window and looked in at Roisin, and Dr Kelley was right, she did appear angelic. She even seemed to have a wistful smile on her lips.

'Sometimes, you know, when they fetch in some young person who doesn't have a mark on them, I wish so much that I could will them back to life,' said Dr Kelley. 'I wish so much that I could say, open your eyes, *breathe*, start your heart beating again, and that they'd throw back the sheet and climb off the trolley and throw their arms around me and say thank you. But of course they never do.'

The door opened, and Roisin's parents came in, accompanied by one of the hospital receptionists.

'Mr and Mrs Carroll,' said the receptionist, and gave Katie an intense look as if to say, *Caution… not very friendly people.*

Roisin's mother was small and plump. She was brushing fluff from the sleeve of her coat, and frowning as if her daughter's premature death had irritated her more than caused her grief. She had a shapeless black felt hat perched on top of her head with a bedraggled black feather in it, and a worn green mock-crocodile handbag was hanging off her arm.

Her father was tall and thin with a large nose and a fine billowing wave of white hair. He was wearing a toffee-brown coat with padded shoulders that were too wide for him. His shirt collar was curled up, and his thin black tie was askew. He had missed a bit when he was shaving, so he had left a patch of prickly white stubble on the left side of his chin.

Dr Kelley introduced herself. 'I'm the Assistant State Pathologist, and this is Detective Superintendent Kathleen Maguire. You have our condolences for your loss.'

Without a word, Mr and Mrs Carroll went up to the window and stared at Roisin lying in the next room.

After a while, Mrs Carroll said, 'She's grown her hair. I never liked her with long hair.'

'I understand you haven't seen her in a while,' said Katie.

'Not since she got herself knocked up, no,' said her father.

'So you haven't yet seen your granddaughter?'

'No.'

'I'm told that she's made a good recovery. Will you be taking care of her, when she's discharged?'

'I suppose we'll have to,' said her mother, still staring at Roisin. Katie could hear the resentment in her voice. *How dare you have an illegitimate child and then die so that we're obliged to look after her for you? Like, how selfish is that?*

'The first thing we'll do is talk to Father Francis to see if we can have the wain baptized,' said her father. 'Otherwise there's no way we'll be able to take her to Mass on a Sunday, will we, and what will the neighbours say then?'

'I thought you'd be thanking the Lord that she survived,' said Katie. 'She could easily have drowned along with her mother if that auld wan hadn't been brave enough to jump in and save her.'

'Maybe it would have been better all around if she had,' her father replied. 'But then the Lord works in mysterious ways, doesn't he? I suppose she was rescued for a reason.'

Katie opened and closed her mouth when he said that. She couldn't think of any response except *That's your own granddaughter you're talking about, you narrow-minded bigot,* but there was no point in antagonizing him. Dr Kelley raised her eyebrows and took a deep suppressed breath, but she, too, held her peace.

'Are you any nearer to catching the fellow who pushed her in?' asked her mother.

'Not yet, to be honest with you,' Katie told her. 'The people he's been pushing in seem to have nothing at all in common, so it's been difficult to understand why he's doing it. But we'll catch him eventually, I can promise you that. He's not going to go unpunished for taking your daughter away from you.'

'Our daughter took *herself* away from us, missus detective,' said Roisin's father. 'She was dead to us long before this happened. The worst of it was, she was our only child. After her, her mother couldn't have any more. We always hoped that she was going to be a son, so that the Carroll family name could carry on. But like I say, the Lord works in mysterious ways. Sometimes you can go to your grave without ever knowing what it was that He was punishing you for.'

'Well, we'll leave you in peace with Roisin now,' said Katie. 'We'll keep you informed if there's any developments.'

With that, she and Dr Kelley left Roisin's parents and stepped out into the corridor.

'Holy Saint Joseph,' said Dr Kelley, under her breath. 'I truly thought we'd outgrown all of that.'

Katie closed the door. 'Really?' she said, as she and Dr Kelley walked back to the morgue. 'I wonder if we ever will. We've shut down the Magdalene Laundries and the mother-and-baby homes, do you know, but putting an end to that sort of intolerance – that's another matter altogether. As far as those two are concerned, that poor Roisin was a fallen woman and there was no redemption. They're not even sorry she's dead.'

Dr Kelley shook her head. 'I think I need another cigarette.'

14

Barry Riordan came home from The Cotton Ball just after three o'clock. He was drunk, and when he drove his Mercedes into the driveway in front of his semi-detached house in Boherboy Road, he collided with the garage doors. He clambered unsteadily out of the driving seat and weaved his way to the front door, jabbing his key at the lock six or seven times before he managed to push it in.

He hadn't even turned the key, though, when the door opened and there was Megan.

'Why didn't you let me in as soon as you heard me come home?' he demanded.

'I was in the back yard, darling, pegging up the washing, that's why.'

'You still could have fecking heard me. Are you deaf or something? Jesus!'

He pushed her roughly out of the way and stumbled into the hall, grabbing hold of the newel post at the bottom of the stairs to keep himself upright.

'Do you want a cup of tea in your hand?' Megan asked him.

'What? No, I'll have a Satz. And you can make me a fecking ham sangwidge while you're at it.'

'You didn't give me the money for the messages yet, Barry. We don't have any ham in the house.'

'What you mean is you've hounded it all, as usual. No wonder your arse is getting so fecking fat!'

He staggered into the kitchen, seizing the back of a chair and tipping it over. He managed to pick it up and sit down on it, searching through the pockets of his jacket for his cigarettes.

'Oh, shite. I've left my fags behind in the boozer. Go up to O'Donovan's, will you, and get me forty Carroll's. And you might as well get another six-pack of Satz while you're up there. And some fecking ham.'

He tugged his wad of euros out of his back trouser pocket, stripped off a €50 note and slammed it on to the tabletop. Megan stood on the other side of the kitchen and looked down at it, but made no move to come over and pick it up.

'Well,' said Barry. 'What are you waiting for? I'm gasping here.'

'I don't have the time to go up to the shopping centre, Barry. I've arranged to meet Ethna and the rest of the girls. We're taking all the kids swimming.'

'You'll have to be late then, won't you? Just feck off and fetch me my fags.'

'No, Barry. Ethna's giving me a lift to the sports complex. I promised to be round her house by half past at the latest.'

'I don't give a shite, Megan. What's more important – me getting my fags or some scratty kids getting themselves half-drownded? Now here – here's the grade – be off with you and fetch my fags and my Satz before I lose my rag altogether.'

He picked up the €50 note and waved it at her, but she said, with her voice trembling, 'I told you, Barry. I have to go now and that's all there is to it. If you want your fags and your booze so bad you'll just have to fetch them yourself.'

'What? What did you say? I'm too fecking langered to fetch them meself. You're not so thick that you can't see that. Jesus Christ, you're me wife! You're supposed to do what I fecking tell you!'

He stood up, but immediately lost his balance and sat down again. His chair tipped over and he fell backwards on to the floor, hitting his head against the door of the washing machine. Swearing and spitting and coughing, he rolled himself over on to his hands and knees and then crawled across the kitchen floor towards Megan, like some mistreated dog.

Megan backed away, towards the door. 'Barry—' she said. 'Barry, don't.'

But Barry took hold of the edge of the draining board and heaved himself up on to his feet. His face was crimson and he was in such a drunken rage that he was squinting. Megan went for the door but he lurched forward and caught hold of her arm, dragging her towards him. Then he punched her on the left cheek, hard, so that her head was jerked back and her knees gave way. She gasped, but she was too stunned to scream.

'Remember what you said in church? Remember your fecking marriage vows, you miserable sketch? "I'll go up the shopping centre whenever me husband tells me to and I'll fetch him the fags and the booze that he needs and I'll come back and make him a sangwidge." Don't you remember saying that, in front of the Lord God Himself? Or words to that effect?'

Although her knees were sagging, Barry was keeping Megan upright by holding on to her elbow. He slapped her across the face, twice, and then he punched her left breast. She let out a high, wavering wail, lifting one arm to shield herself and trying to twist herself away from him. But now, with his right hand, he seized her hair, wrenching it so viciously that she shrieked in pain. Then he slammed her face down against the edge of the kitchen sink, right on the bridge of her nose, so that the bone cracked, and blood spattered on to the porcelain. He paused for two or three seconds and then slammed her face down a second time, on her mouth, splitting her lips and smashing out her top front teeth.

Megan collapsed on to the kitchen floor, shuddering and sobbing. Barry gave her a kick on the hip, and said, 'Look at the fecking state of you la. How're you going to go out and fetch me fags now? You're as useless as you're fecking ugly!'

He staggered back to the table, picked up his chair, and sat down, snorting and wiping his nose with the back of his hand. He rummaged around in his jacket pockets until he found his phone, and after he had closed one eye so that he could focus on the screen, he managed to poke out Feargal's number.

'Feargal! It's Barry, boy, who did you think it was? Listen, I need you to fetch me some fags and a six-pack of Satz. What? I'm at home. I said, I'm at home. Yes. Yes, I know, but she's feeling a bit shook. Thanks a million, boy. I'll see you in a while.'

He sat back. Megan lay where she was for three or four minutes, and then she lifted her head and looked around. Her chin was bearded with blood and her left eye was puffed up and closed. She said nothing, but awkwardly climbed on to her feet and limped out of the kitchen.

'I suppose you want me to feel sorry for you!' Barry shouted after her. 'Well, that'll teach you to do what I fecking tell you when I fecking tell you to do it!'

As he shouted that, he wet himself, and it ran off the vinyl chair seat and dripped on to the kitchen floor. He closed his eyes and whispered, '*Shite*,' because even he knew that he couldn't call Megan back to mop it up, as she usually did.

15

As soon as she returned to Anglesea Street, Katie went down to the laboratory to see Bill Phinner. He was sitting at his desk eating a giant cheese bap and when she came to his office he pointed to his mouth and made muffled noises to indicate that he couldn't speak.

'No rush, Bill,' she told him. 'My ma always used to say that I should chew my food a hundred times.'

She sat down next to him and waited until he had chewed and swallowed his mouthful and taken a swig from a bottle of blackcurrant Mi Wadi. Then she said, 'I've just come back from the morgue to take a sconce at Justice Quinn. I was wondering if you'd had the results yet of his CT scan. Oh – and, by the way, do you know about Billy Hagerty?'

'Billy Hagerty? What, being a trannie? I do of course. But Dr Kelley asked me and my technicians not to say anything to you before you went to see her. She wanted to show you for herself, like. I think she gets a buzz out of being a bit dramatic sometimes.'

'A bit dramatic? That was unbelievable. I've heard of woman-to-man gender reassignment, but it's pure incredible to see what those surgeons can do. Anyhow, I've already put DI Fitzpatrick on to it. He'll be contacting the HSE to see if they have any record of who Billy was before he was Billy.'

Bill Phinner prodded at his computer keyboard, and then angled the monitor so that Katie could see the screen.

'We retrieved very small samples of blood, bile and semen, as well as cerebrospinal fluid. No pleural fluid because his lungs were fried. Unfortunately, all the samples were severely compromised by the intense heat that Justice Quinn's body was subjected to. His blood had literally boiled. We could find nothing to indicate that he was poisoned or drugged – not for sure.'

'But it's still conceivable that he might have been?'

'Yes, it's possible all right. But as you know, most of those knock-you-out drugs like Rohypnol or GHB don't linger in your body for very long. You can sometimes find traces of GHB after twelve hours but that's only if it's been a fierce hefty dose. Then again, if he *was* drugged, I suppose we have to be after asking ourselves how he managed to drive himself up to White's Cross. Not so easy to do if he was unconscious.'

'Dr Kelley said that apart from being burned, there were no physical injuries that might have been fatal. No cuts, for instance. No stab wounds.'

'No. But again, he was so badly burned that it isn't possible to say that one hundred per cent. Look at that Princess Diana. She wasn't burned but she died of a leaky vein that nobody found.'

Katie said, 'Okay, then. Thanks, Bill.' She turned to leave but by the odd way he was looking at her she sensed that he had something more to say to her.

'What?' she asked him.

He opened his desk drawer and took out the phone that had been dropped by the intruder who she had chased away from her house. It was sealed inside a clear plastic evidence bag.

'I'm not sure how to say this, ma'am, so I'll come out with it direct. Conall, our IT expert, was able to unlock this phone with very little trouble at all. It still had the factory password, and he couldn't find hardly nothing on it in the way of texts or emails or stuff like that. I'd say that it was bought specially for that fellow to follow you back to your house. There's a number of photos on it, like.'

'Photos of what, exactly?'

Bill switched the phone on and passed it over. Katie could see at once what the photographs depicted. There were thirteen of them, and they had been taken from her own back garden, into her brightly lit bedroom window, when the curtains were still wide open. They showed Kyna entering the room, wearing nothing but a towel, and then kneeling down naked beside Katie and pecking her on the lips. Two more of them showed Kyna giving her a deep French kiss and fondling her breast.

Katie laid the phone back down on Bill Phinner's desk. 'How many people have seen these?' she asked him. Her heart was beating so hard she wouldn't have been surprised if Bill could hear it.

'Conall, and me, that's all. Here in the lab, anyway.'

'You mean that somebody *outside* the lab might have seen them?'

'They were all sent to an email address – immediately after they were taken, I imagine. It's brendanokane@clovercom.ie.'

Katie felt as if iced water had been poured down the back of her blouse, and she shivered.

'Your man sent these pictures to Chief Superintendent O'Kane?'

'It looks like it, ma'am, I'm sorry to say.'

'You're sure about that?'

Bill Phinner nodded.

'Mother of God, Bill. I can't believe it.'

'C'mere, look – take the phone away with you for your

own safekeeping, and I can swear to you that neither Conall nor me will mention to anyone at all what we've seen. Not unless for some reason we're called to give evidence in a court about it.'

'I appreciate that. I truly do.'

'I've tested the casing myself for fingerprints and DNA. There's both. Clearly your man wasn't expecting to lose it. I sent them off about an hour ago so I should have the AFIS result in about another hour and the rapid DNA result half an hour after, or maybe even sooner.'

'Bill—'

'I've seen what I've seen, ma'am, and so I can't unsee it. But you're the best detective superintendent I've worked with, bar none, and you've stood up and defended me more than once when my findings have been questioned. On top of that, I've always believed that what anybody does when they're off-duty, that's their own business, like, unless it's criminal, and nobody else has the right to judge them. It's up to the Lord God to decide if they've done wrong.'

'Okay, Bill. Thank you. I'll wait to hear from you.'

Katie picked up the phone and left Bill Phinner's office. As she walked across the laboratory, she saw a young bespectacled man with brushed-up ginger hair sitting at a computer in front of the window. He turned to look at her and although he said nothing and almost immediately turned back to his PC, she wondered if he was Conall. If so, he now knew more about her private life than almost anybody except for Bill Phinner and the intruder who had taken all those intimate pictures of her and Kyna together. And, of course, Brendan O'Kane.

★★★

She returned to her office and sat down at her desk. She took one more look at the photographs on the phone. Each picture was so clear and so graphic that there was no possible way that Kyna's nakedness and the passionate kiss that they were sharing could be explained away as accidental, or simply a platonic cuddle between friends.

She switched off the phone, dropped it into her secure drawer and locked it. Then she stood up and walked over to the window. Down in the station car park, she could see Brendan talking to Superintendent Pearse and Councillor Douglas O'Banion from the county council's joint policing committee, and it looked as if they were laughing about something. She knew that it was highly unlikely that Brendan was showing them the pictures of her and Kyna, but all the same she couldn't help thinking that he might be.

Her first reaction had been that she and Kyna could both be dismissed from An Garda Síochána, or severely reprimanded at the very least. Maybe one of them might be posted to another Garda station, as far away as possible. It would be hard to see how she could continue in her position as detective superintendent here at Anglesea Street if those pictures were to be sent to the Garda Ombudsman, or if even one of them went viral on the internet.

She could just imagine how criminals would taunt her if that happened. 'Oh, you're the carpet-munching cop, are you?'

But then she thought: *Don't panic, and think this through.* How could Brendan possibly explain how he had come by such pictures? The phone itself was proof that as soon as the intruder had taken them, he had sent them directly to Brendan's personal email address. So had Brendan paid him to follow her home, on the off-chance that he could take any incriminating photographs of her and Kyna together? Maybe he had wanted them to blackmail her, to make sure that she wouldn't lodge a formal complaint about his rape.

That seemed highly likely – and if it were, Brendan would be equally far up the creek without a paddle, as her late husband, Paul, used to say, and he would be just as much at risk of being sacked.

It looked as if they were deadlocked. The only way they could both hold on to their jobs would be for both of them to say nothing. Brendan might have got his way after all, and escape the consequences of raping her, but losing her career and her reputation would be a very high price to pay for seeing him punished.

She would have to confront him about it, however. It would be absurd for them to carry on with their daily routine without them openly facing up to the hold they now had over each other. When she went to call on him, though, she would make sure she left his door wide open.

She called Kyna up to her office.

Kyna looked around and said, 'Oh. I thought Dr Power had showed up.'

'She should be here in twenty minutes or so. But I needed to talk to you in private first. Do you mind closing the door?'

'What is it?' asked Kyna, approaching her desk. 'What's wrong?'

Katie took out the phone and showed her the pictures. Kyna flicked through all of them in silence, and then said, 'Oh... my... God.'

'It gets worse. Before your man lost the phone, he emailed all those pictures to Chief Superintendent O'Kane.'

Kyna dropped down into one of the couches by the window, still holding the phone. She stared at Katie wide-eyed for a moment, and then she said, 'What are you going to do? What are *we* going to do?'

'For now, nothing.'

'But what if O'Kane passes them on to Frank Magorian, or to Dublin Castle, or the GSOC? Or the media, even?'

'I don't think he will. At least I'm hoping he won't. I don't think he'll want Frank Magorian finding out that he arranged for some gowl to sneak into my garden at night and take compromising photographs, do you? Because I'm sure that's what he's done. There's another reason, too.'

She hadn't meant to tell Kyna about Brendan raping her. She had been unconscious when he had first penetrated her, but she still blamed herself for drinking herself into a stupor that night, even though she had only been trying to numb the shock and the grief of Conor's sudden death.

There was another more secretive reason why she hadn't wanted to tell her. If and when she and Kyna ever became intimate again, she didn't want Kyna put off by the thought that Brendan had been inside her. She knew that Kyna disliked Brendan intensely, not only because he had cheated on Katie when they were young cadets at Templemore, but because she thought that he was glib and vain, and she found dark-haired over-groomed men like him physically repellent. 'They're like snakes,' she had said.

Kyna didn't dislike men, but she liked them scruffy and funny and openly affectionate, and they had to be Ariana Grande fans.

'I'm going to see Brendan after,' said Katie. 'There's no way that we can leave this hanging in the air between us, unspoken.'

'Well, good luck with that.'

There was a knock at the door. Moirin cautiously opened it, and said, 'Dr Power is here, ma'am, along with DI Mulliken and DS Begley.'

'That's grand, Moirin. Please show them in.'

Dr Power came walking briskly up to Katie with her hand held out. She was in her mid-fifties, with a blonde Dutch bob and a scarlet trouser suit. She had huge emerald-green eyes that were lit up as if she were already excited about their meeting.

Detective Inspector Mulliken and Detective Sergeant Begley followed her in, and by the sly, amused glances they were sharing, Katie could tell that Dr Power had already been rattling on to them as they escorted her up here. Katie had met her before, at several criminology seminars in Dublin, and she knew how garrulous she could be. She had heard one professor call her 'the Mouth of the Liffey'.

'How are you, Kathleen?' she said. 'Do you know it's been almost a year since I was here in Cork? A year! I can't think where the time goes flying off to!'

Katie introduced her to Kyna and then they all sat down on the couches by the window. Katie couldn't help noticing that six or seven hooded crows had gathered on the rooftop opposite, and that more were flapping in to join them. She hoped it wasn't an omen. Whenever the crows gathered, something always seemed to go badly or even tragically wrong. They had gathered on the morning that Conor had died.

'I don't know if you saw, but Dr Power recently had a new book out about criminal psychology,' Katie told Kyna.

'*Murder Most Explicable*,' said Dr Power. 'It's twenty-second this week in the *Irish Times* bestseller list. And please call me Ailbe.'

'You've read all the background I sent you on the Lee Pusher?' Katie asked her.

Dr Power reached into her red bucket bag and took out a folded sheaf of papers. 'I read them on the way down here. His victims are all very varied, aren't they – in age, in sex, in background – so I think we can safely say that he picks them totally at random. All they seem to have in common is that they were walking along the riverbank at a location where there's no wall nor railings.'

She unfolded a map of the Lee between the Daly footbridge at Sunday's Well to the west, and Blackrock Castle to the east, where the river widened into Lough Mahon. She had marked with black crosses all the seven sites where the Lee Pusher had knocked his victims into the water.

'The first one was here – at this gap in the wall along Pope's Quay – then the second was here at the dockside at Albert Quay – number three here at Horgan's Quay – number four off the jetty off Tivoli – number five from the Port of Cork Garden – and then six and seven at The Marina.'

'Do you think it's significant that he pushed the last two from the same location?' asked Katie. 'All the others were drowned somewhere different.'

'I don't know if we can read anything into that,' said Detective Inspector Mulliken. 'It seems to me that he took any opportunity that presented itself, and The Marina's by far the easiest place to knock some unsuspecting passer-by into the river. At Pope's Quay you'd have to follow them down the steps, and at Albert Quay and Horgan's Quay you'd have to cross the wide-open dockside before you pushed them. It would be the same with the jetty at Tivoli... they could easily see you coming, although they probably wouldn't guess what you had in mind, like.'

'Personally, I don't think *where* he pushes people into the river is nearly as important as *why*,' said Dr Power. '*Where* is a matter of chance. *Why* is a matter of psychology. I'm convinced from the Lee Pusher's behaviour that he's one of those paranoid people who harbours chronic resentment against the rest of the world. He spends his days mulling over the times that he's been humiliated or rejected – or imagines that he has. He feels that he's a social outcast, and he's deeply envious. He believes that everybody else has a happy and fulfilling life, while he's on his own, out in the cold, with his nose pressed against the window, metaphorically speaking.'

'Do you have any idea at all why he might feel so resentful?' asked Kyna.

'Well – there are many possible reasons. He could have started bearing grudges when he was a child, especially if he had a poor or an underprivileged background. He could have been rejected by somebody he fell in love with. He could have lost his job because of his attitude or his incompetence. His wife or a partner could have left him, or unexpectedly died. It's surprising how much of grief is anger, like "how dare you die and leave me alone". Then again, he could be suffering from a mental illness such as Huntington's disease or Alzheimer's or a stroke, or some form of dementia, or a brain injury. It could be a combination of some or all of these causes.'

'Is there any particular reason why he might feel driven to pushing people into the river?' asked Katie. 'There are plenty of other ways of killing people at random. You know, like shooting them or running them over. And am I right, or is it not uncommon for a serial killer like this to expect to die himself – either by killing himself or by staging things so that the police kill him?'

'It depends on his specific delusion. Some want to go out in a massive orgy of self-publicity. They commit one grandiose act of retribution against a world that failed to recognize their needs – like those school shooters in America, who commit a mass murder followed by suicide. Others, though, prefer to draw attention to themselves with a drawn-out series of killings, like our Lee Pusher. They relish the creeping fear that they create in the community, and they love to build on it, gradually, committing one inexplicable murder after another. "You thought you were so superior, did you? Well, I'll show you!"

'Sometimes they have a delusion that they have a divine mission to carry out, to teach society a lesson. I don't know whether you remember but there was a pusher in Limerick about ten years ago. He drowned nine random people in the Shannon before he was caught. He said they were all sinners and he was carrying out the will of God by baptizing them before they died.'

'I remember him,' said Katie. 'He claimed in court that he was the reincarnation of John the Baptist, so he couldn't be tried by mortal judges, only by angels. Mad as a box of fairies.'

'Frogs,' said Kyna.

'What?'

'It's "mad as a box of frogs".'

'Well, whatever, he was loopers and you can't deny that.'

'So, Dr Power, what do you suggest?' asked Detective Inspector Mulliken. 'Is there any specific type of individual you think that we should be looking for? From the few descriptions we've been given he sounds like he's middle-aged, slender build, like, and he always wears a light grey trackie.'

Dr Power said, 'I guessed at first that he might be unemployed, since he was roaming around in the middle of the day in sports gear. Out of all the murderers and attempted murderers that I've given a psychological assessment, about eighty per cent of them are out of a job for one reason or another. That's usually because they've had some pointless argument with their employer or with another member of staff. But then again I think it's noteworthy that all the pushing incidents took place between one and two in the afternoon, which is when somebody who's in work would have their lunch break.'

'The only exception to that was the last one,' said Katie. 'That took place early in the evening, about a quarter past six.'

'Maybe your man felt like going out for a late push after work,' suggested Detective Sergeant Begley. Then shrugged and said, 'Only a thought, like.'

Katie pointed to Dr Power's sketch map. 'If he *is* employed, then his place of employment can't be too far away from the city centre, although there's a distinct bias to locations off to the east... Horgan's Quay and the Port of Cork Garden and Tivoli Pier and of course The Marina.'

Dr Power said, 'Now this is only supposition, but let's say that there's a strong possibility that the Pusher is in employment. He probably doesn't hold a highly paid position because a man in a highly paid position would be less likely to harbour chronic feelings of resentment, and he'd also be more likely to have time off whenever he wanted it. What's more – if the Pusher has only a limited time frame in which to go out looking for people to drown, I doubt if changing his clothes is a high priority. His grey tracksuit could well be what he wears all day, at work. He may actually keep it on deliberately as a symbol of the oppressed person that he believes himself to be.

'As I said before, many or most mass murderers want to teach the world a lesson of one sort or another. Quite often that lesson is connected to their own job or their own interest in life. I had a Bus Éireann driver in Drogheda once who was sacked after a disabled passenger complained that he wouldn't let her on to his bus, and so the next thing he did was drive his car into a crowded bus stop. He killed three people and seriously injured seven. By that token, I think you could make a reasonable start by checking all the sports teachers and football coaches in Cork, and in particular any swimming instructors.'

Katie looked over at Detective Inspector Mulliken and Detective Sergeant Begley. 'Do we know any schools whose gym teachers wear grey? How about the Ursuline Secondary School in Blackrock? Or GAA club coaches? Or leisure centre instructors? We have the three public swimming pools, don't we, at Bishopstown and Churchfield and Douglas, and then there's the hotel swimming pools, too, like the Clayton and the Maldron and the Montenotte.'

'I don't think that Cork is what you might call overpopulated with sports coaches and swimming instructors,' said Detective Sergeant Begley. 'I'll have Caffrey and O'Crean go round the schools and the pools and the GAA clubs and track down as many as they can.'

'Sean – if they *do* find any likely suspects, I don't need to tell you that they'll need to be approached with the utmost caution. Dr Power's right, and mass murderers like to go out in a blaze of glory. We don't want the Lee Pusher taking his own life, but most of all we don't want him taking any more innocent victims with him.'

'Whatever you say, ma'am. Myself, I'd love to give your man a swimming lesson when we finally haul him in – preferably while he's wearing a pair of concrete badinas.'

16

'Want some ket?' asked the skinny young man with the rainbow sunglasses and the lopsided fade hairstyle.

The broad-shouldered feen standing in front of the urinal shook himself and then zipped himself up.

'Ket? How much are ye asking for it?' He was probably no older than mid- to late-thirties, this feen, but he was bald, with a head that resembled a Halloween pumpkin, both in colour and nubbly texture, and his black T-shirt gaped open at his belly.

'Sixty.'

'Oh, go feck yourself. Sixty?'

'Okay, to you, special offer price. Fifty. But it's quare stuff, like.'

'Not interested, boy. So lay off, will you, you're blocking my road.'

'Forty, then. But I can't go lower.'

'You'll go lower when I shove your head into that there cock manger. Now, out of my road, will you.'

The young man stepped back. 'Your loss, horse.'

'You think so?'

The broad-shouldered feen pushed his way out of the toilet and climbed the narrow stairs back up to the Zombie Lounge. Except for its swivelling strobe lights, the dance floor was pitch dark, with thumping disco music. It was early yet, only 11:30, but the club was beginning to fill up, with a line of young people silhouetted against the orange-lit bar, laughing and jostling each other as they waited impatiently to be served with beer and alcopops. At least twenty or thirty girls were already dancing around the DJ's stage, waving their arms in time to 'Taki Taki'.

The broad-shouldered feen trudged up another flight of stairs to the club's second floor, which was equally dark, except for twinkling red string lights. This floor was partitioned into several intimate booths, where customers could sit around tables drinking the Zombie Lounge's signature rum cocktail, the Walking Dead, and nibbling on their signature snack, the plantain fritters called *tostones*. In the furthest booth, Thomas O'Flynn was jammed in tightly with Muireann, his older brother Doran, his cousin John Mary John, as well as his two henchmen, Darragh and Milo.

'What's the story, Breaslain?' asked Thomas. 'You look like you forgot to unzip your pants when you went for a piss.'

'There's some young guttie down in the jacks flogging Special K.'

'You're codding me, aren't you?'

'No, true as I'm stood here, boy. He offered me a gram for sixty yoyos, then said he'd go down to forty.'

'Did ye reck him?' asked Doran O'Flynn. He was pale and chiselled and even more skeletal in appearance than his younger brother, and his hair was whiter and finer and more flyaway. His left eye was blind and milky, and there was a deep scar underneath it where he had been slashed, twenty years ago, in Portlaoise. 'Was he one of Riordan's scummers?'

'He was nobody that I knew, Doran. I reckon he was one of those young bowsies we've been seeing around lately. I lamped a bunch of them outside Havana Brown's last week and they was definitely selling. They wasn't Riordans and they wasn't any of them Romanians, neither. Like I say, they was only young bowsies, I haven't a baldy where from.'

'They're not this High Five mob I've been hearing about?' asked Thomas. 'Like they're college students who've been getting together to sell Special K and Skippy and G. They've been cooking it up themselves in their chemistry lab and dealing it in the discos to help them pay their way through the university.'

'If that's true, I'd say that was fierce ill-advised of them,' said Doran, in his raspy, hollow voice. He almost sounded as if he were speaking from beyond the grave. 'Don't they understand whose toes they're treading on? You need to be pulling the plug on that one, Tommy, and sooner rather than later.'

'They're not hurting your business *that* much, are they, Tommy?' asked Muireann. This evening she was wearing a shiny emerald-green dress cut so low in the front that it showed the tattoo of a moth, deep down in her cleavage. 'They're only a few students trying to make a bit of grade so that they can get themselves a good education. You don't begrudge them that, do you, surely? You know, live and let live, like.'

'Don't you be deludifying yourself, girl,' said Doran. 'They may be starting off full of shining bright intentions, but you wait until they cop on how much grade they're pulling in for how little effort and how little outlay. They're university students, and that means they're not thick. They'll soon forget all about their fancy degrees, you mark my words, and they'll be on the lang from their classes and setting themselves up as full-time dealers.'

'You're spot on there, Dor,' said Thomas. 'Breaslain... do you want to go back down to the jacks and sling that young feller out on his ear? And make sure you take his stuff off of him, too. Tell him this is our turf and if we ever see him or any of his pals here again, we'll have their mebs off and they'll be singing like the Bee Gees on helium. Darragh – Milo – why don't you two go down with him, just to show him that we're not messing.'

The DJ on the dance floor below them was playing 'Here With Me' by Marshmello, and the club was even more crowded. Breaslain and Darragh and Milo clattered down the two flights of stairs to the toilets, although the music was so loud and the strobe lights were flashing so fitfully that they attracted no attention. Breaslain shouldered his way into the door that had a picture of a male zombie on it, so that it opened with a bang. The skinny young man in the rainbow sunglasses was still in there, talking to another young man with a beard. It looked as if euros and a wrap of ketamine were on the point of changing hands.

Breaslain said to the bearded young man, 'Make tracks, boy. Go on.'

'You what? Who the feck are you?'

'Are you deaf or something? I said, mowsie on. Like, now.'

'I will in me ring. I'm not done here.'

'You are now.' Breaslain grasped his shoulder, swung him around and punched him hard in the stomach. Ten-euro notes fluttered to the toilet floor, mixed with a scattering of white crystals. The bearded young man doubled over, clutching his stomach, so winded that he could only squeak. Breaslain pushed him roughly towards Darragh and Milo, and between the two of them they slung him out of the toilet door so that he fell on to the floor outside, jarring his shoulder against the skirting board. Groaning, he started to climb up the stairs on his hands and knees.

The drug-dealer backed away until he was standing between the two urinals. He drew a large kitchen knife out of the inside pocket of his anorak and held it up high in front of him.

'What the feck's *that* for?' Breaslain mocked him. 'Thanks for the offer, but I have no poppies that need peeling!'

'You stay back and leave me be!' the young man retorted, although his voice was shaking, and he kept anxiously shifting his knife from one hand to the other. 'I have friends upstairs, like, and they'll soon sort you out!'

'Oh, you have friends here, do you? Why don't you whistle for them, then? But I can tell you this, boy, if your friends have been peddling the Special K here, the same as you have, they're going to be in just as much shite as you are.'

He took two steps closer to the young man, and the young man made a jabbing gesture with his knife and said, 'You want some of this? Come on, then!'

Breaslain didn't hesitate. He dodged to his right in a feinting movement, and when the young man stabbed at him he swung back to his left, seizing the young man's wrist and bending it backward so violently that it gave a complicated crackle, like a branch breaking. The young man let out a shrill scream and dropped his knife on to the toilet floor. Breaslain bent down to scoop it up, and while the young man was whimpering and flapping his hand, he stabbed him in the stomach, just above his belt buckle, forcing the knife in right up to the handle.

There was a shocked silence. The only sound was the disco music from upstairs. The young man's rainbow glasses slid from his nose and he stared at Breaslain with a mixture of disbelief and sadness, as if he wished that he had never come here, trying to sell drugs, and that his life had never come to this.

Breaslain stayed motionless for a few seconds. Then he clamped his left hand on to the young man's shoulder and dragged the knife upward as far as his ribs, instantly flooding the front of his pale-blue T-shirt with blood. The young man sank on to his knees on the floor, clutching his stomach with both hands. Breaslain stood over him and said, 'What was it that you was going to give me some of? Remind me, would you, you caffler?'

He looked around until he saw a circular grating in the toilet floor. He used the knife blade to prise it up, and then he dropped the knife down the drain.

Darragh was waiting by the open door and Milo was standing at the bottom of the stairs to make sure that nobody came down and saw what was going on. They were both expressionless, almost bored, showing the supreme disinterest of men who had witnessed so many stabbings and shootings and beatings that they no longer found them entertaining. The bearded young man had already crawled back up to the dance floor and disappeared.

Breaslain rinsed his bloody right hand in the washbasin and shook it. The young drug-dealer was still kneeling on the floor, bent forward, rocking slowly in agony, but making no sound at all. Breaslain looked down at him, gave his sunglasses a kick, and then said, 'Come on, lads, out the gap.' The three of them clambered up the stairs, letting the door of the gents' toilet swing shut behind them.

'Maybe you shouldn't have dropped the blade down the drain, Brez!' shouted Milo, over the music, as they crossed over the dance floor. 'Maybe you should have put it back into the bowsie's hand!'

'What? What for?'

'If you'da done that, the pigs would've thought that he'd committed that hairy kirry, do you know what I mean?'

'No, Milo, I didn't want to chance it. They have the DNA now, don't they, and the infrared? These days, Jesus, I saw it on the telly. They can practically tell if you've let off a breezer in the same street.'

They went back up to the booth where Thomas and Doran O'Flynn were waiting for them.

'Well, did you sling him out?' asked Thomas.

'Not exactly, boss. He pulled a knife on me, so I had to sort him out, like.'

'C'mere to me. What do you mean you had to sort him out?'

'He shanked him, that's what he means,' said Darragh.

'You fecking *what*? So where is he now?'

'Still down in the jacks, I'd say.'

'You know what you are, Breaslain, you're a right fecking daw,' said Doran, in his raspy voice. 'What do you think's going to happen now? Somebody's going to call the shades and the next thing you know they'll be going round the whole club asking everybody questions and taking fingerprints, including you. Did anybody *see* you shank him?'

'No, but there was some beardy fellow in there when we first went in. We threw him out before anything went down, like.'

'But he'd know you again, this beardy fellow?'

'Look, Doran, it was self-defence, like. The bowsie came at me with a fecking knife this long. I took it off him, and what else was I supposed to do?'

'You could have *not* shanked him, and slung him out the club like you was supposed to. Holy Saint Joseph and All the Carpenters!'

Thomas quickly swallowed the rest of his rum cocktail and stood up, pulling Muireann up by her arm. 'Come on, we have to get out of here now. If anybody asks, we were gone before the feller got himself shanked.'

John Mary John had only just ordered himself another drink, and so he plucked out all the fruit, dropped it on to the floor, and gulped down the Bacardi and pineapple juice so quickly that it made him gasp for breath.

The seven of them picked up their coats and their jackets, left the booth and started to make their way downstairs. The club was packed now with over a hundred young dancers, singing along to Sam Smith. 'Look what you made me do... I'm dancing with a stranger!' But before Thomas and Muireann could reach the dance floor, the figure of a young man appeared at the top of the stairs that led down to the toilets. It was hard to make him out clearly because of the epileptic lights, but Thomas could see that he was holding his stomach in both hands and that he was swaying from side to side, as if he were standing on the deck of a ship.

'Oh Christ, that's him, that's the bowsie!' said Darragh.

'How in the name of Jesus did he get up there?' said Breaslain, in a panicky voice. 'I was sure I'd done him in!'

'Well, go and give him a clatter and send him back down,' Thomas told him. 'That should finish him off.'

A rowdy knot of students were laughing and shoving each other at the bottom of the stairs, and before Breaslain could shoulder his way through them, the young drug-dealer had started to stagger towards the middle of the dance floor. His head was tilted right back and his knees were bent and he collided with three girls who were dancing together. They shouted at him and pushed him away, obviously thinking that he was drunk, but this knocked him completely off balance, and he was able to take only two more wobbling steps before he fell heavily sideways. He lost his grip on his sliced-open stomach and his insides spilled out in a slippery tangle, all across the floor.

'Come on, Breaslain, forget it, and let's get the hell out of here,' said Thomas. The seven of them forced their way roughly through the crowd of students and headed for the Zombie Lounge's front door. One of the bouncers said, 'What's the story, lads?' but Thomas ignored him.

Up on the dance floor the music went on thumping and the strobe lights went on flashing and the dancers kept on dancing. They stepped around the young drug-dealer as he lay on his side and one or two of them kicked him. It wasn't unusual for dancers to get so langered or so stoned that they collapsed and ended up unconscious on the floor. But then a tall blonde girl in high heels skidded sideways and almost fell over and when she looked down she realized that her heel had become snagged in a glistening beige coil of small intestine. The young drug-dealer's bowels had been trampled and stamped on to the tune of 'Dancing in the Dark' and the floor all around him was footprinted with blood and faeces.

The blonde girl screamed, and as soon as her friends saw why she was screaming, they started screaming, too. Her boyfriend and another boy elbowed their way up to the DJ's stage together and shouted at him to shut off the music and switch on all the house lights.

For a few moments after the lights went up there was pandemonium. With a noise like a pebbly tide going out, the dancers shuffled as far back from the young drug-dealer's body as they could, leaving a wide circle around him. The girls were weeping and the boys were swearing in shock and knocking over chairs and the DJ was on the phone with one finger in his ear, trying to make himself heard as he called for an ambulance.

By now, Thomas O'Flynn and his companions were walking quickly along Oliver Plunkett Street, which was still crowded with drunks and young revellers from other clubs like Gorby's and Havana Brown's. A soft rain was falling, which made the night sparkle. Thomas's Audi was parked in a disabled bay in Pembroke Street, around the corner from the GPO. Thomas and Doran climbed into the front seats while Muireann and John Mary John and Breaslain squeezed into the back. Darragh and Milo went further up to Smith Street, where they had parked in front of somebody's garage. The garage owner knew who they were, which is why he never complained.

Before he started the engine, Thomas looked into his rear-view mirror. 'Right. We left at twenty past eleven, got it? We were the seven wise monkeys. We saw nothing, we heard nothing, and no matter what you ask us, we're not going to say nothing.'

'I didn't *do* nothing, neither,' put in Breaslain. 'If the pigs ask me about that bowsie being shanked, I'll tell them it wasn't me, no way. And I have no notion at all what might have happened to the knife, afterwards.'

Thomas closed his eyes for a moment, crossed himself, and said, 'Jesus. Please help me.'

17

Katie had just switched off her bedside lamp when her phone played *Mo Ghille Mear*. She was so tired that she was tempted to ignore it, but it kept on and on until her answering service took the message. She switched the lamp on again and when she saw who had been trying to ring her she pressed callback.

Muireann answered almost instantly, as if she didn't want anybody else to hear that her phone was ringing. She spoke so quietly that Katie could hardly hear her, so she guessed that Thomas O'Flynn might be close by.

'Muireann, it's Kathleen.'

'I'll have to be quick, like. But if you haven't heard already, there was a young fellow stabbed to death in the Zombie Lounge tonight.'

'No, I haven't heard yet, Muireann. But I'm off-duty. When I'm off-duty, they usually give me some peace. Who was he, this young fellow?'

Muireann paused, as if she were making sure that nobody could hear her.

'He was one of that lot they call the High Five, at least I think he was. Students making their own drugs and flogging them round the clubs. I don't know what his actual name was. Himself told Brez to throw him out but Brez went and stabbed him instead.'

'Did you see Brez do it?'

'No. He stabbed him down in the jacks and then came up and told us about it. But I never saw himself so angry! I mean, he didn't just give out to Brez, he ate the head off him! We all had to do a legger and swear that we were never there when it happened.'

Katie was about to ask Muireann if she had seen any gardaí arrive at the Zombie Lounge when she heard a man's voice in the background. From what she could make out, he seemed to be asking Muireann what in the name of eff she was doing. Muireann immediately rang off, and Katie knew better than to try and ring her back.

She rang Sergeant Ryan O'Farrell because she knew that he was on duty at Anglesea tonight. When he answered he sounded as if he were in the middle of a shouting match with somebody who was very drunk.

'Sergeant O'Farrell, it's DS Maguire. I've heard that there's been a stabbing at the Zombie Lounge tonight.'

'Will you ever shut your stupid face, you eejit? Sorry, ma'am, I don't mean you. Yes, we had the call about an hour ago. Up the yard with you, you're totally fluthered, go on! I don't want to see you in here again until you're sober! Sorry again, ma'am – your man's off on his way now. We've half a dozen uniforms down to the Zombie already, and we'll be sending more, because there was over a hundred clubbers there and we'll be after taking the names of every one of them. I've informed DI Fitzpatrick and as far as I know Walsh and Cullen are on their way there, too.'

'Do we know exactly what happened?'

'A fellow was stabbed, that's all I know so far. He was attacked in the downstairs toilets but he managed to make his way upstairs to the dance floor before he collapsed. The paramedics were there within less than fifteen minutes but there was nothing they could do for him. He was cut right open and died from shock and loss of blood, that's what Garda Gogarty told me.'

'Any arrests made so far?'

'No, ma'am. And we've found no witnesses yet.'

Katie hesitated, but then she said, 'All right, sergeant. If there's any major developments, please don't hesitate to ring me. I'll be coming in extra early in the morning, once I've grabbed myself a couple of hours' sleep. That's if I *can* sleep.'

She sat on the side of the bed for a long while, thinking. She could have rung Robert Fitzpatrick and told him immediately that the prime suspect for the stabbing was Breaslain Hoobin. Breaslain was one of the hardest of the O'Flynn gang and he had already served two prison terms for assault causing serious harm. Coincidentally, the judge at his second trial had been Garrett Quinn, and he had gone so far as to call Breaslain 'a rabid animal'.

Katie knew, though, that she had to play this with the greatest of care. If there were no witnesses to the stabbing, it was reasonable for her to assume that nobody knew that it was Breaslain who had murdered this drug-dealer except for Thomas O'Flynn and any other members of his gang who might have heard him admit to what he had done. If the Garda immediately went looking for Breaslain and arrested him, it would be obvious to Thomas O'Flynn that somebody had ratted on him, and the most likely rat was Muireann.

If he even had half an inkling that Muireann had informed on him, she would be lucky if she survived until the end of the day. The whole reason that she was staying with him was because of his utter ruthlessness to the women in his life.

Katie looked at her dented pillow and knew that she wouldn't be able to sleep. It was bad enough that she still hadn't been able to confront Brendan. After she had held a briefing that afternoon with Superintendent Pearse and Inspector O'Rourke about her ongoing investigations – especially the Lee Pusher inquiry – she had gone to Brendan's office only to find that he had already left. His personal assistant, Bridie, had told her that he had called in at the dog support unit and tried to pet Laser, one of their German shepherds, while his handler wasn't around. Laser had become aggressive and inflicted some nasty scratches on his face.

'The chief didn't blame the dog, though. He reckoned that because he was new here at Anglesea Street, the dog didn't recognize him and must have thought that he was a criminal.'

Well, that was an out-and-out lie, Katie had thought to herself. *But Laser certainly got that right. He knew a hoor's melt when he met one.*

She dressed and left the house quietly so that she wouldn't wake Barney and Foltchain. Her neighbour, Jenny Tierney, would take them for their walk later. The fine rain was still falling and it felt colder than it had lately, so that she shivered when she sat down in the driving seat.

When she arrived at Anglesea Street she went first to see Sergeant O'Farrell, who told her that gardaí were still taking names at the Zombie Lounge and that Bill Phinner had already sent a team of five forensic technicians to examine the toilet and the dance floor. While she was talking to Sergeant O'Farrell, Detective Inspector Robert Fitzpatrick came in. He looked tired. His chin was prickly with grey stubble and the shoulders of his coat were sparkling with raindrops.

'How's it going, ma'am? You didn't have to show up, like. It's fierce messy, the crime scene, I can tell you, and most of the kids we've been talking to are so high that they don't know whether it's Christmas or Wednesday, but we have it all under control.'

'I could have left it until later to come in, but we really need to talk now,' Katie told him. 'I'll go up and organize us a couple of cups of coffee and then I'll meet you in my office. You take yours white, don't you?'

'Don't bother about the coffee, ma'am,' said Sergeant O'Farrell. 'Garda Caitlin Brady's here on duty tonight. She can fetch them for you.'

'She's not my servant, Ryan. I'm quite capable of fetching my own.'

'Okay. Fair play to you, ma'am.'

By the time Katie had been to the canteen and carried two mugs of coffee up to her office, Robert was already there waiting for her.

'Bill Phinner just texted me to say that they've identified the victim. Guess what from – his student card, found in his back pants pocket. His name's Tadhg Kimmons, and he's taking an elective course in advanced pharmaceutical chemistry at UCC.'

'That makes sense, from what I've heard. But go on.'

'They found more than his student card. They've found nine bags of ketamine shards in his satchel, as well as more than a hundred Blue Ghost PMMA tablets.'

'So it looks likely that he was trying to peddle drugs in the Zombie Lounge – even though we all know that it's strictly O'Flynn territory when it comes to narcotics. That was foolhardy, to say the least, but it makes sense, too. Muireann Nic Riada rang me to tell me what had happened. She said that as soon as Thomas O'Flynn heard that your man was selling ketamine down in the toilets, he sent Breaslain Hoobin after him to kick him out. Only he didn't kick him out, he cut the tripes out of him.'

'Then we actually *know* who killed him? Breaslain Hoobin? Holy Mary, that makes our life a whole lot simpler. I can have Walsh and Cullen lift him before he has time to eat his morning porridge. We even know where he lives... with his old widowed ma, in Farranree.'

'Except that we can't, Robert. You know the situation with Muireann. If Thomas O'Flynn has the slightest suspicion that the tip-off came from her, she'll get the same as happened to her sister, only worse, most likely.'

'What's the plan, then?'

'We keep Hoobin under surveillance for the time being, to make sure that he doesn't pull a disappearing act. If he goes so far as trying to leave the country, we can haul him in on some pretext or other unrelated to the stabbing, but with any luck he'll stay in the area and it won't come to that.'

'But then what?'

'Then we tell Bill Phinner to make the most intensive examination of a crime scene that he's ever done. He checks for fingerprints on the toilet door and any bloody footprints on the floor. At the same time we find out where Thomas O'Flynn was sitting during the evening, so that he can scan for fingerprints and any DNA from Breaslain Hoobin on the table and chairs. And of course you and Walsh and Cullen will be interviewing every single person who was there, and showing them pictures of O'Flynn and Hoobin. I want us to build up a complete scenario of every minute of that night at the Zombie Lounge, up until the time that poor fellow came upstairs and fell on to the floor.'

Katie paused, and sipped her hot black unsweetened coffee. 'All we need is the tiniest shred of forensic evidence that it was Hoobin who stabbed our victim, and then we can lift him without any risk to Muireann.'

Robert was silent for a long moment. He was looking at her in the way that a former lover looks at a woman whose reason for leaving him he hasn't yet been able to comprehend.

She caught him looking at her like that, and said, 'What?'

'Well, nothing, really. Except that what do we do if Bill can't find even that tiniest shred of evidence?'

He doesn't know, does he, what happened between me and Garrett? thought Katie. *He couldn't know. You're being paranoid, that's all.*

'Bill will find something. He always does. Well, at least seventy-five per cent of the time he does.'

'But if he can't? Or if he does, but it doesn't stand up in court? How can we let Hoobin go free when we have a witness who can testify that he did it?'

'I don't know, Robert. Let's cross that shaky bridge when we come to it, shall we?'

At about twenty to nine she saw Brendan's maroon Mercedes turn into the car park, its windscreen wipers flapping. She allowed him enough time to come upstairs to his office and settle himself down, and then she took three deep yoga breaths, *ujjayi pranayama* or 'victorious breaths', and went along the corridor to knock on his half-open door.

'Katie,' he said, looking up from the papers on his desk. A few scratches were still faintly visible on his forehead and the side of his nose, but Katie could see that he had masked them with pale foundation.

She was tempted to ask if he and Laser the German shepherd had made friends now, but what she needed to tell him was too serious for sarcasm.

'You and I need to come to some arrangement,' she said, as coldly as she could.

'Close the door,' he told her, and then added, 'please.'

Katie felt like saying, 'Is it safe to?' Again she said nothing but she stayed where she was, so Brendan had to get up from his desk and close the door himself.

'What do you have in mind?' he asked her.

'You know of course that your pal dropped his phone at my house. One of Bill's technical experts opened it and found the pictures that he took. The pictures that he sent to you.'

Brendan walked over to the window and stood there for a long time looking out at the rain. Six or seven hooded crows had settled on the rooftop opposite, and occasionally shook the rain from their wings as if they were shaking small black umbrellas.

'If you must know, I was jealous,' Brendan said at last. He still didn't look at her.

'Jealous? What are you talking about?'

'I thought you might have a new man friend that I didn't know about. So I asked Stephen to check up on you. I know it was wrong of me, and stupid, but jealousy can make you do some fierce stupid things.'

He turned to face her. 'I have such strong feelings for you, Katie. They're so strong that I don't understand them myself. I cheated on you when we were in college together, but that was one way I felt I could have a relationship with you and still be a man. If you want to know the truth, you frighten me. I've never known a woman as attractive as you, but as scary as you, and I have no idea at all how to deal with you.'

'I see. You thought that if you raped me, that would show me who was in charge?'

'I didn't think that at all. And I didn't see it as a rape. Maybe I was too forceful, but I thought you'd respond to me if I was forceful – you know, considering how strong you are.'

'When you assaulted me in my house, I was wrecked and I was asleep. How could I respond in any way at all? Technically and morally and legally that was rape. And when you assaulted me here in your office, I made it clear that I didn't want to have sex with you. I think the scratches on your face are evidence enough of that.'

'I'm trying to apologize to you, Katie. I'm trying to make you realize that I read you totally wrong. But I can't help being attracted to you. It's something I can't control.'

'Mother of God, Brendan, you're such a liar. I caught you out and I don't believe a single word that comes out of your mouth. But I'm going to make you an offer, God help me. If you swear on your life that you'll delete those pictures that your miserable gobshite of a pal took around at my house, I won't take my complaint about rape to the GOSC. It's not because I think that you don't thoroughly deserve to have the whistle blown on you. It's because we're both experienced and valuable officers and there seems to be no point at all in either of us losing our jobs.'

'All right. I'm truly sorry that you don't believe me. I thought you might even be flattered that I feel about you the way that I do. But if that's how you see it... okay. I'll delete the pictures, and we'll call it quits.'

'There's one more condition, Brendan.'

Brendan raised an eyebrow. 'Oh, yes? And what's that?'

'You never try it on with me again. You never touch me.

You never even stand close enough for me to smell your rancid aftershave or feel your breath on my face.'

'Jesus, Katie. You really know how to lop a man's mebs off, don't you?'

Katie was preparing a media release about the Zombie Lounge stabbing with Mathew McElvey when Kyna appeared. She had knotted her blonde hair up in a little Tyrolean bun and she was wearing a smart ivy-green suit.

She sat by the window and waited until Mathew had finished taking down all the details that he needed. Then, when he had gone, she held up a blue plastic folder and said, 'The Lee Pusher.'

'Oh, yes. What about him?'

'I couldn't stop myself thinking about what Dr Power was telling us about serial killers. You know, why they do it, like. I looked up the book we have on the Lee Pusher, with pictures of all of his victims. I thought they might have something in common, do you know, and that was one of the reasons he wanted to kill them. Here – look, I've printed their pictures out, all seven of them.'

Katie opened the folder and looked at the victims' photographs. Five were men and two were women. Two of the men and one of the women were smiling, little knowing that sooner or later after these pictures were taken, they would be drowned.

'Look at the men there,' said Kyna. 'They could almost be cousins. Same gingery hair, similar pointy noses, similar round faces, similar build – all of them a couple of kilos overweight, like. If he'd had half the chance I reckon our Pusher would have shoved that Ed Sheeran into the river.'

'The two women don't resemble each other, though, do they?'

'No, they don't. But the men are so alike that I'd guess that it isn't the human race in general that the Pusher wants to punish, it's one particular person who's done him wrong.'

'You could be right. Of course we can't tell if he's managed to get his revenge on that one particular person already, and now he's simply getting his revenge on every man who happens to look like him. And even if this particular person is still alive, how in the world are we going to find him? Over ten per cent of the male population of County Cork have red hair, and God only knows how many are overweight.'

'I know that, ma'am. But if we can find a fellow who regularly wears a light grey tracksuit for one reason or another, these pictures could help us when we question him – especially if he has that much bottled-up rage against men who look like this. You remember that time we interviewed that Sean Madden after he'd strangled his wife, and he denied it and denied it until we showed him that picture of her and then he totally lost his cool and admitted it.'

'Thanks, Kyna. This could be useful. I'm only hoping that Caffrey and O'Crean manage to find somebody who dresses like that.'

Katie shrugged on her jacket and together she and Kyna went downstairs for an update meeting with Superintendent Pearse. When they came out of the lift, Katie saw Bill Phinner talking to Detective Inspector Mulliken on the far side of the reception area. He waved to catch her attention, and then he came over and handed her a manila envelope, with a smaller plastic evidence bag inside it.

'I was coming up in a minute to see you, ma'am, to give you these. Dr Kelley gave them to me this morning. It's the rings that were taken from Justice Quinn, his wedding ring and the claddagh band, so that you can return them to his widow.'

'Thanks a million, Bill. How about his post-mortem? Have you made any more progress on that at all?'

Bill Phinner shook his head. 'We found some infinitesimal traces of naproxen. It's an anti-inflammatory drug for treating rheumatoid arthritis or gout. Justice Quinn was probably taking it regularly, but it wouldn't have knocked him out or affected his awareness in any way. That's all, though. He was so badly burned we might as well have carried out a post-mortem on a lump of coal.'

Katie took the rings. She would have done anything to keep the claddagh band, as a souvenir of what she and Garrett had shared together and done together, and the dramatic change that it had made to her life, but she knew that she couldn't. There are some relationships in our past lives that have to remain as secrets, to prevent them from causing even more pain and emotional destruction in the future.

18

Muireann walked into the Mercy University Hospital that morning and there, sitting in the waiting area with a plastic ice pack pressed against her nose, she recognized Megan.

Megan caught sight of her and lowered the ice pack, so Muireann crossed over and said, 'How are you? You reck me, don't you, because I reck you.'

Megan nodded. Both of her eyes were so puffed up that she could barely see and the bridge of her nose was embellished with a crusty crimson scab.

'You can tell me to be off with meself if you want to, girl. I'll totally have you. But my name's Muireann.'

'I'm Megan,' said Megan, in a blocked-up voice. She tried to smile but her lips were swollen and split. 'I won't be after telling you to go, no way. I've been hoping for the chance to meet you ever since I first saw you, but I thought we never would, to be honest with you.'

She turned her head around stiffly to check the other patients in the waiting area and then she said, 'There's none of the lads around, thank God.'

Muireann and Megan had seen each other several times before – once at Mallow Racecourse and three or four times in The Roundy bar on Castle Street and on opposite sides of St Patrick's Street. They had never had the chance to speak, though, or even acknowledge each other, because they had been accompanied every time by the men in their lives – Muireann by Thomas O'Flynn and Megan by Barry Riordan.

Cork was a small city, so their paths had been bound to cross now and again, but whenever they had encountered each other, Thomas and Barry had either ignored each other or exchanged death stares and mouthed silent and obscene threats and given each other the finger, like two bullies in a school playground.

Muireann and Megan hadn't dared to share even a quick sympathetic look. It had been drummed into both of them that their gang rivals were shagging septic cans of piss, and that their old dolls were expected to regard them with equal disgust and hostility. But both women were acutely aware of what they themselves looked like, in the short skirts and the tight slutty tops that their lords and masters insisted that they wear, and that whenever they went out they had to walk three steps behind them. On at least two of the occasions when Muireann and Megan had seen each other they had both had black eyes, which even make-up hadn't been able to conceal.

Muireann knew only too bitterly what a woman in an abusive relationship looked like. It had never mattered to her that she and Megan might never come closer than the far wack of Pana, or if Megan would never want to have anything to do with her. The very first time she had seen her she had recognized that they were sisters in pain.

She was more than ten minutes early for her appointment, so she sat down next to Megan and said, 'How did you come by that, then? Your nose?'

'It was Barry. It was my own fault, I suppose. He wanted me to go to the shop to fetch him booze and fags and I was bold enough to say that I wouldn't. It's only a fracture, and the doctor reset it straight for me, so with any luck I won't need an operation. But I can't tell you how much it hurts.'

'Jesus. With Tommy it's always the clatters. I have only to say one word that riles him and it's *slap*! He wears all these fierce heavy rings, too, and that's what causes the bruises.'

'Why don't you walk out on him?'

'Because I'm with him for a reason. And one day I'll be able to give him what he deserves. Which is everlasting hell. Why don't you walk out on Barry?'

'I'd leave him if I dared but I don't dare, and in any case where would I go, like, do you know? I can't believe that I ever thought that I loved him, or that he loved me. And I can't believe that I went on thinking that he loved me, even when he started to belt me, and tell me what a thick ugly cow I was. But it got worse and worse. I could only leave him if I went to live so far away that he could never find me. He'd have me murdered, if I left him, I'm sure of it. He's said so, more than once. Not because he loves me, but because everybody would say that he couldn't hold on to his woman, and he'd be morto.'

Muireann reached across and took hold of Megan's left hand. 'So we're stuck, then, aren't we, the two of us?'

Megan pressed the ice pack against her nose again, and nodded. After she had given herself a few seconds relief from the pain, she said, 'I've felt like hanging myself, more than once. Or throwing myself in the Lee. Barry hates me but he still wants the sex whenever he's not so langered that he can't manage it. And he always hurts me when he's doing it.'

'Tommy, he's the same. I'm here for a breath test, because I've been having cramps in my stomach, and it wouldn't surprise me at all if he's the cause of it.'

The two of them sat, still holding hands, for over a minute. Patients and nurses and delivery men came and went, and outside on Henry Street the parked cars glittered wet in the grey morning light.

At last Muireann said, 'I'll have to go now, girl. But let's swap phone numbers. If ever you're feeling depressed, like, or if ever your Barry's beating you too much for you to bear, you give me a ring, okay? And I'll do the same if my Tommy's giving out to me.'

'I'm not sure what use that will be.'

'It'll give you a shoulder to cry on, Megan, if nothing else.'

They exchanged numbers, but they had only just finished when Megan glanced towards the door and said urgently, 'Be off with you now, Muireann. Quick. And don't be after looking back at me.'

Muireann immediately stood up and walked over to the information desk, without turning around. She knew why Megan had told her to get up and go, but it was only when she walked over to the stairs that she saw Feargal in a dirty brown trench coat sitting next to Megan, with his arm around the back of her chair. Whatever he was saying to her, he was jabbing his finger as if he were making some kind of a threat.

19

The conference room at Anglesea Street was already crowded with reporters and cameramen when Katie walked in with Superintendent Pearse and Detective Inspector Fitzpatrick.

Katie noticed at once that Owen Dineen from the *Irish Sun* was sitting at the back, manspreading, with his thick-rimmed spectacles perched on the end of his plum-coloured nose and his overcoat undone. Fionnuala Sweeney was there as usual, from RTÉ, as well as Dan Keane from the *Examiner* and Rionach Barr from the *Echo,* but there were three or four unfamiliar faces, which told her that this story had aroused more widespread media attention than usual.

Well, she thought, *that's only to be expected. Young Drug Dealer Disembowelled In Disco.*

She stood up and said, 'Good morning, everyone.' She folded back the press release that she had prepared with Mathew McElvey and was about to read it out when the door swung open and Brendan walked in. He gave Katie a sideways-sloping smile and sat down next to Robert Fitzpatrick.

Katie hesitated, and so Brendan looked up at her, flapped his hand and said, 'Go ahead, DS Maguire,' as if she needed his permission.

'Good morning, everyone. I'm sorry to say that a nineteen-year-old student from UCC was fatally stabbed at approximately midnight last night at the Zombie Lounge nightclub on Oliver Plunkett Street. His name was Tadhg Nicholas Kimmons, and he was living in student accommodation at Carraig House, on the Mardyke, although his parents live at Leslie's Arch in Ballincollig.

'It appears that he was attacked in the men's toilet in the basement of the club. Even though he was gravely injured he managed to make his way up to the dance floor, but then collapsed. When paramedics arrived they found him already deceased.

'A quantity of drugs were found in Tadhg Kimmons' possession, mostly ketamine crystals but also PMMA, known on the street as Blue Ghost. However, we have no witnesses to verify if he was attempting to sell these drugs in the Zombie Lounge, and we have no suggestion that they were connected with his murder, although of course this is one possibility we have to consider.

'There were no witnesses to the actual stabbing and so far no weapon has been found. A considerable number of witnesses saw Tadhg Kimmons fall on to the dance floor and some of those have been receiving treatment for shock and psychological counselling.

'Our investigations are continuing, and as usual we'll be keeping you up to date with any fresh developments. Does anyone have any questions?'

There was a lightning flicker of camera flashes, and then Owen Dineen hoisted up one hand.

'You've a question, Owen?' said Katie. 'I just hope my answer won't be a flop.'

'I don't write the headlines, ma'am. The subs do that. But any road I gather that Tadhg Kimmons' guts were spilled out all over the floor and that about a hundred clubbers were dancing on them before it was realized that he was there.'

'Tadhg Kimmons suffered severe abdominal trauma, yes,

but for the sake of his family and relatives I'm not prepared to go into any more detail than that.'

'Come here, DS Maguire, there he was with over a hundred boys and girls flossing and dancing the triangle on his small intestines.'

'I've no further comment to make on that, Owen. Rionach – do you have a question?'

But before Rionach Barr could open his mouth, Owen Dineen said, 'Was Tadhg Kimmons one of the High Five, DS Maguire? I'm assuming that you know about the High Five, or is that giving you too much credit?'

'I'm aware of the name, Owen, and who they're supposed to be, but so far we have no evidence that their existence is anything but hearsay and we certainly have no evidence that Tadhg Kimmons was one of them.'

'But he was a pharmacy student. And the High Five are all supposed to be pharmacy students, cooking up their own drugs in their college laboratories, to sell on the streets. It seems kind of obvious, don't you think, that Tadhg Kimmons must have been one of them?'

'Again, that's a consideration I have to take on board. But I'm not a detective in a cheap crime novel, Owen. I don't rely on hunches and flashes of inspiration. I rely on evidence. My homicide team will be looking into any number of possibilities, many of which wouldn't even occur to you, and at the same time our Technical Bureau will be examining the crime scene and other likely locations for forensic evidence that will lead us to Tadhg Kimmons' murderer. And, believe me, we'll find him, I promise you that.'

'Oh, well, that's reassuring, I have to admit. You'll find him like you've found out who cremated Justice Garrett Quinn, and who blew Billy Hagerty's head off in broad daylight outside The Weavers?'

'Just because those investigations are not yet concluded, that doesn't mean that they won't be.'

'Fair play to you, DS Maguire. I'm waiting with bated breath here. I only hope I don't spiflicate from lack of oxygen.'

Katie answered more questions from Dan Keane and a woman reporter from the *Irish Times*. It turned out that she had come down especially from Dublin, because a similar group of students from the School of Chemistry at Trinity College had been caught selling drugs in the pubs along Temple Bar. They had called themselves the Holy Trinity.

Finally, Rionach Barr said, 'Is there any kind of reassurance you can give to the parents of young people who'll be going out clubbing tonight to the Zombie Lounge – or any other disco in the city? Are they in any kind of danger?'

'I don't think so, Rionach,' Katie told him. 'The Zombie Lounge is closed for the time being while the Technical Bureau carry out a thorough forensic examination. I've reason to believe, though, that this was a one-off incident, and that there won't be any similar attacks in the Zombie or any other clubs.'

Superintendent Pearse said, 'For the next few days at least we're putting on extra patrols at night, both uniformed and plain clothes, and our officers will be visiting each of the nightclubs in the city centre. As DS Maguire has just told you, we're fairly confident that there won't be any repeats of what happened at the Zombie Lounge.'

'What makes you so confident, superintendent?' asked Owen Dineen. 'Is there something you're not telling us?'

'This is an ongoing investigation, Owen,' said Katie. 'I'm telling you as much as I reasonably can. I'm sure you can understand that I have to hold some information back because it might compromise our ability to identify the murderer of Tadhg Kimmons and bring him to justice.'

'And you still won't confirm that the clubbers at the Zombie Lounge were dancing all over his tripes?'

'I have respect for a young man whose life has been violently cut short, and for his family. Murder isn't an entertainment, Owen. That's all for now.'

After the media briefing, Brendan left immediately and went back to his office, closing his door just as Katie walked past. She had nothing to say to him, but she had the feeling that he was making a point. *Let's keep away from each other.*

It was 10:05 a.m., and she had arranged with the governor of Rathmore Road Prison to interview Donal Hagerty at 10:30 a.m. Rathmore Road was the committal prison for Cork, Kerry and Waterford, a two-tone grey block that stood on the hill by Collins Barracks, overlooking the city to the north. Donal Hagerty was being held there while he waited for his sentencing.

Katie was driven up there by Robert, with Detective Caffrey sitting in the back eating an oat bar, because he hadn't had time for breakfast. Robert said, in the flattest of voices, 'I'm not looking forward to tomorrow's *Sun*, ma'am. I definitely have the feeling that Dineen fellow has it in for you, and I don't think he's finished with you yet, not by a long chalk.'

'I can't be bothering about him, Robert. He'll get tired of slagging me off sooner or later. Any news story has only so much life in it.'

'Well, I know that, but I'm pure bemused why he's being so hostile towards you. It's almost like it's something personal.'

The prison gates were opened up for them and they parked inside, next to a van delivering Clonakilty sausages. The governor came down to greet them in person. He was bald and plump and cheerful in a navy-blue suit, more like a friendly hotelier than a prison governor. The prison itself had been renovated not too long ago, at a cost of millions, so that its grey and yellow paint still smelled fresh; but no amount of renovation could change the familiar sounds of a prison – the clanging of metal doors and the weird howling echoes from the upper landings.

'I'm not so sure that you'll be able to get Hagerty to say anything,' said the governor. 'He hardly utters a word... even to tell us what he wants for his dinner.'

'He's frightened,' said Katie. 'He doesn't want to say anything that sounds as if he might be ratting on the O'Flynns, even if he's only asking for bacon and cabbage.'

The governor led them to the interview room, plain and chilly, where Donal Hagerty was already sitting at the table under the window, with two bored-looking prison guards sitting on either side of him. One of the guards reminded Katie so much of her late husband, Paul, that she could hardly bring herself to look at him, in case he spoke with Paul's voice.

There was no solicitor present, and no need for one, because they hadn't come here to discuss Donal Hagerty's own case, or his committal.

'This is Detective Superintendent Maguire, Donal,' said the governor. 'And this here is Detective Inspector Fitzpatrick and Detective Caffrey.'

Katie and Robert and Detective Caffrey sat down opposite Donal Hagerty. He was bent forward in his chair, his shoulders sloping, and his eyes were fixed on the table. He didn't look up to acknowledge his visitors, or speak. He was forty-one years old, but looked much older, with thinning brown hair, a long bony nose like the rudder of a rowboat, and cavernous cheeks. His agate-coloured eyes seemed to have no life in them at all, as if they were simply tired of looking.

'Donal, we're not here to talk about your case, or your sentencing hearing,' said Katie. 'We've come to talk only about your brother Billy. Before we ask you anything at all, I want to offer you our condolences for your loss. The way that Billy was taken, that was no way for anybody to lose their life, especially so young. He was only thirty-seven, wasn't he?'

Donal said nothing, and didn't raise his eyes, but started to pick at one of his fingernails.

'I've seen Billy in the mortuary, Donal, and there's a question I have to ask you. What name was he given when he was baptized? He *was* baptized, wasn't he? We've had fierce difficulty finding his records, and there was nothing we could find in his flat to enlighten us.'

'His name was Billy,' said Donal, so quietly that Katie could hardly hear him. 'That's what he always called himself. Billy.'

'But what did your parents name him, when he was born?'

'How should I know? We never knew them. We was brought up in St Hilda's. It was the nuns that gave us our names and we was never baptized, the neither of us.'

Katie took a deep breath, trying to stay patient. 'So what name did the nuns give to Billy, when you first went to St Hilda's?'

Donal didn't answer, but continued to pick at his fingernail.

After almost half a minute, Katie said, 'Billy was born a girl, Donal. To begin with, she was your sister. Don't tell me the nuns called her Billy when she was a girl.'

Donal still didn't answer, but Katie could see that his lips were tightly pursed and his scrawny Adam's apple was rising up and down, and suddenly two large teardrops rolled down his cheeks and dripped off his chin.

At last he managed to say, 'I've lost her not only the once. I've lost her twice.'

Katie waited, because she could tell that he desperately needed to explain what he meant. He might never have said this to anybody else before, but now that Billy was dead, it had to come out. He couldn't keep it bottled up inside him for the rest of his life, especially now that he was probably going to be locked up in prison for more than a decade.

'The nuns – the nuns they called her Neala,' he whispered. 'She was my little sister. I always took care of her because nobody else did. I even used to change her if she wet herself, like, and what was I, five years old? I loved her. I loved her to death.'

He wiped his eyes with his sleeve, and gave a rueful smile, still looking down at the tabletop as if he could see a model of his life with Neala being played out on it, in miniature.

'She was always a round little thing, even when we didn't have much to eat. The other kids used to tease her and call her "Balloony". She used to fight them back, though. She was always having a scatter with them and it didn't take long before they learned to treat her with respect. I mean, holy Jesus, she was tougher than me. I loved her. But I lost her. And now I've lost her again.'

'How old was she when she realized that she wanted to change?' asked Katie.

Donal sniffed and pulled a face. 'I think she always knew it, right from the very beginning. That was why she always called herself Billy. But she'd only just started at the Mercy College in Sligo when she told me that she didn't feel right there. She talked to one of her teachers but the teacher said it was only a kind of a phase she was going through, like, and she'd soon get over it. After that she tried so hard to be a woman, I'll tell you. She growed her hair long and she painted her nails and she started jagging with boys. But, you know. Inside her head she still felt like a feller.'

'So when did she decide to go for the operation?'

Donal glanced left and right at the two prison guards sitting either side of him. Their faces were impassive but Katie was quite sure that they had been listening with suppressed relish to Donal telling her all about Billy, and that they would be repeating all the gory details in the staff canteen as soon as they had the chance.

'Three years ago, the first treatment,' Donal told her. 'Only the pills at first. The what-do-ye-call-thems. The hormones.'

'Did something happen in her life to make her decide to start transitioning? I mean, any stressful event?'

'I can't tell you that.'

'Why not, Donal? It won't be going any further.'

Donal didn't answer, but looked down at the table again.

'But I'm guessing that something *did* happen, even if you don't feel that you can tell me about it?'

Still Donal said nothing.

After a while, Katie said, very gently, 'Can you think of any reason why somebody would want to kill Billy? Maybe they were aiming for Thomas O'Flynn and they missed, but what if they weren't? What if it was Billy they were after? Can you think of any motive they might have had?'

Donal remained silent.

Katie and Robert and Detective Caffrey waited patiently, but after three or four minutes of silence it was clear that

Donal had said all that he had needed to say, and that he had no intention of answering any more questions.

'Right,' said Katie. 'Thank you for what you've told us, Donal. It would have been pure helpful if you could have told us a little more, do you know, but Billy was your brother, and we respect your grieving for him. If you have second thoughts about it, you have only to ask the prison staff here and they'll arrange for us to talk some more, either in person or on the phone.'

She stood up, giving him a few more seconds to change his mind, but he didn't speak or raise his eyes, and so she turned around and left the interview room, followed by Robert and Detective Caffrey. They said goodbye to the governor and walked out into the chilly afternoon.

'That last question was critical,' she said, as they climbed back into their car.

'He didn't answer it,' said Detective Caffrey, from the back seat.

'That was why it was critical. He didn't answer it because he didn't want the guards to hear what the answer was.'

'So?'

'He didn't want the guards to hear what the answer was because it's connected somehow with the reason why he shot Michael Riordan and his family. I reckon that it could well have been a giveaway that Thomas O'Flynn contracted him to do it.'

'That's a stretch, isn't it, ma'am?' asked Robert.

'Not at all. What else does he have to hide? Nothing. Nothing that could jeopardize his safety in prison, any road. Well – not more than it's jeopardized already, by the Riordans. But he's already being kept segregated from any pals of the Riordans who might be likely to do him harm.

If he never admits that Thomas O'Flynn put him up to the killing, then at least he doesn't have to worry about any pals of the O'Flynns as well.'

'I have you, ma'am. But I still don't see how Billy Hagerty's sex change could have anything to do with Thomas O'Flynn ordering Donal Hagerty to shoot Michael Riordan.'

'Neither do I. Not yet. But there couldn't be any other reason why Donal wouldn't tell us what made Billy make up his mind to transition. She'd struggled all those years to be a woman… if she'd simply decided it was time for her to change, and become a him, Donal would have had no qualms about telling us, would he? But you saw his reaction for yourself. He clammed up like somebody had put a gun to his head.'

'Holy Saint Dymphna,' said Robert, shaking his head. 'Bring back the days when the boys knew they were boys and the girls knew they were girls and they didn't keep lopping bits off and sticking them back on again.'

20

When they reached Anglesea Street, Katie asked Robert to drop her off outside the law courts. Stephen Herlihy's secretary was out at lunch, so she went straight through to his office and knocked at his door.

He called out, 'Come!' and when she went inside she found him sitting at his desk, talking to a broad-shouldered man in a dark grey suit.

'Oh, I didn't mean to interrupt you, Stephen. I'm sorry. I can come back later, if you like.'

'No, please stay. In fact I was going to ring you in any case and ask you if you could join us. DS Maguire, this is the Honourable Mr Justice Kieran Connolly. Justice Connolly, this is Detective Superintendent Kathleen Maguire.'

Justice Connolly stood up. He was very tall, at least six foot three or four, with swept-back flax-coloured hair, which was beginning to glisten silver at the sides. He could have been Scandinavian rather than Irish, with a broad forehead and high cheekbones and washed-out blue eyes that looked as if they had faded to that colour because he had been standing for too long on the prow of a longboat, staring out to sea.

He cupped her hand between both of his and said, 'DS Maguire. I've heard a great deal about you.'

'Some of it complimentary, I hope,' said Katie.

'Oh, sure. You have quite a reputation. All that business with the Garda whistle-blowers, and how you handled that – that didn't go unnoticed up in Dublin.'

Katie immediately liked Justice Connolly's voice. It was rich and soothing, halfway between a rumble and a purr, but it also had a hint of amusement behind it, as if he didn't take himself too seriously.

She sat down, and Stephen Herlihy said, 'Justice Connolly has come down to Cork to support Justice O'Rafferty for the next two months or so on serious cases. He'll be kicking off with the sentencing hearing for Donal Hagerty.'

'Legally, Justice O'Rafferty could hand down the sentence on her own,' said Justice Connolly. 'But we wanted to show the public and the criminal fraternity that the death of Justice Quinn has done nothing to weaken or deter the judiciary. You may take one of us down, but there'll always be another to step up in their place.'

He picked up a thick manila folder from Stephen Herlihy's desk. 'I've studied the court reports on Donal Hagerty, and discussed them in detail with Justice O'Rafferty, and we're in total agreement about the length of the prison term that we intend to impose.'

'He'll be sentenced on Monday morning,' said Stephen Herlihy. 'Then on Tuesday we have the Moody case listed, all things being equal.'

Katie could understand why they wanted two judges for the Moody case. Declan Moody and two of his brothers were accused of supplying semi-automatic rifles and pistols to anyone who wanted to buy them, including a group of Republican activists who called themselves the True IRA and a gang of Nigerian pimps known as the Dudu.

'I've just this minute come back from an interview with Donal Hagerty up at Rathmore Road,' she told Justice Connolly.

'Oh yes? And was he co-operative?'

'Not about shooting Michael Riordan. I'm still convinced that he was paid to kill Michael Riordan by Thomas O'Flynn. In fact I'm even more convinced now than I ever was, but you'd have to waterboard him or pull out his fingernails with red-hot pliers to get him to admit it. Sure like, he was friendly with the O'Flynns, enough to have a scoop with them if they ever met up in a bar. But he wasn't a paid-up member of their gang, and he had no personal beef against Michael Riordan, no matter what he said in court.'

'Oh yes,' said Justice Connolly. 'That cock-and-bull story about Michael Riordan having threatened to kill him because he'd overheard the Riordans planning some robbery and he'd tipped off the law.'

'That's right. The Riordans were going to hijack an excavator from a building site near the Blackpool Shopping Centre and then dig the ATM out of the wall of the Bank of Ireland. We *were* tipped off about that, yes, and we foiled it by putting the excavator out of commission, but we doubt that it was Donal Hagerty who told us. He was in Sligo at the time, and it wasn't until five months later that he shot Michael Riordan. If he was that scared of Michael Riordan coming after him, surely he would have done it sooner.'

'But you're still trying to find evidence that Thomas O'Flynn was behind it?'

'I'm determined to, Your Honour. I'm totally determined to.'

'What about Justice Quinn? How's that investigation coming along?'

'Pure slow, I'm afraid. But again, I won't let up until I find out who murdered him.'

'You think the O'Flynns might have had something to do with that, too?'

'I can't be sure. Again, we have our suspicions. But it's no use coming up in front of a judge with suspicions – even if they're strong suspicions – as you know yourself.'

'True,' said Justice Connolly, and he looked at his Rolex. 'Listen, Stephen, I think we've covered everything we need to. I'll see you on Monday morning so. I had no breakfast, and I'm starving, so I'm going to find myself some lunch. Maybe you could suggest somewhere, DS Maguire?'

'I've had no lunch either, Your Honour, so why don't we go together?'

'Sure, that sounds like a plan.'

Katie could hardly believe herself that she had invited him. She was still numb with grief from losing Conor and the shock of seeing Garrett's incinerated body. When her previous lover, John, had died, she had wanted to do nothing for weeks but shut herself away and talk to nobody, although of course that had been impossible. But this time she felt she needed company, especially since she was having such complicated trouble at work.

More than that, she found Justice Connolly's presence warm and reassuring. She felt that she would be able to tell him about some of her current difficulties at Anglesea Street, and that he would understand them. Her sisters and her friends in Cobh, even if they were sympathetic, wouldn't have the first clue what she was talking about.

'You don't mind a five-minute scove, do you, Your Honour?' she asked him, as they left the court office.

'I think outside of office hours you can call me Kieran.'

'In that case, you can call me Kathleen. Or Katie, if you like.'

'I'd prefer to call you Katie, if that's all right with you. I had an aunt called Kathleen, and she was a bit of a Cailleach, I'm afraid.' By that, he meant a witch, or an old hag.

They walked across the Parnell Bridge over the south channel of the River Lee. A damp south-west wind was ruffling the surface of the river, and three ducks were noisily squabbling over a grey mullet that one of them had caught.

'I was deeply sorry to hear about Garrett Quinn,' said Kieran. 'I'd met him a fair few times, and I liked him a lot. Did you know him at all?'

For a moment, Katie was breathless with emotion, and she could barely speak. *Oh dear God, don't let me start crying, not halfway across the bridge, on the way to lunch.*

'Yes,' she said at last, as they stopped and waited to cross over South Mall. 'He and I were good friends. He gave me a rake of very sound advice when I was making my way up the ladder at Anglesea Street.'

'I'm sorry. I didn't mean to intrude.'

Katie looked up at him, and by the expression on his face she couldn't help thinking that he already knew how intense her relationship with Garrett had been, or at least had guessed it. *Do I really give myself away that much? I always thought I was the one who could read other people's minds, and that I myself was inscrutable.*

They arrived at the Market Lane restaurant on Oliver Plunkett Street, and they were shown to a table upstairs, by the railing that overlooked the ground floor. Lunchtime was almost over, and so it was less crowded and noisy than usual, but in any case Katie had no trouble in hearing Kieran's deep, clear, distinctive voice. She could almost follow what he was saying by the look in his eyes, and by a kind of professional osmosis. They understood each other.

'You wouldn't believe it, but I never intended to be a lawyer, let alone a judge,' Kieran told her. 'I wanted to join the navy and go to sea.'

'It's strange, but I would have guessed that, if you'd asked me.'

'Really? But now I'll never know. My oldest brother got himself into trouble with a hotel business that he'd started up, and he was accused of fraud. I boned up on the law about what he was supposed to have done, and when he went to court I stood up and I spoke in his defence. He was found not guilty, and I was so pleased with myself for getting him off, and so pumped up about performing in court, that I decided then and there that I was going to take up the law.'

They ordered lunch. Kieran went for the slow-cooked bacon collar with parsnip mash, while Katie chose a salad of torn ham hock with roast butternut squash and sundried tomatoes.

'I could murder a glass of Chardonnay,' said Kieran. 'But I don't think that would be a great idea with a detective superintendent as a witness. Let's go for the sparkling Ishka spring water, shall we?'

They talked for over two hours. Katie told Kieran about her late father being a Garda inspector, and how she had been the only one of his seven daughters to follow him into An Garda Síochána, so as not to disappoint him.

Kieran told Katie about his upbringing in Portobello, an idyllic suburb close to Dublin city centre with a canal running through it. As a boy he used to paddle a kayak up and down the canal, which is how he had become interested in joining the navy. His father had been a highly successful surgeon while his mother had been an actress in the popular TV soap *Fair City*. When his mother's character had been killed off, though, she had found it impossible to find regular acting work in Ireland, and she had taken to drinking. She had died five years ago of liver failure.

'She was beautiful. I miss her every day. Whenever it rains, or the sun comes out, I think to myself, why aren't you here to see this, ma?'

He was silent for a while, his eyes focused on nothing at all. 'So – are you married?' Katie asked him, to break him out of his reverie.

'Oh, yes – well, no. I was for three years. Siobhan her name was, and she had this fierce frizzy hair. We met at a friend's wedding. All I can say about our marriage is that we were both too young, and our personalities didn't match at all. There was a whole lot of shouting and slamming of doors, that's what I remember most about it. I was lucky to get out of it without going stone deaf.'

Katie told Kieran briefly about her marriage to Paul, the fast-and-loose building contractor;, with John, the farmer, whom she had hoped to marry; and her deep relationship with Conor, the pet detective. He listened to her carefully, never taking his eyes off her once, and nodding from time to time.

'I had the feeling you were hurting,' he said, when she had finished.

'Why?'

'I don't know. Maybe the same way that you knew that I wanted to be a sailor.'

She went on to tell him about all the problems at Anglesea Street that were currently putting her under so much stress. She didn't mention Brendan, or his rape, or the pictures that he had arranged for his crony to take of her and Kyna together. However, she did tell him about the grumpy sexual discrimination she was still suffering every day from some of her senior male officers, and the hostile media reports she had been given by Owen Dineen. It was his blistering attack in the

Irish Sun that had upset her the most, because it accused her of being incompetent in a job to which she was devoted.

Kieran laid his hand on top of hers. 'Listen, Katie, crime is on the increase everywhere – not only in Cork, not only in Ireland, but all over the globe. It's the drugs trade, it's the people-trafficking, it's the prostitution, and more than anything else it's the social media that make it so much easier for gangsters to run a criminal racket. On top of that, it's the cuts in government spending on law and order, with so many local Garda stations closing down – what is it, a hundred and forty stations shut in the past ten years? You know all this as well as I do. But so long as you're confident that you're doing the very best you can under the circumstances, you should pay no attention at all to the shite that the newspapers and your senior officers are giving you. You know you're good, Katie. To be totally crude about it, just give them all the middle finger.'

Katie couldn't help smiling. 'I think I'll ask you to repeat that, so that I can record it, and play it back to myself when I go to bed tonight.'

Kieran stared at her, and she felt a tingle up the back of her neck. He didn't say it, and maybe he wasn't even thinking it. Maybe it was only her imagination, and her grief, and her jumbled confusion. But she almost expected him to suggest that when she went to bed tonight he could be lying next to her to repeat it for her in person, if she wanted him to.

They drank coffee, and Kieran paid the bill, and then they walked back across the river to Anglesea Street. Slate-grey clouds were looming overhead like a dark collapsing roof, and the orange streetlights were already starting to flicker on. Outside the law courts Kieran took hold of Katie's hand again and said, 'I might as well tell you that we'll be giving Hagerty life. That's mandatory. But we're going to be imposing a sentence of twenty-two years.'

'If he'd come out and informed on whoever paid him to do it, would you have recommended less?'

'We couldn't have given him any less than twelve, could we, even if he'd been more co-operative. But he murdered an innocent woman and two young children, too, and I don't think even the softest-hearted penal reformer would say that he doesn't deserve at least twenty-two years for that.'

'Well, I agree. But the real murderer is still walking free, and believe me, Kieran, that's really burning me up inside. I won't have any rest until I see Thomas O'Flynn hauled up in front of you, too. But – Jesus – look at the time! I have to go now. My team have been texting me every two minutes and they'll be wondering what in the name of God has happened to me.'

'Katie – we must talk some more. When can I see you again?'

'Let me check my roster, and I'll ring you.'

'You promise?'

They stood there, holding hands, and it began to rain, softly pattering on the pavement all around them. Katie didn't answer, but Kieran said, 'Off you go. You don't want to get yourself wringing, now, do you?'

21

Detectives Caffrey and O'Crean were waiting for her when she returned to her office.

'How's the tracksuit hunt coming along?' she asked them.

'Dead end so far,' said Detective O'Crean. 'We've found no GAA coaches who wear grey tracksuits, nor any private gyms, nor school sports teachers. Nobody.'

Detective Caffrey said, 'We called in at JD Sports and Cummins and Intersport Elverys but all the grey tracksuits they sell have two broad white stripes down the legs. Finn's Corner sell a solid grey tracksuit but they're only for the girls at St Catherine's Secondary School in Ardpatrick. To be honest with you, ma'am, we're running out of places to look.'

'Your man could have bought his tracksuit anywhere,' put in Detective O'Crean. 'He could have bought it in the UK, like, or America, or online. I mean, we've given it our best shot, but I think we're on something of a wild tracksuit chase here.'

'All right,' said Katie. 'You can leave it for now. Go over to Oliver Plunkett Street and give Walsh and Cullen a hand with the Zombie Lounge stabbing. They've still dozens of witnesses left to interview.'

Moirin put her head around the door. 'Coffee, ma'am?'

'No, thanks, Moirin. I've only just had a double espresso. If I have any more I think I'll be treble-jigging around the room and jumping on the furniture.'

'Assistant Commissioner Magorian was looking for you.'

'Is he still here?'

'I think so. He said he'll be off to Limerick at five.'

'Well, I'll go find him in a minute. Just now I need some time to sit and sort my thoughts out.'

'Is everything okay, ma'am?'

'I'm grand altogether, Moirin, thanks. The world isn't about to come to an end yet.'

Katie sat down at her desk and looked through the memos and the files that had been left for her. Revenue had been tipped off about a large shipment of heroin that might be smuggled in through Ringaskiddy in the next two or three days. Apart from that, there was nothing of desperate urgency.

She couldn't stop thinking about the Lee Pusher. Maybe it was the ghostly picture of him that she had in her mind, rushing up to innocent people in his grey tracksuit and knocking them into the river. Maybe it was the concept that Dr Power had given her of a lonely, isolated man who always felt that he was rejected by society and needed to take out his frustration on people who looked happy.

She thought, too, about Billy Hagerty, originally Aoife Hagerty, and how lonely and isolated she must have felt, never fitting in, because she always felt like a boy.

In one of those unexpected flashes of recall, she remembered a friend of hers at her secondary school, Margaret Finlay, who had been relentlessly teased by all the other girls because she was so tall. One day when they were walking home together Margaret had sobbed all the way back to her house, saying that she wished she had been born a boy if she was going to be so tall. Either that, or she wished that she had never been born at all. She hated everybody, she wept, because she had no friends apart from Katie, and none of the other girls would share secrets with her or let her join their clubs.

Two weeks later Margaret had wrapped her school scarf around her neck and hanged herself in her bedroom.

Katie went to the window and looked out at the rain dredging across the car park. The hooded crows were still there, huddled on the rooftop opposite. Her mind was all jumbled up like a kaleidoscope. *'I'd kill all those bullies if I could,'* Margaret had told her. *'They've taken my life, why shouldn't I take theirs?'*

Katie went back to her desk and switched on her computer. She looked up St Catherine's Secondary School in Ardpatrick and found photos of this year's athletics team. They were all wearing grey tracksuits, but none of them could have been much taller than five foot four and most of them had long hair or plaits so it was highly unlikely that any of them could have been mistaken for a man.

She scrolled back to previous seasons and saw that they had started to wear light grey tracksuits only eight years ago, so she started to check through their team photographs year by year, starting with the earliest. After only three seasons, she came across a photograph of St Catherine's senior girls winning a trophy at the South Munster Schools Track and Field Championships. Standing at the back of the team was a thin, sad-looking girl who was even taller than the smiling official who was presenting the team with their shield.

Katie enlarged the picture and studied the girl carefully. Her hair was cut short and she had a long, masculine face, with unplucked eyebrows.

She picked up her phone and rang Kyna. 'Kyna – come up and take a sconce at this, would you?'

Kyna appeared wearing her yellow raincoat and swinging her yellow rain hat on her finger, ready to go home. She came around and stood behind Katie and peered closely at the photo of the athletics team.

'That was five years ago, so she'd be twenty-one or twenty-two now,' said Katie.

'You really think the Pusher could be female? What are the odds she'd still have that same tracksuit, all those years after leaving school?'

'I have no idea. Maybe she kept it, and maybe she wears it when she goes out to push people into the river because it symbolizes the time when she was bullied. But then again, it's far more likely that she wasn't bullied and she isn't the Pusher. She could be happily married and living in Crosshaven with a husband and two kids and a cat. But you have to admit that she looks fierce miserable in this picture, and she's not the most feminine girl you've ever seen. Apart from which, she's the only tall thin person in a grey tracksuit that we've been able to find.'

'I'll contact the school then, and find out who she is,' said Kyna. 'It's probably best if I go up there in person. I'll call in there on my way home.'

'It'll probably come to nothing at all, do you know? I don't believe in hunches. But there's no harm in checking.'

She told Kyna about Margaret Finlay committing suicide, and Kyna said, 'That's so sad. And it's worse these days, the bullying, on Twitter. You're never allowed to be different. Look at us – being threatened by Brendan O'Kane, and for what? For finding each other attractive? When has that ever been a sin?'

Katie went down to see Assistant Commissioner Magorian. He, too, was just about to leave the station, and was buttoning up his trench coat.

'Ah, Kathleen... thanks for dropping by. How's it going on?'

'Slow but sure, sir. I could do with about twenty more detectives to be honest with you, but we're making progress.'

'Nothing new on Justice Quinn? I've had the Commissioner nagging me about it, because the Minister's been nagging the Secretary General about it and the Secretary General's been nagging him.'

'We're still working on the possibility that the O'Flynn gang was behind it – maybe to warn the judges not to hand down too severe a sentence on Donal Hagerty. But we have to be open-minded. Justice Quinn made a rake of enemies over his years on the bench, as all judges do.'

'And the stabbing at the Zombie Lounge?'

'Again, we're still interviewing witnesses and assessing the forensics.'

'And the High Five drug-dealers?'

Katie looked at him narrowly. 'Has that Owen Dineen been on to you, sir, from the *Sun*?'

'Yes, he has. And he asked me a whole lot of fierce difficult questions. Like, why is the Garda allowing gangs to run riot in Cork city, and why aren't we solving more murders and assault cases and hauling in more pimps and people smugglers? It's even worse in the countryside. Farmers are having their tractors and their livestock stolen and their houses broken into and we seem to be doing nothing to catch the gangs responsible. He said that many members of the public are feeling pure apprehensive when they go out at night, especially the older generation. A county councillor has complained to him that Cork is like the Wild West these days, only worse.'

'You've seen the figures, sir. So far this year we've cleared up five per cent more cases than we did this time last year, and our conviction rate has gone up by three-point-five per cent.'

'It's still not good enough, Kathleen, if the public are feeling unsafe.'

'Then get me more money, that's all I can say.'

'It's not just a case of more money. It's a question of competence.'

Frank Magorian took a deep breath, and paused, as if he were undecided about what he should say next.

'Go on,' said Katie. 'What else did the charming Owen Dineen have to say to you?'

'He asked me when we were going to let you go and replace you with a detective superintendent who could actually catch criminals.'

'I see. And may I ask you what you replied?'

'I told him that I have complete trust in you and your team, and that if he looked back over your record he would see that your performance as a DS has been exemplary. I said that you've cracked some of the most complex crimes that have been committed in Cork city and county in the past few years, and that you've put behind bars some of the most dangerous men in Ireland.'

'Thank you. But I sense a "but"?'

'Of course I defended you. But the public perception is that you've lost your grip. You're going to have to up your game, Kathleen, and fast. Right now we have too many high-profile cases that you haven't been able to solve, and the media are going to go on giving you a hard time until you track down the offenders and fetch them up in front of the courts.'

'And what if it takes longer to track them down than the media would like? Why doesn't Owen Dineen try his luck at finding out who set fire to Justice Quinn or who stabbed that student in the Zombie Lounge? Why doesn't *he* try to trap the Lee Pusher?'

'I hear you, but I have to put you on notice. We can't tolerate very much more of this bad media coverage. It's not only the *Sun* now. I've had the *Times* and the *Examiner* on to me, too. I know your arrest figures are marginally improved on last year, but what we're talking about here is a crisis of confidence.'

Katie said nothing. Inside, her stomach had knotted up and she felt that she could burst out with rage, in the same way that Conor had exploded when he had blown up the Foggy Fields puppy farm. But she also remembered what Conor had said to her when they had first lived together, and she had raged on to him about some misogynistic comment at work. *Fanacht socair*. Stay calm. Hold your peace. Don't throw all your cards on to the table. The time will come when you'll be vindicated.

'Fair play to you, sir,' she told Frank, at last. 'Let's see what the papers have to say tomorrow, shall we?'

Before she left the city centre, Katie drove up to Oliver Plunkett Street, where Detective Inspector Fitzpatrick had requisitioned two upstairs offices at the Zombie Lounge as interview rooms. He had chosen to bring potential witnesses to the club rather than the Garda station because he believed that it would make it easier for them to picture in their mind's eye anything they might have seen when Tadhg Kimmons was stabbed. It would be less intimidating, too.

Six young clubbers were waiting in the booth where Thomas O'Flynn and his cronies had been sitting, four boys and two girls. They looked bored and restless, even though they had each been given a free bottle of Pepsi-Cola and a package of Taytos.

'I'm Detective Superintendent Maguire,' Katie told them. 'I just want to tell you how much we appreciate your cooperation with this investigation.'

'I don't know what I'm doing here to be straight with you,' said one of the lads. 'I didn't see feck-all, and neither did none of the rest of us here. I didn't even notice the feen when he was panned out on the floor.'

'Well, you never know,' Katie told him. 'You might have seen something important without even realizing it. That often happens.'

The lad looked at his watch. 'So long as they don't keep us here too much longer. I'm supposed to be meeting the ould doll at six, and she'll have my mebs for meatballs if I'm late.'

Katie knocked and went into the interview room where Detectives Walsh and Cullen were talking to a young girl with a tangly blonde Madonna hairstyle.

'You saw him fall over, then?' Detective Cullen was asking her. 'Did he say anything before he fell over?'

'If he did, I wouldn't have been able to hear it, like. The music was like deafening. I thought he was buckled at first, and I was dancing around him. It's happened before, like, when one of the lads gets off his face. But then I felt this squelching and I looked down and I tell you I almost gawked.'

'How's the form, Cailin?' Katie asked her.

Detective Walsh looked up and gave her a jaded smile. 'We're slowly getting through them, ma'am. Only another forty-seven to go, after this. It's been a bit like a jigsaw, one twinchy piece at a time, but I'd say we're gradually building up a picture of what happened.'

'Good work,' said Katie. 'We'll have a full briefing tomorrow afternoon, when you've finished.'

She went into the adjacent office, where Detectives Caffrey and O'Crean were trying to get some sense out of a boy with gingery dreadlocks and a baggy green tracksuit. He was slumped in his chair and obviously half-stoned.

'What's the story?' she asked them.

'Snow White and the Seven Dwarfs, according to this feller,' said Detective O'Crean. 'He's mad out of it.'

'Oh well, do your best. I'll catch up with you in the morning so.'

Katie left the Zombie Lounge and drove north across St Patrick's Bridge to MacCurtain Street and then north-eastwards up Summerhill, passing the guest house where she and Conor had first made love. She didn't look at it, because it was too painful to think that it was less than a year ago, and how little time they had been able to spend together.

She remembered something else that he had said to her. 'I didn't realize until I met you that I was living in pitchy-black darkness. When I first saw you, it was like I was opening up the curtains in the morning and the sun came bursting in.'

She drove to Tivoli Park and stopped outside the Quinn house. It was a six-bedroomed mansion, painted pale green, with a terraced garden lined with sculpted yew hedges and a view to the south over the River Lee and the distant hills beyond. The lights were on and inside she could hear the indistinct burbling of the *Six One News*.

When she rang the bell at the front door, the television was immediately turned down, and she could hear voices. After a long pause, the front door was opened and a stocky grey-haired man with a red face appeared.

'Yes? Can I help you?'

'Detective Superintendent Maguire, from Anglesea Street Garda station. I've dropped by to give Mrs Quinn some property that belonged to her late husband.'

'Property, is it?'

Orla Quinn appeared behind him, wearing what looked like silky black pyjamas. 'It's all right, Andrew. You can let her in. I'm sorry to be so cautious, Katie. After what happened to Garrett, you can understand that I've been pure fearful of somebody coming after me. Andrew's my cousin. He was a boxing champion back in the day. He's staying for a while as my bodyguard.'

'You've had no threats, have you?'

'Only three or four gowls on Twitter saying they're delighted that Garrett's dead. Ex-cons that he sent down, I expect.'

Andrew opened the door wider and Katie followed Orla into the living room. It was huge, high-ceilinged, with two elephantine grey leather sofas, four armchairs and a monumental red-marble fireplace. At least a dozen framed family photographs were clustered on the mantelpiece, and in the centre was an oval portrait of Garrett, with a black ribbon tied in a bow around it.

'Please, sit down,' said Orla.

But Katie said, 'I can't stay. I've come only to give you this.'

She handed Orla the evidence bag with the claddagh band and the wedding ring inside it. Orla opened the bag and took them out, one after the other.

'So… this is all I have left of him. Well, apart from all his clothes and his shoes and his books and his golf clubs, and they're all going to the ISPCC.'

'You have your memories, Orla, and they're the most precious.'

Orla held up the claddagh band and gave a rueful smile. 'Garrett always told me that he would never take this off, because it represented the greatest love that he had ever known. He bought it himself about two years after we were married. To you, Katie, it may make no sense at all, but it reassured me that he still wore it even when he was being unfaithful to me.'

'You don't need to think about him like that any more. Remember the good times you had together and forget about the times that he strayed. We're all human, after all.'

'I used to blame myself for him being unfaithful, can you believe that? I used to think I must be ugly, or stupid, or that I was no use in bed. But I met a very handsome fellow at a big legal party last St Stephen's Day, and this fellow gave me so many compliments and was so flirtatious that the scales fell away from my eyes, do you know what I mean? I suddenly understood that the fault had never been mine, not in any way at all. It was simply the way that Garrett always was, and always would be. As far as he was concerned, the only reason that God had put women on Earth was for Garrett Quinn's personal pleasure – the pretty ones, anyway. It would have been deeply ungrateful of him not to enjoy what God had so generously given him. Sacrilege, almost.'

'But he never took off the claddagh band, or the wedding ring. So – like you say – he was still being loyal to you, in his own disloyal way.'

Orla turned to the photograph of Garrett above the fireplace. 'I miss him so much that it's making me ill. I can't eat, I can't sleep. When you find out who murdered him, don't let me anywhere near them, because I swear that I'll scratch their eyes out.'

'I have to go now,' said Katie. 'My dogs will be pining for their supper and their evening walk. But I'll keep you informed so. I promise.'

She gave Orla a brief hug, and like before, she could feel her bony ribcage through her black silky blouse. Then she smiled and nodded goodbye to Andrew, and left. It was chilly outside, and she shivered and quickly buttoned up her coat.

As she unlocked her car, she noticed that one of the houses further up Tivoli Park had a CCTV security camera under the eaves. The owner had obviously angled it to cover his own front garden, but when Katie looked up and down the street, she considered that it might possibly have caught an image of the silver Range Rover that Orla said she had seen there on Monday and Tuesday.

She crossed the street. A bright light popped on when she entered the front gate, and she could see lights inside the hallway and behind the curtains in the living room. However, there were no cars parked in front of the garage, and when she knocked there was no response. She knocked again, and waited, but it was clear that there was nobody home. She made a note of the house number and went back to her car. She would send Detective Scanlan up here in the morning to see if she could download the past week's CCTV footage from the owners' hard drive or cloud server, depending on how they stored it.

As she drove back to Cobh, with reflections glittering in the darkness from the River Lee, she felt a wave of loneliness. She could picture the January evening when she had met Garrett in the bar of the Hayfield Manor hotel as if it were only a week ago, instead of years – the evening she had given him the claddagh band.

He had twisted it on to the third finger of his right hand, and kissed her, and said, 'I promise you this, Katie. I'll still be wearing this the day I die.'

22

They huddled together at the far end of the laboratory, keeping their voices down so that nobody could overhear them. Beside them, the sun was shining on the shelves that were stacked with glass bottles of propylene glycol and sorbitol solution and sodium citrate and all the other inactive ingredients that go into medicinal syrups and pills and pessaries.

Only three other students had arrived so far and they were too preoccupied with prodding at their smartphones to take any notice of them, and Dr Griffin had yet to appear to start them off on their morning's pharmacy project.

There were only four of them now: Eoin Keating, Cormac O'Driscoll, Kevin Moynihan and Lorraine Byrne. Lorraine was wearing a black armband but Eoin told her to take it off.

'It's to show that I'm in mourning for Tadhg,' she protested. Lorraine had dark brown undulating hair and she was quite pretty in a plump, pouting, droopy-eyed way, although her wide hips made it difficult for her to fasten the bottom two buttons of her lab coat.

'I know that, Lorraine,' said Eoin. He was short and round-shouldered, with a snub nose and tightly curled hair, so blond that it was almost white, like unwashed lambswool. 'But somebody's going to wonder why you're wearing it and we don't want them to find out that any of us were friends with him. Otherwise they'll start to suspect that the High Five is us. Not that we can call ourselves that any more.'

'But what do we say if the guards come around asking questions?' put in Cormac. He was tall and skinny and mournful and he always swayed from side to side when he talked, like a poplar tree in the wind.

'We act mongo sap, like we never knew what Tadhg was up to.'

'Don't be an eejit,' said Kevin. He was the oldest of them, bull-necked and bearded, with a prickly black crew cut, and he already held a BPharm degree. 'They *know* that there was five of us. It was all over the news, for God's sake.'

'Still and all, if we say nothing—'

'Oh, cop on to yourself, will you? Tadhg wouldn't have been after calling himself the High Five if there was only one of him, would he? And now that they know who he was, and that he was studying here at the Cavanagh, they're bound to put two and two together and realize that he was cooking his drugs up right here in this lab – and that he likely wasn't doing it on his ownsome. Get serious, Eoin, you might think the guards are thick as bottled shite, but my brother Sean knows one of their detectives, and believe me, that fellow is the cutest hoor you could ever hope to meet. He'd know at once if you was wearing your grundies back to front, just because you was looking guzz-eyed.'

'I still say we act schtum,' said Eoin. 'The cops can't find any evidence here that we've been breaking the law, can they, because all the chemicals we've been using are one hundred per cent legit. And even if somebody grasses on us, like somebody we've been selling to, we only have to say that they're spoofing, and it wasn't us. If they was out looking to buy dope, the chances are that they were half-baked to begin with, so how they can swear on the Bible that it was one of us?'

'I don't think it's the law we have to worry about the most,' said Lorraine. 'It's whoever killed poor Tadhg. I can think of only one reason why he got himself stabbed, and that's because somebody didn't want him selling ket at the Zombie Lounge. I mean, that was something else they said on the news, wasn't it, that the drugs gangs in Cork, they're fierce territorial. I think we've been putting ourselves in much more danger than we know.'

'Lorraine's right, you know, Eoin,' said Cormac. 'We need to call it a day. If we don't get ourselves lifted by the law we're sure to get ourselves murdered by one of the mobs.'

'Oh, come on,' Eoin coaxed him. 'I agree with you that we'll have to be doggy wide for the next three or four weeks. But we'd have to be crazy to give it up altogether. You know how much grade we made last month – more than three thousand five hundred between us. And we're already starting to build up regular customers. We could be millionaires by Christmas.'

'Tadhg's *dead*, Eoin,' Lorraine protested, and her eyes suddenly brimmed with tears. 'It was his twentieth birthday in two weeks' time but he's never going to see it because he's *dead*. He's never going to graduate, he's never going to be a pharmacist, he's never going to get married, he's never going to have children. He can't see the sky today. He can't see the sunshine. This isn't a temporary inconvenience as far as he's concerned, like it seems to be for you. His life is over for ever, Eoin. You'll be throwing shapes all around the city centre next week but he'll be lying under the ground, in the dark, not breathing, inside a box.'

Eoin shrugged and looked away, with his lips pursed, as if he didn't want to hear.

Cormac said, 'Maybe we should talk this over later, like. What happened to Tadhg, Jesus, it put all of our hearts crossways, you have to admit. Myself, I keep thinking that I only dreamed he was murdered, and that any minute now he's going to come strolling in as usual with his Egg McMuffin, stinking out the lab like he always used to.'

More students were arriving now, taking their places at the laboratory benches with a loud scraping of stools and chattering loudly to each other. Their professor, Dr Griffin, would be coming in soon to outline what medications they would be preparing today, and explaining their effects and possible side effects – how the very same preparation could cure one patient but make another patient seriously ill, or even kill them.

The four remaining members of the High Five separated and sat down. Eoin was sulking and when he lit his Bunsen burner he kept turning the flame up so high that it roared and then back down again, as if he were expressing his frustration in a fiery Morse code.

Kevin was about to go over and try to calm him down when a broad-shouldered man in a red baseball cap and a black leather jacket came backing in through the laboratory door, carrying a large cardboard box.

'I've a delivery here from Medisure,' he announced. 'I think it's a sentifroogway.'

Cormac stood up and looked at the label. 'Oh. You mean a centrifuge.'

'Whatever it is, it's fierce heavy so is there somewhere I can set it down?'

'Put it on the side here,' said Cormac, so the man shuffled his way along the aisle and heaved the box down on the workbench that ran along the right-hand wall, grunting with effort.

'They've signed for it already downstairs,' the man told him. 'I only fetched it up here myself because it weighs a fecking ton. There. Whatever it is you young geniuses do with a sentifroogway, I wish you joy of it.'

He gave them a salute and walked out, leaving the door open behind him.

Exactly twenty-seven minutes and thirty seconds later, just as Dr Griffin was explaining how the drug prednisolone could ease inflammation but possibly cause peptic ulcers, the box blew up.

The blast devastated the laboratory, blowing out all the windows into College Road, and shattering every single bottle and test tube and retort flask into a blizzard of sharp glass shards. Cormac, who had been sitting closest to the box, was shredded into a long, ragged string of red muscles, tangled with bones. Next to him, Lorraine's head was knocked off by the blast and sent spinning out of the window with her dark hair whirling, while her body burst open and her bloody lungs flapped up as if they were wings.

In the row in front of them, Eoin's head was torn off, too, leaving him with a bony stalk of vertebrae for a neck. Kevin was standing with his back to the box, stretching. Both of his arms were ripped off and whirled away in different directions, as if they were frantically signalling, while his stomach exploded out of his lab coat and his intestines unravelled like a speeded-up film, piling over the window sill in pale slippery loops.

Dr Griffin had just turned away from the whiteboard to face his students when the box was detonated, and he was caught in the hailstorm of thousands of sharp glass fragments. His entire face was instantly flayed into thin scarlet ribbons of skin, and his Donegal tweed jacket was shredded into shoddy.

He was thrown backwards and sideways and disappeared under his desk.

Half of the laboratory ceiling collapsed at an angle. Pipes burst and electricity cables were torn apart, so that water began to shower down over the bodies and the wreckage, and sparks jumped and crackled through the indoor rain. In all, Dr Griffin and eleven students had been killed, and three students devastatingly injured. One girl had survived because she had bent down to pick up her pen when she had dropped it, but her right hip and most of her right buttock had been blasted away.

The School of Pharmacy was over two kilometres away from the city centre, but the bang was so loud that it had been heard by shoppers on St Patrick's Street. They stopped, and looked up, and many of them thought that a plane could have crashed, up at the airport.

Katie had just opened her office window to let in some fresh air, and she heard it, too. She had heard bombs going off before, and she knew at once what it was. She rang down to Superintendent Pearse and said, 'Michael – did you hear that?'

'Did I hear what?'

'It sounded like a bomb going off. I can't be sure what direction it came from. To the west, I'd say.'

'Sorry, no. I had on my earphones. I was listening to last night's interview with Minister Flanagan.'

Katie was about to say something else when she heard Superintendent Pearse's phones starting to ring, and then two of her own phones started to ring, too, and within seconds phones all over the station were ringing.

She picked up the nearest phone. It was Detective Sergeant Begley.

'There's been a bomb at UCC. The Cavanagh building. It's a major explosion by what's been reported, with multiple casualties.'

'All right, Sean. We need to get out there right away. Who do you have available?'

Before he could answer, Katie heard sirens from the fire station across the road, first one engine and then another, followed by a third.

Mother of God, can this week get any more catastrophic?

23

Katie stood on the pavement outside the School of Pharmacy on College Road with Kyna and Detective Sergeant Begley for over three hours. It was sunny but the wind had a bitter edge to it. Her breath smoked and she wished she had worn her gloves.

Detective O'Donovan came over from Anglesea Street to view the devastation first-hand and to collect the CCTV hard drive from the Cavanagh building's reception area. He didn't stay long. Katie had also assigned him to look for any footage from the Lough area that might show the delivery van that had brought the box containing the bomb, and hopefully its driver, too.

Kyna and Detective Sergeant Begley had interviewed the school's principal and its two receptionists, as well as five other witnesses who had been in the lobby when the driver had carried in the 'centrifuge'. His delivery note from Medisure had appeared to be genuine, and the receptionists had agreed to him taking it up to the laboratory himself because it was so heavy.

They hadn't been able to describe his face clearly, because the peak of his red baseball cap had been pulled down low over his forehead and he had kept his head down and his collar turned up. All they could distinctly remember was his worn black leather jacket and that he smelled strongly of stale cigarettes and Fisherman's Friend lozenges, as if he had been trying to mask the fact that he had bad breath, or that he had been drinking alcohol.

Inspector Francis O'Rourke had deployed sixteen uniformed gardaí around the building and cordoned it off with crime scene tapes. Ambulances had taken away the injured to the Mercy Urgent Care Centre at St Mary's, although the dead had been left untouched until Bill Phinner's technical experts could photograph and examine them, and Dr Mary Kelley could arrive to give them a preliminary post-mortem. First of all they had to wait until the bomb squad from Collins Barracks could give them the all-clear to enter the devastated laboratory, in case a secondary device had been planted there to catch the first responders.

It was nearly three o'clock before Sergeant Harvey of the Army Ordnance Corps came out of the building, followed by a bomb disposal expert who was taking off his khaki Kevlar armour piece by piece.

Sergeant Harvey came up to Katie and said, 'All clear, DS Maguire. There was only the one bomb, but by God that was one hell of a bomb. Almost certainly Semtex, I'd guess nearly fifteen pounds of it. You could have brought down St Patrick's Bridge with that. None of the victims stood a chance. It was a miracle that anybody survived at all.'

'Any telltale signs about it?'

'Too early to say for sure. We have parts of the detonator and the outer casing that the explosive was packed in. It wasn't a centrifuge and it certainly didn't come from Medisure. It was a stainless-steel pressure cooker, a big one, fifteen litres. We found no timing device so it was probably set off remotely. The last time we came across one like that was when the Fermoy Boys were planning to blow up that Elton John concert.'

'Oh, the Fermoy Boys. I remember them all right. They were all loopers, that lot. Most of them couldn't even spell

IRA, let alone know what it stood for. But whoever they got to make their bomb really knew what they were doing, didn't they? And we never managed to track down who it was.'

'Well, forensics have come a long way since then, ma'am. Maybe your technical experts will be able to find fingerprints or DNA on the bits of the cooker we have left. It wouldn't surprise me at all if this bomb-maker doesn't have any strong political affiliation, but simply makes the bombs to order. I know there's been two or three pressure-cooker bombs found fairly recently up North, and when I'm back at the barracks I'll be getting in touch with 321 EOD Squadron in Belfast. You know, to see if there's any similarities.'

'Thanks a million, sergeant. Let me know if you come up with anything at all that might help us.'

After Sergeant Harvey had gone to rejoin his men from the bomb squad, Bill Phinner came up to her, looking even more miserable than usual.

'We're going in now, ma'am. Do you want to come in with us? I think you'll need to see this first-hand.'

Katie looked up to the first floor of the pharmacy building. The Cavanagh had been opened as recently as 2003, as part of UCC's expansion, and it was rectangular and modern, with a shiny glass frontage. Bill's technicians had draped a wide blue plastic sheet over the hole where the laboratory window had been blown out, partly to protect any forensic evidence from the elements, but mostly to hide the bloody remains of the victims from public view. The grass verge below the window sparkled with broken glass.

Katie and Kyna and Detective Sergeant Begley followed Bill Phinner inside. They were given shoe covers and surgical masks, and then they climbed upstairs. Inside the laboratory, five technical experts were already at work, taking photographs and videos. If they hadn't been so bulky in their white Tyvek suits, and if they hadn't rustled so loudly as they walked around, and their feet hadn't crunched on the debris that was scattered all over the laboratory floor, they could have been a family of ghosts. They didn't speak, and the only other sound they made was the cricket-like clicking of their camera shutters as they recorded the grisly dismembered corpses that were strewn all around them.

Katie said nothing, but stared at the massacre for almost five minutes. Some of the bodies were so comprehensively blown apart that their ribcages looked like baskets filled up with dark red balloons. Others appeared to be hardly injured at all. Three of them were lying next to each other on the floor in their blood-spattered lab coats, their heads together as if they were taking a selfie, their faces white and their eyes staring in shock. It was by far the worst crime scene she had ever witnessed. Next to her, Kyna whispered, 'Holy Mary,' and retched behind her mask. Then she immediately turned away and hurried off along the corridor.

'Do you have any notion who might have done this, ma'am, and why?' asked Detective Sergeant Begley. 'So far we've had nobody claiming responsibility for it.'

'Who would want to blow up a college laboratory? There could be any number of motives, do you know? Maybe it's connected with those stories we've been hearing about the High Five. I can think of at least five gangs who might have decided to put a stop to what they were doing.'

'They've gone way over the top, though, wouldn't you say? That lad that was stabbed, he was likely one of the High Five. Surely killing him would have been warning enough to the rest of them. Jesus. They didn't have to blow up half the fecking School of Pharmacy.'

'Maybe they wanted to do more than wipe out the High Five. Maybe they also wanted to send a message to every other gang in the city. You know – don't mess with us or we'll be blowing you up to kingdom come, too.'

They went silently back downstairs to the lobby. Katie found Kyna waiting for her, looking shivery and pale.

'How are you going on, Kyna?'

'A little less gawky, thanks, now that I've said goodbye to my breakfast. But I'll be having the most desperate of nightmares when I go to bed tonight.'

'Did you get the names of all the students who were in that class? And do you know which ones lost their lives and which ones didn't?'

Kyna held up a sheet torn from a notepad. 'I have them here. The principal just wrote them all down for me. Poor fellow could barely hold the pen.'

'Okay, good. What we need to do now is to go around to all their relatives and friends and try to find out any reason at all why somebody might have been motivated to kill them. Either *one* of them, or *some* of them, or maybe the whole lot of them.'

'Like you said, though, this is most likely the work of a drugs gang,' put in Detective Sergeant Begley. 'The Riordans, I'd place them top of the list, or maybe the O'Flynns. Or those headers from Lithuania, what do they call themselves, the Iron Wolves.'

'It's the most likely explanation, sure, that a drugs gang was responsible, but in the meantime we have to consider every possibility, no matter how unlikely. Maybe it was a mad jealous boyfriend. Or a student who was kicked off the pharmacy course for one reason or another, taking drugs maybe, and wanted his revenge. Or a Jehovah's Witness or some other religious fanatic who thinks that medicine is tampering with the will of God.'

'Right, then,' said Kyna. 'I'll get Buckley and O'Sullivan on to it. And maybe Geoghegan too. I think he's just about wrapped up that robbery at Michel Jewellers.'

Almost as soon as she had said that, her phone rang. She answered it and said, 'Yes,' and 'yes,' and, 'thanks a million, yes, if you could text it to me.' Then she said to Katie, 'That was the secretary at St Catherine's. I went to see her last night. It took her a bit of time but she's been through the school records and identified that tall girl for me.'

'That's grand. Does she have a last known address for her, too?'

'She's sending it over. I can have Cushley find out if she's still there, or if she's moved away.'

'Once you've located where she's living, though, I want *you* to question her, Kyna, yourself. You're the best we have when it comes to cajoling some babbling psychopath into explaining why he did what he did. Or *she*, in this case. Apart from that – well, maybe it'll help you to take your mind off all that desperate mess we've seen upstairs.'

'Well, I doubt it. But I'll talk to her anyway, once we find her. *If* we can find her. Here's her name and address pinging up – Doireann Greaney, 29 Inniscarra Road, Fair Hill.'

Detective Sergeant Begley nodded his head towards the opposite side of College Road. 'There's all the press over there, ma'am. Swarming like flies around dog shite. You'll have seen the papers this morning, I expect.'

'What, why? I haven't had time to have a cup of coffee, Sean, let alone read the papers.'

'There's a fierce derogatory story about you in the *Sun*, I'm sorry to say. Not deserved at all, but they seem to have it in for you.'

'Go on. What does it say?'

'I didn't read all of it, but there's a picture of you on the inside page and the headline's something like "The Detective Who Hasn't Got The Guts". It's referring to that young feen being stabbed at the Zombie Lounge and how you wouldn't release any details of him being disembowelled all over the floor, like.'

Katie shook her head. 'It's that Owen Dineen. For some reason he's doing everything he can to bring me down. Well, all I can do is ignore him. He'll grow tired of it sooner or later.'

'There's stories about the Zombie Lounge in the *Times* and the *Examiner,* too. They don't criticize you personal-like, but the *Examiner* says that Cork is becoming like a war zone. Worse than Limerick, they say, back in the days of the McCarthy-Dundons and the Collopy-Keanes.'

'Right at this moment, Sean, I don't give a purple damn what the newspapers are saying about me. There's eleven young students upstairs who came to college today to learn how to live a full and useful life, helping the sick to get better. Instead of that, they've been blown into pieces – their professor, too. For some reason I can't understand, the newspapers seem to have turned against me. But that's not going to stop me finding out who murdered all these innocent people today, and making sure that we gather enough evidence to have them locked away for life.'

Katie was breathing hard. She paused, and then she said, 'I'm sorry. I'm angry. I didn't mean to take it out on you. I'm going to go over now and take it out on the press.'

★★★

She walked across the road to where the reporters were all waiting behind an orange plastic Bord Gáis barrier. They were always eager to question her when she held a news conference, but this morning they looked more than eager, they looked like a ravenous pack of wolves who couldn't wait to get their teeth into her. Even Fionnuala Sweeney from RTÉ was holding out her microphone as if she were a character in *Game of Thrones*, holding out a sword.

'I've a short statement to make,' Katie told them. 'After that I'll answer questions, but we'll have to be brief because this is the golden hour and we can't waste a minute of it.'

'Can you confirm that it was a bomb?' called out Rionach Barr, from the *Echo*. 'The gas engineer who was here said it sounded more like a gas main explosion.'

'How many casualties?' asked Douglas Kelly, from the *Irish Times*. 'Is there many dead?'

Katie waited until the reporters had all stopped shouting out. Then, slowly and clearly, she said, 'An explosive device was planted in the junior laboratory on the first floor of the UCC's School of Pharmacy and it was detonated at nine-sixteen this morning, probably remotely. I'm sorry to tell you that eleven pharmacy students and their professor were killed instantly and three suffered life-changing injuries.'

'Was there any warning given at all?'

'Not that we're aware of.'

'Has anybody claimed responsibility for it?'

'Not yet.'

'Do you have any theories about who might have planted it?'

'As in all investigations, we're pursuing several possibilities.'

'Such as?' called out Owen Dineen, from the back of the crowd.

'It's too early for me to speculate, Mr Dineen.'

'But come here to me, ma'am, who would plant a bomb in a college pharmacy laboratory unless they had good reason to put a decisive stop to what was going on there? Like the students in there cooking up their own recreational drugs, for example, to sell in the discos, and putting the noses of Cork's esteemed drug gangs out of joint?'

'As I've just said, Mr Dineen, we're looking into a number of different scenarios. You're entitled to your interpretation of what happened here, but it would be poor police work if we were to jump to conclusions at this early stage without irrefutable proof.'

'I love hearing you saying those words "irrefutable proof", DS Maguire. They trip off your tongue like a line out of a poem by Yeats. But it seems to me these days that you and your detectives have fierce difficulty in finding any proof at all about anything, irrefutable or not. Why aren't all these drug gangs already behind bars? Why aren't the streets of Cork safe any more?'

'I've no further comment to make to you at this stage, Mr Dineen. I'll be holding another media conference later today to give you the names of all the victims of this appalling atrocity, once their next of kin have all been informed. If we've made any progress with our investigation, I'll be able to give you an update on that, too. I want to conclude by offering our heartfelt condolences to the families and friends of those deceased, and our prayers for the survival and rapid recovery of those injured. That's all.'

'Do you reckon it was the High Five they were after?' shouted Owen Dineen. 'They've gutted one of them, after all, so maybe they were going for the rest. Could you not have found a way to warn those daft young eejits that their lives were in imminent danger?'

Katie lifted her hand to show that she wasn't going to say any more, despite the clamour of questions from the other reporters. She turned around and crossed back over the road with her heart beating hard. She was even angrier than she had been before.

Detective Sergeant Begley said, 'What's wrong with that fellow, eating the head off you like that? You'd think that you'd spat in his drink or something.'

'You know what really makes me mad? He's probably bang on, and it *was* one of the gangs that did it. You say the Riordans. I reckon the O'Flynns.'

'What's the plan now, then?'

'I've already asked Sergeant Murphy to start combing through the CCTV footage. We can question any students here who knew the deceased and see if we can find out for certain if they *were* this High Five. We can ask around the clubs, too, when they open up tonight. And we can only hope that Bill Phinner can identify whoever put that bomb together. If we can find the bomb-maker, we can find out who paid him to make it. I might even talk to Frank Magorian and see if he'll agree to us offering a reward for any information that leads to a conviction.'

She looked back at the reporters, some of them returning to their cars, others talking on their phones with one finger stuck in their ears.

'They don't get it, do they? They don't understand that it's almost impossible to get people to come forward with evidence when they're ten times more afraid of the gangs than they are of the law.'

'It depends what you offer them,' said Detective Sergeant Begley. 'Years ago, when I was the only guard on patrol up in Castletownroche, some gouger was stealing sheep and I couldn't find anybody to grass on them till I offered a year's free scoops at the RockForest Bar. I was able to haul him in the very next day.'

Katie gave him a wry smile. 'Some hopes of that, Sean. But after this, I swear that I'm going to wipe out these drug gangs if it's the last thing I do.'

24

Patrin was following his mongrel, Sooblik, along the Ballyhooly Road when he saw seven or eight hooded crows fluttering and squawking by the hedgerow about fifty metres up ahead of him.

Sooblik saw them at the same time. He let out one of his aggressive barks, which was more like a smoker's cough, and started to shamble along the pavement a little faster. Although his name meant 'boy', Sooblik was fifteen years old at least, a tangled brownish cross between a lurcher and a water spaniel, with perhaps a dash of Irish terrier, too.

Patrin was nine, and he should have been at school today but he was on the hop. His pa and his ma had gone to Cloughmacsimon for a Pavee wedding and his Uncle Bartley, who was supposed to be taking care of him, had a monumental hangover and had still been too drunk this morning to speak, let alone make him breakfast and drive him to school. Patrin was a thin boy, with slitty eyes that always made him look suspicious, and hair that stuck up on top of his head like a thistle.

Sooblik began to shamble along faster as he neared the spot where the crows were fighting with each other. He barked again, and they flapped away, but they didn't go far, perching on a nearby fence and the branches of an overhanging ash tree as if they were waiting reluctantly for Sooblik to mowsie on so that they could carry on squabbling.

Patrin caught up with Sooblik just as the dog went snuffling into the undergrowth. It was then that he saw what the crows had been bickering over. Half-hidden beneath a blackthorn bush was a grey-haired man, lying on his side with his back towards the road. He was wearing a tan leather jerkin and a check shirt, although the crows had already torn at the shoulder of his shirt and pecked at the flesh underneath, which was crawling with white maggots.

To his horror, he recognized the man by his jerkin. It was Timbo Coffey, who had gone missing from the halting site at Water Lane three days ago. Timbo was notorious for going out on the lash and spending the night in shop doorways and bus shelters and people's front gardens, but this was the first time that he had been away for so long.

'Sooby, come away from there, boy!' Patrin snapped at him. He could smell Timbo's decomposing body from more than three metres away. It was sweet and putrid, like the dead goat that had once been caught by its horns in the cables underneath their caravan. They had thought it was a blocked toilet and it had been almost a week before they had discovered where the stink was really coming from.

Sooblik kept nosing and nudging at Timbo's back, but Patrin took hold of his tail and dragged him away.

'Come on, you munikin! You'll catch a dose, you will, sniffing at that!'

He wasn't sure what to do. He thought of flagging down the driver of a passing car, but then he was worried that the driver would make him stay there while he called for the guards, and that the guards might think that he had something to do with Timbo being dead and ask him a whole rake of questions. His pa had always impressed on him that he should never say a word to the guards. He shouldn't even tell them his name.

He carried on walking as far as the first side road, which led up to a small housing estate. He could see a man digging in the garden of the second house, and so he went up to his fence and stood there for a while, wondering what he ought to say to him. Eventually, the man noticed him standing there with Sooblik, and stopped digging, and said, 'What's the story, boy? Something you wanted, was there?'

'No,' said Patrin. 'But there's a feen lying by the road back up towards The Bridle and he's looking fierce shook, like.'

'What, is he langered?'

'I don't think so. I think he might be sick, like. Or maybe he was runded over.'

The man hesitated for a moment, but then he chopped his spade into the soil and said, 'Okay. Let me fetch my coat from indoors and then you can show me where this fellow is.'

He went into his house, leaving the kitchen door open behind him. As soon as he had disappeared inside, though, Patrin started to run down the side road, with Sooblik clumsily bounding along beside him. He reached the Ballyhooly Road and carried on running, until the side road was out of sight.

It was only when he reached the entrance to the Water Lane halting site that he stopped running, screeching for breath. Sooblik had fallen behind, but caught up with him at last, his tongue flapping out like a long grey scarf.

Patrin crossed over the muddy ground to his own mobile home and climbed up the steps. His Uncle Bartley was hunched over the Formica-topped dining table, wearing only his trousers, his green braces looped over his round hairy shoulders. He was holding a mug of strong tea in both hands and staring at the television, although the sound was muted and his eyes didn't appear to be focused.

'Uncle Bartley,' said Patrin. 'Uncle Bartley!'

'Jesus, Pat, do you have to shout so fecking loud?'

'Uncle Bartley, I found Timbo Coffey. He's lying by the road above there by The Bridle and he's pure dead.'

Uncle Bartley looked at him as if he were speaking in a foreign language. Then he said, '*Timbo?* Timbo Coffey? Well, that's no surprise at all. I always knew that he would come to a sticky end. Sorry about your breakfast. Do you fancy a mug of scaldy in your hand?'

'I told this one feen I saw digging his garden, but we should be after telling the guards, too, shouldn't we? We don't have to give them our names or nothing.'

'No, boy, no. You've told that one fellow that you've found him, haven't you, so there's no need to bother. He'll be ringing the guards himself, won't he? It's not like Timbo was related to us or nothing like that. Not that I know of, any road. I'll go to his wake, though. A wake, that's always a good excuse for a couple of gatts or more.'

He paused, and then he said, 'I think there's some biscuits if you've a mouth on you.'

Gardaí Micky Phelan and Neasa O'Connor were the first to arrive at the scene where Timbo Coffey had been found. The man who had been digging his garden was standing by the side of the road and flagged them down.

'Macklin Delaney,' he said, as they approached him. 'It was me that called you.'

'You say there's a body?' asked Garda Phelan.

'Just along there, in the bush, like. An old fellow by the look of him.'

'And you're sure he's dead?'

'The crows seem to think he is. They've been pecking away

at him something desperate and I haven't noticed him raising any objection.'

Garda Phelan walked along the road and as soon as they saw Timbo Coffey's body with his tan jerkin and his check shirt they recognized him immediately.

'Oh, God in Heaven,' said Garda O'Connor. She took several tissues out of her pocket, folded them over, and held them up against her nose before she leaned closer to make sure that it was really him. 'By the state of him, I'd say he's been here since we slung him out of The Bridle. I told you we should have given him a ride back to Water Lane.'

'What, and have him croak in the back of the car? He's probably had a heart attack or multiple organ failure. Jesus Christ, Neasa – he smelled bad enough when he was alive!'

Macklin Delaney was standing well back, his arms folded, looking glum and impatient. Garda Phelan went up to him and said, 'So, like, how did you find him?'

'It was a young lad who found him first. I was planting my poppies and he came up to me and said there's a feen lying sick or dead by the side of the road. But the second I went into the house to fetch my coat the lad ran off. By the look of him and the way he spoke I'd say he was a Pavee from the halting site down there. He had a brown mongrel with him. A pure sorry apology of a dog. It looked like some manky old fireside rug had decided to grow itself legs.'

'A dog like that shouldn't be too hard to find,' said Garda O'Connor. 'You don't happen to know this dead fellow, do you? Or ever seen him before?'

'Never seen him before in my life, and I hope to God I never see him again. Is it okay if I go now? The auld doll's not well and I don't like to leave her for long. I live only up the boreen there.'

'You can of course. Just give us your name and address and your phone number because we'll be needing to talk to you again.'

An ambulance arrived, silently, but with its blue lights flashing. Almost immediately afterwards a black van from the Technical Bureau pulled up behind it, followed by two SUVs carrying technical experts, two Garda squad cars and a Garda van. Five uniformed gardaí climbed out, and once they had peered with wrinkled-up noses at Timbo Coffey's body lying half-hidden in the blackthorn bushes, they set up a barrier of cones and tapes.

Two technical experts in white Tyvek suits took photographs of the body from every angle. They also scrutinized the grass verge for footprints and broken twigs and the surrounding blackthorn bushes for any scraps of fabric in case Timbo had been forced into the bushes by an assailant. Then they knelt beside the body and bowed down as if they were praying. They were looking for any indication that he might have been beaten or stabbed or struck by a passing vehicle and flung into the bushes by the impact.

All the while this was going on, the hooded crows were watching from the trees, occasionally thrashing their wings impatiently and letting out a sinister chorus of soft death rattles.

After less than twenty minutes, a forensic expert came up to Gardaí Phelan and O'Connor, pulling down her face mask and pushing back the hood of her Tyvek suit so that her tight chestnut curls sprang out.

'He's been shot,' she said.

'Get away out of here. Serious?'

'One bullet wound in the back of the head. A hollow-point, too. When we turned him over, we found that he has only half a face.'

'I can't believe that,' said Garda Phelan. 'He was a pest, all right. Always twisted and causing a ruction in pubs. The last time we saw him we were throwing him out of The Bridle for gawking all over the floor. But not so much of a pest that he needed shooting.'

'Well, I'll have to call it in to DI Fitzpatrick. There's no question that this was a homicide. We'll be setting up a tent in a minute and seeing how quick we can get a pathologist up here.'

'I'm totally confubbled,' said Garda Phelan, once the technical expert had returned to the body. 'Why in the world would anybody want to shoot a smelly old knacker who couldn't even tell you what day it was?'

'Maybe Patrick from The Bridle went after him because he'd had enough of him and one thing led to another.'

'Oh, come on, *Patrick*? He's as soft as a sofa, that feller. He'll have to be questioned, of course, but he wouldn't even squash a wazzie. No – I reckon that dead feen was involved in some shady Pavee business that we don't know about, and it caught up with him. Maybe he owed another Pavee money. You know what those knackers are like. They'd shank you over a missing hubcap.'

'I hate bodies. They're so dead.'

'That's the definition of bodies, Neasa – dead. What do you expect him to do? Jump up and sing "Don't Forget Your Shovel"?'

The afternoon wore on, and the shadows lengthened, and at last Timbo Coffey's body was disentangled from the blackthorn bush and carried on a stretcher to the waiting ambulance. Cheated of their supper, the hooded crows squawked in annoyance and flew away.

25

Katie was still trying to cope with the chaotic aftermath of this morning's explosion at the School of Pharmacy when Detective Inspector Fitzpatrick came in to tell her about the traveller's body that had been found by the Ballyhooly Road.

She sat back. 'Mother of God, that's all I need. I think I must have answered a hundred and fifty phone calls about that bombing since lunch. Not that I *had* any lunch.'

'All we know so far is that he was a traveller from the Water Lane halting site, by the name of Timbo Coffey. He'd been living there for nearly five years, first of all with his wife, but then she passed away and since then his only partner has been Paddy's, from what we can tell. He was well respected in the traveller community before he hit the bottle. He was mentioned in that famous book about bare-knuckle boxers. Coffey the Conker, they called him.'

'But he was shot in the back of the head, like an execution, almost?'

'That's what it looks like. But I'll be going up to Water Lane later with Buckley and O'Sullivan and maybe we can find out if there was anybody who held a grudge against him.'

'Good luck with that. The day I meet a traveller who's prepared to co-operate with the Garda, I swear to you, I'll go on a pilgrimage and light a candle for Black Sara, the patron saint of all the gypsies. No – make that *five* candles, *and* I'll sew her a dress. With bells on.'

Robert nodded towards the three couches under Katie's office window. Spread out untidily on the coffee table in between them were this morning's newspapers – all of them open at the pages that carried critical reports about Katie's detection rate. On top of them was the *Sun* story, 'Detective Who Hasn't Got The Guts'.

'I hope you're not letting these gowls get to you, ma'am. If they knew only half of what we have to deal with, day in, day out.'

'I'm trying to put a brave face on it, Robert. But what really gets to me is why they've suddenly turned on me like this. Especially that Owen Dineen.'

Her phone rang. It was Assistant Commissioner Frank Magorian, asking for an update on the bombing. He was about to go into a security meeting about domestic terrorism at Dublin Castle, and he wanted to know if there was any suggestion that the bomb might have been planted for political or religious reasons.

'We've no firm evidence yet, sir. But I can't see any political terror group or any bunch of religious fanatics being behind it. Well – apart from Jehovah's Witnesses and that's about as far from likely as I can think of. What point would any terrorists be making by blowing up the School of Pharmacy? Even jihadis have to take Imodium, now and again. More than most of us, probably.'

She didn't know why she had made a joke of it. She had rarely felt more harassed in her whole career. But almost as soon as she had hung up on Frank Magorian, her phone rang again. It was Bill Phinner, and he sounded unusually upbeat.

She raised her hand to tell Robert to wait, and then she said, 'How's it going on, Bill?'

'I believe we're making a fair amount of progress here, ma'am. Sergeant Harvey's sent me an email from Collins Barracks. He's contacted the British Army bomb disposal unit in Belfast and they've identified four telltale signatures that link our bomb with three large bombs that they defused in the North.'

'How long ago was that? I don't recall reading anything about three large bombs up in Ulster. Not in the last six months or so, anyway.'

'The most recent was at Thiepval Barracks, which of course is the British Army headquarters in Ireland now. That was in March last year. Another was found at St Lucia, in Omagh, which used to be a British Army barracks but now it's a PSNI station. The third was discovered at Ballykinlar, but that barracks was abandoned in 2018, so they reckon the bomb must have been planted there sometime before then but failed to go off. It probably dated from 2009, or even earlier.'

'So what are the similarities between those bombs and ours?'

'I'll come up and show you if that's okay. That'll be the easiest way.'

Bill appeared a few minutes later. He was accompanied by Conall, the same young gingery-haired IT expert who had downloaded the pictures of Katie and Kyna from the mobile phone that had been dropped by their intruder. Conall looked at Katie defensively through his thumbprinted spectacles and quickly offered her a selection of three different smiles – first puckered, then wide and then toothy – as if he couldn't quite decide which would be most diplomatic.

'They always say that the more trouble a bomb-maker takes to hide his identity, the more obvious it becomes who it is,' said Bill. 'It's the amateurs who cobble IEDs together out of all kinds of bits and pieces they've bought at Hickeys – they're the toughest to track down.'

He plugged a USB into Katie's desktop computer and stood close behind her to explain what she was looking at. Conall stood a little further away, but every time Katie turned around to look at him he gave her another flustered smile. She wondered if he was visualizing her in bed, being kissed by a naked Kyna.

'The container itself was the first signature,' Bill told her. 'It's a fifteen-litre Artame pressure cooker, and that was exactly the same make and model that was used for all three of the bombs that they found up North. You can buy them online of course and we can check with the UK manufacturer to find out who might have ordered one from Ireland. The only place in Cork that stocks them is Kitchen Magic on the Grange Industrial Estate at Ballycurreen, and they should have a record of any that were bought in the past few weeks. They cost over three hundred and fifty euros each, so I doubt if they've sold too many of them.'

'Expensive tastes, these terrorists,' said Robert.

'I think it was the casing they were going for. The best-quality shrapnel money could buy.'

'Jesus. You have to wonder how anybody can think like that. Don't they have brothers and sisters of their own?'

Bill Phinner clicked to the next picture on the screen, which showed a stack of purple-coloured bricks. 'The second signature was the unusual type of charge that was used in all four bombs. It was this Semtex-1K, which was formulated for blasting work in very confined and risky surroundings, like collapsed mineshafts and half-demolished buildings. It's very malleable and stable, but it's also fierce high explosive. As you know, there are more than forty types of Semtex, and they're all made by Explosia in the Czech Republic, but these four bombs are the only ones that have ever been found in Ireland to contain this particular variety.

'The third signature was the activator, and this was a mobile phone. After he'd planted the bomb in the pharmacy lab, the bomber could set it off at any time, from any distance away, simply by ringing it. Now, look – the phone was blown to pieces, but we found the SIM card. It was locked, and it was damaged, but our IT genius here, Conall, was able to unlock it and retrieve a limited amount of information from it. Tell them what you found, Conall.'

Conall stepped forward and held up a sheet of notepaper. 'I was able to find two incoming phone calls. My guess is that they were made to test that the phone was working properly, and that the device would go off without a hitch. They're both from the same number in Ballincollig – and you won't believe this, the number's listed in the name of Brendan Moley.'

'Well, that's mockery for you,' said Katie. She was well aware that Brendan Moley was a famous IRA activist who had been blown up by his own bomb in February 1988, along with another activist, Brendan Burns.

'Sergeant Harvey spoke to a British Army captain up at 321 EOD,' Bill went on. 'It seems like British intelligence had always suspected that the three bombs they found in the North were made by an IRA bomb expert from Cork, or thereabouts. They identified him as a market gardener by the name of James MacGreevy, but they could never find watertight proof that he was their man. MacGreevy was questioned by the Garda Special Detective Unit but he flatly denied having anything to do with the IRA and they could find no evidence on his property that he'd been making bombs, so they had to leave it at that.'

Bill was silent for a few moments, with his hands clasped together, as if he were a priest about to give a benediction.

'You said you found *four* signatures,' said Katie. 'That's only three.'

'The fourth could be the clincher, even though the SDU ignored it when they went to interview MacGreevy. They could find no trace of explosives even though they had a sniffer dog with them, because you know that Semtex smells of nothing at all to humans – only to dogs. Neither could they find any of the usual paraphernalia that bomb-makers have around the place – wiring and batteries and kitchen timers and that kind of thing.

'From what Sergeant Harvey was told by the British captain, the report came back that MacGreevy was fully co-operative and friendly and there was no record of him ever having been a member of a dissident group. *But* – and this is what the SDU failed to check up on, for some reason. If you ask me, they were probably too busy chatting with MacGreevy about the latest runners at Mallow or how to grow prize turnips, or else they decided that if there were no explosives on the premises, it wasn't worth looking into.'

'Go on. Don't keep us in suspense.'

'In each bomb the mobile phone was taped to the detonator with that sticky brown parcel tape, you know the kind of stuff. And in *each* bomb – including ours – there were dog hairs stuck to the tape. Only a few. In the bomb they defused at Thiepval Barracks, only two. But they were all the same greyishy colour and it's likely they all came from the same dog, almost certainly mixed breed, but mostly Kerry Blue. We're carrying out a DNA test on the hairs right now, and that will give us its ancestry, back to three generations anyway, as well as its approximate size and weight and appearance.'

'Do we know if this James MacGreevy owns such a dog?'

Robert said, 'Not yet. We've checked with An Post and he doesn't hold a current dog licence. But if it *is* his, this dog, or if we can prove that it was, he's going to find it fierce difficult to explain what its hairs were doing inside four of the most powerful IEDs since Enniskillen.'

'We know where he lives?'

'Oh, sure. MacGreevy's Garden Centre. That's at Classes Lake, on the west side of Ballincollig.'

'Right—' said Katie, 'let's set up surveillance while we're waiting for the dog's DNA. First of all to make sure that he really *does* have a dog, and also to see who comes and goes. And let's start tapping into his phone and hacking into his computer.'

'Okay, ma'am. I'll find out who his service providers are and make the necessary applications. And if it seems likely that he's the fellow we're looking for, I'll ask for a search warrant, too, from the District Court.'

'Don't bother about the applications. Under the circumstances, I've sufficient judicial authority myself to authorize you to access his telephone and internet data. If it *was* James MacGreevy who made this bomb, he's a mass murderer and a serious terrorist threat, and I need no more justification than that.'

Bill said, 'I'll have Conall go upstairs to the control room and give them a hand. He's your man when it comes to—'

Katie was sure that he was about to say 'tapping into phones' but then decided it might not be appropriate, especially since Kyna had now walked in.

Robert and Bill left Katie's office together, talking to each other. Kyna stayed by the window, with her back turned, so Katie guessed she had come up to say something personal, and it could wait until everybody had gone. But just as Conall was about to walk out through the doorway, Katie caught up with him and said, 'Conall—'

Conall looked startled and actually blushed.

'Conall – it's not about what you found on that fellow's phone. The fact is, I need you to do something for me. It's pure important, but it must stay totally confidential. Like, nobody must know about it for the time being, only you and me. They mustn't even catch a whisper.'

'Well, I don't know, ma'am. It depends what it is.'

'I want you to hack into that *Irish Sun* reporter's phone calls and email messages. Owen Dineen. Do you think you can do that?'

Conall blinked at her. 'Sure, like. That'll be easy, even if his phone's encrypted – a Blackphone or one of those. But isn't that kind of—'

'Don't worry. I'll take full responsibility for it, so you won't find yourself in any legal trouble at all. But I'd appreciate it if you could start doing it as soon as you can, and give me updates maybe three or four times a day. And also keep a record of everything he says and every text and email he sends out, no matter who it's to.'

Conall looked back into Katie's office at Kyna, who was now sitting down on one of the couches. Katie couldn't quite read what must have been going through his mind, but he nodded, and kept on nodding, and after a while he said, 'Sure. I'll do that for you, ma'am, no bother at all. Come to think of it, it should be fierce interesting, shouldn't it, catching up on all the day's news before anybody else gets to hear about it?'

Katie gave Conall a quick smile. She was well aware what a risk she was taking, asking him to do this for her. Even if he found evidence to back up her suspicions, it could still be disastrous for her career. But she remembered what Conor had done. He had stayed true to his beliefs, never giving up or turning back, even though it had meant sacrificing his life.

'Thanks a million,' she said, almost silently. Conall stayed blinking at her for a few moments, as if he were trying to think of some pithy rejoinder, but then he simply swivelled around and went off along the corridor with a strange loping walk, like a cartoon character.

Kyna said, 'We've found Doireann Greaney. She doesn't live at Inniscarra Road any more. That's her parents' address. Well, her da and her stepma... her real mother died giving birth to her. She used to live there until she was nineteen years old but then she and her da had some kind of a falling-out about her never going to college like she was supposed to and never even trying to look for a job, so she moved out.'

'So where is she now?' asked Katie, returning to her desk.

'She's living in a rented bedsit in Ballyphehane... right on the end of St Nessan Street. So far as her parents know, she's still not studying or working, but then they haven't spoken to her for almost a year. In spite of that, they've seen her around town from time to time. And... this may be the clincher... on every occasion when they saw her, except for one, she was wearing a light grey tracksuit.'

'Serious?'

Kyna nodded. 'Her stepma was pretty sure it must be the same one she used to wear at school. Like, being in the school sports team and winning prizes, that was the high point of her life. After she left school she had no friends at all – never had a boyfriend, neither. When she lived at home she spent most of her time in her bedroom, playing Fortnite or whatever. Now and again, though, she'd go out jogging, or at least that's what she told her ma she was doing. It was maybe once or twice a week, but then she'd be out for hours.'

'What do you think?' said Katie. 'It sounds like she's a pure close match to the psychological profile that Dr Power gave us, do you know? Somebody who feels isolated from the rest of the world and grows more and more resentful about it as the time goes by. We can't jump to conclusions. I mean – maybe this Doireann Greaney is just a lonely young woman who can't seem to get along with anybody. Maybe the fact that she wears a grey tracksuit is just a coincidence. But you do need to go and talk to her, at the very least.'

'I will of course. I'll take Jack Cushley with me, but he can stay in the car unless things go pear-shaped. I have the feeling this is going to be one of those interviews that needs to be one-to-one, whether she's the Pusher or not.'

She hesitated, and then she said, 'How's it going with himself?'

'Brendan? Stalemate, at the moment. I think that's what you would call it. If he tries to report *us*, he knows that we could just as easy report *him*.'

'I know. But this is keeping me awake at night, I tell you.'

'Well, don't let it. We've done nothing illegal. I'm keeping my eyes and my ears open as far as Brendan's concerned, that's all. I don't trust him thicker than a sheet of paper.'

'Okay. I know I'm sounding like a jibber, but I just can't help it. I don't want to see you hurt.'

'Everything will work out, Kyna, don't you worry.' Katie got up from her desk and was about to give Kyna a quick reassuring hug and a kiss when Moirin walked in.

'I'm so sorry, ma'am. I clean forgot to tell you, what with that bomb going off over at the college and all the confusion.

While you were out, Justice Connolly rang you. He wanted to know if you might be free tomorrow evening maybe for dinner. Here – he's left his private number for you.'

'Justice Connolly? Thanks a million, Moirin. Tomorrow evening? I'll have to see how things go.'

When Moirin had returned to her office, Kyna looked at Katie and raised one perfectly arched eyebrow. 'Justice Connolly? Isn't he the tall fair-haired feen who looks like that He-Man out of the Masters of the Universe?'

'That's your man. They've sent him down from the Central Criminal Court to back up Justice O'Rafferty.'

'So why does he want to take you out to dinner?'

'I don't know. He'll be sentencing Donal Hagerty on Monday so maybe he wants to discuss the whole gang situation in Cork – the O'Flynns and the Riordans and all the rest of the scummers. It could be that he wants my opinion on whether he should hand down Hagerty a mandatory life sentence. If he did that, maybe it would give those gangs a warning that they can't ignore.'

'Over dinner?'

'Ah, come on. Even judges have to eat. They're only human.'

'That's what bothers me. Well, the "man" bit of "human" does, anyhow.'

'Kyna, I get hungry too.'

'That bothers me even more.'

Katie went up to her and kissed her on the lips, twice.

'You don't have to be bothered. He's a judge, not some local lecher, and he knows that I've only just this minute laid Conor in his grave. And if there's any leftovers, I'll fetch you back a doggy bag.'

26

Detective Cushley parked in the disabled bay at the end of St Nessan Street and switched off the engine.

'You're sure you don't want me to come with you? What if she's a black-belt karate expert? What if she attacks you with a knife?'

'Jack, I'm perfectly capable of taking care of myself, and if I do get myself into any trouble I can always give you a shout, can't I?'

'Fair play to you, sarge. I like to think of myself as a visible deterrent, that's all.'

Detective Cushley was built like a minotaur, so bull-chested that he could barely button up his jacket. He had a bull's head, too, with an abrasive grey crew cut and deep-set eyes, and he looked permanently frustrated and furious, as if a nun had jumped the queue at O'Brien's sandwich bar ahead of him.

'Sure like, I know exactly what you mean,' Kyna told him, trying to sound soothing. 'And if this Doireann Greaney needs to be visibly deterred, I promise you I'll call you.'

Kyna climbed out of the car and crossed the road. St Nessan Street was a short, narrow street with small terraced houses on both sides, all of them pebble-dashed but painted in a variety of colours, grey and white and cream and one blue. Neat white net curtains were hung at every window and wheelie bins were standing on the pavement outside every front door.

Three boys were playing long slogs up and down the street, hitting a leather ball with a hurley as hard as they could so that it banged into the wheelie bins or the cars parked along the left-hand kerb. Two little girls were skipping on the pavement and singing, 'Datsie-dotsie, miss the rope, you're outie-o!'

Kyna paused for a moment to watch the girls before she rang the doorbell at the house where Doireann Greaney was supposed to be lodging. They brought back her own childhood, which now seemed so long ago: days of skipping in the schoolyard, and rain, and innocence, and hair-pulling, and wondering why she didn't fancy boys like the other girls did.

The girls sang, 'If you'd have been, where I'd have been, you wouldn't have been put outie-o!' and Kyna rang the doorbell.

A short woman in a floral housecoat opened the door almost immediately, as if she had been waiting on the other side. She had a face that put Kyna in mind of a pug dog, with bulging eyes, a squashed-up nose and a turned-down mouth, as well as a large brown mole on her upper lip.

'Whatever it is, I'm not interested,' she snapped.

'I'm not selling anything,' Kyna told her, holding out her identity card. 'I'm a detective, from Anglesea Street Garda station.'

The woman peered at the card short-sightedly for a moment, her lips moving as she read out *An Garda Síochána*, and then she said, 'That doesn't look like you at all. Your hair's different.'

'Yes, it is, but I've grown it since this picture was taken. It *is* me, though, I can promise you.'

'All right. If it is you, what do you want?'

'I'm looking for Doireann Greaney. I understand that she rents a room here.'

'Doireann, is it? What's Doireann done?'

'All I want to do is have a word with her. Is she in?'

'Did I say she lived here?'

'No, but I've been reliably informed that she does, and you seem to know her.'

'Well, she does, but she's not here now. You've missed her by only a minute but she told me she wouldn't be back till maybe five, like. She's gone off joggling.'

'Really? What was she wearing?'

'What do you think? Her tracksuit, like always. The only time she never wears that tracksuit is when it's in the laundry.'

'What colour is it, this tracksuit?'

'What colour? Sort of grey, I suppose you'd call it. About the same colour as them clouds up there.'

'Do you know where she's gone?'

'How would I? I couldn't go with her. I have the desperate arthamiritis in my knees. I can hardly stagger to the shop, let alone joggle.'

'You say she left here only about a minute ago. Did you see which way she went?'

'She went the way she always goes.'

'You'll excuse my not knowing, but which way is that?'

The woman puffed out her cheeks, as if she couldn't believe Kyna's ignorance. 'Up St Kevin's Street. After that, though, only the good Lord knows. Sometimes she's away for hours.'

'But *up* St Kevin's Street, towards the river?'

'That's what I said, like, didn't I?'

Kyna didn't answer. She left the woman standing in her doorway and hurried back across the road. She climbed into the car, slammed the door and said, 'She's gone off jogging in her grey tracksuit. We've only just missed her. According to Mrs Haggerty there, she's heading north towards the river. If we're quick we may be able to catch up with her.'

Detective Cushley started the engine, slammed the gearstick into reverse, and they backed out into St Kevin's Street on slithering tyres, right into the path of a slow-moving Murphy's coal truck. The truck driver blasted his horn and Kyna could hear him shouting but Detective Cushley ignored him, changed gear, and they sped as fast as they could up to the junction with Barrack Street. Kyna looked left and right into every side turning but she could see no sign of Doireann Greaney jogging in her grey tracksuit.

As it approached the river, Barrack Street sloped downwards, passing the Flying Enterprise Lounge. It ended up at French's Quay, which was one way westward, so Detective Cushley would have to turn left. The traffic lights were red, so he slowed down, and as he did so, Kyna looked over to the right and said, 'There she is! There! See her? Behind that fat fellow in the hat! Just waiting to cross the road!'

Detective Cushley stamped on the brake pedal, so that the van behind him almost hit their rear bumper. Kyna flung open the passenger door and scrambled out, dodging across Barrack Street in front of an oncoming car just as the lights changed and Doireann Greaney started to run across the junction. On the other side of the junction was South Gate Bridge, with a low stone wall leading up to it. A young woman in a red raincoat was sitting on the wall, tying up the laces of her knee-high boots, while her small gingery terrier sat on the pavement waiting for her.

Doireann Greaney in her pale grey hooded tracksuit looked like a flickering ghost as she ran diagonally across the road, thin and inhuman. Kyna could see that she was running faster and faster, and she was heading directly for the young woman in the red raincoat.

'Look out!' Kyna shouted, her voice hoarse. And then, 'Doireann! Stop! *Doireann!*'

She was too late. Doireann Greaney ran straight up to the young woman without slackening her pace and pushed her backwards off the wall. The young woman must have had her dog's lead tied to her wrist because the terrier was plucked up off the pavement like a conjuring trick and disappeared after her.

Kyna reached the wall seconds later – in time to hear the young woman splash into the river only three metres below and scream out for help.

She turned to face Doireann Greaney, and for two or three seconds they stared at each other. Underneath her grey hood, Doireann Greaney was thin-faced, sallow, with a pointed nose and unplucked eyebrows and huge dark eyes, but she was strangely attractive, in the same way that witches or banshees could be attractive. She was breathing hard but she said nothing.

'Stay right where you are, Doireann,' Kyna snapped at her. 'I'm a police officer and you're under arrest. I mean it. Don't fecking move a muscle.'

The young woman screamed again. Kyna could see that Detective Cushley had parked on the opposite side of French's Quay and was climbing out of the car to come and help her. Without any further hesitation, she unbuttoned her coat and tugged it off, and then her jacket, and kicked off her boots. She swung her legs over the wall and carefully climbed down the craggy limestone embankment until she reached the river's edge.

The young woman was about twenty metres away by now, the tails of her red raincoat curving out on either side of her like wings. She was thrashing her arms to stay afloat, although every few seconds her head disappeared under the surface, and when she reappeared she spat out water and coughed and tried to scream.

Beside her, her terrier was furiously paddling, but one of its legs was tangled up in its lead, and so it was having difficulty in keeping itself upright.

'*Sarge!*' shouted Detective Cushley. Kyna looked up and saw him leaning over the wall. He had untied one of the red-and-white lifebelts from the railings along the other side of the bridge. He dropped it down and it bounced off the stones at the brink of the river and slowly floated towards the young woman. The tide was going out, and she had already been drawn downriver until she was underneath the bridge.

'Hold on, sarge! I've called for backup!' Detective Cushley told her.

The young woman went under again. Kyna took a deep breath and dived into the river. She had always been a strong swimmer, but the water was stunningly cold – so cold that she felt as if she had been electrocuted and gone into shock. She struggled to the surface, gasping to get her breath back, but ripples from the river smacked her across the face, again and again, like a petulant lover, as if it were punishing her for diving into it.

Gradually, though, she began to gain on the young woman, and as the current carried them underneath the bridge together and out to the other side, she was able to snatch at her hand. The young woman tugged at her desperately, her eyes wide with fear. She was panicking so much that she pulled them both under the water, kicking and flailing her arms, and Kyna heard her let out a gargling sound.

As they surfaced again, Kyna wrestled with all her strength to turn the young woman around, so that she was floating on her back. She was still kicking her legs and splashing with her arms and so Kyna gasped, '*Still! Keep still!*' She wanted to say more but she had swallowed too much icy water and she was already out of breath.

The lifebelt was now within reach, so Kyna caught hold of it and pulled it towards them. The young woman grabbed hold of it, too, and its buoyancy calmed her down, because she stopped struggling so frantically and allowed Kyna to tilt her head back against her shoulder.

With one arm around the young woman, Kyna began to swim backwards towards the embankment. It seemed to take forever, because the current was so strong, and she began to think that she wouldn't have the strength to make it. Her swimming arm was aching and her hands were so cold that she felt as if they had been amputated. She closed her eyes and thought, *Help me, dear God. Don't let me die like this, in this filthy freezing river, with only the grey mullet to mourn me.*

She began to think that she was dreaming. She could hear nothing but her own breathing and the lapping of the water against her face, and she imagined that even if she didn't drown she would have to go on paddling like this for the rest of her life, trying to reach an embankment that never came any closer.

But then she heard sirens, and when she turned her head around she saw blue flashing lights. A crowd of people had gathered along the quayside, and after only a few seconds three firefighters pushed their way through them and climbed over the railings.

'Don't you worry, girl, we're coming for you!' one of the firefighters shouted. The three of them lowered themselves on ropes down the mossy limestone wall, and then held out their hands, ready to help her out of the water.

She could also see that the young woman's terrier had managed to reach the embankment. Another firefighter had abseiled down to pluck him out of the river, and now she was holding him up, dripping and bedraggled, so that she could hand him to a garda who was leaning over the railings.

At last Kyna's shoulder bumped against the embankment. Immediately the young woman was lifted off her and rose up as if she could levitate, with streams of water running from her red raincoat. Kyna tried to turn herself around, but as she did so she knocked her forehead hard against the wall, just above her left eye. For a split second her world went inky black, and she slipped down underneath the surface. She was semi-concussed and numb with cold, but she still had a tiny speck of consciousness so that she felt that sinking under the water was almost a relief. *You've done what you set out to do, Kyna, you can rest now.*

She didn't hear the firefighter plunging into the water next to her, or realize that he was heaving her up and fastening a canvas sling around her so that she could be hoisted up the side of the embankment. She wasn't aware that she was lifted over the railings, wrapped in a crinkly silver blanket and laid gently down on a stretcher. She didn't feel a woman's lips pressed against hers, giving her five deep rescue breaths.

She couldn't feel the first thirty chest compressions, followed by two more rescue breaths, and then thirty more chest compressions. But then she spluttered, and blurted out water, and opened her eyes. Looking down at her she saw Katie, frowning with anxiety.

She opened and closed her mouth, trying to say 'Katie', but all she could do was cough.

'Oh, Kyna, I thought I'd lost you. I really thought I'd lost you.'

Kyna coughed again. She was shivering violently, but she managed to say, 'That young girl—'

'Don't you worry. She's going to be fine. They've just taken her off to the Mercy. You saved her life, Kyna. There's no doubt at all that she would have drowned if you hadn't jumped in.'

Kyna tried to sit up but Katie gently pushed her back down. 'Relax, darling. You've got yourself a fierce nasty debt on the forehead there. They'll be taking you off to emergency, too, just to make sure.'

'What about D-Doireann Greaney?'

'Don't you worry about her, either. She didn't try to do a legger. I'd guess that she didn't see the point. Just as soon as Jack had called for the blue lights he lifted her. She's sitting right across the road there in the back of that squad car.'

'Oh Jesus, I'm so cold. I feel like my spine's rattling, top to tail.'

A freckly-faced woman paramedic came bustling up to them.

'How're you going on there, girl? We'll be whizzing you off to the Mercy now. You might need the blood rewarming, or a hot mug of scaldy at the very least.'

Katie leaned over and kissed Kyna on the forehead.

'There's photographers over there,' said Kyna.

'I don't care. You're the bravest person I ever met, and I love you.'

27

When she returned to Anglesea Street, Katie held her news conference about the explosion at the School of Pharmacy. It was twenty minutes later than scheduled, and the assembled reporters were growing restless, but it was just in time for RTÉ's *Six One News*. She was accompanied by Superintendent Pearse and Mathew McElvey.

Dan Keane and Douglas Kelly both asked her if she was any closer to identifying the bomber. She could tell that they suspected her of knowing more than she was giving out, which of course she did. Operationally, though, it was far too early to give them any information about the telltale signatures that might link the device with the three bombs discovered up North; and she made no mention of James MacGreevy.

All she did was release the names of the eleven dead students and give an update on the condition of the three who had been seriously hurt. They remained in intensive care, but were expected to survive, although two of them had life-changing injuries. One had lost both of her forearms below the elbows and the other had suffered catastrophic brain damage.

'But you *still* have no inkling of who might be responsible?' called out Owen Dineen. 'You can't even hazard a guess?'

'Like I told you earlier, Mr Dineen, we can't arrest a guess.'

'Oh, sure like. I forgot. It's the "irrefutable proof" you're after. You're sure it's not the eighty proof?'

'What exactly do you mean by that?'

'Nothing at all, Detective Superintendent. Well – let's say nothing at all and something. Nothing that we haven't been suspecting for quite a long time, and something that a little bird told us.'

'Come on, then, out with it, whatever it is.'

'I'm not in a position to say more for the moment, ma'am. But it'll all become clear in the fullness of time.'

'Right, then. I'm up the walls right now, as you can probably imagine, so I can't be bothered with riddles. But before you go, I do have one more important announcement to make. We've detained a young female on suspicion of being the Lee Pusher.'

'The Lee Pusher is a *woman*?' asked Fionnuala Sweeney.

'That's correct. We'll be releasing her name and any further details once she's been interviewed and formally charged. She was arrested after that incident by South Gate Bridge this afternoon when a young woman was pushed into the river and subsequently rescued by a Garda detective sergeant.'

'So that young woman didn't fall in accidentally? She was pushed?' said Dan Keane. 'That puts an entirely different complexion on the story altogether. It looks like we all have some major rewriting to do. Were there any witnesses?'

'There were several passers-by in the vicinity. But it happened so quickly that nobody saw the suspect push the young woman into the water except for Detective Sergeant Ní Nuallán who saved her – not even her partner, Detective Cushley. As you know, that's been one of the defining characteristics of all the Lee Pusher's attacks. They've all been totally unexpected and carried out so quick that nobody's ever sure of what they saw. That's one of the reasons that it's taken us all this time to catch her – apart from us not realizing until very recently that she was female, because of how tall she is.'

'So she's pushed in eight now that you know of, including this one?'

'That's correct. But it's quite possible that she may have pushed in more. We'll be questioning her about some of the drownings in the Lee that have so far been unaccounted for.'

'And was she wearing the same grey tracksuit, the same like she was wearing for all the other times she pushed somebody in?'

'She was, yes. That was partly how we managed to track her down.'

'I was going to ask you,' said Dan Keane. 'How is DS Ní Nuallán? I've already written a grand "Heroine Cop Saves Drowning Woman" piece.'

'She was suffering from hypothermia and she also took a nasty knock to her head, so she'll be staying at the Mercy overnight for observation. But it looks like she's going to be fine altogether, thank you. I'll be giving her a couple of days off to get over it.'

'We have a fantastic picture of you giving her the kiss of life, DS Maguire.'

'Well, it's only a couple of minutes from here to the South Gate Bridge, and I went straight there as soon as Detective Cushley called it in. I managed to get there just as they were lifting DS Ní Nuallán out of the river.'

Owen Dineen raised his hand. 'Here's a question for you. If it had been Chief Superintendent O'Kane who needed CPR, instead of DS Ní Nuallán, would you have given *him* the kiss of life?'

'I would have given it to anybody who had almost drowned, Mr Dineen,' said Katie. 'Even *you*.'

She answered him tonelessly, as if she were neither insulted nor amused. However, she was sure that in asking that question he had inadvertently let slip more about his vendetta against her than he had intended. Perhaps it wasn't irrefutable proof, but it was highly revealing.

She smiled, said 'Thanks a million' to all the reporters, and went back upstairs, feeling that at last she might be getting the edge.

Three people were waiting in her office for her: Bill Phinner, his new ballistics expert Aoife Shaugnessy and Detective Padragain Scanlan.

'So, what kind of a mood were the hungry wolves in?' asked Bill. He was wearing a mustard-coloured sweater with a shawl collar and wooden buttons that made him look even more like somebody's miserable uncle than ever. Aoife, standing close beside him, was still in her lab coat. She had bouncy brunette hair and a snub nose, which made her look more like his shy teenage niece than his new ballistics expert.

'The press?' said Katie, sitting down at her desk. 'I told them that I didn't have the first notion who might have built that bomb but I don't think they swallowed that for a moment. Even Owen Dineen knows I'm not as thick as that, no matter what he writes about me. But of course I don't want to give James MacGreevy even a hint yet that we suspect him. If I'd mentioned those three bombs up North, he would guess straight away that we have him in the frame.'

'If MacGreevy owns the dog that those hairs came from, then he's our man all right. The DNA tests have shown that it's a billion to one that they were all shed by the same animal.'

'Okay. We have him under surveillance but if we don't see him with a dog within forty-eight hours I'll ask for a search warrant. We can check then to see if we can find any more of those hairs around his house. And any bomb-making equipment at all. Even a screwdriver with a trace of that Semtex-1K on it would do it.'

'Did the press ask you who might have had a motive for blowing up the School of Pharmacy, of all places?'

'They did, yes, but I told them that we still had no definite leads. I'm afraid I fibbed a little. I said that we had reason to believe that the bomber could have been harbouring a personal grudge against UCC. Maybe it was a student who was kicked off his course for misconduct – stealing drugs from the lab, like, or sexual harassment.'

'So you didn't mention the O'Flynns or the Riordans, or some other gang?'

'No. I want them to believe that they might have got away with it. With any luck they'll get complacent and start boasting about it.'

Bill gave her a thumbs up. 'That's good thinking there, ma'am. And since we're talking about the O'Flynns and the Riordans, we've come up with something that will interest you. Aoife – show DS Maguire what you have there, would you?'

Aoife came forward and set down two small plastic evidence bags on Katie's desk. Katie picked them up and saw that each of them contained a brass cartridge case.

'Nine-millimetre Parabellum?' she said. She peered at them more closely. 'They look pretty much alike to me.'

'They're much more than alike, they're twins,' Aoife told her, speaking softly but very clearly in a Galway accent. 'They both have headstamps that show they were manufactured by Prvi Partizan in Serbia. Not only that, they have identical indentations caused by the firing-pin of the pistol they were shot from. They also have identical face-marks caused by the ejector after they were fired. And to top it all, they have matching fingerprints on them. I've sent off copies of course to see if AFIS has a record of them.'

'Take a sconce at the labels on them,' Bill put in. 'You'll see that one was found in the burned-out Honda Accord that was found at Bottlehill after Billy Hagerty was shot. And you'll never guess where the other one was picked up.'

'Go on. Surprise me.'

'We raked it up out of the grass verge next to the body of Timbo Coffey. Billy Hagerty and Timbo Coffey were shot by one and the same gun.'

'Why in the name of Jesus would anybody have wanted to shoot both a tragic gombeen like Billy Hagerty and an old alky Pavee like Timbo Coffey? Always assuming that the same perpetrator shot them both, and that one shooter didn't lend another shooter a borrow of his gun.'

'That's the sixty-five-thousand-euro question,' said Bill. 'Even if the shooter who killed Billy Hagerty had been intending to kill Thomas O'Flynn, but missed, why would he have shot Timbo Coffey?'

Katie sat back and shook her head. 'I give up, Bill. I think the whole world's gone off its head.'

Bill and Aoife left, and Detective Scanlan came forward.

'Padragain,' said Katie. 'Tell me you have some good news.'

'I just heard about DS Ní Nuallán. That took some nerve, jumping into the river like that, especially this time of year. Is she really okay?'

'She's grand altogether, thanks. But she had me worried for a minute or two, I have to admit.'

Detective Scanlan looked as if she were about to say something sympathetic, like, 'I know what you two feel for each other'. But all she did was give Katie an understanding smile, and say, 'I went round to that house in Tivoli Park earlier this afternoon.'

'Oh yes? And did you find anybody in?'

'There was still nobody home but one of the neighbours told me that the family would be back from their holliers later, so I went round again at four. The Dalys, that's who they are. Stephen Daly from Mulligan and Daly, the solicitors from South Mall.'

'I know him of course. He's on the board of the ISPCC. He and my husband, Paul, used to play golf together.'

'Anyway, he was pure accommodating and gave me this USB from his CCTV.' She opened up her purse and held up a 64GB memory stick. 'It covers the whole of the past month, at least. He had an alarm installed already but he added the camera after he found that some burglar had tried to force open their kitchen window.'

'That's fantastic, Padragain. If you can take it upstairs and ask Sergeant Murphy to run through it for us. He's been going back over all the CCTV footage that might relate to Justice Quinn's last movements, so he has a fair idea of what we're looking for.'

'What *are* we looking for? I mean, anything specific?'

'I'm not at all totally sure, to be honest with you. Anything that might tell us why he drove up to White's Cross, instead of heading directly for the law courts. There could have been any number of reasons. Maybe there was somebody up near White's Cross that he'd arranged to visit, although there's no evidence of that in his phone records. Maybe he was tricked into going there. Maybe he just decided that he wanted to drive around the countryside to clear his mind.'

'I know how *that* feels,' said Detective Scanlan.

'You're all right, are you? I know I've been overworking

everybody but right now there's so much to cope with and we're so short-staffed.'

'I've been having some boyfriend trouble, that's all. Nothing serious. It's mostly the crowd he mixes with.'

Katie thought of her late husband, Paul, and how he had become involved in so many shady building-supply contracts, such as lorryloads of bricks that were sold twice over, and hundreds of bags of cement that never were. Even if she hadn't been a senior police officer his scams would have troubled her, so she could understand why Detective Scanlan was feeling so stressed.

'If you need to talk about it—' she began.

'Thanks a million, ma'am, but I'm sure you've enough troubles of your own to be getting on with.'

She left, and Katie stood up and went to the window. It wasn't raining, but it was already beginning to grow dark, as if God had drawn the curtains early because the world was giving Him a migraine. Not only that, but the hooded crows were clustered on the rooftop opposite – so many of them that they were fighting with each other for footing on the ridge tiles. If that wasn't a sinister omen, she didn't know what was.

Her iPhone played *Mo Ghille Mear* and her eyes filled with tears.

For some short time I was a gentle maiden,
Now I am a spent, worn-out widow,
My darling has crossed the wild waves,
Gone far away.

28

There were two short rings at the doorbell, followed by a long ring. Barry Riordan said, 'That'll be Nocky. Go let him in, will you, Gavin?'

Gavin went out into the hallway and returned with Nocky following close behind him. Nocky was short, with a bulbous forehead and one of those thin moustaches that Norries called a 'thirsty eyebrow'. He was wearing a brownish tweed jacket with sagging pockets and baggy corduroy trousers.

'That's the third motor for you,' he told Barry, dropping a set of car keys on to the kitchen table. 'It's a white VW Passat Estate, semi-automatic. It's parked along with the other two in that unused unit at the Árd Álainn Business Park. I've switched the number plates already.'

Barry said, 'That's grand, boy, thanks.' He lifted himself up from his chair and tugged a thick bundle of euros out of his back jeans pocket. 'Are you sure I can't twist your arm to join us on this one? I'll pay you double what I'm paying you already.'

Nocky shook his head. 'I'm still under licence, Bazza, with three and a half years to go. If they snare me again, God knows how long I'll be banged up.'

'I'm only needing you to drive. Nothing else.'

'I'm not even going to ask you what you're planning. Look, I've hobbled your motors for you, haven't I, and that's only because I owe you a favour.'

Nocky spoke cautiously, because he knew how unpredictable Barry's temper could be. But Barry shrugged and licked his thumb and counted out three hundred euros in fifties. Before he pushed them across the table, though, he said, 'You're *sure*, like? I could double it and pay you another ton on top. All you have to do is drive a couple of the fellers up to The Weavers on Saturday afternoon and wait outside for a couple of minutes. Then – when they come out – you'll drive them up to O'Brien's builder's yard at Boreen Dearg.'

'And then what?'

'They'll be torching all three motors but you'll be picked up from there and taken home. The problem is that I have only the five drivers so far and I need six.'

'I don't know, like. What will you be doing at The Weavers? Don't tell me you need three cars just to rob the place. Besides, that's where the O'Flynns usually hang out now, isn't it – The Weavers?'

'Well, I'll be straight with you. The O'Flynns are holding a twenty-first birthday bash there, and all we're going to do is mess it up for them good and proper. Kick the tables over, spill all the drinks, smash the band's bodhrán and drop the birthday cake down the jacks. They'll be too scunderated to report it to the cops.'

'And that's all? You won't be giving nobody a beating or nothing like that?'

'Nocky – they deserve a million times worse for murdering Michael and Saoirse and their two little wains. But the whole of Cork will get to hear about their birthday party getting wrecked and they'll be morto.'

'Well... I won't say that I couldn't use the grade.'

Barry counted out another four hundred euros and pushed the notes towards him. Nocky hesitated for a moment, and then picked them up, clutching them in both hands like a child clutches a bag of sweets. His expression was still one of desperate indecision.

Feargal was standing in the far corner of the kitchen, by the fridge. He finished smoking his cigarette right down to the filter and then he flicked the butt into the sink and turned on the tap. 'You'll be fine, Nocky. Don't you worry. It'll be a piece of piss.'

'Fetch one of the motors around here at 2.30 Saturday arvo and we'll be set to go,' said Barry. 'But don't be wearing that stupid fecking orangey cap of yours, otherwise you might as well stick a sign "Here Comes Nocky" in the windie.'

'Okay, Bazza. I might as well take the Passat, then.' Nocky picked up the car keys from the table, juggled them once in his hand and left, closing the kitchen door behind him.

Barry took out a cigarette himself, and Gavin leaned over to light it for him. Barry breathed two long streams of smoke out of his nostrils, and then said, 'Right, then, Gavin, let's see what you have in them bags of yours.'

Gavin lifted up two long black nylon bags and laid them side by side on the table. He unzipped one of them and opened it. Packed inside in three separate pieces was a Ruger SR-556, a semi-automatic rifle that could be taken apart and reassembled in a matter of seconds. The bags in which they were stowed looked completely innocuous, like shopping bags, and they had padded interiors so that the two receiver assemblies and the barrel system didn't clank together when they were carried.

'Johnny had only the two of these, like. But he gave me three handguns, too – two Glock ten-millimetres and a Sig-Sauer – and he swore that none of them was traceable.'

'Holy Jesus!' Barry choked on his cigarette smoke and he coughed and coughed, flapping his hand until he could get his breath back. 'We won't be needing more than them two Rugers. But I tell you, boy, this birthday party's going to be one to remember. For us it is, any road. Not for those fecking O'Flynns. The whole lot of them will be lying in St Michael's Cemetery with more holes in them than a kitchen colander.'

With the cars and the guns and all the arrangements for Saturday sorted, Barry decided that they should all go off to the Top of the Hill to meet the rest of the gang and have a few scoops. He took down his dark green coat from the peg in the hallway, and while he was buttoning it up, he opened the door of the front living room with his elbow.

Megan was sitting curled up on the leatherette couch watching *Dancing on Ice* and she didn't even turn to look at him.

'I'm off out, girl. I don't know how long I'll be, but I'll be starving when I come back, do you hear me? Make sure you have that pot of colcannon soup bubbling up good and hot for me and plenty of soda bread buttered.'

'I will, yeah,' said Megan.

'So what's that supposed to mean? You will or you won't?'

'It means I will.'

'Then fecking look at me when you say it.'

Megan turned and stared at him. Her eyes were circled with black bruises and she still had a bulky white gauze pad stuck to the bridge of her nose, which gave her the appearance of a curious swan.

'It'll be ready for you so. I wouldn't want another belt.'

Barry fixed her with a hostile stare, as if he were minded to come into the living room and give her a slap, but then, without another word, he turned and left. Gavin and Feargal followed close behind him. Gavin glanced at Megan as he passed the open door, shaking his head as if to say, *Why does he do it to you, and why do you fecking let him?*

As soon as the front door had slammed behind them, Megan turned down the volume on the television, lifted the seat cushion and picked up her phone. She jabbed out Muireann's number and waited while it rang. She knew that Muireann may not be able to answer straight away, especially if she was in The Weavers with Thomas O'Flynn and some of his scummers, and maybe she may not be aware at first that she was being called. Her phone was set only to vibrate, and not to ring, like Megan's own.

Megan was almost ready to give up when Muireann said, 'It's okay. I can talk now. I'm in the toilets.'

'Are you at The Weavers? There's a party there on Saturday afternoon.'

'That's right. It's Maddie O'Flynn's twenty-first. There's at least thirty coming, maybe more.'

'You need to give it a miss, Muireann, I'm warning you.'

'Why? What's going to happen?'

'I can't say. It'd be more than my life's worth. But give your Tommy any excuse you can think of not to go. I don't know – tell him you have the scutters or you're jamming or your ma's passed away. Anything.'

'Megan – he'll expect me to be there no matter what.'

'Then don't make any excuses. Simply don't go.'

'But he'll be fuming if I don't.'

'No, he won't. I swear to God.'

'How can you be so sure of that? You know what – hold on, I have to go. Somebody's just walked in.'

With that, Muireann abruptly ended their conversation, and Megan was left with a dead phone and the muted sounds of 'Tango Argentino' on the television.

She chewed anxiously at her swollen lip. She was desperately undecided as to what she should do. After Nocky had arrived, she had crept to the kitchen door and eavesdropped. She had heard only snatches, because none of the men spoke very distinctly, and she was partly deaf in her left ear from when Barry had smacked her across the head on Christmas Day. All the same, she had picked up enough to realize that they were planning to invade The Weavers and wreck Maddie O'Flynn's birthday party.

When Nocky had left she'd nearly been caught, but he had hesitated for a moment before he had opened the door wide and that had given her time to dodge back into the living room. After he had gone, she had crept back to listen to what Barry and Gavin and Feargal were talking about. Again, it hadn't been easy to make out what they were saying, but she had distinctly heard Gavin say 'handguns' and 'Glock' and Barry say 'Rugers' and 'St Michael's Cemetery'.

She had been married to Barry for long enough to know what a Ruger was. And she had heard him come out with that threat about St Michael's Cemetery more than once. It wasn't difficult to guess that he was planning on shooting at least one of the O'Flynns at the birthday party, and maybe more. But if she warned the guards, she would be the first person that Barry would suspect of ratting on him, and she was terrified of what he would do to her, even if he had no proof. He had suspected her once before of letting slip the time and place of a major drugs deal, and it was only after he had done appalling things to her with a broom handle that he had given up and admitted that perhaps she hadn't sneaked on him after all.

She waited with the television still turned down to see if Muireann would ring her back, but her phone remained dead.

29

Before she left the station that evening, Katie went down to the holding cells to look in on Doireann Greaney. Halfway along the corridor she met the duty physician, Maebh Dorgan, who had just finished examining her. Dr Dorgan was a short woman with a double chin and glasses and a triangular brown-dyed hairstyle that made it appear as if she had a large slice of barmbrack balanced on top of her head.

'You've come to see Doireann?'

'I have, yes. How is she?'

'Unconscious. I did a blood test earlier and she's taken a high dose of lisdexamfetamine. Not dangerously high, but enough to knock her out. Plus she has a blood alcohol level of sixty-three milligrams, so she's over the drink-drive limit.'

'Lisdexamfetamine?'

'That's usually prescribed for attention deficit hyperactivity disorder – ADHD. One of its side effects is that it can make you aggressive and give you violent mood swings, but if you take too much it can make you pure drowsy.'

'How about her general health? Any other symptoms?'

'She has multiple scars on the insides of her wrists, which indicate self-harming, although not recently. She's also twenty kilos underweight for a young woman as tall as she is, so we can almost classify her as anorexic, or maybe bulimic.'

She looked back towards her cell and said, 'The best we can do now is let her sleep it off and see what she's like in the morning – physically and psychologically. I'd say myself that whatever she's guilty of, she's had a fierce hard life, one way or another.'

The next morning's *Irish Sun* was no kinder to Katie than the previous two days' issues. She could see it lying on top of all the other newspapers as she hung up her coat. LEE PUSHER SUSPECT SEIZED – *But why did 7 have to drown before cops caught on?*

Detective Inspector Fitzpatrick knocked and came into her office even before she had sat down. He nodded towards the newspapers on the coffee table and said, 'I've seen it. That Owen Dineen really has his teeth into you, doesn't he?'

'I'm ignoring it,' said Katie. 'There's no point in getting my knickers in a twist.' She didn't tell him about her growing conviction that Owen Dineen's attacks on her were entirely personal, rather than a serious media campaign for more effective policing.

'You should lodge a complaint with the Press Council.'

'I might, in the fullness of time. Right now I've far too much on my plate to be bothered about the press giving me grief.' She sat down and flicked through the memos and files that Moirin had left on her desk for her, and then she looked up. 'So what do you have for me, Robert? Hey – you're smiling, so you are. You look like you lost a fly-button and found a bitcoin.'

Robert handed her a folder. 'See for yourself.'

When she opened the folder, Katie saw that it contained at least a dozen photographs of a black Range Rover parked outside a white fence with a privet hedge behind it. The pictures had been taken at night, but there was sufficient light from a nearby lamp post and they had been taken with a camera with very high ISO sensitivity.

The Range Rover was half obscuring a sign so that all she could see was MacGr Gard Cen. A man in a black oilskin raincoat and a chequered cap was opening up the vehicle's tailgate so that a grey curly-haired dog could jump out.

'James MacGreevy,' said Katie. 'So he *does* have a dog. And the right breed, too. Or *breeds*. Holy Mother of God, just take a sconce at him, the poor little fellow. He's a right old mash-up, isn't he? Mostly Kerry Blue, I'd say, but with at least two or three other varieties mixed in.'

'MacGreevy went to fetch the dog about half-past eight from his son's house in Inishannon. It turns out his son's a vet, so I can only assume that he was treating it for some illness or other. Anyway, he has it there now, back at the garden centre. We've seen him walking around the greenhouses with it just this morning.'

'Right,' said Katie. 'Let's apply for the necessary warrants and haul him in. And haul the dog in, too. Bill Phinner will be needing to take dog hair samples.'

She rang Detective O'Donovan so that he could come downstairs with her and question Doireann Greaney.

If Kyna had been available to join her it would have been ideal, because Kyna had such a knack for coaxing sensitive information out of suspects who were aggressive or cagey or wildly disturbed. All the same, Detective O'Donovan was blunt and plain-speaking and his directness had often triggered the most reticent of offenders into an unexpected outpouring of guilt and remorse. Detective Sergeant Begley had once told him that he had missed his vocation, and should have been a priest, taking confession every Sunday.

As she stood up to leave, Chief Superintendent O'Kane appeared in the doorway. She imagined that she could smell his Boss aftershave, even though she probably couldn't, and she briefly pressed the back of her hand against her nose.

'Kathleen – do you have a minute?' From the tone of his voice, she could tell that it wasn't a question.

'I'm just on my way to interview the Pusher,' she said. 'Can it wait until later?'

'Not really. I have to head off for Phoenix Park in a minute. I've been called for a meeting with the Director of Communications and Superintendent O'Hare, the Garda Press Officer. It's likely that the Commissioner will join us, too.'

He paused, and pointed towards the copy of the *Irish Sun*. 'I'm sure you can guess what we're going to be discussing.'

'What do you want me to say? I think the press are being grossly unfair and I totally refute all of their accusations that crime in Cork is getting out of hand. But then I have no control over what they choose to print in the newspapers. I only wish I knew why they're being so personal, and so vindictive.'

Brendan stared at her for at least ten seconds, tentatively licking his lips with the tip of his tongue. She felt as if he were undressing her with his eyes. At last he said, 'I can't tell them at Phoenix Park, then, that you're considering your position?'

'"Considering my position"? You mean am I thinking of resigning?'

'The media coverage gets ten times worse every day, Kathleen. You can't deny it. Frank Magorian's spitting tin tacks.'

'I have a job to do, and whatever the press say I'm doing it well, and so is every single member of my team. If Frank Magorian wants to sack me, then all I can say is let him try. You know that both my detection and conviction rates are up on last year, and the year before, *and* the year before that. And let me tell you this: if you and Frank think that you can do to me what the Garda did to my father, you'll wish you'd never heard the name of Kathleen Maguire, the both of you.'

'You're not still holding those pictures against me, are you? I promised on my honour that I'd delete them, and I have. But this media coverage, Kathleen, come on, this is something a thousand times more serious. This is about more than the Garda's public image. It's about our whole reputation for keeping law and order. Even the Commissioner's asking questions about it now – like, what can we do in the way of damage limitation?'

'And you all want me to be your sacrificial lamb, do you? "Oh – we tried promoting a woman to detective super-intendent, but do you know, just as we always thought, women can't hack it. They're too emotional, too feather-brained, too menstrual, too argumentative. And they don't have prunes, or play golf."'

'Kathleen—'

'"Detective Superintendent" to you, sir, or "ma'am" if you prefer. I'm not going to beat around the bushes. If you try to have me removed from this office, I swear to God that you'll be coming out the door with me. I'll be lodging a formal complaint against you of bullying, sexual harassment, attempted blackmail, and rape.'

'For Christ's sake, Kathleen. I'm human. I couldn't help having feelings for you, and believe it or not I still do. Can't you take what happened as a compliment? How was I to know that it wasn't consensual?'

Katie was breathing hard. 'You'll have to forgive me, sir. I have to go down now to question the young woman we've arrested as the Lee Pusher. Another investigation successfully closed. Perhaps you'd care to report *that* to the Commissioner, and the Director of Communications, and the Garda Press Officer, and any other misogynists within earshot.'

30

She met Detective O'Donovan in the reception area, with his phone held to his ear. He sounded as if he were chatting to a woman because he glanced at Katie and said, 'Gotta go,' and then blew her a kiss before he rang off.

'How're you going on, ma'am?' he asked. 'You have kind of an agitated look about you if you don't mind my saying so.'

'Agitated? Is that all? Have you not read the *Sun* this morning?'

'Well, yes, but only the racing tips, and the horoscopes. You can't believe any of the rest of it.'

They walked along the corridor to the interview room. Doireann Greaney was waiting for them, along with her duty solicitor, Sionha Barrett, and a female garda. Doireann was sitting slumped behind the table in a floppy grey jumper and a pair of dark blue tracksuit trousers that were at least two sizes too large for her. Her arms were folded and she was staring up at the ceiling as if she were bored beyond measure. She had tied back her hair with elastic bands into a long stringy ponytail.

Sionha Barrett wore a thick heather tweed suit. Her huge pink-rimmed spectacles looked like two goldfish bowls with her eyes swimming around inside them. They kept threatening to drop off the end of her snubby little nose, so that she constantly had to prod them back up.

Katie and Detective O'Donovan sat down. 'Doireann – I'm Detective Superintendent Kathleen Maguire and this is

Detective Patrick O'Donovan. May I ask you how you're feeling this morning?'

Doireann shrugged but said nothing. Sionha said, 'I think you should try and answer DS Maguire, Doireann. She's only concerned for your welfare.'

'How am I *feeling*?' asked Doireann. It was almost a sneer.

'The doctor said that you'd taken a high dose of lisdexamfetamine and a few gatts too.'

'So if you know that, how the feck do you think I'm feeling? Like shite warmed up.'

'Would you care for a cup of tea in your hand?'

'No. But a Tanora if you have one.'

'I believe we can find you a Tanora. Are you hungry? We could fetch you a sandwich or some biscuits maybe.'

'I'm never hungry.'

'How old are you, Doireann?'

'I already told the guard that yesterday when he charged me.'

'Still, but we're recording this conversation and it's just for the record.'

'Twenty-two. Twenty-three on April the sixteenth. That's my official birthday anyway.'

'Your *official* birthday?'

'Saint Drogo's Day.'

'Is there a reason for that?'

'Saint Drogo's my patron saint. He was the same as me. His mother died when he was being born, like mine. And he's the saint of unattractive people, like me.'

'Who said you were unattractive?' asked Detective O'Donovan.

Doireann let out a bitter bark of a laugh. 'Are you fecking blind or something? Look at me.'

'You're not unattractive.'

'Well, you're the only person in the whole world who doesn't think so. How many other girls do you know who are six feet two and weigh fifty-six kilos? I've been bullied ever since I was eleven. "Hand me down the Moon", that's what all my classmates used to call me. And they'd throw peanuts and biscuits at me because they said I need fatting up.'

'That was at St Catherine's?'

Doireann nodded, and whispered something. It sounded venomous, and obscene, although Katie couldn't hear what it was.

'I thought you were happy at St Catherine's,' she said. 'You did well in the athletics team.'

'That was the only time I was anything close to happy, when I was running. I was always way ahead of all the other girls, and I won all the cups. But that only made them hate me even more.'

'Have you never had a close friend you could confide in – girl or boy?'

'Only Saint Drogo. He understood me. He was ugly, too – so ugly that he shut himself away so that people wouldn't have to look at him. He lived off nothing but water and the Eucharist, which was pushed through a hole in the wall. But he mortified his flesh, to remind himself that God had made him, even if he *was* ugly.'

'And you did the same? You cut yourself?'

'When you feel the pain, and when you see the blood, there you are, like – that's proof.'

'Proof of what, Doireann?'

'Proof that you're not imaginary. Proof that you're real.'

Katie opened the folder that she had brought with her and

took out two sheets of paper. She passed one to Doireann and another to Sionha.

'As you can see, these are the names of all seven people you've been charged with murdering, with the dates, times and places of each of the alleged offences listed beside them. Plus the attempted murder of that young woman yesterday at South Gate Bridge. I'm asking you to read through these names and give me your response to each of the eight charges.'

'You don't have to answer, Doireann,' said Sionha. 'You're entitled to say nothing at all. In fact, my advice to you is to hold your peace.'

The interview room was silent for almost three minutes while Doireann studied the list of people she was charged with drowning. At length, she laid the sheet of paper flat on the table and tapped one of the names hard with her finger.

'I never drowned seven of them. Only six. This one I never.'

'Which one, Doireann?'

'This one here. This what's-her-name.' She leaned forward to see the name more clearly. 'This Roisin Carroll. It says here that I pushed her into the river off The Marina at a quarter to five on the Tuesday. Well, I never did.'

'An eyewitness saw you. He not only saw you, he jumped into the river and saved Roisin Carroll's young wain from drowning.'

'He couldn't have seen me because I wasn't there. I was back in my room on St Nessan Street because I had the cramps. I didn't go out all day. You can ask Mrs Haggerty, she'll tell you.'

'Very well, we will. But let's put Roisin Carroll aside for a moment and ask you about the others. Are you admitting that you deliberately drowned all of them?'

Sionha shook her head so vigorously that her glasses almost dropped off. 'Now, you don't have to admit to anything, Doireann. It's up to them to prove to the satisfaction of a judge and jury that it was you.'

'But they deserved it. Can't I say that?'

'You can, sure,' said Detective O'Donovan. 'But maybe you can explain to us *why* they deserved it. They'd upset you in some way, but how?'

Doireann sat up straight and banged both her fists on the table. 'Of course they'd upset me! There they were, strolling beside the river, the very picture of happy! And when the feck have I ever been happy? Not once! Not once for one minute for the whole of my life! Not once for one second, from the moment the midwife lifted me out my dead mother's womb until today! Upset me? Are you codding me? *Upset* me?'

Now Doireann was almost screaming, and banging the table again and again to emphasize every word. 'They might just as well have been throwing peanuts and biscuits at me, and laughing, and dancing around me like the girls did at school, saying that I was the last surviving maypole in Ireland! And you're asking me what they'd done to deserve it?'

She sat back again, her flat chest rising and falling under her jumper. Sionha laid her hand on her arm to calm her down.

Very gently, Detective O'Donovan said, 'Did you know any of them personally – these people you pushed?'

Doireann stared at him. 'Did I *what*? Did I *know* any of them? Of course I didn't know any of them! I don't know nobody! Only my stupid da and that geebag of a woman he calls his wife, and Mrs Haggerty, and Mrs Haggerty's gom of a son Charlie who keeps waving his langer at me whenever he comes out of his bedroom and asking if I want some. Why should I need to know somebody to know that I'll never have what *they* have?'

Shaking with anger, she held up one hand and counted off on her fingers the things that she believed she would never have. 'Never have friends. Never have a job. Never have enough money for a holiday, nor somebody to go with. Never have a boyfriend who loves me. Never have a husband. Never have children.'

She paused for breath, and then she leaned forward and said, much more softly, 'Do you know something, I've never had somebody cuddle me. Never. Nobody has ever put their arms around me and told me that I'm the one for them.'

'But you're alive,' said Detective O'Donovan. 'You're alive and God loves you for a start, otherwise you wouldn't be here at all. And you're as beautiful as you feel, not as other people judge you. It's just tragic that you took so many other people's lives away from them so that you could have your revenge for being bullied.'

Doireann burst into tears and started to rock backwards and forwards in her chair, making a thin keening sound. Sionha looked across at Katie and raised her eyebrows.

'I don't think there's much point in taking this any further,' Katie told her. 'It seems that she's going to plead guilty to all but one of the charges, the murder of Roisin Carroll, and we'll have to question her about that again later. First, though, we'll have to talk to her landlady about her whereabouts on Tuesday, and interview the eyewitness again, and see what other evidence we can come up with. Doireann may not have pushed Roisin Carroll into the river, but somebody did.'

Once the garda had ushered Doireann back to her cell, Sionha said, 'Well... you saw for yourself how unstable she is. I think we need to have a psychiatric report, don't you, before we take her prosecution any further?'

'I agree. And I'll make sure that we keep a twenty-four-hour watch on her, too. I've come across young women like her before, who feel they have nothing to live for.'

Sionha folded up her spectacles and stood up. 'I think there are times when we all feel a bit like that, DS Maguire. When we're caught between the devil and the deep blue sea.'

31

Katie was sitting in the canteen with a cup of tea and a hand pie when Detective Inspector Fitzpatrick, Detective Cullen and Bill Phinner came looking for her.

The rain was trickling down the window beside her. She was reading the latest report on Oberstown Children's Detention Campus in Lusk, where seventeen-year-olds were sent by the courts these days instead of adult prisons. Last week there had been an outburst of serious violence there, including a stabbing in which a boy had lost one of his eyes – not at all like the TV comedy series *The Young Offenders*.

Eighteen months ago, in Cork, she had set up her own specialized team of young detectives to investigate juvenile crime, headed up by Detective Sergeant Alanna McPhail. So far they had made good progress in bringing down the incidence of petty theft and clashes between rival gangs and drug-peddling. But Katie was keen to know how well the young offenders were being rehabilitated, or if they were simply going to come strutting back from Lusk even more hardened and antisocial than they were when they went in.

'Sorry to interrupt your lunch, ma'am,' said Bill. 'I've heard back now from my team who've been searching James MacGreevy's house. So far they've come up with nothing that could possibly be bomb-related. Not even a clock or a box of matches.'

Katie raised an eyebrow. He was usually so miserable that she could always tell when he was feeling pleased with himself.

'You've come up with something, though, haven't you?'

Bill held up two printouts, one with rainbow-coloured stripes on it, and the other with three columns of figures. 'These here – these are the DNA tests on the sample of hairs that we clipped from MacGreevy's dog. We compared them with the hairs we found stuck to the parcel tape that was used in making the bomb. The probability that they belong to the same dog is ninety-nine point nine-nine per cent.'

'So – whoever planted it – it's almost certain that MacGreevy made it.'

'He's been downstairs for a while now, ready to be interviewed,' said Robert. 'He's called in his own solicitor, too, and no prizes for guessing who *that* is.'

'Don't tell me. Aidan O'Mahoney.'

Katie knew Aidan O'Mahoney well: he had a long record of defending Republican activists. It was in his blood. After the IRA had ambushed a detachment of British soldiers at Dripsey in 1921, his great-great-uncle Patrick O'Mahoney had been caught, tried, and executed by firing squad at Victoria Barracks, and the O'Mahoney family had nursed a grievance about it ever since – a grievance that had smouldered down the years like a peat fire, occasionally dying down but never completely going out.

'Go on, finish your pie, ma'am,' said Robert. 'We can wait.' But Katie pushed her plate away, picked up her purse and stood up.

'No, Robert. All of a sudden I have no appetite at all. This creature made a bomb that killed twelve innocent people and I want to talk to him face-to-face right now.'

When Katie and Robert and Detective Cullen entered the interview room, James MacGreevy was standing up and talking to his solicitor. MacGreevy was a burly man with tightly curled white hair and a bristling white moustache and a crimson face, his eyes bloodshot from drink. Aidan O'Mahoney, on the other hand, was slender and ivory-faced with shiny black hair parted in the centre, and he was wearing a dark grey three-piece suit. He looked as if he had stepped right out of a black-and-white photograph from the Easter Rising.

'Ah! *You!*' blustered James MacGreevy, pointing at Katie as soon as she walked in through the door. 'Three fecking hours I've been waiting here! Three fecking hours when I could have been tending me chrysanthemums!'

'Please sit down, Mr MacGreevy.'

'No, I will not sit down! What's this fecking nonsense all about, I'd like to know? I've been hauled in for what? "Offences against the State?" What "Offences against the State"? I'm a fecking market gardener! Since when has it been an offence against the state to grow tomatoes?'

'It's all right, James, I'll handle this,' said Aidan O'Mahoney, patting him on the shoulder.

'No! This is a fecking outrage! Hauling me in here and searching my house! This is a blatant invasion of me yooman rights! It's this woman, that's who it is! She's been in all the papers lately because she couldn't catch a dose of the garronarhea, let alone a criminal!'

'Please advise your client to sit down, Mr Mahoney,' said Katie, drawing up a chair. 'And please advise him to keep his language and his insults to himself.'

'I will in me ring, girl,' James MacGreevy retorted. 'Where's Fear first?'

'Fear?'

'Me dog. Why did you have to fetch him in, too? Who's

taking care of him? The poor gom's been suffering from the ear mites. If anything happens to him, I'm warning you.'

Katie opened up the file of reports on the School of Pharmacy bombing. 'Is that why you took him to see your son?' she asked, without looking up at him.

James MacGreevy scraped out a chair and sat down. 'How did you know that?'

'Because whatever your low opinion of my abilities, Mr MacGreevy, it's my business to know the movements of all the suspects in every investigation that I'm dealing with. Especially a serious investigation like this, in which there's been massive loss of life.'

'What the feck are you raving about, "massive loss of life"? I've just told you, girl. I'm a market gardener. The only massive loss of life that I'm responsible for is bindweed and aphids.'

'Please ask your client not to spit so much when he speaks, Mr O'Mahoney. You will have noticed that the District Court not only gave us the authority to bring in Mr MacGreevy's dog, but gave us permission to take hair samples from him.'

Aidan O'Mahoney's eyes narrowed. He had dealt with Katie before, and he knew that she never made accusations without having watertight evidence to back them up. 'May I ask where this is leading, Detective Superintendent?'

'It's leading to the conclusive proof we now have in our possession that your client was responsible for constructing the explosive device that was detonated two days ago at the UCC School of Pharmacy.'

'What proof?' James MacGreevy burst out. 'You don't have any fecking proof! Come on, I'm asking you, *what* proof? Found any explosive in me house, have you? Found anything at all that I could have used to make a bomb with? You've not, have you? You've found *squat*, that's what you've found! Squat and double-squat! I'll bet you pigs went trawling through me computer trying to see if there was any bomb-making information on there, but all you found there was the wholesale price of Delaway cabbage!'

'It was your client's dog, Mr O'Mahoney. He was right to call him Fear.'

'Oh, feck off. "Fear" only means "Man", you know that. And so what's me poor fecking dog got to do with it? Are you trying to tell me that *he* made the fecking bomb, and I told him how? Ever since he's had them ear mites he's been too busy scratching to dig up bones, leave alone make bombs.'

'I could have reserved this evidence until later, but if it'll stop your client from cursing then I'll share it with you now. Stray dog hairs were found by forensic experts stuck to adhesive tape in the remains of the UCC bomb. These have been shown by DNA testing to match beyond any reasonable doubt the hairs of Mr MacGreevy's dog.'

'What?' demanded James MacGreevy. 'Dog hairs? Are you fecking serious?'

'Totally. They also match hairs found by bomb disposal experts in Belfast in three other high-explosive devices – all of which were discovered and defused before they could be detonated, thank God.'

Aidan O'Mahoney said, 'I'll need to have sight of this so-called evidence myself, DS Maguire. I smell something here.'

'You can smell something? Semtex doesn't have a smell. Unlike the blown-up bodies of pharmacy students.'

'I smell a fix between you and the PSNI.'

'Oh, yes?'

'The PSNI have never been able to find out who made those three devices, have they? So my guess is that when they heard about this device, they got in touch with you, and between you you're trying to frame my client for making all of them. That would tie everything up pure neatly for the both of you, now wouldn't it?'

'If that's what you can smell, Mr O'Mahoney, I suggest you pay a visit to Mr MacGreevy's son the vet. He's sorted out Fear's ears. I'm sure he could sort out your nose.'

She turned to Robert and said, 'Charge him.'

Robert said, in his flattest voice, 'James Pearse MacGreevy, I am arresting you under the Offences Against the State Act for the construction of an explosive device, knowing that its purpose was to inflict multiple loss of life. You are not obliged to say anything unless you wish to do so, but anything you say will be taken down in writing and may be given in evidence.'

'Feck off over the wall,' said James MacGreevy. 'I'll give you fecking dog hairs, you *amadán*.'

32

After James MacGreevy had been charged and taken away, Katie and Robert found that Sergeant Murphy was waiting outside in the corridor for them.

'You need to come up and take a sconce at that Tivoli Park footage,' he told them. 'I can't be one hundred per cent sure, but if it shows what I think it shows, it's pure incriminating.'

They followed him up to the station's top floor, into the dim, hushed communications room. Six gardaí were sitting in front of the forty CCTV screens that covered Cork city from almost every angle, occasionally panning their cameras to track a shopper who was acting suspiciously, or focusing on a car driver's face. They could zoom in so close that they could read the titles of the books in Eason's shop windows, and the price tickets in Penneys.

They found Detective Sergeant Begley already peering at one of the screens – so intently that his nose was almost touching it. He was stopping the footage and backing it up and running it over and over again.

'Sean here's been trying to identify the fellow who planted the bomb in the pharmacy lab,' said Sergeant Murphy, and Detective Sergeant Begley sat back so that they could all see the screen.

'Here – this beige Volvo pulls up in front of the School of Pharmacy. There's the front view of it from the camera outside the AIB Bank just past Highfield West, and the back view of it from the camera outside the Bon Secours Hospital. Now this fellow gets out, opens up the boot and takes out a large cardboard box. The trouble is, his face is hidden first of all by the boot lid, and then he lifts the box on to his shoulder, so that you still can't clearly see what he looks like.

'He's wearing what looks like a black leather or nylon jacket and jeans. The receptionists said it was black leather but they couldn't be sure.'

'I'm assuming the car's number plate is false?' Katie asked him.

'It's a genuine Limerick County LK plate but it doesn't belong to that car. It was registered to a Kia that was stolen two years ago and never located.'

Detective Sergeant Begley froze the image of the man lifting the box on to his shoulder. 'There – between the boot lid and the box, before he closes the boot lid and turns around, you can just see part of his chin. Kind of cleft, like. I swear I recognize that chin, but I can't quite put a name to it. And there's something else, too. Look at the gatch on the fellow. Maybe it's the box he's carrying that makes him walk like that, but it seems to me like he's limping slightly, with his right foot turned outward. And *that* reminds me of somebody, too.'

'If you can put the chin together with the limp, maybe you'll be able to remember who he is,' said Robert.

'I'm wracking my brains, I'll tell you.'

'Well, keep wracking.'

Sergeant Murphy said, 'Let's leave aside the bombing for a moment, DS Maguire. Come and take a lamp at this.'

He ushered Katie over to the next room, where there was another bank of CCTV screens, with two gardaí operating them.

'Maura – would you run that Tivoli footage for us, please?'

'From the beginning, sir?'

'From the beginning, yes, but speed it up. I'll tell you when to go slo-mo.'

Katie sat down next to the garda. 'This is the footage from the house opposite Justice Quinn's?'

'That's right,' said Sergeant Murphy. 'Like I say, most of it is hours and hours of nothing at all. But you can see Justice Quinn taking his Jaguar out of his garage every morning and driving off, and then driving back again in the evening and putting it away. You can tell that it's his pride and joy, because he always puts it away, out of the rain, except when he fetches it out on Saturday and gives it a wash and a polish. The way he does it, it wouldn't surprise you if he gave it a kiss.'

Katie said, 'I don't see him coming out of his front door, so there must be access to the garage from inside the house.'

'Now and again you see his wife coming out and driving off in her Lexus. There, see – there she goes. Each time she's back about two or three hours later so she's probably been shopping or out for lunch. The only times you see Justice Quinn himself is at the weekends, when he comes out to sign a letter for the postman or take a sconce at his front garden. But now let's fast forward to that morning when he was murdered.'

The garda ran through the footage until she reached the day that Justice Quinn had died. As usual, the garage door was raised, and Justice Quinn's white Jaguar reversed out on to the drive. This time, though, the garage door remained open, and the Jaguar stopped on the drive with its engine running. Orla came out of the front door in a long white towelling dressing gown and a paisley headscarf and walked around the front of the car. As she did so, the driver's window was let down, and it could be seen that the driver was saying something to Orla and gesticulating with his right hand. Even though she now had her back to the camera, Orla seemed to be arguing with him, because she was raising both hands and making chopping gestures.

Katie said, 'Maura – could you pause it, please. No, back a bit. Back a little more. That's it, there.'

She leaned closer to the screen, although she had already seen what she needed to see. The driver of the Jaguar wasn't Garrett. It was a bald, pouchy-cheeked man with glasses, wearing what looked like an olive shawl-neck sweater. He reminded Katie of some comedian that she had never found funny.

'That's obviously not Justice Quinn,' said Sergeant Murphy. 'Do you reck him at all?'

Katie slowly shook her head. 'I've never seen him before. He looks like a bit of a gouger, though, don't you think? And how did he get into the house without the CCTV picking him up?'

'Maybe there's a back door. Maybe he'd been staying there for days. Who knows?'

'So where's Justice Quinn?'

'Take a screenshot, will you, Maura?' Sergeant Murphy asked the garda. Then, to Katie, 'Watch.'

Orla went back into the house and the Jaguar continued to reverse out of the driveway, bumping over the kerb as it went, so it was clearly not being driven by somebody who cared for it, or who was used to taking it out of Justice Quinn's driveway. It stopped for a few seconds in the road while the driver changed gear, and Sergeant Murphy said, 'That's it, freeze it there.'

Through the rear window of the Jaguar, it was just possible to see the silhouette of somebody sitting in the front passenger seat.

'See the recorded time here?' said Sergeant Murphy. 'It was less than twenty-three minutes between the Jaguar being driven away from Tivoli Park to the moment when those two officers heard the first explosion up at White's Cross. That means the passenger has to be Justice Quinn. It would have taken approximately fifteen minutes to drive from Tivoli Park to White's Cross – maybe a few minutes longer depending on the traffic. Then a few minutes more to shift Justice Quinn into the driver's seat, depending on his condition.'

Katie said, 'He wouldn't have gone voluntarily, that's for sure, and there's no way in the world that he would have let anybody else drive his precious car. Either he was threatened and he was under duress or else he was drugged and he was unconscious – or at the very least so doped-up that he was incapable of putting up any resistance.'

Sergeant Murphy nodded. 'It's not irrefutable proof, of course, but it all seems to fit, wouldn't you say? It looks like Mrs Quinn and this unidentified fellow conspired together to kill him.'

Katie thought of Orla saying, '*I should have divorced him, shouldn't I, years ago? But I could never think of it, Katie. I couldn't bear to think of us living apart. I loved him so much. I adored him.*'

She sat looking at the silhouette of Garrett's head in the passenger seat of his beloved Jaguar. Then she turned to Sergeant Murphy and said, 'I only pray that he was gone before they set his car on fire.'

Katie and Robert and Detective Sergeant Begley went back down to Katie's office.

'So what's the plan?' asked Robert.

Katie turned to Detective Sergeant Begley. 'Sean – you said you might have an inkling who that fellow is who planted the bomb in the pharmacy lab. If you give yourself some time, do you believe that it might come to you? Myself, I have a little leprechaun in my brain who's sitting there smoking and reading the paper and if I've forgotten anything like somebody's name I have only to ask him. Nine times out of ten he comes back after a while and gives me the answer.'

'I'm pretty certain it'll come to me, sure like,' said Detective Sergeant Begley. 'It's the way he walked, more than anything else. Like somebody with a gammy hip, do you know what I mean?'

'Right, then. In the meantime, can you tell Cullen and Walsh to contact the Facial Recognition unit and see if they can find a match for that fellow who was driving Justice Quinn's Jaguar.'

'Do you know, I have the distinct feeling that I've come across him before, too.'

'If you can remember who he is, all well and good, but you may not need to, and we may not need the AFR, either. Let's pay a visit to Orla Quinn. It's plain that she knows him, so maybe we can persuade *her* to tell us. Robert – can you see if Padragain Scanlan's free to come with us? And ask Superintendent Pearse for two uniforms to back us up. If what we saw in that CCTV footage is anything to go by, we'll be hauling her in for questioning, no doubt about it. I'll see you downstairs.'

Once Robert and Detective Sergeant Begley had left her office, Katie put on her shiny black raincoat with the pointed hood. It was starting to rain, and if Orla really had organized Garrett's murder, then she couldn't think of anything more appropriate to wear.

Although it was hard to draw any other conclusion from the CCTV footage, she still found it difficult to believe that

Orla would have wanted to harm him. She and Garrett had been married for such a long time, and her grief had seemed so genuine.

She went to tell Moirin that she was going out again, but she hadn't even reached her office door before her phone rang. She was tempted to leave it, but it kept on ringing so she went back and picked it up.

'DS Maguire.'

'Kathleen? It's Muireann.'

'What's the story, Muireann?'

'They're holding a big twenty-first birthday party tomorrow afternoon at The Weavers.'

'The O'Flynns, you mean?'

There was a lengthy silence, and Katie thought she could hear music in the background, and a man shouting. Then Muireann said, 'I've been warned off going. It seems like the Riordans are planning to mess it up, like.'

'When you say "mess it up"—'

'I don't know. I'm not sure, like. But it was Megan Riordan who told me not to go.'

'You and Megan Riordan – you're friends? I didn't know that.'

'We've seen each other around the city, now and again. But we met by accident at the Mercy this week and that was the first time we've been able to talk. We're both in the same boat, Kathleen – except that I'm staying with Tommy for a reason and she's stuck with Barry because he'll kill her if she tries to leave him.'

'All right, Muireann. What time is this party?'

'Two thirty it's supposed to start. I'm going mental trying to think up some excuse not to go. After what Megan told me, I have such a desperate feeling about what's going to happen there, I tell you. You know how much the Riordans hate the O'Flynns. They're sure that it was Tommy who paid Donal Hagerty to shoot Michael Riordan and his family. It's not Tommy I care about. I don't care a flying flea if they beat Tommy to a jelly. But there's so many other members of the family going to be there, like Maddie herself, whose party it is, and Maddie's a darling, so she is, and there'll be wains, too, and I don't want to see any of them hurt.'

'Listen, I'll think of a way to deal with this, I promise you.'

'But you'll let nothing happen to Megan? I'm fierce worried about her, Kathleen. If the guards show up, the first thing that Barry's going to think is that it was Megan who ratted on him – because how else could you have found out what he was planning? God alone knows what he might do to her. He smashed her nose the other day just because she wouldn't go out and buy him some beers. That's what she was doing in the Mercy, when I met her.

'If Barry gets even the slightest notion into his head that the tip-off came from her – she'll be lucky if she doesn't end up strangled and buried two metres deep in Glanmire bog.'

'I have you, Muireann. Find yourself some reason not to show up, that's all, and leave the rest to me.'

There was a click from Muireann's phone and the background music abruptly stopped. Katie said, 'Muireann? Muireann?' but she was gone.

By the time she came downstairs, Robert and Detective Sergeant Begley and Detective Scanlan were all waiting for her, as well as two uniformed gardaí, one male and one female. They hurried across the car park in the scattering rain and climbed into an unmarked Toyota and a squad car.

'It never rains but it lashes,' said Katie, as they crossed the Michael Collins Bridge and headed east towards Tivoli. 'And I'm not talking about the weather. I've just had Muireann Nic Riada on the phone.'

'Muireann Nic Riada? Now there's a girl with a nerve of steel, no mistake about that. How's she going on?'

Katie explained what Muireann had told her about the party at The Weavers, and Detective Sergeant Begley whistled and shook his head.

'Jesus. That might start out as nothing but a scrap but there'll be blood on the walls before you know it. Them Riordans and them O'Flynns – they've been champing at the bit lately. They're bursting to knock chunks out of each other.'

'I'm not going to give them the chance,' said Katie. 'The papers have slagged me off more than enough because I haven't yet stamped out all of the local gangs. Well, now's the time I'm going to do it, even if it means turning a blind eye to their so-called human rights. By the end of tomorrow I want to see Barry Riordan and his thugs behind bars, and by the end of next week I want to see Thomas O'Flynn and *his* thugs locked up. I don't care what the charges are. I'll make them up if I have to. Picking their noses in public, anything. And after the Riordans and the O'Flynns, I'm going to go after all the rest of them – the Romanians and the Nigerians and the Real IRA – even if I have to spend my whole year's budget in a month.'

Detective Sergeant Begley was driving, but he turned around and looked at Robert, who was sitting in the back seat behind Katie. He gave him a look that meant, *Holy Mary, have you ever heard DS Maguire talk like this before – like, ever? She's fuming!*

33

By the time they reached Tivoli Park, it was raining hard. They pulled up outside the Quinn house, and as they did so, Orla appeared at the front door, wearing a beige trench coat and opening up an umbrella.

Katie raised her witch's hood and walked quickly across to the porch.

'What are you doing here?' frowned Orla. 'What's that police car for?'

'We need to have a word with you, Orla. Can we go inside?'

'I'm on my way out. I have a hairdressing appointment and then lunch with my solicitor.'

'I'm afraid you'll have to cancel the hairdresser. You may need to see your solicitor, though. Not for lunch, but later.'

'What's this all about? I don't have to talk to you if I don't want to. Besides, I have nothing to say to you that I haven't said already.'

Katie had now been joined by Robert, Detective Sergeant Begley and Detective Scanlan. They stood behind her, impassively, with the rain pattering on to their shoulders.

Robert said, 'Even if you don't want to talk to us, Mrs Quinn, we'd appreciate it if we could come in out of the wet.'

Orla hesitated, but then she folded her umbrella and unlocked the front door. 'Come on inside, then. But take off your shoes, please. I don't want my carpet ruined.'

They took off their coats and prised off their shoes and followed Orla into the living room. She stood in front of the red-marble fireplace with her arms folded, her lips tightly pursed.

She didn't invite them to sit down on the large grey leather sofas. Behind her, on the mantelpiece, a framed photograph of Garrett was smiling cheerfully at the back of her head.

'We need you to tell us who was driving Garrett's car on the morning that he died,' said Katie.

'Garrett, of course. Who else?'

'Well, no, he wasn't. And we have evidence that he wasn't.'

'What evidence?'

'We have CCTV footage that plainly shows another man sitting in the driving seat of Garrett's car. Not only that, it shows you coming out of the house and talking to this man before he drives off.'

'I don't believe you.'

'I think a judge will believe us when we show that footage in court.'

'I've no comment to make. I know what you gardaí are like. You'll tell any kind of lies to coax a false confession out of people. And then you'll conveniently lose all the proof that you lied, the same as you did with Sergeant McCabe and Lynn Margiotta and Majella Moynihan.'

'Orla, there's no doubting this footage. It's as clear as day. I'm asking you now to tell me who was driving Garrett's car on the morning that he died.'

'I've no comment.'

'All right, you've no comment. But we have a screenshot of this fellow's face and even if you won't tell us who he is, it won't take us long to identify him, and then we can ask *him* why he was driving Garrett's car.'

'I still have nothing to say. I'm not going to let you trap me into admitting something that I haven't done.'

'Garrett was sitting in the front passenger seat that morning, wasn't he?'

'No comment.'

'It must have been him, because he was found in his burned-out car at White's Cross only half an hour later. But why would he agree to be a passenger in his own car? Was he threatened? Or did he not agree at all? Was he drugged? Or was he knocked unconscious?'

'No comment.'

'Orla, you told me how devastated you were by Garrett's death. But you did also tell me that you resented his affairs. Is that what this was all about? Were you trying to teach him a lesson but it went too far? Did you hire this fellow simply to frighten him, or to give him a bit of a beating maybe, by way of punishment?'

Orla looked down at the floor and said nothing.

'If it wasn't your intention that Garrett should be killed, Orla, you'll have at least something to tell a court in mitigation. But you do need to co-operate with us, and tell us exactly what you expected to happen. You also need to tell us who the fellow was who drove Garrett away.'

Orla looked up.

'Can I speak to you alone, Kathleen?' she asked. She didn't seem at all abashed, more impatient, and it sounded like more of a demand than a request. Not only that, but Katie had never heard her call her by her name before now.

Katie turned to Robert and Detective Sergeant Begley and Detective Scanlan. 'Sure,' she said. 'If you three wouldn't mind waiting in the car for a while.'

The three of them laced up their shoes again and shrugged on their coats and went out into the rain. Once they had closed the front door behind them, Katie said, 'So, Orla – what is it that you can only tell me in private?'

Orla took down the photograph of Garrett. She gave it a wry, regretful shake of her head before she carefully placed it back on the mantelpiece, next to a photograph of her daughter and two sons. 'I don't know why I keep this picture. I suppose it reminds me that we did have some good times, on and off, in between the arguments, and in between the other women.'

'Did you arrange to have him killed? Is that what you wanted to tell me?'

'Of course not. Like I said to you before, I've no comment to make about that. What I wanted you to know is that one day about five or six years ago I threatened to throw Garrett out of the house and divorce him. I told him that I'd only change my mind on one condition. He would have to confess to me all the times that he'd been unfaithful, and beg for my forgiveness, and swear on our children's lives that he'd never be unfaithful ever again.'

'But he broke that promise? Is that why you wanted to punish him?'

'No. That's neither here nor there. What I'm telling you is that he described to me every one of his affairs in every detail. The women's names, their ages, the places they met. Whether they were single or married. He told me he'd made two of them pregnant, and that he'd arranged for the both of them to travel to the UK to have abortions.'

'Oh, God. I'm hardly surprised that you felt resentful.'

'That's not what I'm trying to say to you. That was all part of his mortification, yes. But it was what he told me about *you* that I'm getting at.'

'I don't understand.'

'I'm sure you will if I say the name Phinean Joyce.'

Katie stared at her. 'Garrett told you about Phinean Joyce? Why would he have done that?'

'I suppose because he was proud of how much he helped you. As I understand it, you would never have been promoted to detective superintendent if Phinean Joyce hadn't been convicted. The beast who was supposed to have raped and murdered the wife of Cork's incumbent Lord Mayor?'

'What do you mean by "supposed to"? He did. There was a rake of evidence to convict him.'

'Oh, really? That's not what Garrett told me. Garrett told me that you suspected Phinean Joyce only because the council had refused him planning permission for a factory extension. Because of that he'd warned the Lord Mayor that he'd regret it for the rest of his days.'

'That's partly true, yes. But what he actually said was that he would personally make sure that the Lord Mayor's life was hell on earth. He even threatened him in a signed letter.'

'Well, whatever. But a threat isn't evidence, is it? And the only witness who was supposed to have seen Phinean Joyce leaving the Lord Mayor's house on the night of the murder was a well-known local drunk and a fantasist.'

'There was forensic evidence, too.'

'Oh, yes. A single footprint in the hallway that matched one of Phinean Joyce's shoes – even though they were loafers from Schuh and half of the middle-aged men in Cork walk around in loafers from Schuh.'

'Orla – there was a deep and distinctive cleft in that footprint. It was unique.'

'Unique enough for you to arrest Phinean Joyce on that evidence alone and charge him with rape and murder. No semen sample, no bruising, no fibres, no fingerprints on the poker that the poor woman was beaten to death with.'

'The footprint was enough.'

'Obviously. After only a three-day trial His Honour Mr Justice Garrett Quinn directed the jury to find Phinean Joyce guilty, without letting them know that he and Detective Inspector Kathleen Maguire were lovers. The Central Criminal Court didn't know about their affair, and the Garda didn't know, and the press didn't know. Nobody knew but the two of them – until His Honour Mr Justice Garrett Quinn confessed it to his wife years later by way of atonement.'

'It was Phinean Joyce who raped and killed the Lord Mayor's wife, nobody else.'

'Oh, really?'

'Fair play to you, Orla, the witness who saw him coming out of the Lord Mayor's front door had downed a few scoops, I'll admit, but his description was totally accurate, right down to the corduroy cap that he was wearing. It would have made no difference if our relationship had come to light.'

'Oh, but you're so wrong there. It *would* have made all the difference in the world. If your affair had come to light then Phinean Joyce would have been able to appeal for that reason alone. But of course he suffered a stroke after only six weeks in jail, which rendered him speechless and unable to lodge an appeal, and less than a year after that he passed away. Detective Inspector Kathleen Maguire, on the other hand, was feted for her detective work and promoted to detective superintendent – the first female detective superintendent in Cork.'

Katie stood silent for a while. She could see herself reflected in the mirror over the fireplace, and the back of Orla's head with its coronet of tightly braided hair, as if the two of them were figures in a surrealist painting by René Magritte.

Orla said, 'I can't imagine that you're so dim that you haven't caught on to why I'm telling you this. If you arrest me and try to charge me with anything relating to Garrett's death, I'll find myself obliged to make it known that he was having an affair with you when he was hearing the charges against Phinean Joyce, and that you would never have been promoted if Garrett hadn't convicted him.'

Katie wasn't sure how to respond to that. She felt a surge of anger at Orla's superior attitude, and she was tempted to say that Garrett wouldn't have needed to seek out the comfort of other women if she had been anything like the perfect wife that she clearly imagined herself to be.

Her first instinct was to tell Orla to do her worst. She was sure that Phinean Joyce's conviction had been sound. In the footprint that Bill Phinner's technicians had found on the parquet flooring in the Lord Mayor's hallway, there had been a fish-hook shaped cleft, and this had exactly matched a nick in the sole of Phinean Joyce's left loafer. Plenty of other criminals had been convicted on evidence as slight as that.

Apart from the footprint, no other forensic evidence had been found to confirm Phinean Joyce's presence in the house, but he had been unable to give Katie and her detectives a plausible explanation of where he had been on the night of the murder. In fact, he had given them three different explanations, and every one of them had turned out to be a lie. Along with his repeated threats to make the Lord Mayor's life 'hell on earth', both verbal and written, that evasiveness had been sufficient to send him down.

Katie began to say, 'Come here to me, Orla—' but then she abruptly stopped herself. What if Orla carried out her threat, and *did* reveal that she had been having an affair with Garrett during Phinean Joyce's trial? Brendan of all people would go for it like a hungry mongrel. He would have no compunction about reporting her both to Assistant Commissioner Frank

Magorian and the Garda Ombudsman, and immediately suspending her from duty, pending a full investigation. He might use it as an excuse to demote her, or even to sack her altogether.

Sure, she could retaliate by reporting him for rape and sexual harassment, but if she did that she would be in danger of looking like a slut who was simply trying to justify her own lack of morals. Brendan would have only to say, 'Ah come on, she gave me the impression that she was crying out for it,' and her counter-accusation would stand no chance at all of being believed. In the notorious case when Garda Majella Moynihan had come within a hair's breadth of being dismissed from the force for having a baby out of wedlock, the garda who had made her pregnant had only been cautioned and fined £90. An Garda Síochána was still a man's world.

And Katie couldn't help thinking of the consequences, not only for her career but for preventing crime in Cork. If she were suspended, she would no longer be able to go after Thomas O'Flynn and Barry Riordan and all the other Cork gangs she wanted to rout out. She would also be forced to abandon every other case that she was working on, like the Lee Pusher, and the fatal stabbing in the Zombie Lounge.

Not only that, she would have to abandon her investigation into Garrett's murder, and that would cause her more grief than anything else. After all these years and everything that had happened, she still loved the memory of him, and he had still been wearing her claddagh band when he died.

'I'll tell you, Orla, you can threaten me all you like,' she said, trying to sound calm. 'But the Phinean Joyce trial was years ago now, and you'll be fierce hard put to prove that Garrett and I were involved with each other, especially now that he's no longer here to be questioned about it. On top of that, you're bound to be asked why it took you so long to report it, if you thought it was such a desperate miscarriage of justice.'

'Don't fool yourself, Kathleen. There's bound to be some evidence that you and he were having an affair. Emails, hotel receipts. *Billets-doux.*'

'If I were you, I'd be considering your own defence before you start worrying about mine. You know that we'll identify that fellow who was driving Garrett's car. And sooner rather than later.'

'Good luck to you is all I can say.'

'Well, until we do, I have nothing further to ask you. That's unless you change your mind and want to volunteer some information about who that fellow was and what he was up to.'

'I do not.'

'I'm not going to arrest you today, but I have to advise you not to leave Cork for the time being. I'll be needing to question you again.'

'You can question me until you're purple in the face, Kathleen, but whether I'll be giving you any answers, that's a different matter altogether. I'm a lawyer and I know my rights. And what I said to you will still apply. If you try to accuse me of having anything at all to do with Garrett's death, just remember the name of Phinean Joyce.'

Katie was close to telling Orla that she wasn't going to give in to blackmail, but she closed her mouth tightly and kept it closed. Without saying anything else, she went out to the hallway, tugged on her rushers and buttoned up her raincoat, and opened the front door. Outside the rain was still pelting down – harder than it had rained for weeks.

Orla followed her out on to the porch and watched her as she hurried across to her waiting car. By the time Katie had climbed into the passenger seat, though, and turned around, she had gone back inside and closed the front door behind her.

'So what was that all about?' asked Robert. 'Will we not be taking her in?'

'We will, but not yet. She refuses to co-operate and so far we don't have enough evidence to arrest her.'

'We have the CCTV.'

'Yes, but she knows her legal onions and who knows what story she could come up with? She could say that fellow was a motor mechanic who'd come to fix Justice Quinn's car – or maybe some acquaintance of his that she'd never met before, and he was letting him have a go driving it. Until we find him, Robert, we'll have to put it on the long finger.'

'I'll bet you twenty-two to one that herself had a hand in Justice Quinn getting cremated,' said Detective Sergeant Begley. 'In fact, I'll bet you she paid the fellow to do it. But what if we never find him? He could have left the country by now.'

'Don't be a pessimist, Sean. Just because the sea is full of herring, that doesn't mean you can't catch the one herring you're after.'

'Who said that?'

'I did.'

34

As soon as she returned to Anglesea Street, Katie convened a meeting with Superintendent Pearse and Inspector O'Rourke, as well as Sergeant Mullally and three other officers of the station's armed response unit. They sat in a circle in the squad room while the rain continued to gurgle in the gutters outside. It was so gloomy they had to switch the lights on.

Katie explained to them what Muireann had told her about the O'Flynns' twenty-first birthday party, and how the Riordans were planning to invade it and 'mess it up'.

'Holy Saint Peter,' said Inspector O'Rourke. 'If I know Barry Riordan, and his idea of "messing things up", him and his gang will be charging in there armed to the back teeth.'

'Ah you're spot on there, sir,' said Sergeant Philip Mullally. At forty, he was the oldest of the armed response unit, but fit and tense and muscular with a bald, bullet-shaped head and a nose that looked as if it were being pressed hard against an upstairs window. 'This is going to be sheer bloody revenge for Micky Riordan and his family, you mark my words. They'll be doing a whole lot worse than throwing sponge cake around.'

'What I'm desperately anxious to avoid is a three-way gunfight between the Riordans, the O'Flynns, and us,' said Katie. 'That's obviously my main concern, but there's another consideration, too. When we show up, Barry Riordan is bound to realize that we must have been tipped off, and the first person he's going to suspect is his wife, Megan. He treats her badly enough, always beating her, and he'll probably assume that she did it to get her own back on him – which of course is partly why she did.

'Not only that, but Muireann will have made an excuse not to be there, and there's a strong possibility that Thomas O'Flynn will want to know why. It's vital that neither of those women are put at risk, especially Muireann. She's an invaluable informant when it comes to the O'Flynns, even though I've told her time and time again that she's putting herself at fierce grave risk.'

'I don't see there's too much we can do about that,' said Sergeant Mullally. 'We've been given the advance information so we can't ignore it. We *have* to show up, or else it's going to be a massacre. There's going to be innocent women and kids there, and we can't risk any of them being hurt – or killed, even, God forbid. Surely we can offer this Muireann and this Megan witness protection afterwards, can't we?'

'We could,' Katie told him. 'But Muireann has a compelling reason for wanting to stay with Thomas O'Flynn. And I'm not sure that either of them would ever feel safe, even if we did give them protection. According to Muireann, Megan won't walk out on Barry Riordan because she's convinced that he would find her and kill her if she did, no matter where she went.'

Inspector O'Rourke raised his hand like a boy at school who knows all the answers. 'I hope I'm not being presumptuous here, ma'am, but I have the distinct feeling that you've thought up some way of getting around this particular problem.'

'I have, Francis. And that's to arrange it so that the O'Flynns don't hold their party in The Weavers at all.'

'How in the name of Jesus can we do that? And even if we can – what's Barry Riordan going to think if he and his gang show up at The Weavers all ready to do battle and there's no sign of the O'Flynns? He's going to know at once that somebody's ratted on them. He may have no proof that it was his wife – but like you say, he'll probably blame her anyway.'

'Well, you're right,' said Katie. 'But you remember the Bord Gáis barriers that we put up in the street when the School of Pharmacy was bombed? That's what gave me this idea. What we do is, we send two officers to The Weavers early tomorrow morning wearing jackets that we've borrowed from Bord Gáis. They'll be carrying false identity cards to show that they're emergency response gas fitters.'

'Okay... I think I see where you're going with this.'

'Our two fake fitters will tell the landlord that there's been a strong smell of natural gas detected in the street and that there's a suspected mains leak right outside their front door. Remember that this part of the city still has the old cast-iron gas pipes. The fitters will say that there's a serious risk of an explosion, which might even demolish the whole pub. After that they'll put up the barriers and they dig up the pavement. The landlord will have to contact the O'Flynns and tell them that their party is either cancelled or postponed or that they'll have to hold it somewhere else.'

'And what happens when the Riordans roll up?' asked Inspector O'Rourke.

'Give them a count of ten after they go bursting into the pub, Philip, and then you and your unit go in after them. Michael – your officers can deal with any vehicles that they've left outside in the street, can they not? It's vital that we give the impression that we've been called to the incident by one of The Weavers' staff, or by some bystander in the street. This must never look like a set-up.'

'Right,' said Superintendent Pearse. 'I'll get the Bord Gáis side of it sorted. I know Denis O'Halloran, the area manager, so that won't be any problem. I beat him at golf last week and he still owes me seventy-five yoyos.'

'We can follow Barry Riordan all the way from his home in Farranree tomorrow,' added Inspector O'Rourke. 'Pure discreetly, though. We want to make sure that we catch him *in flagrante* this time. Those cute lawyers of his have managed to get him off too often. Either that, or they always slip his judges a backhander or two.'

'Do you know, I've wondered that myself more than once,' said Robert. 'If any of our judges can be bought, like, or blackmailed.'

He looked across at Katie but there was no expression on his face and no hint of a question in his voice. Katie thought: *Stop feeling guilty. And stop thinking about Garrett, and the way he smiled at you across the courtroom as soon as he had directed the jury to find Phinean Joyce guilty of rape and murder.*

When she returned to her office, Katie found Detective O'Donovan and Dr Ailbe Power waiting for her. Dr Power was wearing a plain grey tweed suit but a strong musky perfume and a pair of dangly crystal earrings.

'What's the story, doctor?' she asked her. 'How did you make out with Doireann?'

'Oh, dear Lord, she's one tragic individual, that girl.'

'But she opened up to you all right?'

'Oh yes. But, like I say, tragic. She fits almost exactly the stereotype that I was telling you about before – the person who always feels that they're excluded from society for one reason or another. She believes that her height and her appearance will always make it impossible for her to find love and be happy. That's why she's been so determined to make sure that nobody else could be happy, either.'

Katie said, 'Is she still insistent that she didn't drown that Roisin Carroll?'

'Totally.'

'Do you think there's a reason for that? She freely confessed to the first six murders, and we have an eyewitness who saw her push Roisin Carroll into the river.'

They sat down on the couches under the windows and Moirin came in to ask them if they would like coffee or tea. Katie couldn't help noticing that the hooded crows were still crowded on the rooftop opposite. Usually, when it was raining as hard as this, they flew off to find shelter under the roof of the Merchants Quay car park. When they stayed, it almost always meant trouble.

'I questioned her again and again, using several different approaches. First I was gentle with her, and sympathetic. Then I was remote and made out that I wasn't particularly interested in what she had to say. That technique often works with psychopathic subjects like her. No matter how much they say they hate the world, and don't care about it, they're desperate to be heard and understood.'

'What results did you get from that?'

'Only the same answer again and again. "I pushed the first six into the river, but not the seventh." "I wasn't there on that afternoon, I swear it. I was tucked up in bed with the terrible cramps."'

'So where did you take it from there?'

'I really gave her down the banks. You were *seen*! I told her. You were seen by the old fellow who saved that poor woman's baby from drowning! Do you seriously think he wouldn't recognize you? In fact, I got so angry with her that her solicitor told me to ease off and treat her more gentle. But of course I was only putting it on. I was trying to rile her into shouting back at me. I wanted to provoke her into admitting that yes, she *had* pushed Roisin Carroll into the river, and she was only denying it to show the rest of the world that she could stick up two fingers to us and there was nothing we could do about it.'

'But if that's the way she felt, why didn't she deny the other six murders? Why only that one?'

'That's exactly what I asked myself, DS Maguire. Why only that one? And with that one, there was an interesting anomaly. All of the other times she'd pushed somebody into the river, she'd done it at a different location. But this one was at precisely the same spot as the previous incident – The Marina, midway between the rowing club and the park.'

'Did you ask her about that?'

'I did, and again she insisted that it wasn't her. She was adamant that she'd always chosen a different location to push people in, and she had a reason for that. She wanted the people of Cork to come to believe that nowhere along the riverbank was safe. Living by the Lee is one of the things that makes Corkonians happy, she said. It was her intention to make them dread the river, to the point where they might even move away from Cork altogether. She said she wanted the Lee to be more frightening than the Styx.'

'What's your professional opinion, then? That it really wasn't her who killed Roisin Carroll?'

Dr Power was about to carry on, but hesitated, and looked across at Detective O'Donovan as if she wasn't sure what she should say next.

'It's okay, doctor,' he told her. 'You're grand altogether.

You can tell DS Maguire about it. I don't think she'll be after giving you a hard time for it.'

'If you're sure,' said Dr Power. 'What I did was kind of illegal, and it certainly wouldn't stand up in court. The thing was, Doireann's solicitor asked if we could have a five-minute break because she needed to use the toilet and make a couple of phone calls to her office. So while she was out of the room, I hypnotized Doireann.'

'You *hypnotized* her? You can actually do that?'

'I did a study on hypnosis at Trinity a couple of years ago. I was trying to evaluate how effective it is as a medical treatment. At the time I interviewed several famous stage hypnotists like Keith Barry and I also talked to Martin Keiller, who runs a hypnosis clinic here in Cork. Between them they taught me how to put people under, and it's not as difficult as you might think.'

'You're absolutely right, though, about it being "kind of illegal",' Katie told her. 'We have fierce strict rules about questioning suspects. Only two gardaí are allowed to question a suspect at any one time, and only three are allowed altogether into the interview room. Hypnosis – well, that's totally out of the question. Even if Doireann admitted under hypnosis that she'd pushed a hundred more victims into the river, as well as fifty dogs and ten babies, I couldn't possibly use that as evidence. Quite apart from the fact that her solicitor was out of the room.'

'I told her to fix her attention on one of my earrings, and she went under just like that,' said Dr Power, snapping her fingers. 'But – she wouldn't admit to killing anybody else. In fact, she stuck to her original story, word for word.'

'You don't think she was codding you? You know – pretending to be hypnotized?'

'No, she was in a deep hypnotic trance, no doubt about it. I asked her to tell me two or three intimate details about herself, and when she came out of the trance she couldn't remember telling me at all. In my opinion, Doireann did *not* push Roisin Carroll into the Lee. Whoever it was, it wasn't her.'

'It seems like we could be looking for a copycat killer,' said Detective O'Donovan. 'But a copycat killer who didn't copy close enough. He didn't realize that Doireann always picked a different stretch of the river to push her victims in.'

Katie sat back. She sipped at her cappuccino, and then she said, 'What do you think, then? We have another local psychopath who's bitterly jealous that the rest of the world is happy and they're not? Or do we?'

'It's a strong possibility, sure,' said Dr Power. 'He or she must have read about it in the news or seen it on TV and thought – "This is how I can get my revenge on the world but somebody else can take the blame for it."'

'But if it really wasn't Doireann, there must have been *some* differences in his or her appearance,' said Katie. 'We may be talking about the doonchiest detail. Maybe a curl of hair, peeking out from underneath the hoodie, or a ring on the pusher's fingers. I think we need to go right back to square one and interview our witness again. This time, though, with much greater care. In fact, I have an idea. If you're willing, Dr Power, perhaps you could come along with us and listen to us question him. And then, if it's appropriate—'

Katie put down her cup and made a hypnotist's gesture with both hands.

'You mean put him under?'

'Maybe he'll be able to recall some detail that he couldn't visualize the first time we talked to him. He was in a desperate state of shock, remember. He'd seen a woman drown and he'd jumped into the freezing cold river himself to rescue her baby. And he's over eighty years old.'

'All right,' said Dr Power slowly. 'I'm willing to give it a try. So long as you realize that I can't guarantee the veracity of anything your man might tell us, and it won't be admissible in court. And so long as I don't get my name in the papers. I have a serious academic reputation to uphold, and I don't think the Provost of Trinity College would be very approving if he found out that I'd been using a stage act to help the Cork Garda to track down a murderer. Or the Dean of Health Sciences, for that matter.'

35

Before she left the station, Katie rang Kyna to make sure that she had fully recovered. Kyna was back at her flat now, 'and I'm all snuggled up with Merrow my one-eyed cat and a mug of hot chocolate'.

'Will you be fit to come in tomorrow? I'll be needing you so.'

Katie told her about the O'Flynns' birthday party, and the plan that she had been devising to ambush the Riordans.

'Oh, my God. I'll be there for that, Katie, don't you worry. Besides that – well, besides that – I miss you.'

'I miss you, too. I'm so glad you're feeling better.'

She hung up and headed for the door, but before she could reach it, her phone rang. *Mother of God. Please don't land me with another crisis. It's a quarter to seven and I'm shattered and all I want to do is get home to Barney and Foltchain.*

She went back to her desk, picked up her phone, and snapped, 'Yes? What do you want? I'm finished for the day.'

But a deep warm voice said, 'Katie? It's Kieran – Kieran Connolly. How are you going on? I've been waiting to hear from you.'

'Kieran... I'm so sorry. Moirin did pass me your message but I haven't had a second to myself.'

'I was only wondering if you'd be free for dinner this evening. If you're too tired, there's no bother, we could always make it another day. Sunday, maybe, or one day next week. I've had you on my mind and it would be grand to see you again.'

Katie closed her eyes for a moment out of sheer relief.

'I'm a little weary, Kieran, to tell you the truth. But if you don't mind my nodding off halfway through the soup, I'd love to come for dinner. I feel like there's a whole circus going on inside of my head, elephants and clowns and all, and it would be heaven to fold up the big top and forget about it, if only for a few hours.'

'I'll pick you up in five minutes, then.'

'Make it ten. I need to fix my face. I've been out in the rain today and I look like I've seen a ghost.'

She went into her toilet, switched on the light over the washbasin, and stared at herself. She was wearing no make-up apart from her blotchy mascara, and so she did look pale and freckly and vulnerable. All the same, she recognized that hard, determined stare in her sea-green eyes – the stare that she always gave to the world when she was stressed. Her late husband, Paul, had called it 'that fecking ice-pick look'.

She smoothed on some light foundation and blusher for her cheekbones, brushed some fresh mascara on her lashes, and combed out her short, dark red bob. By the time she had given herself a finishing squirt of Flowerbomb, she felt composed and pretty and ready to take on anything, including Mr Justice Kieran Connolly.

Kieran took her to Greenes restaurant, behind Hotel Isaacs in MacCurtain Street, on the north side of the River Lee. It was busy and warm, and they sat by one of the floor-to-ceiling windows at the back, overlooking the courtyard, so that Katie could see that it was still raining hard.

'You know, sometimes we need to get away and think about something else apart from law and order,' said Kieran, picking up the menu. Katie noticed for the first time that he had a zigzag scar over his left eye. *Maybe he's a wizard. Maybe he's Cian, the shape-shifter. Maybe he's Conor, come back to me in a different form. No, stop thinking like that, because you'll well up with tears if you start thinking about Conor, and make a mess of your mascara.*

Kieran put down the menu, reached across the table and took hold of Katie's wrist. 'I know all about grief and grieving, Katie. When you lose somebody you love you never get over it, no matter what people tell you about time being the great healer. That's total shite, if you'll forgive me for saying so. If anything, time makes it hurt all the more. When my ma died, I felt like I'd left her abandoned on a train station platform, while my train pulled away, and all I could do was look out the window and watch her getting smaller and smaller until she disappeared into the distance.'

He beckoned the waitress, and said, 'Let's start with a couple of glasses of champagne. I don't know what we're celebrating. Maybe it's the start of a long-lasting friendship.'

Katie couldn't help smiling. Kieran was the first man she had met in a long time who had neither been trying to come on to her nor to belittle her.

Although they had agreed not to spend the evening talking about their work, Katie gave him a quick update on the major cases that her team was investigating. They were still front-page news, after all – the bombing at the School of Pharmacy more than any other story, but the arrest of the Lee Pusher, too.

'And how about Justice Quinn? Are you any nearer to finding out who might have done for poor Garrett?'

Katie thought for a while, and then she said, 'Can I tell you something in the strictest confidence? I can't discuss this with anybody else – not at the station, anyway. You already know what my situation is with Chief Superintendent O'Kane. To say that we have our horns locked – well, that would be an understatement. And Frank Magorian – well, he's been supportive in the past, now and again, but if I were to lose my job I don't think he'd be reaching for the man-sized Kleenex.'

'Ah yes,' said Kieran. 'Stephen Herlihy at the courthouse gave me a hint about your problems with Chief Superintendent O'Kane. He didn't know all the whys and the wherefores, but he told me that one minute your man couldn't be too complimentary about you, saying that you were too glam to be a garda. The next he was calling you worse than a *cailleach feasa,* and it was a pity we didn't still burn witches at the stake.'

'That just about sums it up, I'd say. I won't bore you with all the reasons why Brendan's turned against me, because they're pure personal, and not really relevant. But let me tell you about this dilemma I'm facing at the moment. As I say – I can't ask anybody else, but maybe you'd be willing to give me the benefit of some of your judgely advice.'

The waitress had approached their table. 'Before you tell me all the gory details,' said Kieran, 'let me recommend the Ballyhoura mushroom risotto.'

'You read my mind. The last thing I feel like at the moment is anything with blood in it.'

'But I'll have the Skeaghanore duck, crispy on the outside, rare in the middle. That won't put you off, will it?'

Once they had ordered, Katie leaned forward over the table and quietly told Kieran about Orla Quinn's threat to reveal that she and Garrett had been lovers during the Phinean Joyce trial.

'We've not yet been able to identify the fellow who drove off with Garrett that morning, but it's hard not to make the assumption that Orla arranged for him to punish Garrett in some way – maybe even paid him to do it. I wouldn't say for certain that she intended for the fellow to kill him. Maybe Garrett fought back and it all went pear-shaped and that was how the fellow thought that he'd get rid of the evidence. I never believe in coming up with too many suppositions. The truth almost always turns out to be a whole lot stranger.'

'If she hadn't threatened you, would you have arrested Orla Quinn? Or at least taken her in to ask her some more questions?'

'Arrested her? I suppose I could have, based on the CCTV footage. But even if she hadn't threatened me, I probably would have waited until we'd located the fellow in the driving seat. I need to know who he is, and what his relationship is with Orla, and what he has to say for himself about driving off with Garrett. But I would have taken her in for questioning... yes. She's a lawyer herself and she knows her rights, but underneath all that she's a passionate and angry woman, and I wonder how long she'd be able to keep that bottled up.'

Kieran said, 'I think you made the right decision, though. Why jeopardize your whole future career because you made one historic lapse of judgement? We all make mistakes, even us judges. Yes – you should have declared your relationship to Justice Quinn before Phinean Joyce was sent for trial. But equally so should Justice Quinn. In fact, more so, because he was responsible for handing down the sentence. But he's dead now, so he can't be censured, and Phinean Joyce is dead, too, so he can't be retried.

'Katie – your value to this community in terms of what you do for keeping the peace, it's beyond measure. If you're suspended, or sacked, then the Cork Garda are going to lose all your experience, all your talent, and most of all they're going to lose one of the few people who can drag them out of the masonic lodges and the golf club bars and into the open, where they're accountable for everything they do.'

'That sounded like a summing-up,' said Katie.

'It was, in a way,' Kieran told her, and he banged the table with the handle of his knife as if it were a gavel. '"Detective Superintendent Kathleen Maguire, on this occasion I find that the charges that you've levelled against yourself are unproven. You're free to go, but only after you've finished your risotto. And I hope you'll be wanting some chocolate pecan torte to finish up with. And one more glass of champagne."'

They spent the rest of their dinner talking about Kieran's passion for sailing, both cruising and racing. He was a member of the Clontarf Yacht Club and he promised to take Katie out on his yacht when she could find the free time to come up to Dublin.

'No offence meant,' she told him. 'But I hope that'll be later rather than sooner.'

Kieran rang for a Satellite taxi, and then they left Greenes to stand under the arch that led to MacCurtain Street to wait for its arrival. It was still pouring with rain and the street was sparkling wet.

'I hope I haven't kept you up too late,' said Kieran. 'How long will it take you to drive home?'

'No more than twenty minutes, this time of night. I have to take my dogs out for their last hurrah when I get back, although they can't expect anything more than a short high-speed hod when it's bucketing like this.'

'We had a dog, when I was a boy. You'll never guess what we called him.'

Katie looked up at him. His height and his masculinity made her feel physically protected, but he was so relaxed and so amiable, and that was why she found him attractive – that, and his understanding that all she needed so soon after losing Conor was support, and friendship, and somebody with whom she could occasionally become tearful.

'So what did you call him, this dog?' she asked him – but before he could answer she saw two men crossing the street towards them from the entrance to Dan Lowrey's pub, directly opposite.

It was the quick, jerky way that these two men were walking that caught her attention. Both wore black nylon puffer jackets and baseball caps. One had spectacles and the other had wraparound sunglasses, and both had scarves covering the lower half of their faces. When they were halfway across the road, she saw that the one with spectacles was pulling something out of his pocket.

'*Kieran!*' she screamed, and she kicked at the back of his legs with an *ashi barai* foot sweep. He fell heavily backwards on to the cobbles underneath the arch and Katie dropped on top of him to make sure that he didn't lift his head. As they fell, she heard two sharp cracks, and the framed Greenes' menu on the wall beside them was shattered, showering them with sharp fragments of glass.

She heard one more crack, and a man shouting, followed almost immediately by the slithering sound of a car pulling up. The car's doors were slammed, and then it roared away. It must have driven through a red light at the junction with Summerhill because she heard an angry barrage of horns blowing.

She looked up cautiously, and then sat up. Kieran sat up, too, rubbing the back of his head where it had knocked against the cobbles. Two of the waitresses came out of Greenes, followed by the manager, and several passers-by came across the street to see if they had been hurt.

'Are you all right?' Katie asked Kieran.

Kieran brushed bits of glass from the front of his coat. 'I think so. Jesus – those fellows were trying to kill us, weren't they?'

They both climbed awkwardly on to their feet. A young man came up to them and said, 'I seen it all, like. That feen was only shooting at you. You was dead lucky you fell over like that, or else you could have been dead, like.'

A middle-aged man came up behind him, with a gravy-stained napkin still tucked into the front of his sweater. 'They shot a hole clean through the window of Cask's, right next door there. It was pure chance there was nobody sitting there.'

'Did you see the car they got away in?' asked Katie.

'Silver, it was. Range Rover or something like it.'

'You didn't see its number plate?'

'Don't even think it had one, to be honest with you.'

Katie took out her phone and rang the station. As she was waiting to be answered, Kieran laid his hand on her shoulder and said, 'You saved my life there, Katie. God in Heaven, you saved *both* of our lives.'

'Sergeant O'Farrell? This is DS Maguire. I'm outside Hotel Isaacs on MacCurtain Street. There's been a shooting here, not three minutes ago. At *me*, would you believe, and Justice Connolly. No, nobody hurt. No. But the shooters left the scene in a silver car, heading east along the Lower Glanmire Road, at speed. Maybe a Range Rover but a witness says it had no registration plates.

'Yes, we'll need the area cordoned off. And we'll need to take statements from everybody who saw it happen. And if you can contact Bill Phinner for me so that we can have the technical experts up here as soon as they can pull on their rushers. It's lashing out, and if there's any cartridge cases or other forensics I don't want them washed down the shores.'

When she had finished calling for backup, the restaurant manager came up to Katie and said, 'Come here, why don't you both come back inside? Have a brandy on the house. You must be fierce shaken up, the both of you.'

'I'd kill for a brandy, but I'll have to make do with a strong cup of coffee. I'm back on duty now.'

They sat down at a table near the door and waited to hear sirens and see blue flashing lights in the wet street outside. Kieran took hold of Katie's wrist again, and said, 'You're extraordinary, do you know that? You've just had two gowls shooting at you, trying to kill you, and you're as cool as if somebody had done nothing more than let one of your tyres down.'

Katie gave him half a smile. 'Don't tell me you don't hear evidence in court that makes you want to gawk up your breakfast. But you don't, do you? You stay calm, and listen, and you make a considered judgement, because that's your job. Staying calm when bullets are flying around, that's *my* job. That doesn't mean I won't go to bed tonight and have nightmares that wake me up screaming. That's if I *do* get to bed tonight, which I doubt.'

They heard the wailing and scribbling of sirens and Katie stood up.

'Time to go to work,' she told him. She didn't tell him how relieved she was that he was unhurt. She had suffered so many losses that she was almost beginning to believe that she was a living *Sluagh*, a restless spirit who could never find peace, and whose only purpose was to bring death and misery to others.

36

It was still raining the following morning when Detectives Walsh and Cullen drove out to Blackrock with Dr Power.

'If it carries on like this I'm going to start building myself a fecking ark,' said Detective Cullen.

They turned into Sunnyside and drew up outside Peadar Ó Dálaigh's bungalow, with its dripping overgrown yew hedge and its gate hanging on by only one hinge. Detective Walsh had phoned Peadar earlier, and Peadar had said that he was more than happy to talk about Roisin Carroll and little Ita being pushed into the river.

'To be honest with you, I think it would do me the power of good. I keep thinking about that poor unfortunate Roisin over and over, and how I wish to God that I'd had the strength in me to save her, too.'

Detective Cullen knocked at the door and after a few moments Peadar came shuffling along the hallway to open it. His white hair was sticking up like a dandelion puff and he was wearing a droopy oatmeal sweater with tomato ketchup stains on the front of it. The inside of the house was dark and damp and hazy with cigarette smoke.

'Come in, come in,' said Peadar, waving his hand. He led them into the living room, where a sullen peat fire was burning. A gloomy reproduction of *The Croppy Boy* hung over the fireplace, a dark painting rendered even darker by smoke. It showed a young Irish rebel on his knees, confessing to a priest that he was going to fight for the nationalist cause, without realizing that the priest was an English soldier in disguise.

Detective Walsh couldn't stop herself from sneezing, twice.

'*Dia leat!*' Peadar blessed her, and then said, 'Please, have yourself a seat. There's some tea in the pot if you'd care for some. It should be well stewed by now.'

'We're grand, thanks,' said Detective Walsh.

They sat down on Peadar's damp, lumpy settee. Detective Walsh noticed that there was a rag doll perched on the back of it, with a grimy white mob cap and a wide, inane smile. She had the strangest intuition that the doll had once belonged to a child who was now dead.

Detective Cullen cleared his throat. 'As you know, Peadar, we've arrested the Lee Pusher and we have her in custody. We're preparing the book of evidence against her, and now that you've had some time to get over the shock of Roisin Carroll being drowned, we thought we'd ask you to think again about what you saw. Maybe there's one or two extra details that didn't come to mind when you first described what happened. Sometimes it's details like that can help to make absolutely certain that an offender gets convicted.'

Peadar thought for a while, and then took a packet of Major cigarettes out of his sweater pocket and lit one. 'I can see it now – Roisin pushing her stroller along the path by the river. Then this tall feller in the grey trackie running towards her. Well, I thought it was a feller at the time, because he looked like a feller. Tall, and skinny, like. And he ran faster and faster and *crash!* straight into her, and *splosh!* into the river she went, go-car and babby and all.

'The feller ran off but I didn't pay no mind to him after that because I was too busy jumping into the river meself and fishing out the babby.'

'Can you describe him again, this feller?' asked Detective Walsh. 'Let's call him a feller for now, because that's what you thought at the time. You've already told us that he was tall, and thin, wearing a light grey tracksuit with a hood. Do you remember if he was wearing gloves? And what kind of shoes he had on? Was there anything unusual about the way he ran? I mean, did he run like a girl, with his arms waving?'

Peadar took a long drag at his cigarette and then blew smoke out of the side of his mouth. 'I can't think of nothing more, like. Gloves? I couldn't tell you. As for the way he was running, it was like sprinting, you know, with his arms chopping up and down on either side of him. Not like girls run, not at all, no.'

Dr Power was sitting closest to Peadar. Now she leaned towards him and said, 'Could you do me a favour and lift one finger for me? No – not with your cigarette hand, your other hand.'

Peadar did as he was told and lifted his left index finger. He had allowed the fingernail to grow so long that it curved over, and it had a black semi-circle of dirt underneath it. 'What's this for, then?'

'It's a way to help you remember,' said Dr Power. 'Stare at the tip of your finger, don't take your eyes off it, and blink as little as you can. Try and think about nothing else at all. Not the pusher, not Roisin going into the river – only the tip of your finger.'

'Okay, I have you,' said Peadar, and glared at his fingertip as if it had mortally offended him.

'Now lift up your hand and press your fingertip down on the top of your head. But keep staring at it. Imagine that you can look upwards right through your brain and your skull and you can see that fingertip just as clearly as you did before. Keep staring up at it.'

Again, Peadar did as he was told, and pointed his fingertip

into his wispy white hair. At the same time, he rolled up his eyes so that he was keeping his gaze fixed on where it was, even if he couldn't actually see it. Within only a few seconds, his eyelids closed.

'Keep looking at that fingertip, Peadar,' said Dr Power. 'Keep looking at it and think back to that moment when you first saw Roisin pushing her baby along The Marina.'

Peadar was silent for almost half a minute, but the two detectives could see that his chest was rising and falling more slowly as he breathed, and he started to make a high-pitched wheezing sound, as if he were asleep. His right hand suddenly dropped down to the arm of his chair and his cigarette fell on to the shaggy chocolate-coloured hearthrug. Detective Cullen picked it up and tossed it into the fire.

'Can you see Roisin coming?' asked Dr Power.

'Roisin...' said Peadar, in a blurry voice. He sounded like somebody talking in another room. 'How're ye going on, girl? I don't never normally see you at this time of day.'

'What happens now, Peadar?'

'What? Oh, I'm telling Roisin all about Sinéad... my little Sinéad. Then she says that Ita's poorly and she has to take her home, and into the warm.'

'When do you first see the feller in the grey tracksuit?'

'I can *hear* him... I can hear him now. Like, his rubber dollies are slapping along the path, *slap-slappity-slap*. And it sounds like he's running, so I turn around. He's left the path now and he's crossing the grass towards Roisin, and he's going faster and faster and his arms going like them connecting rods on a steam engine.'

'Can you see his face at all?'

'No... he has his hood up... and by the time I turn around he's like side-on to me.'

'Is there any hair protruding from his hood?'

'No. It's pulled too far down. I can see the end of his nose but that's all.'

'Is he wearing gloves?'

Even though his eyes were closed, Peadar leaned forward as if he were trying to focus more narrowly on something that he could see in front of him.

'Yes,' he said at last. 'He's wearing gloves all right. Grey knitted gloves by the look of them.'

'And how about his trainers? What does he have on his feet?'

'They're navy blue, with a big silvery N on the side of them.'

'That's perfect, Peadar. And his tracksuit, just to confirm, it's light grey, yes, with no decoration on it at all?'

'It's light grey all right, but it does have this thin white stripe down the side of the leg.'

'A thin white stripe? You're positive about that?'

'Sure, like. I can see it now. This very thin white stripe.'

Detective Cullen looked at Detective Walsh. Neither of them had to say, *Doireann's tracksuit had no stripe. Maybe she's been telling the truth and she didn't push Roisin Carroll into the river.*

Dr Power said, 'What can you hear, Peadar? The fellow in the tracksuit, does he speak at all?'

'I can hear somebody shout, but I'm not sure if it's him.'

'Is it a man or a woman's voice?'

'Oh, it's a feller all right.'

'And what does he shout, this fellow?'

'It's hard to hear. The wind's blowing, and that makes the trees rustle, and the river's clapping up against the bank, like. But it sounds like "*fraoch Ún!*"'

'Is that all? "Whore!" Just that one word?'

'That's all I can hear. And the feller's running off now, and I'm hobbling fast as I can towards the riverbank, and all I can hear is screaming and splashing.'

Peadar jerked his hand away from the top of his head and clawed at the collar of his sweater as if he were trying to pull it off. But then he abruptly opened his eyes and stared at Dr Power and the two detectives in bewilderment.

'I thought I was—' he began, looking around the living room. 'I thought I was *there*, like, by the river, and Roisin had just fallen in.'

'You were remembering, that's all,' said Dr Power.

'But, *Jesus,* I was sure that I was really there. And where's me—?' He lifted his right hand and turned it this way and that. 'I was smoking a fag a minute ago, wasn't I? Or did I imagine it? Don't tell me I'm going doolally.'

'No, you're as sane as the rest of us, Peadar,' Dr Power told him. 'You went through a fierce traumatic experience that afternoon, and stress can play some mad tricks on our brains sometimes. Your memory of it will fade a bit in time, I promise you. The only thing that you should never let yourself forget is that you were a hero, and that you saved a little girl's life.'

'On top of which, you've given us some pure valuable information,' said Detective Cullen.

Peadar looked baffled. 'Information? You have me there, boy. What information? I don't follow you.'

'You told us a couple of important details about what happened that we didn't know before. If they lead to a conviction, I'll see if I can persuade the powers that be at Anglesea Street to give you some kind of reward.'

'What did I say? You have me pure bamboozled like, now.'

'Don't let it bother you, Peadar,' said Dr Power, patting the knee of his worn brown corduroy trousers. 'These two detectives, they're almost psychic. They know what you're thinking before you can think it.'

Detective Cullen pressed his hand to his forehead and said, 'Like, I know what you'll be eating for your lunch today. O'Neal's Irish Stew.'

Peadar burst out laughing. 'Holy Saint Joseph! How in the name of God Almighty did you know *that,* boy?'

It was only when the two detectives and Dr Power were back in their car that Detective Walsh asked Detective Cullen the same question.

'Easy,' he said, as he steered out of Sunnyside and headed back towards the city centre. 'I saw the tin on his kitchen table when we walked in. My mam used to feed it to us almost every week because she couldn't cook for shite.'

37

At a quarter past ten the next morning, Katie's phone rang and it was Muireann. Her voice was breathy and furtive.

'Tommy's cancelled the party. Something about a gas leak, and so The Weavers is closed. You didn't fix that, did you? If you did, I'm so relieved I can't tell you.'

'What's he planning to do?' Katie asked her. 'Cancel it altogether or arrange to hold it at some other pub?'

'He's going to wait until the gas leak's been fixed because he wants to hold it at The Weavers. Besides, it's too late now to shift it to anywhere else. Maybe we'll be having it next week.'

'All right. Perfect. Just make sure you stay well away from Gerald Griffin Street. And – please, whatever you do, don't let on to Megan that the party's cancelled. Barry Riordan mustn't catch even a whisper of it.'

'Megan won't be in any danger, will she? Jesus Christ, I think the poor girl's suffered more than enough.'

'No, Muireann. But I'm hoping that finally – *finally*, we're going to wipe out Barry Riordan and his gang of gowls for good and all. And as soon as we have *them* locked up, I promise you, we'll be going after the O'Flynns.'

'I'll be saying a prayer for you, Kathleen. And for myself. And for Bryanna. It's the least she deserves.'

Katie called Moirin and asked for another cappuccino. It had been 2:15 in the morning before she had been able to leave MacCurtain Street. Only twenty minutes after the shooting, a team from the Technical Bureau had arrived to search for forensic evidence, as well as three squad cars and two unmarked Garda cars, all with their sirens screaming and their headlights flashing, closely followed by a Garda Transit. Along with Detectives Caffrey and Buckley, Katie herself had spent over two hours interviewing passers-by and customers from Isaacs and Dan Lowrey's.

Kieran had stayed with her until she had finished, his coat collar turned up against the rain, although he had plainly been tired and shaken by being shot at. Eventually, a taxi had taken him back up to the Ambassador Hotel, where he was staying, and Katie had returned to Anglesea Street, to spend the night there. She had rung her neighbour, Jenny Tierney, and asked her if she would take Barney and Foltchain out for their late-night walk.

Her phone rang again. It was Brendan's assistant, Bridie, telling her that Brendan had returned from Dublin and had just walked into his office.

'Please tell him I'll be along in about ten minutes, Bridie.'

'He has a rake of catching-up to be catching up with, ma'am.'

'I can understand that. But this is urgent.'

As detective superintendent, she had full authority to set up her operation to surprise the Riordans when they raided The Weavers this afternoon to 'mess up' Maddie O'Flynn's birthday party. All the same, she needed to brief Brendan about it, if only as a matter of protocol. It would also give her some insurance if anything were to go catastrophically wrong, and either a gang member or a garda got shot. If Brendan knew about it beforehand, she couldn't be held solely responsible.

Had her relationship with Brendan been less than daggers drawn, she would have rung him or emailed him yesterday evening when he was up at Phoenix Park, or even early this morning, and told him all about it. But she strongly suspected that he might have vetoed the operation to make her appear indecisive and incompetent – if only in the eyes of her fellow officers.

It didn't help that this morning's *Irish Sun* carried a front-page story about last night's attempt on her life – POTSHOT AT TOP COP. It was written under the byline of Owen Dineen, and it strongly suggested that Cork was now so lawless that criminals could shoot with impunity at the city's leading detective.

She had waited until Brendan returned to Anglesea Street because she wanted to tell him about the operation in person – Operation Hubbard, she had called it, after Old Mother Hubbard who found that her cupboard was bare, just like the Riordans would go to The Weavers and find no O'Flynns there. He would find it much more difficult if he had to tell her face-to-face to pull the plug on it. She could suggest that he was lacking the nerve to tackle the Riordans head-on, in case they retaliated, as they once had before by setting a Garda squad car on fire.

'You don't have to wait until they're so buckled they're dead to the world,' she could tell him. 'Not like you did with me.'

Apart from that, the operation was now well advanced, and he would have to face serious questions about his motives if he were to call it off. Overtime had been allocated, vehicles had been diverted, armaments had been withdrawn, and a great deal of time and money would have been wasted.

Earlier this morning, Superintendent Pearse had arranged with the local Bord Gáis manager, Denis O'Halloran, to borrow fluorescent jackets and ID cards, as well as a Bord Gáis van, and two gardaí dressed as emergency gas fitters had visited The Weavers to warn the landlord of a major gas leak. Obviously, from what Muireann had told her, that part of Operation Hubbard had already worked, and the O'Flynn party had been called off.

Katie sipped her coffee and unhurriedly ate one chocolate biscuit to keep herself totally calm. Although she had assured Kieran that she wasn't frightened by flying bullets, her nerves were still seriously jangled by yesterday evening's attempt on her life, and last night she had managed to sleep for less than half an hour. She had sat up in bed, shaking, not sure where she was, feeling as if somebody had suddenly shouted in her ear, and she had settled herself down again only by saying a prayer.

'*Go raibh maith agat, a Thiarna, as ligean dom a fheiceáil, Bás ag teacht nuair a bhagair sé orm* – Thank you, Lord, for allowing me to see, Death coming when he threatened me.'

She had said that prayer twice before during her career, and she had always hoped that she would never have to say it again.

Brendan was talking on the phone when she knocked at the door of his office, but he flapped his hand to beckon her in, and once she was in he flapped his hand again to indicate that she should sit down.

'That's sound, Sonny, thanks for arranging all of that,' he was saying. 'And you won't be forgetting the fizz?' As he spoke, though, he picked up a copy of the *Irish Sun* from his desk and held it up, waving it, so that Katie could see the front page. Katie made a point of looking away, out of the window, where the rain was still trickling down and the gutter was spouting down to the car park below.

'Okay, then, I'll catch you at the weekend at Fota,' Brendan finished off, and put down the phone. Fota was Cork's most prestigious golf club, so Katie could guess what kind of weekend he had been planning.

'Well, Katie, you're all over the papers again,' he said, standing up. 'Thank God you weren't hurt – neither you nor Justice Connolly. Is he okay?'

'Shaken, like we both were, but otherwise grand. He rang me this morning to ask after me, and he didn't sound so bad.'

'Do you have any notion at all who was shooting at you?'

'They both had their faces covered, and it all happened so quick. And like Owen Dineen says, there's plenty of criminals in Cork who'd be happy to see me dead and spit on my grave.'

'You should have taken the day off so. You must be exhausted.'

'I can't, sir. I've far too much to take care of today. I'm up the walls.'

'Well, I hope you have a few minutes to spare because I need to tell you what was decided at my meeting at Phoenix Park yesterday.'

'I don't think so, I'm afraid. There's something critical I have to tell you about first.'

'Katie – Kathleen—'

'Detective Superintendent, if you don't mind, sir. And I'm sure that your discussion with the Director of Communications was all wonderfully upbeat. Going forward, as they say, I've no doubt that you'll be able to portray An Garda Síochána in a glowing light that's almost holy. You'll show the public that you're not a tight-knit secret society of misogynists who won't tolerate whistle-blowers, and who conveniently lose embarrassing files, and whose only fearful misjudgement was to appoint a woman to lead Cork's detectives. You're saints in uniform.'

Brendan took a deep breath and tightly puckered his lips. Katie could see that she had seriously riled him, and he was doing everything he could to stop himself from shouting at her.

'It was nothing like that at all,' he said, with a controlled tremble in his voice. 'But we *did* discuss in detail how to refocus the negative image that the media have of policing in Cork. Statistically, yes – we may not be doing so badly. It's the way that you've been presenting yourself personally that's led to the media giving us such poor publicity.'

'And your answer to that was—?'

'For the time being at least, I'll be taking over any and all press conferences we hold about our ongoing investigations here at Anglesea Street. You'll be taking what you might call a back seat.'

'Oh, they didn't want me to quit altogether? Just to become less visible?'

'If you want to put it that way, yes.'

'Fair play, sir, even if I briefed you fully before any press conference, the media could still ask you some unexpected questions that you wouldn't be able to answer. More important, they could well ask you some unexpected questions that you wouldn't know how *not* to answer. And that would very quickly make you appear as if you didn't really have a grasp on what you were talking about.'

'I'm sorry, but I totally disagree with you. I believe I'm more than capable of handling the media and giving them all the information they want in a way that makes us look empowered and efficient and totally dedicated to a Cork with only minimum crime. Which we are.'

'In that case, you'll need to know all about the operation that we're carrying out this afternoon. Operation Hubbard.'

Brendan was standing very close to her now, and she knew why he was doing it. She would either have to look up to him when she spoke or suddenly push her chair back and stand up herself, which would make her look clumsy and intimidated. She had seen him do it too often before, even with other men. But when she said 'Operation Hubbard' he jerked his head back a little and frowned, because she had caught him off balance.

'Operation *what*?'

'Hubbard. It's a bit of a joke, do you know? "Old Mother Hubbard went to the cupboard to fetch her poor dog a bone."'

'*What*?'

Katie explained how the Riordans would go bursting into The Weavers in the expectation that the O'Flynns would be holding their birthday party there, and how officers from the armed support unit would be waiting for them.

Brendan stared at her as if she had told him that his car had rolled backwards into the River Lee.

'You're not serious? You've arranged for an out-and-out shooting match with Barry Riordan and his gang? What do you think this is? The Wild West? The gunfight at the OK Corral?'

'What option did we have? Once we were tipped off about what they intended to do, we couldn't very well ignore it, could we?'

'This is in the middle of the city in the middle of the day! What if there are collateral casualties? What if innocent bystanders get themselves shot?'

'That whole stretch of pavement outside The Weavers is fenced off with Bord Gáis barricades, and as soon as the Riordans go inside, we'll be stopping all traffic at both ends of Gerald Griffin Street, both cars and pedestrians. There'll be no landlord or staff in the pub, they've already been evacuated.'

'Why the hell didn't you tell me this before you set it all in motion?'

'Because I know exactly what you would have said. You know it's the right thing to do, but you would have found a reason to call it off. You wouldn't have wanted me to take the credit for it.'

Katie stood up now, and snatched up the *Irish Sun* from Brendan's desk, shaking it angrily in his face so that the pages all fell out across the carpet.

'You don't want to see me on the front page of tomorrow's paper, do you? TOP COP SMASHES CORK'S WORST DRUGS GANG. Who do you think the media will want to talk to tomorrow? It won't be *you,* will it, for all of your top-level politically correct pow-wow up at Phoenix Park?'

Brendan took three stiff steps towards her and raised his fist. She had never seen a man so angry. He still had faded fingernail marks on his face from when she had scratched him and he looked as fierce as one of the grotesque gargoyles on Saint Fin Barre's Cathedral.

'Go on, then, sir,' she said quietly, lifting her chin. 'You want to hit me – hit me. I knew you never really loved me, no matter how many times you said it.'

Brendan's nostrils flared, and he made a peculiar snarling sound. Then he picked up the leather chair that Katie had been sitting in, held it high above his head and threw it across his office. It crashed against his glass-fronted bookcase and broke a triangular piece out of one of the windows.

Almost immediately, the side door opened and Bridie appeared, holding her spectacles.

'What in the name of God was that noise?'

She looked at Brendan, and then she looked at Katie, and then she saw the chair lying on its side on the floor.

"'Twas nothing at all,' Brendan told her.

But now Bridie had seen the cracked pane of glass. She looked again at Katie and silently mouthed something that could have been 'What in the world is going on?'

'I *said* – 'twas nothing at all,' Brendan repeated. He was breathing heavily and it was obvious to Katie that even Bridie could hear the menace in his voice. 'I was carrying the chair, as it happens, and I tripped over the carpet. Nothing for you to be bothered about. Haven't you those letters to be getting on with?'

Bridie retreated, and quietly closed her door behind her.

Katie said, 'If that's everything, I have to be getting off to see how Operation Hubbard's coming along.' She couldn't bring herself to call him 'sir'.

'I'm sorry,' he mumbled.

'No, you're not. With me you never will be.'

He looked across at her and gave her a rueful shrug. 'We seem to be star-crossed, don't we, you and me?'

'It's lovers who are star-crossed, and we've never been lovers. All you've ever wanted to do is have your way with me, and because I won't let you have your way with me, you want to destroy me. Well, come here to me – I'm not giving you the pleasure of either.'

She went to the door and opened it. 'I'll keep you up to date on Operation Hubbard. I'll do it because you're the chief superintendent and it's proper procedure. But don't you ever dare to threaten me again, do you hear me?'

Brendan looked down at the sheets of newspaper strewn around his feet. Then he looked at Katie again, with a strange mixture of hostility and regret, but he didn't answer.

38

When the tide began to rise on the River Lee that morning, it had already been raining heavily for twenty-eight hours, and a strong south-east wind had slowed the usual eastward flow of water into Cork Harbour.

By 10:45, the quays were under water and South Mall and the lower part of Oliver Plunkett Street were flooded ankle-deep. The county council were putting out warnings that it was going to get 'worse before it got better', and that free sandbags could be picked up from the council depot.

Katie glanced out of the rain-dribbled window from time to time but she was concentrating now on making sure that everything was ready for Operation Hubbard.

She had downloaded photographs from The Weavers Facebook page so that she could see the wood-panelled interior of the two adjoining bars and how all the tables were laid out. On their estate agents' website she had discovered floor plans not only of both bars, but of the pub's upstairs rooms.

Sergeant Mullally and four officers from his armed support unit came up to her office to work out second by second how they were going to respond when the Riordans arrived outside, depending on how many of the gang showed up, and what weapons they were carrying, if any. They discussed what positions they were going to take up once they were inside the bars, especially if any of the gang ducked down behind the counter for cover.

No matter what happened inside The Weavers, none of the gang would be able to get away. Katie had arranged that seven unmarked cars would be parked in tactical positions in every side street all around. As soon as the Riordans arrived they would move in to block every exit. Gardaí would be staked out in the back yard too, so that they couldn't escape that way.

'Most of the members of Barry Riordan's gang we know well,' said Katie. 'He still has his old-time hard cases that he keeps close around him – what you might call his imperial guard. As we're aware, though, he's recruited more than a dozen young local gurriers in the past eighteen months. He's done that so that he can extend his drug-trafficking as far west as Mallow, as far north as Fermoy and at least as far east as Youghal. But of course he's also done it to replace those eleven members of his gang who we've been able to haul in and successfully put behind bars – for the time being, anyway, until they get parole.

'So it's not the old-timers I'm so concerned about today. They know when they've been snared rapid and they usually give up without a fight, so that they don't end up with too long a prison sentence. It's the young ones whose only experience of detention is Oberstown and who spend most of their time whacked out of their brains on coke or krokodil or Molly or the Lord God only knows what. They're the ones who worry me.

'I'm hoping and praying that they'll all give up without a fight, do you know, but you have my express authority to open fire instantly if any of our officers' lives appear to be at risk.'

She hesitated, and then she said, 'I want this day to be the turning point. I want this to be the day when we start to eliminate the drug gangs in Cork for good and all. Then we can tell the *Sun* to stick their stories where the sun doesn't shine.'

Only a few minutes after Sergeant Mullally and his fellow officers had left Katie's office, Kyna knocked at her door. She was wearing a smart black trouser suit and a blouse with a crisp white collar and her blonde hair was tied up with a black silk scarf.

'Look at *you* la,' said Katie, getting up from her desk. 'Perhaps you ought to go swimming more often.'

'Oh, stop. I've never been so cold in my entire life as I was then. I was *Baltic*, right down to the bone. I thought that I was never going to feel warm again, ever.'

'I'm glad you've made it in, anyway. I've just finished planning the final details of Operation Hubbard with the ASU. We have twenty-two uniforms, five armed support officers and four detectives, plus of course you and me.'

'And you've told himself?'

'Chief Superintendent O'Kane? I have of course. And what do you think? He threw a rabie. In fact, he threw a chair across his office. But there's nothing he can do about it.'

'Jesus. What about Frank Magorian?'

'He's above in Dublin at the moment. I'll tell him all about it when it's over.'

'But not before? I hope you know what a risk you're taking. If this should go at all wrong—'

'Kyna, I don't care about the risk. Not now – not with Brendan threatening me on one side and Orla Quinn threatening me on the other. If I can pull this off, and if I can find a way to take down the O'Flynns soon after – that's it, I'll be untouchable.'

'Ah now,' said Kyna with a smile, and she lifted up a clear plastic envelope. 'I may be able to help you when it comes to the O'Flynns. In fact, God may have helped you already.'

She handed Katie the envelope. Inside was a photograph of a large kitchen knife, with its measurements marked alongside it, and its evidence reference number.

'That was fetched in less than twenty minutes ago, by a plumber.'

'A *plumber*?'

'Yes – he'd been called in to the Zombie Lounge because of the flooding. The drain in the men's jacks was blocked and so they were waist-deep in water. He managed to find the grating and pull it up, and inside he found that it was clogged with bits of old paper towels and other rubbish – and this knife.'

'That's the same toilet where that Kimmons lad was stabbed.'

'It is, yes... and there's a fair chance that this is the knife he was stabbed with. Like, why else would somebody drop a knife like this down a drain, except to hide it?'

'Thank goodness for a plumber with a scrap of brains.'

'I was downstairs by the front desk talking to Cailin Walsh when he fetched it in, having a quick catch-up. Cailin took down his name and all his particulars and I took the knife straight across to the lab. Bill said that if there's any latent fingerprints on it or even the twinchiest trace of blood, they'll be sure to find them.'

'I don't doubt it. Do you know, about two months before you were posted here we had a case in Glanmire when a farmer was beaten to death by one of his casual labourers, a Polish fellow. It was six weeks before we found the shovel that he'd been beaten with, and all that time it had been lying on the bottom of the Glashaboy River, where your man had thrown it. Bill's people still managed to find fingerprints and DNA on it.'

'Well, if we can prove that this knife was the knife that stabbed Tadhg Kimmons, and if we can prove that it was one of Thomas O'Flynn's gowls who did the stabbing—'

'Don't let's get ahead of ourselves, Kyna. The road to miscarriages of justice is paved with hunches – that's what my da always used to tell me. It could have been that a handyman was using the knife to try and dig out the bits of paper towels, and accidentally dropped it.'

'You're such a pessimist.'

'No, I'm not, sweetheart. I'm a realist. I've learned how to face up to loss and disappointment and things going wrong. Even if you make a bags of today, there's always tomorrow.'

'Tomorrow – or this afternoon,' said Kyna. 'What time will we be setting out?'

'One thirty. But we'll be taking up our positions in stages – one and two at a time – in case any of Riordan's gang are keeping sketch in the area. We don't want to be after driving up there like the Mayor of Cork's motorcade.

'Here – let me go over the plan of action with you. Then you can go down to the armoury and draw out your pistol. And whatever you do, don't forget your ballistic vest.'

Katie took out her own pistol, a Smith & Wesson Airweight .38 Special, finished in stainless steel. It wasn't standard Garda issue, but it was small and light with a short barrel and easy to conceal. She flipped open the chamber to make sure that it was clean and then she reloaded it with five 38 +P bullets, which were overloaded for extra punch.

She had only just tucked it into her hip holster when Conall appeared at her open door and gave her a jerky little wave. 'Would you have a moment, ma'am?'

'Conall,' she said. 'Come on in.'

He approached her desk so awkwardly and so shyly that she wondered if he could still visualize the pictures of Kyna and her together, in her bedroom. 'What's the story, Conall? Do you have something for me?'

He came up to her desk and held up his iPhone.

'Two voice recordings. You didn't tell me if you wanted me to hack Owen Dineen talking to any specific people, but I made an educated guess that this was the kind of discussion that you were interested in. They're both using Silent Circle, which encrypts end-to-end conversations, but that wasn't a bother.'

'Good man, Conall... let's go over and make ourselves comfortable, then, and you can play them for me.'

They sat on one of the leather couches by the window and Conall held up the phone so that she could hear it clearly.

First of all she heard some fluffing noises, and a cough, and then Owen Dineen's distinctive growl saying, 'It won't be at all easy to put a critical angle on this... I mean—'

He was interrupted by another man's voice. At first it was difficult to hear what he was saying because it sounded as if he were bending over or turning around and his phone wasn't close to his mouth. Suddenly, though, his voice barked out loud and clear and there was no mistaking that it was Brendan.

'She's supposed to be in charge of law and order, for Christ's sake! She's supposed to be breaking up the gangs so that the city's streets are safe! And yet even *she* gets shot at! *There's* your critical angle!'

'Yes, Brendan, I have you, but even after all the stories that we've been running to knock her, you need to bear in mind that a fair majority of the public are still rooting for her. She's attractive to look at, and she speaks on the TV like she's not trying to make excuses for herself, and that counts for a lot.'

'But she was *shot* at, Owen, along with Justice Connolly! In the open street! It's unbelievable that neither of them were killed!'

'Of course. But there's every chance that she'll be given sympathy for that like, more than condemnation. Even you have to admit that she's had a pretty reasonable track record over the past few years. A whole lot better than her predecessor, for sure. What was his name – that DS Daithi MacClancy? What a plank he was. If his brains had been Semtex they wouldn't have blown his hat off.'

'Talking of Semtex, what about the bomb at UCC?'

'Granted, that shook her reputation quite a bit, but what you have to realize is that the ordinary people of Cork don't feel threatened on the streets when they're going about their daily business, and that's what matters more than anything.'

'Owen – listen to me – I'm paying you an eye-watering amount of grade to make sure that they *do* feel threatened, even if they aren't, and that she takes the blame for them feeling that way. And you couldn't have a better start than this shooting, could you? Think how you can put it: if the gangs aren't frightened to shoot at the city's top detective, they can't be frightened to shoot at anybody, can they?'

There was a pause, and a sigh of resignation, and then Owen Dineen said, 'All right, leave it with me. I'll see what I can do so.'

That conversation abruptly came to a close, but then Conall fast-forwarded to another brief exchange. 'This one I recorded this morning, about eight o'clock.'

It was Brendan again, and again he was talking to Owen Dineen. From the background noise, Katie could tell that he was still on the train coming back from Dublin.

'Did you receive that payment yet?'

'I don't know. I haven't had the time to check my account.'

'Well, check it now. I don't want it going astray like that last one.'

There was an interval of nearly half a minute, during which Katie could only hear the train, and what sounded like a newspaper rustling. Then Owen Dineen said, 'Yes. I've just checked. It's landed.'

'Great, good. And that story this morning – that was fantastic. Well done yourself. If you can follow that up tomorrow with another one just as good there's another five hundred in it for you.'

'Don't worry about it,' Owen Dineen told him. 'Like I said before, I can always find *something* to chip away at her reputation – even if it's some case she made a hames of years ago when she was only a detective garda.'

'You just keep chipping away, Owen. Chip, chip, chip! Now – will you be coming to Fota on Sunday? We can talk some more about it then.'

Katie sat back. She had suspected that Owen Dineen's hostility wasn't entirely genuine, and that Brendan may have been briefing him against her, but she was still shocked that Brendan could actually be paying him to destroy her career. It almost made her feel concussed, as if she had unexpectedly knocked her head very hard against an open cupboard door.

'I don't think I need to hear any more, thanks, Conall. Can you please make me a copy of those recordings, and anything else you have between the two of them?'

Conall switched off his iPhone. 'This is dead serious this, isn't it, ma'am?'

'You'll keep it to yourself, won't you? At least for now. Don't say anything to anybody, not even Bill.'

'I didn't really understand why you wanted me to hack Owen Dineen... but now that I've heard what he's been doing – like, deliberately writing bad things about you – and the chief superintendent actually *paying* him to do it – I can hardly believe it.'

Katie smiled and patted his arm. 'Conall – I owe you more than I can tell you. In fact, you've made my day. So far, at least.'

'Thank you, ma'am. And – well – I don't quite know how to say this – but the other thing – the pictures. My sister's LGBT – so, you know, that won't go any further, either.'

He blushed, and then stood up, and left Katie's office with his odd loping walk, almost colliding with the door frame.

39

The rain continued, heavy and relentless, and when Katie hurried across the station car park to climb into the car with Inspector O'Rourke and Kyna and Detectives O'Donovan and Buckley, she heard a rumble of thunder directly overhead. It sounded like a hundred empty beer barrels rolling down the steps into a cellar.

'Grand weather for fishing,' said Inspector O'Rourke. 'The salmon can't tell the difference between the river and the sky.'

'Let's hope it's grand weather for hauling in Riordans,' said Detective O'Donovan.

They were squashed tightly together in the Toyota, because they were all wearing ballistic vests underneath their raincoats. They drove along Merchants Quay to St Patrick's Bridge, with the floodwater swilling across the road with herringbone ripples. Then they crossed over the river and headed north-westwards, up the steep incline of Roman Street, with its small multicoloured houses stacked up on either side. It took them no more than ten minutes to reach the grey Gothic tower of St Mary's Cathedral and Gerald Griffin Street – only a hundred metres north of The Weavers.

They parked in Cathedral Walk, next to a deserted school playground. Katie thanked God that the O'Flynns had decided to hold their party on a Saturday, when there would be no children around. Inspector O'Rourke was in radio contact with all of the other Garda vehicles, and he was following their arrival in the area, in ones and twos, on a map on his laptop.

Their fake gas fitters had erected a red PVC work tent on

the corner of Cathedral Walk – not only because it was raining but to conceal the fact that they had only lifted up a few flagstones and weren't actually carrying out any repairs. They had also fenced off the pavement from Cathedral Walk up towards Cathedral Road with Bord Gáis barriers, although they had left a two-metre gap to give access to the front door of The Weavers.

'I saw the *Sun* this morning, ma'am,' said Inspector O'Rourke, as they sat and waited in the car with the rain drumming on the roof. 'They have some axe to grind with you, like, don't they?'

'Oh, water off a frog's back,' Katie told him. Nobody corrected her and said 'duck'. They didn't realize that her father had always liked to mangle well-known expressions and that she had never known any different.

She sorely wished that she could tell Inspector O'Rourke about Brendan bribing Owen Dineen to write derogatory stories about her, but she knew that she had to bide her time. She would have to choose her moment with the utmost care if she was going to protect her reputation, and her career.

At 2:21 p.m., a grey Volvo came up Gerald Griffin Street and parked on the wide pavement beside the playground railings. This was the last of the unmarked Garda cars.

'All in position now, ma'am,' said Inspector O'Rourke. 'All we have to do now is wait for the Riordans to show up. That's unless somebody's tipped them off.'

'That lippy young barman at The Weavers, isn't he in with Barry Riordan?' asked Detective O'Donovan.

'Lenny Malone, you mean?' said Detective Buckley. 'Sure. He sells Es and coke for him under the counter. "Two pints of Murphy's, a package of cheese-and-onion Taytos and a bag of crack, please!"'

'Surely *he* would have found out that the party's been cancelled, wouldn't he?' asked Katie. 'The landlord would have rung him and told him not to come into work.'

'Oh no, I shouldn't think so. Lenny's only part-time. Weekends he's down at Kinsale, mostly, working on the yachts for the yacht club and scamming the amateur sailors with coke mixed with cow-worming powder. Half of them are sailing round Old Head stoned out of their minds and with a chronic case of the runs, with nowhere to go but over the side. I've pulled Lenny in three times myself, but somehow mysteriously he always seems to get away with nothing more than a fine and a finger-wagging.'

Inspector O' Rourke shook his head. 'They really have things sewn up between them, don't they, the Riordans and the O'Flynns?'

'Not any more,' said Katie. 'This is where they start to get unstitched.'

When it happened, it happened with dreamlike speed. A white VW Passat estate car came up Gerald Griffin Street at nearly fifty, and slewed to a halt a few metres past the entrance to The Weavers. It was followed by a Ford Mondeo and a Datsun.

As soon as the three cars had stopped, their doors were flung open and eight men in balaclavas and hoodies jumped out, leaving their drivers behind the steering wheel, ready for a getaway. From where she was sitting, Katie could see only the third car, the Datsun, but she could see that one of the two men who climbed out of the back seat was carrying a Ruger automatic rifle.

'Right,' she said. 'Five seconds, Francis, and then let's go.'

Inspector O'Rourke counted down *five – four – three – two – one* over the radio, and then they all pushed open the doors of their car and scrambled out. On the opposite side of Gerald Griffin Street, the doors of five more unmarked cars were opening up, and the armed support officers came running across the road, dressed from head to foot in black, holding up their Heckler & Koch assault rifles. At the same time, two Garda squad cars appeared at the top of the hill, their headlights on full and their blue lights flashing, blocking off the junction with Cathedral Road, and two more turned into Gerald Griffin Street from Farren Street, approaching The Weavers side by side to prevent the Riordans reversing and trying to escape the way that they had come.

Katie ran through the rain with Detective O'Donovan beside her and Kyna close behind her. She rounded the corner by the Bord Gáis tent just as the last of the armed support unit was entering The Weavers' front door. She lifted the flap of her raincoat to pull out her pistol and then she followed him inside, through the narrow entrance hall and into the first of the two bars. The bar was dark and smelled of stale beer and furniture polish.

Three of Riordan's gang were standing in front of the counter, looking bewildered, and a fourth was standing behind it. Five armed support officers were pointing their assault rifles at them and screaming, 'Don't move! Drop your weapons and put up your hands! *Now!*'

Two of the gang were carrying automatic pistols. One dropped his on to the floor with a loud clatter while the other carefully laid his down on a nearby table, on top of a beer mat. The third appeared to be armed only with a baseball bat, which he swung once and then tossed towards the fireplace, knocking over the fire irons.

'Put up your hands!' one of the officers shouted at them. 'And you – behind the bar! Lay down that weapon ye fecking gom – like *now*!'

The gang member behind the counter was holding up a Ruger semi-automatic rifle. He hesitated for a few seconds and then he started gently to lay it down on top of the bar, two-handed, as if he were offering up a sacrifice. As he did so, though, there was a deafening bang from the next bar, and then another, and then a sharp *brrrrp!* of sub-machine gun fire.

The gang member behind the counter lifted up his Ruger again, swung it around and fired two shots at the armed response officers. One of them was hit on the collarbone and knocked sideways, colliding with Katie and bringing down two chairs with him as he sprawled on to the floor. Katie was thrown off balance for a moment, until Detective O'Donovan took hold of her shoulders and steadied her. Before she could fire back at the gang member behind the counter, two of the armed response officers had let loose an ear-splitting salvo of bullets at him. They hit him in the head and the chest so that his eyes exploded out of the holes in his balaclava and he was thrown backwards with such violence that he crashed into the rows of bottles on the shelves behind the bar. He dropped down and disappeared from sight in a shower of broken glass and cascading whiskey.

The armed response officers jostled the three surviving gang members into the centre of the bar, fastened handcuffs on them and pulled off their balaclavas. One of them she recognized: it was Gavin Garvey, one of Barry Riordan's longest-serving thugs, with a record for drug-dealing and theft and assault causing bodily harm. She didn't know either of the others, although she could tell by the glazed, unfocused look in their eyes that both were under the influence of some drug or other, probably crack.

'All right, get them out of my sight,' said Katie. As they were ushered away, Katie heard shouting from the next bar, and a strange self-pitying moaning, like a woman begging for a man to stop beating her. Together with Kyna and Detective O'Donovan she went through to see what was happening.

Two gang members were lying on the floor, one with his head half-hidden underneath a table. A third was crouched beside them, the knees of his jeans soaked in blood. He was clasping his hands together and bowing up and down like a penitent at prayer. As Katie came into the bar, he was still moaning, but more softly now. The three remaining armed response officers were standing around the bodies, including Sergeant Mullally. He was talking on his radio, giving an update to the paramedics who were stationed in one of the four ambulances that Katie had arranged to have on standby.

'Two deceased – no, I've just been told three – and one of us is badly bruised apparently. Otherwise no other injuries. I'll get back to you as soon as we're happy that the premises are totally secure, but at the moment it looks like you won't be required. Except for carting the bodies off to the morgue, in due course.'

Katie said, 'What's the story, sergeant?'

Sergeant Mullally took off his helmet and wiped his forehead with the back of his hand. 'They'd realized that the place was empty, and that there was no party going on, and they were on their way out again when we came in and confronted them. These three ran in here, but we stopped them before they could get away upstairs. Not that it would have done them any good. We still would have caught them.'

Sergeant Mullally's two fellow officers lifted up the whining gang member under his armpits and dragged him limp-legged out of the bar, his trainers scumbling on the floor.

'We ordered them to put down their weapons, but they told us to eff off and a few other choice phrases. I've no doubt at all that they were high on something or other. Monkey dust is my guess. We ordered them again, but they still refused, and then one of them fired a shot at us, and even though he missed, and they were high, we had no option but to shoot to kill.'

Katie leaned over the bodies. 'Patrick – let's take a lamp at their faces.'

Detective O'Donovan pulled a pair of forensic gloves out of his raincoat pocket and snapped them on. Then he bent over the two dead men and rolled up their balaclavas.

Neither man could have been older than his mid-twenties. One had a wispy scobe moustache and a silver ring through his septum, while the other had snakes tattooed on his neck. The one with the moustache had a bullet hole right in the centre of his forehead, and the back of his balaclava was a bagful of soft bloody mush.

'Barry's not among them,' said Katie. 'It looks like the lord and master sent his minions out to do his dirty work for him while he stayed drinking at The Cotton Ball.'

She looked around the bar. There was a door at the back, which was slightly ajar, and she could see stairs, carpeted in worn-out green hessian. From the floor plans that she had downloaded, she knew those stairs led up to The Weavers' back bedrooms, where any live-in staff presumably slept. She looked down at the bodies on the floor again, and then she said to Sergeant Mullally, 'How many were there altogether?'

'Three came out of the front car... three from the second... but only two came out of the third car.'

'That makes eight. We've killed three of them and lifted four. That's seven.'

She pointed towards the open door. 'Number eight must have bolted upstairs. In which case, he must still be up there. There's no access to the back.'

'I didn't see any of them go up there. Maybe I miscounted when I saw them coming out of their cars. But, okay, let's go up and make sure. We don't want the landlord coming back to find a half-baked Riordan hiding in his hot press.'

He pushed the door open wider and started to climb the stairs, holding his pistol high up in front of him. Katie and Detective O'Donovan followed him.

At the top of the stairs there was a narrow landing, with two doors on either side. It smelled even stuffier than the bars downstairs. At the far end there was a stained-glass window in amber and red, with two broken panes that had been blocked with cardboard.

Sergeant Mullally turned the handle of the first bedroom door and then kicked it open. Inside there was a single unmade bed, a side table and a cheap plywood wardrobe. He looked under the bed and then flung open the wardrobe doors, but there was nobody under the bed and nothing in the wardrobe but blouses and dresses and wire coat-hangers.

They went on to the next bedroom, and the next, and the next. In one of them, the bed had no mattress and the rest of the room was stacked with boxes. In another, the bed was neatly made and there were photographs on the wall of children and elderly grandparents. But there was nobody hiding in any of them.

'Definitely must have miscounted,' said Sergeant Mullally, holstering his pistol. As he did so, one of his unit shouted up the stairs, 'Sarge! They're calling for some backup outside!'

'Right with you!' Sergeant Mullally told him, and he clumped his way back down the stairs to the bar. Detective O'Donovan holstered his pistol, too, and followed him, ducking his head down as he went through the door.

Katie took a last look around the landing and was about to go after them when she heard a soft scraping sound, and then a dull bump, and another scrape.

She stood still, her pistol half-lifted, listening. At first she couldn't be sure where the noises were coming from, but then she heard another bump, and she realized it had come from the ceiling. She stayed where she was, waiting; and then suddenly the attic door flapped down, swinging from side to side. With a creak of hinges, a sliding aluminium ladder came down, and two legs appeared, in faded blue jeans and worn-out brown boots.

Katie held her pistol in both hands and aimed it directly at the foot of the ladder. She didn't shout out for Detective O'Donovan or Sergeant Mullally because that would warn the man climbing down that she was waiting for him, and it was highly likely that he was armed.

As he climbed down he had his back to her, and when he reached the floor he paused for a few seconds, still holding on to the ladder, as if he were listening to make sure that the gardaí had all gone downstairs.

Her voice sharp and clear, Katie said, 'Keep your hands raised up and turn slowly around.'

Even under his black puffer jacket she could see the man's shoulders tense.

'I *said* – keep your hands raised up and turn slowly around. You're under arrest.'

He turned to face her. He was fortyish, with spiky grey hair, baggy cheeks, and glasses. Even though he had his back to the light, Katie recognized him at once as the man who had been driving Garrett Quinn's Jaguar on the morning when Garrett had been burned to death.

'Patrick!' she shouted. 'Patrick – get yourself up here, will you? Quick as you can!'

The man stared at her through his thumbprinted lenses and then he said, 'Holy Christ and all the fecking Holy Ghosts, it's *you*! Talk about the worst fecking luck! I swear to God I'll kill that fecking optician!'

Katie heard no answer from downstairs, so she shouted out again, '*Patrick! Sergeant Mullally!*'

Still no answer. If they couldn't hear her, she would have to reach inside her raincoat for her TETRA radio to call them for help, but the bespectacled man was sure to be armed, and so she wanted to keep her pistol aimed at him as steadily as she could.

'What's your name?' she demanded.

'What the feck is my name any business of yours?'

'It's my business because you're under arrest for threatening behaviour and on suspicion of homicide, and because you're under arrest you're required by law to give me your name and address.'

'Aha. But the law also says that you're required to show me *your* ID, girl, since you're not in uniform. You could be fecking anybody for all I know.'

'You know who I am.'

'Ah, but you could be your twin sister. Or maybe some other bean-garda who's the bulb off of you.'

'Are you going to tell me your name?'

'Why don't you fecking guess? I'll give you a clue – "Sharky".'

Katie said, 'I'm going to back slowly downstairs and I want you to follow me, keeping your hands up. If you don't follow me, or if you make any suspicious moves, I won't hesitate to shoot you. Do you understand?'

The man suddenly lost his temper. 'You fecking scrubber!' he screamed at her. 'You *cailleach*! How the hell did I miss you? You should be lying in your fecking coffin by now with all your relatives weeping around you!'

Katie thought, *My God, he was one of the two fellows who tried to shoot me and Justice Connolly outside Greenes.* She could see now that he was wearing the identical pair of glasses.

She could have retreated downstairs, leaving him up here on the landing for the ASU team to deal with. But that would give him the opportunity to take out his gun, and the stairs were so narrow that the armed support unit could climb up them only one at a time to confront him. Even if they used tear gas to smoke him out or a thunderflash to shock him, there was still a risk that a garda could get shot.

'Come here to me – if you give yourself up now, things will go much easier for you,' Katie told him. 'It wasn't you who set this raid up, was it? It was Barry. And you wouldn't have done it at all if you weren't so scared of him.'

'*What?* Are you trying to say that I'm a jibber? I'm not scared of nobody and that's Barry Riordan and you included!'

He staggered slightly on his left leg, and from that, and from his posture, and the way he was talking to her, Katie was sure that he was drunk. If he had been sober, he probably would have waited up in the attic for much longer, to make absolutely sure that the last of the gardaí had gone.

Almost immediately she was proved right, because he suddenly shivered and urinated, flooding the front of his jeans.

'*Now look what you've fecking done!*' he screamed at her. He was obviously so mortified about wetting himself in front of her that he didn't care if he was risking his life. He dropped both arms and thrust his right hand into the pocket of his puffer jacket, yanking out a black Glock automatic.

Katie shot him through the hand, so that he dropped the pistol on to the carpet and shouted out '*Shite!*', flapping his hand in the air so that blood sprayed all over the mustard-coloured wallpaper. She shot him a second time in the left knee, so that he pitched over sideways, hitting his head against the frame of one of the bedroom doors. He lay there, alternately groaning and swearing, holding up his bleeding right hand as if he were appealing to God and clutching his bleeding knee with his left.

Sergeant Mullally came storming up the stairs with his gun raised, followed by Detective O'Donovan and Kyna. The landing was pungent with gun smoke, and Katie's ears were singing.

'Are you okay, ma'am?' asked Sergeant Mullally. First of all he bent down to pick up the Glock automatic, hooking his finger through the trigger guard, but when he stood up straight again he saw the attic door hanging open and the aluminium ladder. Katie could tell by the expression on his face that he was cursing himself for not having thought of searching the attic himself. It had seemed so unlikely that anybody could have sprung open the door, brought down the ladder and climbed up out of sight, closing the door behind them, all in such a short space of time. But Sharky was drunk and his bladder had been bursting and he must have acted with all the jerky frenetic speed of a man who is desperately trying not to wet himself.

'You can call in the paramedics now, sergeant,' said Katie. 'Kyna – Patrick – you don't reck this character, do you?'

Kyna shook her head and Detective O'Donovan said, 'No, ma'am, I can't say that I do. But then the Riordans have never strutted around town throwing shapes, have they? Not like the O'Flynns.'

'When I asked him for his name he refused to tell me, but he said that a clue was "Sharky", so I'm making a wild guess that his first name is Feargal. You know – like Feargal Sharkey the singer.'

The man on the floor continued to groan and curse, and when Detective O'Donovan leaned over him to take a photograph of his face, he spat at him and said, 'Feck off, will you? Go and shite yourself, you fecking shade!' He then brought up about a tablespoonful of cream-coloured vomit.

It was only a few minutes before two paramedics came panting up the stairs, lugging their emergency trauma bags.

'Your man's been shot in the hand and the knee,' Katie told them. 'I don't think you'll have any trouble stopping the bleeding but I don't know how you're going to stop the stream of filth that's coming out of his mouth.'

'Not a bother, ma'am,' said the older paramedic placidly, as if he had handled cases like this a hundred times before. 'We'll give him a hefty shot of fentanyl and that'll shut him up.'

Katie waited for a while, watching the paramedics clean the hole in the man's hand and cut open his sodden jeans to expose the lumpy bullet wound in his knee. She found it hard to take her eyes off the man who may have been responsible for murdering Garrett. Eventually, though, she turned and went back downstairs to join Kyna and Detective O'Donovan. As she went, the man lifted his head and shouted out, '*Cailleach!*' one more time. '*Witch!*'

Katie and Kyna and Detective O'Donovan walked through the bars, past the bodies of the three dead gangsters. In the street outside it was still raining hard. Uniformed gardaí had arrested the drivers of the three getaway cars, including Nocky. Even though Nocky hadn't been wearing his trademark orange cap, he had been recognized at once. He was standing in the middle of the road, handcuffed and soaking wet, rain dripping from the end of his nose, the picture of human misery. A Garda van had been reversed down the slope, its blue lights flashing, and the remaining seven gang members were being jostled inside.

'I'm only sorry that Barry Riordan wasn't here in person,' said Katie, looking around. 'In fact, I'm amazed. I would have thought that nothing in the world could have stopped him from coming to see Maddie O'Flynn's twenty-first birthday party being wrecked.'

'I don't know... it doesn't surprise me that much,' said Detective O'Donovan. 'I'm not the only one who's noticed that your man's been keeping a pure low profile in the past few months. Even lower than usual. DS Dempsey mentioned it to me only last week. Like, where's Barry?'

'You're right. There was no sign of him at all, was there, when we lifted those five fellows at The Shamrock Club with all that crack, and they were all Riordan's men. And you can't tell me that he wasn't behind that hit on Billy Hagerty. In the old days he would have gone looking for Billy and shot him himself.'

'Do you know, I firmly believe that it's *you* that's keeping his head down,' said Kyna.

'Me?'

'Yes, I'm sure of it. The papers may have been putting you down all right, but I think Barry Riordan wised up to the fact quite some time ago that you've been putting plans together to break up his gang, and all the other gangs, too, and he respects you.'

'Mother of God. I don't know if I'm flattered to be respected by the sleaziest scummer in Cork.'

'This raid today, ma'am – my guess is that it was supposed to be a warning to everybody in Cork not to mess with the Riordans, do you know? Informers, enemy gang members, rival drug-dealers, you name it. And *us*, too. This was supposed to show that Barry Riordan is the King of Crime. Untouchable.'

'Right,' said Katie. 'Let's ship the survivors down to the station to be interviewed. We only need one of them to squeal and admit that this raid was initiated by Barry Riordan and we have him. With any luck, the king is about to lose his crown.'

She watched as Sharky was carried out on a stretcher to a waiting ambulance, with an umbrella held over him.

'Believe it or not, that fellow there was one of the two feens who tried to kill me and Justice Connolly in MacCurtain Street. He pretty much admitted it. More than that, though, he was driving Justice Quinn's car just before Justice Quinn was murdered. I recognized him from the CCTV.'

'Serious? It was him who shot at you? And it could have been him who killed Justice Quinn? Like, one and the same fellow?'

'There's a strong possibility, yes. He's totally buckled at the moment. I mean like *wrecked*. He must have had more than a few scoops before he set out on this raid to give himself some Dutch courage. But once he's sobered up and recovered from his painkillers, maybe we can persuade him to tell us who paid him to kill Justice Quinn and to try to kill me and Justice Connolly.'

'You think he will? Barry Riordan's been known to take his revenge on squealers, even when they're in jail.'

'We could offer to persuade the judge to give him a lighter sentence, and to give him protection once he's inside. I want that information, though, Patrick. It's personal. You don't even know how much.'

40

'Declan! Take a sconce up in front, boy! Jesus! We could make this a tourist attraction and sell tickets!'

Declan Hennessy looked up from his laptop. He and Peter Bale were driving down the main access road of the Waterfront Business Park, nine kilometres to the east of Cork city. The rain was hammering against their windscreen and drumming against the side of their van. The road was flooded up to their axles and they were towing a hydro jet pump on a trailer, so they could only creep along slowly.

Both sides of the road were lined with factories and warehouses. Outside the entrance to the next warehouse up ahead of them, a huge geyser of water was spouting over thirty metres up into the air. It was being blown by the strong south-east wind so that it was topped by a ragged plume of spray.

Peter stopped the van and they both turned up the collars of their yellow waterproof jackets and put on their white protective helmets with *Irish Water* stencilled on the front. They were leak detection technicians, although this leak needed nothing at all in the way of detecting. Since the latest trough of low pressure had moved in over Cork and brought continuous heavy rain, this was the fifth overflow they had been called out to deal with, three of them in the city centre, but this one was by far the most spectacular.

They waded over to the open manhole. The manhole cover had been blown off by the force of the flooding and was lying under the water nearby.

'See, the tide's coming in and the sewer's already full to capacity and that's why it's backing up,' Peter shouted, so that Declan could hear him over the gushing water and the blustering wind.

'Yes, but with *this* amount of pressure?' Declan shouted back. 'If you ask me, there's something obstructing it. Or, like, *partially* obstructing it. Like when you squeeze a garden hose, do you know what I mean?'

They waited for a few minutes, and the geyser gradually started to subside. It sank lower and lower until it was only knee-high, but then it suddenly surged up again, until it was almost as high as it had been when they had first seen it.

'That's the tide,' said Peter, and checked his watch. 'It's on the turn soon. We should be able to check then if anything's blocking it.'

They sloshed back to their van and climbed back in, shaking the rain from their jackets. Peter switched on the radio to RedFM and then they both took out plastic boxes of sandwiches, and sat there listening to the Colm O'Sullivan music show and solemnly munching.

'What's your old doll given you today, boy?'

'Turkey again. If you ask me she still has a load of it left over from Christmas. What's yours?'

'Some kind of cheese it tastes like, but I wouldn't lay money on it.'

It took nearly an hour for the geyser to sink down as far as the surface of the flood water. After that, it simply bubbled and occasionally let out a belch of foetid sewage gas. Declan uncoupled the hydro jet pump trailer from the back of their van and wheeled it around next to the manhole. The pump would blast water at such high pressure into the drain that almost anything that was blocking it would be cleared away:

tree roots, solidified fat, slurry, and almost any kind of waste from wet wipes and cardboard to industrial sludge and animal intestines from abattoirs.

Both Declan and Peter covered their eyes with goggles and their faces with protective masks, and then Declan lowered the jet pump nozzle into the bubbling water. He was able to feed it down hand over hand for about six and a half metres before he suddenly stopped and said, 'Hello. There's something here all right, boy. And it's *big*, by the feel of it.'

He prodded the pipe down again and again. 'It's almost completely blocking the outflow, so that all this floodwater has nowhere to go except up... especially when the tide comes in. I'll give it a blast and see if I can shift it.'

He switched on the hydro jet pump and instantly the water over the manhole looked as if it were boiling. A few tangled tree roots came dancing to the surface, followed by lumps of sodden paper. The roaring of the pump was deafening and Declan had to mime to Peter that the blockage hadn't budged. He jabbed the pipe down again and again and he still couldn't shift it.

He was just about to give up when the water suddenly swirled and gurgled like a whirlpool. Out of the flooded manhole a human figure shot up, almost waist-high. It was a man in a wet white shirt and sagging red braces. His bloated face was pale green, mottled with black, and his eyes were as blind as two poached eggs. His lips were swollen into a monstrous pout, as if he were furious at having been dislodged.

He bobbed up and down in the froth from the jet pump, but Declan immediately switched off the motor, and he sank down to float just below the surface. Both Declan and Peter stumbled away from the manhole, almost falling over each other, their waders splashing in the floodwater.

'Christ almighty, Peter, that put my heart crossways!' Declan panted, bending over and grasping his knees, as if he had just run a marathon.

'You and me both, boy. Jesus. How do you think your man got himself stuck down there?'

'What difference does it make? The poor soul's dead and perished, however he did it.'

'But the cover was closed, like, and you wouldn't think that anybody would go down there and shut the lid down after themselves. I mean, that would be suicide. Or sewercide. Christ, this is no time for me to be making jokes.'

'I don't know, Peter. I have no idea at all. But we have to ring the guards.'

'God, Declan. I think that turkey sandwich is getting itself ready for a second coming.'

Detective Inspector Mulliken stood in the rain with his collar turned up and the peak of his tweed cap pulled down, watching as the man's body was lifted out of the manhole. As soon as the tide had turned, the manhole had started to empty, and the body had sunk back down into the sewer. Peter Bale had called in a flusher from Irish Water and the flusher had climbed down to attach a harness under the man's arms so that he could be hauled out.

An ambulance was parked by the side of the road, as well as two squad cars, two unmarked Garda cars, and two cars and a van from the Technical Bureau. Even as the body appeared, a van from RTÉ news came down the road, followed by a battered blue Mondeo that Detective Inspector

Mulliken recognized as belonging to Dan Keane from the *Irish Examiner.*

'Who the hell tipped off the press?' asked Detective O'Sullivan. Then he looked across at the nearby furniture warehouse where he could see the staff all lined up, staring out of the windows. 'I don't even know why I said that.'

The man's body was lifted out of the manhole by two gardaí, who laid him on a stretcher with a sound like somebody dropping a sodden mattress. Detective Inspector Mulliken and Detective O'Sullivan crossed over to take a closer look, while technical experts were taking so many flash photographs that they appeared to freeze the raindrops in mid-air.

Bill Phinner was crouched down next to the body. He was wearing a fluorescent yellow raincoat with a hood, although he had pushed the hood back. He looked as miserable as ever, as if the dead man had been a relative of his.

'His skull's been fractured,' said Bill, and he lifted up the man's head. 'See, look, at the back here, there's this triangular piece sticking out, and it's pierced his scalp. In fact, his whole head has been crushed like an egg, although you wouldn't think it because his face is so swelled up.'

Detective Inspector Mulliken bent over the body and stared at it for almost a quarter of a minute without saying anything. Then he turned back to Detective O'Sullivan.

'It's Eamonn O'Malley. No question. I thought it must be him, because of his braces. But he has that gold anchor earring in his left ear, too. If you can imagine his face not so puffed up, and his head not so pointed, and his eyes blue.'

'Eamonn O'Malley – that's Thomas O'Flynn's hit man, isn't it?'

'Bang on, but "hit man" would be paying him too much of a compliment, to be honest with you. More like "head-the-ball hard chaw". Violent, and dangerous, but mental with it. The sort of gowl who'd only have to think that you were looking at him funny and he'd claim you.'

'He won't be causing anybody any more bother now,' said Bill. 'It's my guess that whoever killed him thought that he'd decompose quickly and be carried out to sea. Maybe they didn't know that bodies stay intact for longer in running water, even in sewage, with all its bacteria. You can still identify a body that's been lying in running water after seven weeks, or even longer.'

Detective O'Sullivan looked back at the warehouse. 'We may have a stroke of luck, and they've CCTV over there that covers the road. Or maybe one of their staff saw somebody out here by the manhole acting suspicious-like. I mean, look at them. They're nosy enough.'

'Let's hope so,' said Detective Inspector Mulliken. 'It's going to be the devil's own job, otherwise, trying to find out who wanted O'Malley dead. He had more enemies than a hedgehog has fleas.'

'Don't be too glum about it,' Bill told him, standing up. 'The autopsy should give us a fair number of leads. It'll tell us roughly how long he's been dead, so at least we'll have a time frame for when his killers dropped him down the drain. And the way that his head was smashed, I reckon that's going to tell us the most.'

'How's that, then?'

'It's what it was done with. I've seen heads that were bashed in with sledgehammers and heads that were run over by cars and heads that were crushed against factory walls by reversing lorries, but I've never seen a head smashed in exactly like this before. You see the deep indentations here on each side, and the angle they're at, and the damage that's been done to his ears? Those tell me that his head was struck with considerable force at least three times and possibly more, and in some kind of pincers like a massive pair of nutcrackers. All we have to do now is work out what could cause injuries like that, and whatever it is, who owns it.'

'Piece of cake,' said Detective O'Sullivan. 'All we have to do is get on to Amazon and see who's bought a massive pair of nutcrackers recently.'

Detective Inspector Mulliken gave him a sharp look and he said, 'Sorry. Just trying to lighten the mood, like.'

Katie was back in her office when Kyna came in to tell her that Sharky had been identified. One of the arrested gang had heard Katie's two pistol shots and assumed that she had killed him. He had asked if Sharky's sister who lived in Ardnacrusha could be notified, so that she could make funeral arrangements for him.

Sharky's name was Feargal Grífin, sometimes known as Feargal Darsey, and he had been a member of the Keane-Collopy gang in St Mary's Park in Limerick before he had met Barry Riordan and been recruited to come below to Cork. He had a criminal record that went back to his fifteenth birthday party, when he had picked up a cake knife and stabbed one of his friends because he had shifted his girlfriend. After that he had been in and out of jail three times, once for robbery and twice for assault. Seven years ago he had been attacked in Limerick Prison and hit in the face with a metal chair, which had permanently affected his eyesight. After that he had been nicknamed Feargal the Four-Eyed Fecker, although the story was that he had slashed and permanently disfigured a gang member who had dared to call him that to his face.

'At least we know now what kind of a creature we're dealing with,' said Katie. 'An unadulterated scumbag. No wonder Barry Riordan wanted him to come to Cork and work for him. Our Barry has a keen eye when it comes to picking the dregs of the Earth.'

She was still talking to Kyna when Detective Inspector Mulliken knocked at her door.

'Tony…' she said. 'How's it going with the body down the drain?'

Detective Inspector Mulliken came in, followed by Detective O'Sullivan.

'Would you believe it's Eamonn O'Malley. Yes, *that* Eamonn O'Malley, the hit man for Thomas O'Flynn. At least that's what he liked to call himself. More like blustering bully-boy.'

'Can you believe it? Two hit men in one day. I think the angels must be smiling on us.'

'Well, you reap what you sow. O'Malley's remains are on their way to the morgue at CUH and I've notified Dr Kelley. Bill Phinner's promised to expedite the forensics. He reckons that O'Malley's head was crushed in something like a giant pair of nutcrackers.'

'Giant nutcrackers? That's a first.'

'Of course it wasn't really nutcrackers but he seemed confident that his people could work out what actually did it. What's the story with that fellow you shot at The Weavers?'

'He's over at the Mercy, under guard in the emergency room. I'm waiting to hear from his doctor when he's fit enough to be questioned. Feargal Grífin his name is, apparently.'

'I've heard the name, I'm sure of it,' said Detective O'Sullivan. 'But the Riordans, they're a tight-lipped lot, aren't they? They wouldn't tell you how many sausages they had for breakfast, even for money.'

'What about the media?' asked Detective Inspector Mulliken. 'They're gagging for more information about what happened at The Weavers. Dan Keane and Fionnuala Sweeney both turned up at the Waterfront Business Park when we were fetching Eamonn O'Malley's body up out of the manhole, and Dan Keane asked me about it then.'

'What did you tell him?'

'Nothing at all. I didn't even tell him that the body was Eamonn O'Malley. I thought I'd leave that up to you. You'll be holding a media briefing, won't you?'

Katie said, 'I'm not sure yet. I may be, but first of all I need to have a word with Chief Superintendent O'Kane.'

She didn't add 'to find out if he'll give me permission'.

41

Barry Riordan had started up the engine of his Mercedes when Dougal Dolan came leaping down the steps at the back of The Cotton Ball pub two at a time. He came running across the car park and rapped on his window with his knuckles.

Barry put down the window, took the cigarette out of his mouth and snapped, 'What?'

'It's all gone arseways, Bazza! I've just heard from Molan! There was no O'Flynns there at all and when our boys went rushing in, a whole crowd of cops went rushing in after them!'

'*What?*'

'He says he heard shooting and then the cops fetched the boys out all cuffed up and loaded them into a paddy wagon. But he saw no sign of Feargal coming out, nor Jimmy, nor Padraig nor Cathal neither.'

Barry gripped the wheel so tightly that he looked as if he were going to wrench it right off the steering column. Dougal remained by the side of his car, panting in the rain like a Labrador waiting to have a stick thrown for him.

'We've been stitched up!' Barry breathed, with smoke still puffing out of his nose and his mouth. 'We've been fecking stitched up! I'll bet you anything you like that Tommy O'Flynn set this up deliberate! I'll bet you there never *was* no birthday party! He *knew* we'd want to mess it up, and he tipped off the shades! I'll fecking kill him with my bare hands! I'll fecking shoot him and run him over and cut off his mebs and toss him in the river!'

'But if there wasn't a party, why did Lenny tell us that there was?'

'How the feck should I know? O'Flynn must have bamboozled him, too, or paid him off.'

'No... Lenny wouldn't rat on you. Not Lenny.'

'Every feen has his price, Dougal. You know that.'

'Not me, Bazza. I'm with you all the way. But what are you going to do now?'

'What do you think I'm going to do? I'm going to go home and do nothing. Absolutely fecking feck-all. You know what's bound to happen now, don't you? The shades'll be knocking at my door trying to haul me in for conspiracy to murder.'

'But you wasn't there, Bazza.'

'That's where I'll have them on toast. I wasn't there personally myself in person, like you say. And there was nobody there at The Weavers to be murdered, so I couldn't conspire to murder somebody who wasn't there, could I? And I'll swear on the Bible that I knew nothing whatsoever about any of this at all. They can't arrest me for something I never even heard of.'

'So long as none of the lads squeal.'

'What? Are you taking the Michael? Lenny might've been paid off, and if he has I'll find out about it, and he'll pay for it ten times more, I promise you. But none of our boys would dream of squealing. They know too well what would be coming their way if ever they did.'

Barry paused, his nostrils flaring, still gripping the steering wheel tightly. Then he said, 'Keep me in the loop, all right, Dougal? Minute by minute. If it wasn't Lenny who shopped us then I'm going to find out who it was and by all that's holy I'm going to make them beg on their bended knees for me to kill them.'

***

When he reached home he found Megan in the kitchen, ironing his shirts. She was still wearing a plaster across the bridge of her nose, but her face was much less swollen and the bruises under her eyes had faded to a dull yellow.

He had slammed the front door and when he came into the kitchen he went straight to the bottle of Paddy's whiskey on top of the fridge, half-filled a teacup, and swallowed it in one.

'What's the matter, Barry?' Megan asked him. 'Is it still lashing out?'

He couldn't speak for a few moments, because of the whiskey, and he had to punch his chest before he could say, '*What?* Has God struck you blind or something? Look out the window and you can see for yourself it's still lashing. What you can't see is that the whole world's gone arse over tit.'

'I don't know what you mean.'

'Well you wouldn't because you're too fecking thick. But somebody's shopped us and it looks like four of the boys have been shot dead by the shades and another seven have been lifted.'

'Mother of God, Barry. When was this?'

Barry poured himself another half-cupful of whiskey and lit a cigarette. 'You don't need to know about it and if the shades come around asking about it you don't know nothing. Do you have me?'

'But who's dead?'

'I told you. You don't need to know about it. Feargal, as it happens. Feargal and Jimmy and Cathal and Padraig. And you're stupid enough to ask me what's wrong?'

'How did it happen?'

'I told you, you stupid ganky. You don't need to know. Now shut your bake and carry on with your pressing, will you? Christ almighty!'

Megan stood behind the ironing board, genuinely shocked.

'Well, get on with it,' Barry barked at her. 'Those fecking shirts aren't going to press themselves, are they?'

'But what are you going to do?'

'What can I do? If they're dead they're dead. You want me to go round to the funeral parlour and give them the kiss of life?'

'Aren't you going to get in touch with their families or nothing? Cathal's sister, she's going to be devastated. And Jimmy's ma.'

'You don't get it, do you? I don't know nothing about them being shot and neither do you.'

'What were they up to? Was it some job they were on?'

Barry blew out a column of smoke and then he tossed his cigarette into the sink. He stalked across the kitchen, wrenched the steam iron out of Megan's hand and then knocked over the ironing board so that it crashed sideways on to the floor.

'You—!' he shouted. 'You are getting on my fecking wick, you are! Why the hell can't you keep your yapper shut and do what any good wife is supposed to do – cooking and cleaning and laundry and opening your legs when I tell you? Don't you remember the promise you made to me in front of the priest? Honour and fecking obey! That's what you promised! Honour and fecking obey! But no! What do I get? Nothing but fecking lip! You weapon!'

He dug his fingers into the hair at the back of Megan's head and held up the steam iron in front of her face, dripping and hissing.

'You think that breaking your hooter was bad? Your hooter's healing, isn't it? But let's see what you look like if I give you the full-face branding! Then everybody's going to be asking you, how did you get that iron-shaped scar on your face, Megan? Was you being careless when you was pressing your old fellow's shirts? And you'll have to tell them, no, I was always fecking nagging, like, and Barry needed to teach me a lesson that I'd never forget!'

He pressed the button on the iron, so that a jet of steam was puffed into Megan's face. She squealed and flinched and tried to twist her head away, but Barry gripped her hair even tighter, and gave her another puff.

'Don't, Barry, for the love of God,' she pleaded with him, but he held the iron even closer – so close that she could see her face reflected in it, her brown eyes staring at herself in panic. 'I swear I won't ever nag you again, not ever. I'll do whatever you want me to, and I won't ever argue.'

'That's what you said the last time, I seem to remember – *and* the time before that. I don't fecking believe you. Didn't I ask you pure polite-like to buy me some beer and some fags and what did you say? Go on, what did you say?'

'I said I wouldn't.'

'Chalk it down. That's exactly what you said. And is that what a wife should be after saying to her husband, when she's promised to honour and obey him?'

He held the iron closer still, almost touching the tip of her nose, and Megan went rigid, trying to tilt her head away from it, and she let out a thin whining sound in the back of her throat. At that moment, though, the front doorbell rang, and rang again, and yet again, and the ringing was followed by a thunderous knocking.

Barry immediately let go of Megan's hair. He set the iron down on the drainer next to the sink and bent over to pick up the ironing board. The bell-ringing and the knocking went on, and now somebody was kicking at the door panels too.

'Listen, I was only codding about branding you,' said Barry. 'Do you have me? I just wanted to put the fear of God into you, that's all.'

Megan stared at him, unable to speak, fingering her nose where it had been scorched by the heat of the iron.

'That'll be the shades, girl, no question. Remember what I said to you. You don't know nothing and you never heard nothing and you don't know none of those feens that was shot. Not Feargal not Jimmy not Padraig not Cathal and you don't know Cathal's sister or Jimmy's ma neither.'

With that, Barry went out into the hallway screaming, 'All right! All right! I heard you the first time! Stall the fecking ball, will you? What are you trying to do, kick my fecking door in?'

He opened the door and there was Detective Sergeant Begley and Detective Cushley, with four uniformed gardaí behind them. Barry could see that most of his near neighbours had opened their front doors or drawn back their living-room curtains to see what all the disturbance was about.

'How's the form, Barry?' asked Detective Sergeant Begley. Both he and Detective Cushley were holding up their IDs. 'Having a restful afternoon at home, are we?'

'I was, yeah, until you lot started beating four colours of shite out of my poor defenceless front door. Look what you've done to the fecking paintwork. I'll be sending you the tab for that, you can count on it. What are you after?'

'Have you been watching the news on the TV at all? Or listening to it, on the radio?'

'No. I've been having a few gatts with my pals in The Cotton Ball since about twelve. I've only this minute come back. So what's been on the news? Something important?'

'Important to *you*, I'd say, Barry. We'd like you to come down to the station with us, if that's all right with you, so that we can ask you one or two questions.'

'Questions about what?'

'Let's leave that till we get to Anglesea Street, shall we? But once we've told you why we want to talk to you, you can ring your solicitor if you want to, or we can provide a duty lawyer for you.'

'What if I tell you to go and stick your head up your arse?'

'Then I'd have to tell you that you were suggesting something physically impossible and arrest you.'

'Arrest me what for?'

'Barry – you know the score. How many times have we done this before? I'm asking you to come to the station voluntarily so that we can clear up a couple of points without having to go through the whole arrest procedure. It's in your interest as well as ours.'

Barry stared back at Detective Sergeant Begley with that expression he had seen on so many criminals over the years. It was boredom, more than anything – the look of men and women who feel nothing at all for the rest of humanity and its morality. The only times they will ever cry is when their own comfort or their own freedom is in jeopardy. Then they will sob like babies, even the toughest of them.

'I'll just give the old doll a kiss and tell her where I'm off to, if that's all right with you, and then I'll get my coat.'

'Take your time, boy.'

Barry went back into the kitchen. Megan said, 'They've not arrested you, have they?'

'No. But I'm playing Mister Co-operative and I'm off to the cop shop with them so that they can ask me some questions, which I won't be giving them the answer to. Give Molan a bell, will you, and tell him that's where I am. But if the shades come asking you questions, you don't know nothing at all, remember?'

'Barry – I don't know nothing anyway.'

'Jesus's under-grundies, you can say that again.'

42

Katie found Brendan upstairs in the communications room, his arms folded, watching the aftermath of Operation Hubbard on CCTV. The Bord Gáis tent was being dismantled, although the pavement outside The Weavers was still cordoned off. An ambulance had backed down the hill and the bodies of the three dead gang members were being carried out on stretchers.

'Ah, Kathleen,' said Brendan. 'I was on my way to see you so. I suppose some sort of congratulations are in order. Not that I'm overjoyed about the death toll. There'll have to be an inquest of course and there'll be all kinds of prickly questions asked by the press. One minute we're not doing enough to combat crime in Cork and the next we're overreacting and firing guns off all over the place. Yourself included, so I'm told.'

'Those Riordans were armed to the back teeth, sir. They had two AR-15s and half a dozen automatic pistols, Glocks and Sig-Sauers. We were haunted we didn't suffer any casualties ourselves, apart from one badly bruised shoulder. I'll be filing a full report.'

Although Sergeant Murphy and the rest of the gardaí in the communications room appeared to be giving their full attention to the CCTV screens in front of them, Brendan could see that they were half-listening to him and Katie, too.

'Let's go back down to my office, shall we?' he suggested.

'Maybe the canteen, sir. I could do with a coffee.' When Katie said that, she gave Brendan a look that meant, *I don't want to be alone with you in your office – not now, and not ever again.*

They went down in the lift together, not speaking. When they reached the canteen they sat by the window, out of earshot of three gardaí who were having a late lunch of bacon and cabbage and talking loudly about hurling. Outside, the rain had eased off, and the clouds were tearing apart like damp grey tissue paper.

'So that's three of Riordan's gang down and eight lifted?' said Brendan. 'But Barry Riordan himself wasn't among them. That kind of defeated the whole object of the exercise, didn't it? All he has to do now is find himself eleven more gurriers and that's the Riordans back up to strength. There must be dozens of corner boys who'd give anything to say they're one of his gang.'

'Sean Begley's fetching Barry Riordan in right now for questioning. And we'll be questioning all of his gang individually. They're not the brightest bunch that you'll ever come across, so there's a fair chance that one of them will slip up and give us the evidence we need to hold your man on a charge of conspiracy. One in particular.'

'Oh, yes?'

Katie told him about Feargal Grífin, and the strong possibility that he had murdered Justice Quinn.

'He's fierce unstable. In fact he's a header. There I was, not three metres away and pointing my pistol directly at him and he still tried to pull out his own gun. If we can charge him with Justice Quinn's murder he could well go for a plea bargain and testify that Barry Riordan organized the raid on The Weavers.'

'But we have no firm evidence that he killed Justice Quinn.'

'We have the CCTV of him driving off with him less than an hour before his car was set on fire. And I firmly believe that I can come up with more evidence, too.'

'Like what?'

'Like who paid him to kill him.'

'Kathleen, this is all pie in the sky. The number of times I've heard you saying that you don't believe in hunches. But admit it – you're making this up as you go along, aren't you, just to make the media believe that you're getting on top of the gangs, when you're not. This Operation Hubbard was nothing but a fiasco. We've ended up killing three men and wounding another with almost no legal justification. They were armed, yes, but you knew that they weren't going to be shooting anybody because you'd already arranged it yourself that there was nobody in the pub for them to shoot.'

'Sir – they opened fire on us first.'

'Yes, but they wouldn't have fired on you if you hadn't gone in after them. Why didn't you wait until they came out and pull their cars over separately?'

'Don't think I didn't consider that. But even then there would have been a high risk of them opening fire on us, and that would have endangered not only us but any passers-by, too. Or they might have tried to drive away at high speed, which could have caused a serious traffic accident.'

'I don't know. What am I going to tell the media? "Don't worry, Detective Superintendent Maguire is turning Cork into a fairground shooting gallery. She's decided that the easiest way to get rid of the gangs is to use them as target practice."'

'That's what I wanted to talk to you about. We have to hold a media conference about Operation Hubbard, and we have to hold it within the next hour or so. But even after what you decided at Phoenix Park, I want to be the one to brief them – not you.'

Brendan said nothing, but sipped his coffee, staring at her.

'I know exactly how this needs to be presented,' Katie told him. 'What needs to be said and what needs to be kept totally confidential. We can't explain to the media that the gas leak was nothing but a ruse. If we do, Thomas O'Flynn will realize that somebody told the Riordans about Maddie O'Flynn's birthday party and that somebody then told *us* that the Riordans were going to attack it. If Thomas O'Flynn and Barry Riordan put two and two together that could possibly put both Muireann Nic Riada and Megan Riordan in danger of their lives.'

'So how do we tell the media that we found out what the Riordans were planning to do? Because they're bound to ask us.'

'Simple. We'd heard rumours of a major drug deal in the offing and we were hacking the Riordan gang's phones.'

'Is that possible? Don't they use those smartphones that can't be hacked, the same as we do?'

'Bill Phinner has a phone expert, Conall. He can explain how we do it.'

She was sorely tempted to tell Brendan that Conall had been hacking *his* phone calls, even though they were encrypted, and that she had found out that he had been bribing Owen Dineen to write smear stories about her. But she knew this wasn't the right moment. For the time being, that knowledge was her insurance policy.

'I still believe this Operation Hubbard was incredibly ill thought-out, Kathleen, especially in the way that the public are going to see it.'

'That will depend on how we present it, sir. And I'd still prefer you to call me Detective Superintendent.'

Brendan sipped more coffee, and then he said, 'Can't we bury the hatchet? I mean – are we really going to spend the rest of our careers at loggerheads?'

'The rest of our careers? Who knows how long that's going to be. Or how short, for that matter.'

'In this case anyway, yes, you can lead the media briefing. I'll be frank with you, though. It's mainly because I don't want the press to think that I was the one who set up Operation Hubbard.'

'They might well applaud me for it, sir, and then you'd get no credit at all. "And so the poor dog had none."'

Brendan looked at Katie in almost exactly the same way that Feargal Grífin had looked at her after she had shot him, and she could imagine him thinking the same word that Feargal Grífin had spat at her: '*Cailleach!*'

Katie asked Mathew McElvey to arrange the media briefing as late as he possibly could, so that the reporters would be pushed for time to make their deadlines for the *Six One News* and tomorrow morning's papers.

As it was, they were much more interested in the gory details of the shootings that had killed three of Barry Riordan's gang than the wider picture of what this could mean for crime-fighting in Cork and the safety of her citizens.

Only Owen Dineen asked her a critical question, and now she knew that he was being paid to write negative articles about her, she wasn't upset by it at all. He would have his comeuppance. Once his editors at the *Irish Sun* discovered that he had taken bribes to twist his stories, it was unlikely that he would ever be employed by them again. They liked sensational news, but they were always punctilious about the facts.

Owen raised his hand like Bottler the schoolboy. 'Would you not admit that you've put your own officers and the population of this city as a whole in very grave danger, DS Maguire?'

'In what way, Owen?'

'Sure like, those Riordans are going to be thirsting for revenge, aren't they? I know Barry Riordan well, and there's no way he's going to be taking this lying down. Why do you think Billy Hagerty was shot? That was payback for Michael Riordan and his family being murdered by his brother Donal, and I challenge you to tell me anything different.'

'We have no proof yet who shot Billy Hagerty, or why. It's conceivable that whoever shot him was aiming for Thomas O'Flynn, who was right behind him at the time, and missed.'

Katie looked across at Brendan, who was sitting on the other side of Detective O'Donovan, and said, 'You know what a stickler I am for hard evidence, Owen. Guesswork is all well and good, but guesswork doesn't stand up in front of a judge and jury.'

'But do you not agree that this operation has made Cork a more dangerous city to live in?' Owen Dineen persisted. 'All you've done is poke a hornets' nest, haven't you? Barry Riordan is still a free man, and so is Thomas O'Flynn, and tonight the drug peddlers will be round the clubs as usual and the brothels will be open for business on Grafton Street but your officers had better be wearing bulletproof vests.'

Katie stayed calm. 'I can't divulge to you all of the progress we're making against the gangs in Cork, for operational reasons. But I can assure you that Operation Hubbard was only the beginning. What you're going to be seeing in the next few weeks and months is a purge of crime in this city like you've never seen before – a disinfection. From St Luke's Cross down to Togher, it's going to be cleaner and safer than any other community in the country.'

'Chief Superintendent O'Kane, what do you have to say about that?' asked Rionach Barr from the *Echo*. 'That's quite a target to be aiming for, isn't it?'

Brendan blinked, as if he hadn't been listening. 'What? Oh. Well. I suppose you could say that I'm a little less sanguine than DS Maguire, but I'm never one to put a damper on anyone's optimism. And of course I'll be giving her my unqualified support – always provided that she and I see eye to eye on the operations she has in mind to carry out this "purge".'

'What about this Operation Hubbard? Did you see eye to eye on that?'

Brendan stood up abruptly. 'I'm sorry, but that's all we have time for this afternoon. Thank you all for coming. If you need any further information, have a word with Mathew McElvey here.'

'You didn't answer my question, sir!' called out Rionach Barr. But Brendan had already stepped down from the platform and walked out of the door.

Rionach Barr turned to Katie. 'DS Maguire?'

'It's been a hard day for all of us, Rionach. We very much regret the fatalities that took place this afternoon during Operation Hubbard, and Chief Superintendent O'Kane is obviously anxious that we don't have more. All I can say is that men who carry guns with the intention of killing other men are endangering their own lives, too.'

'Especially when DS Maguire is on the warpath,' said Owen Dineen.

You just wait, thought Katie. *You're next in the firing line, my fat friend.*

Before she left for home, Katie went down to the cells to see Doireann Greaney. She was due to be sent to Limerick Prison in the morning, where committal prisoners for all of Munster were held pending trial.

Doireann was lying on her bunk reading a book when Katie entered her cell. She didn't even look up.

'How are you going on, Doireann?' Katie asked her.

'Peaceful,' said Doireann, still without looking up. 'At least I was until you came in.'

'What are you reading?'

'*The Collected Poems of W.B. Yeats.*'

'You like Yeats?'

'I wouldn't be reading it if I didn't, would I?'

'Read me one.'

Doireann was silent for a long time. Katie could see that she was struggling with herself – whether to be aggressive and refuse to do as she was asked, or whether to be gentle, and comply. If she complied, that would mean conceding that she was not completely an outsider, and that she could make friends, but that pushing innocent people into the river had been even more inexcusable.

Her face was even whiter and more witch-like than when she had first been arrested, and her long-fingered hands holding her book were almost transparent, so that Katie could see the tracery of her blue veins through her skin.

At last, still without raising her eyes, she whispered,

Come away, O human child!
To the waters and the wild
With a faery, hand in hand.
For the world's more full of weeping than you can
    understand.

Katie said, '"The Stolen Child". I used to read that, too, when I felt that all the world was against me.'

'At least you had a "when". For me it's been always.'

'I know. And you still have a long and hard road ahead of you, Doireann. You'll be sent off to Limerick Prison in the morning pending your trial. I'm not here to offer you my forgiveness, because that's God's job, not mine. But you'll find that there are plenty of people in the prison service who can give you guidance and support.'

Doireann at last looked up at her, with those dark, limpid eyes.

'How can you bear it, doing what you do?' she asked Katie. 'Doesn't it crucify you sometimes?'

'It's saints who get crucified, Doireann. I'm not a saint and never have been. That's why I can do this job. You need to be something of a sinner yourself to understand why sinners sin, and to catch them at it.'

Although Jenny Tierney had already taken Barney and Foltchain out for their evening hod before she arrived home, Katie took them out again, because she needed some fresh air herself. The two of them stayed very close to her, nearly tripping her up, and every now and then they would turn their heads and look up at her as if they were reassuring themselves that she was still there behind them.

She could tell that they missed Conor almost as much as she did, and how keenly they sensed her grief. In the days after he had died, Barney had sat in front of her whenever she was at home, resting his head in her lap, his ears spread wide like Falkor in *The NeverEnding Story*, and both of them had followed her from room to room.

She walked as far as Rinacollig, a narrow side road that led down to the estuary's edge, and she stood there for a while looking out over the night-glittering water.

Be peaceful, she told herself. Forget all the shock of shooting Feargal Grífin and all the hostilities and complications of the day's investigations. It was a chilly evening, so she kept her hands thrust deep in her overcoat pockets, but at least it wasn't raining, and the moon occasionally showed its face behind the clouds.

She was still standing there when her phone played *Mo Ghille Mear.*

'Katie? It's Kieran. I saw you on the news a couple of minutes ago talking about that raid in Blackpool this afternoon. Three men dead! You're okay yourself, though?'

'A little shaken, Kieran, to tell you the truth. But I wasn't hurt. And would you believe the fellow I took down was one of the two who tried to shoot us outside Greenes. He admitted it. Well, he didn't exactly admit it. He cursed himself for having missed me, which was pretty much an admission. Not only that, but he was the same fellow who drove off with Garrett Quinn on the morning that Garrett was killed.'

'Hold on. Does that mean that it could have been Barry Riordan who arranged to have Garrett done away with?'

'Well, Feargal Grífin is one of his gang, after all. One of his inner circle, from what I gather.'

'Yes, but I can't see the logic in Barry Riordan having Garrett killed, can you? Garrett was all ready to pass down a life sentence on the man who shot his brother and his family. And I can't see the logic in him arranging to have me and you done away with, either. It was you and your detectives who arrested Donal Hagerty, and it's me who'll be sentencing him on Monday morning in Garrett's place. It makes no sense at all. You would have thought Barry Riordan would have wanted to pat us on the back rather than shoot us in the front.'

'You're right, Kieran. But I'm too tired to think about it any more tonight.'

'Will you be free at all tomorrow?'

'Sunday is supposed to be my day off but I'll be going in to the station in the morning to sort out one or two things. I should be clear by lunchtime, though.'

'Let's meet for lunch, then. A couple of glasses of fizz and some roast prime rib should restore your faith in humanity.'

'It's never humanity that worries me, Kieran. Only inhumanity.'

43

The following morning Katie allowed herself an hour extra in bed. She always found that her mind was much clearer just after she had woken up, and problems that had seemed impossibly knotted the night before would untangle themselves as if by magic.

Despite that, she was still unsure what to think about Feargal Grífin. Had Barry Riordan ordered him to murder Garrett, and if he had, why?

Maybe he had hoped that suspicion for the killing would fall on Thomas O'Flynn, but that seemed like a very shaky explanation. No anonymous calls had been made, blaming the O'Flynns, and no false evidence had been planted at the scene of the murder that might have led Katie's detectives to believe that one of O'Flynn's gang might have committed it.

It was still possible, of course, that neither Barry Riordan nor Thomas O'Flynn had any hand in Garrett's murder at all, and that he had been killed by some vengeful ex-con who had been sent to prison by Garrett at some time in the past, and had recently been released. Maybe this ex-con had known Feargal Grífin and had arranged for him to pick up Garrett and drive him to White's Cross to be executed. But why would Garrett have agreed to go with him – and on top of that, why would he have allowed him to drive his cherished Jaguar?

Again and again, Katie's thinking kept returning to Orla Quinn. She knew from her own affair with Garrett that Orla was really the only woman in his life. He had always returned to her, no matter how often he had strayed. He had proved it, hadn't he, by telling her the intimate details of every one of his affairs, including his affair with Katie herself? And there was no question that Orla had loved him dearly. Not just dearly – desperately. So would she really have gone so far as to have him killed?

Orla was a criminal lawyer herself, so it was likely that she had come across Feargal Grífin at some point in her career, and from the way she had been talking to him on the CCTV footage it was apparent that she knew him at least reasonably well.

Katie wondered if she had been right in thinking that Orla had simply wanted him threatened or beaten up, but that the punishment had all gone horribly wrong, and his car had been set on fire to obliterate any forensic evidence.

She had only coffee and two ginger biscuits for breakfast because she would be meeting Kieran for lunch, and then she took Barney and Foltchain for a walk as far as the Passage West ferry terminal. It was a windy morning, and all the boats were bobbing up and down like *Riverdance*. She hadn't crossed the river to Monkstown for over a month now, ever since she and her sisters had put her father's house up for sale. She couldn't help remembering the smile on her father's face when she had told him that she wanted to join An Garda Síochána, the only one of her sisters to keep up the family tradition.

'You'll make your mark all right,' he had told her. 'You'll see. You'll have every criminal in Cork begging you for mercy.'

She arrived at Anglesea Street at a quarter past eleven. When she walked into her office she was surprised to find Bill Phinner and Aoife Shaughnessy, his new ballistics expert, sitting on the couches by the window, drinking tea and eating chocolate fingers.

'How's it going, ma'am?' asked Bill. 'We came up to see you and Patrick O'Donovan said you'd be here in a jiffy so we decided to wait for you. We thought you'd be wanting to see this in person.'

'What have you found, Bill?'

Aoife held up an evidence bag with two cartridge cases in it, and another bag with the Glock automatic pistol that had been taken from Feargal Grífin after Katie had shot him.

'We picked these cartridge cases out of the gutter in MacCurtain Street after you and Justice Connolly were shot at. They match the rounds exactly that were found in that burned-out Honda at Bottlehill after Billy Hagerty was shot and next to Timbo Coffey's body. Not only that, all four rounds were fired from this same pistol.

'AFIS had no record of the fingerprints we sent up to be checked from the first two cartridge cases, but no matter. There are partial fingerprints on these other two here that match them, and they all match the fingerprints on the pistol itself. There are no other prints on it, so I think we can reasonably assume that whoever shot Billy Hagerty was the same offender who shot Timbo Coffey and who shot at you and Justice Connolly, too.'

'Feargal Grífin,' said Katie. 'He was the fellow I brought down at The Weavers. He virtually confessed that it was him who tried to kill us in MacCurtain Street. He may well retract what he said or try to make out that he only said it under stress, but he should be fit enough to be questioned tomorrow. Grand work, Aoife. All I need to find out now is *why* he shot Billy Hagerty and Timbo Coffey and why he wanted to shoot us. He's also my prime suspect in the murder of Justice Quinn.'

'He was the fellow in the car, in that CCTV footage?'

'That's right. Either him or his identical twin brother.'

Bill picked up the Glock and turned it this way and that. 'Whatever you say about your man, then, you can't accuse him of not being prolific.'

It was less than half an hour before she was brought more evidence – this time from Detectives Walsh and Cullen. They had obviously come straight up to see her from outside: Detective Walsh was still bundled up in her fur-collared anorak and Detective Cullen had not yet taken off his droopy camel-coloured duffel coat. They both appeared pleased and excited.

'Holy Mary,' said Detective Walsh. 'We must have visited every single sports kit shop within a twenty-kilometre radius.'

'If I never again see a GAA T-shirt or smell the smell of Nike runners, I tell you, that'll be too soon for me,' Detective Cullen put in. He was normally so glum but today he couldn't stop smiling and running his hand through his curly red hair.

'Well, come on,' said Katie. 'You look like you've made some kind of a breakthrough.'

'We have, yes – at least we think so,' Detective Walsh told her. 'Until yesterday afternoon we thought we'd drawn a total blank. We'd been in and out of every sports outfitters all the way from Sports Direct in Ballincollig to the Mahon Point shopping centre. But then we called into the FitNess shop in Wilton. We noticed that they sell a light grey Donnay tracksuit with a thin white stripe down the leg and also a pair of runners with an N on the side – New Balance, that's who makes them. But what caught our attention was – they're the only shop that sells *both*.'

'The manager had already gone off home so we couldn't go through the sales records there and then,' said Detective Cullen. 'But we went back there as soon as they opened this morning, like, and he couldn't have been more obliging. It turned out that only one customer in the past month had bought both that tracksuit and those runners together in the same purchase.'

'He showed us the "be" Visa card receipt and guess who that card is registered to.'

'Go on. Don't keep me in suspense.'

'Nolan Carroll. Roisin Carroll's father.'

'Mother of God,' said Katie. She sat back in her chair, shaking her head in disbelief. 'Maybe I should have guessed it when I met him at the morgue to view Roisin's body. He was bad-tempered enough all right, and he deeply resented Roisin getting herself pregnant. I mean he was unbelievably bitter about it. But she was his daughter, and his only child at that. It's hard to believe that he'd dress himself up like that and push her into the river… her and his baby granddaughter, too.'

'What's the plan, then?' asked Detective Walsh.

'You have a copy of that FitNess receipt? Good. What with that, and his raging about Roisin when he came to the morgue to view her body, I think we have more than sufficient cause to arrest him on suspicion of murder. Dr Kelley was there with me at the viewing, and she'll testify to what she heard him say.'

She looked at her watch. 'Inspector O'Rourke's in today, isn't he? I'll have him arrange for a couple of uniforms to back us up. I'm supposed to be meeting somebody for lunch today, but this is one arrest I want to witness in person.'

Detective Cullen drove them down to the suburb of Ballyphehane in a dark blue unmarked Toyota, followed by a squad car with two uniformed gardaí. For the first time since Owen Dineen's first derogatory story about her in the *Sun*, Katie was beginning to feel upbeat and confident, and that she and her team were at last getting on top of a tragic and chaotic week.

One or two things still rankled. She still had to find a way to deal with Brendan's knowledge of her closeness to Kyna. She didn't believe for a moment that he had deleted the compromising pictures of them together. Knowing him, he would have kept them so that he always felt he had a hold over her, as well as for his own lubricious enjoyment. But her discovery that he had been bribing Owen Dineen might be enough to keep him quiet, even though Conall had hacked his phone illegally.

Then there was Orla's threat to expose her affair with Garrett, and how the conviction of Phinean Joyce had favoured her promotion. But that had been a long time ago now, and if she managed to tie up the most serious investigations that she was having to handle now – the bombing at the School of Pharmacy and the murder of Garrett Quinn above all – she hoped that it wouldn't affect her career as much as she had first feared.

'You're quiet, ma'am, if you don't mind my saying so,' said Detective Walsh.

'Yes,' said Katie. 'I'm just thinking how sad life can be sometimes. The world's full of weeping.'

They turned into Friary Gardens, a crescent of small terraced houses, most of them shingled in grey, with front gardens that had been concreted over for the owners to park their cars and store their wheelie bins. The Carroll's house was one of the few that was hidden behind a high privet hedge.

Katie and her detectives stood back while one of the uniformed gardaí went up to the front door and banged its brass knocker, hard. It was opened almost at once, but by less than ten centimetres, still on its security chain. Nolan Carroll, with his wave of white hair, peered out from the gloom of the hallway. He looked to Katie like a suspicious badger poking its nose out of its sett.

'What do you want?' he demanded. 'It's Sunday.'

Katie stepped forward. 'Nolan Carroll, I'm here to arrest you on suspicion of the murder of Roisin Carroll. You are not obliged to say anything unless you wish to do so, but anything you say will be taken down in writing and may be given in evidence.'

There was a long silence. Nolan Carroll continued to look out at them, but made no move to slide off the security chain or to open the door any wider.

'Would you please open the door, Mr Carroll, and step outside.'

'It's Sunday. It's the Lord's Day.'

'I'm perfectly aware of that, Mr Carroll, but whatever day of the week it is, you're under arrest. Now will you please open the door or else we'll be obliged to open it ourselves by force.'

Nolan Carroll hesitated a moment longer, and then closed the door, which he would have needed to do in order to slide off the security chain. However, he didn't open it again, and

Katie heard him calling out to his wife. '*Hilda! Hilda, where are you?*'

'Knock again,' she told the garda.

The garda knocked six or seven times, and shouted out, 'Open up, Mr Carroll!'

'Is there any way he could sneak out round the back?' asked Katie.

'I'll go down the side alley there and make sure that he doesn't make a run for it out of his yard,' said Detective Cullen.

Katie went up to the door, bent over and opened the letter-box flap. 'Mr Carroll, you need to open the door and come out now! You're only making things worse for yourself!'

There was still no response, so she stood back again and said to the gardaí, 'Okay... kick it in, if you can.'

At that moment, though, the front door opened, and Mrs Carroll appeared, wearing a bulky red cardigan, her hair in nylon curlers.

'What's going on? What do you want here?'

'Your husband, Mrs Carroll. He's under arrest. Will you tell him to come out or else we'll have to come inside and fetch him ourselves.'

'You've no right.'

'We have every right. We can legally enter your house and we can search it, too. Which we will. Now would you please tell your husband to come out here, without any more delay, before he gets himself into even more trouble.'

'But he's done nothing. What do you want him for?'

'Mrs Carroll, I've arrested him for murdering your daughter. That may be "nothing" to you, but I'm afraid it's the most serious offence there is in the eyes of the law. And the eyes of God, too.'

Mrs Carroll flinched, as if Katie had thrown a cup of cold water in her face.

'I don't understand. *What?* He never would have done such a thing. What in the name of Jesus makes you think it was him?'

'Mrs Carroll – I'm not standing here arguing with you any longer. We're coming in to fetch out your husband and that's all there is to it.'

'He's – he's gone into his shed.'

'Come on,' said Katie, to Detective Walsh and the two gardaí. She pushed Mrs Carroll to one side, so that she stumbled backwards against all the coats that were hanging in the hallway.

'Hey! You can't—!' Mrs Carroll cried out, but Katie ignored her. She hurried through the kitchen and the washroom extension, and out through the open back door to the brick-paved yard.

There was a row of concrete plant pots along the right-hand fence, and a wooden shed in the left-hand corner. Detective Cullen was standing in the alleyway on the left-hand side, looking over the fence.

'I haven't seen him come out this way, ma'am!' he called out.

'He's in the shed, Daley! Get yourself over here!'

One of the gardaí went up to the shed and tugged at the door. An open padlock was hanging from the handle, but the door wouldn't budge.

The garda rattled it again, but then he said, 'It's no use, ma'am – he's bolted it on the inside, top and bottom. Not a bother, though. I have a pry bar in the car.'

Katie and Detective Walsh went around to the side of the shed, where there was a window. It was dark inside, and the clouds were reflected in the grimy glass, as well as the two of them, but behind their reflections Katie could make out shelves with pots of paint and weedkiller on them, and tools hanging up, although she couldn't see Nolan Carroll.

'Nolan!' she shouted. 'There's no use you hiding yourself in there! We'll have that door pried open in less than a minute! Resisting arrest – that's an offence, too!'

Nolan Carroll must have been crouched down out of sight on the floor of the shed. He stood up suddenly and shook his fist at Katie and she could see that he was mouthing something, although she could hear him only faintly. In his left hand he was holding up a red plastic petrol can, and she could see that he had already screwed off the lid.

He mouthed something more, and even though she couldn't make out what it was, she could judge by his expression that it must be angry and abusive. Then he lifted the can up higher, and started to pour petrol all over himself, his eyes and his mouth tight shut, drenching his wave of white hair and soaking the shoulders of his mustard-coloured shirt.

'*No!*' Katie shouted at him, and she immediately turned to Detective Walsh and the garda who was standing beside the shed door. 'Jesus! He's just emptied a can of petrol over his head! Cailin – call the fire brigade! Tell them it's desperate!'

Detective Cullen had just appeared at the back of the house, and she called out, 'Daley! Go and fetch the fire extinguisher out of the car, will you! Double-quick!'

The garda with the pry bar was right behind Detective Cullen and Katie beckoned to him frantically. 'Quick! Hurry! Get that shed door open! Your man's dripping head to foot with petrol!'

The garda came running across the yard, but before he could reach the shed door, Katie saw Nolan Carroll holding up a box of matches, almost ostentatiously, as if he were performing a conjuring trick in front of an audience. Ladies and gentlemen, I have here an ordinary box of matches. Guess what I'm going to do next!

'*No, Nolan! Don't do it!*' she screamed at him, but he struck a match. It flared up, lighting up his face. He looked triumphant, but only for a split second, because then he was totally engulfed in leaping orange flames.

He didn't cry out – not that Katie could hear, anyway. She couldn't see him clearly, because the inside of the shed was rapidly filling up with smoke and the window was turning a dark amber colour, but he appeared to be hopping up and down and swaying from side to side, a column of flames with a human being inside it that was dancing some kind of last self-sacrificial dance.

With a splintering crackle, the garda with the pry bar forced the shed door open. As soon as he did so, the air rushed in, and the inside of the shed exploded into a fireball. Katie went around to the open door, shielding her face with her hand. Somehow, in the middle of that inferno, Nolan Carroll was still standing, and he managed to take two or three jerky steps towards the door. Tins of gloss paint were bursting and bubbling on either side of him and blazing loops were dripping down from the shelves.

He nearly managed to reach the door, although by now he must have been blind, and his nerve endings all seared away, so that he wouldn't have been able to feel anything. He raised one arm as if in salute, or an appeal for help. But then he sagged and fell forward, half in and half out of the shed. He lay at Katie's feet, blackened and smouldering now, with only a few small flames flickering across his back.

Detective Cullen came panting up with the fire extinguisher, and squirted foam all over him, and then squirted more into the open shed door. It was futile, though. The whole shed was burning too ferociously, spitting and popping, with pungent black smoke piling up into the clouds, peppered with sparks.

Katie waited for a minute or two. She felt numb. Nolan Carroll's body reminded her too painfully of Garrett, sitting incinerated in his car. After a while she laid her hand on Detective Walsh's shoulder because she could see how shocked she was, too. Then, without a word, she turned away and went back into the house. As she made her way around the kitchen table, she could hear the fire brigade's sirens approaching.

She found Mrs Carroll sitting on her own in the living room, her hands clasped together, with tears streaming down her cheeks. Katie was aware that her clothes smelled of smoke.

Mrs Carroll looked up at her. 'Did he really do that? Push Roisin and her baby into the river?'

'Yes, Mrs Carroll. We have every reason to believe that it was him.'

'It must have been him. He always used to say that if he ever committed a mortal sin, he would take his own life, rather than allow God to punish him for all eternity. I never met another man so frightened of God.'

'You saw the fire?'

Mrs Carroll nodded.

'I'm afraid that he's passed away,' Katie told her. 'We tried to get him out of there, but he'd bolted the door. There was nothing we could do to save him.'

Mrs Carroll lifted the hem of her brown pleated skirt and used it to wipe her eyes. 'I blame Roisin. It was all her fault, utterly. I don't know how I could have given birth to such a slut of a girl. Well, Nolan gave her the punishment she deserved, did he not? And now he and I have both been well and truly punished for conceiving her.'

Katie raised her eyes to the large wooden crucifix hanging over the fireplace, with a plaster Jesus nailed on to it. Jesus looked back at her, and she thought that he looked bewildered, as if he had woken up from a hangover and couldn't understand what he was doing up there. Dear Lord, she thought, is *this* what you gave your life for? Were you so offended by Roisin giving birth out of wedlock that she had to die, drowned by the very man who conceived her? And were you and your Holy Father really going to torture him for ever and ever for what he did, so that he preferred to burn himself to death?

The fire engines arrived outside, and their blue flashing lights made it look as if Jesus were jerking up and down, trying to tug himself off the cross. Katie heard the firefighters shouting and running down the side alleyway, unravelling their hoses.

'You have my condolences, Mrs Carroll,' she said, and then she left the living room and went back into the yard. There was nothing left of the shed except for a smoking black skeleton, and all the firefighters could do was spray water over it to extinguish any stray sparks.

44

While she was waiting for the technical experts to arrive, Katie rang Kieran.

'I'm so sorry, Kieran. There's been an incident. I won't be able to meet you for lunch. Even if I could, I'm afraid I'd have no appetite.'

She explained how Nolan Carroll had committed suicide. As she spoke, she could even taste the smoke from his self-immolation in her saliva. She was glad that she had eaten so little for breakfast, or else she was sure she would have brought it all up again. As it was, she couldn't stop herself from retching and spitting into her handkerchief.

Kieran said, 'Take care of yourself, Katie. Could you ring me again when you're safely back home? It's your well-being, that's all that matters. We can meet for lunch any time at all.'

It was growing dark by the time she was ready to leave Friary Gardens. The press had arrived, and she had given them an impromptu briefing in the street. There was no sign of Owen Dineen among them, although Stephen Ó Fallamhain turned up – a stringer who sometimes wrote for the *Sun*. The only question he asked her was what evidence the Garda had for arresting Nolan Carroll, but when she declined to tell him he didn't persist.

She drove back with Detectives Walsh and Cullen to Anglesea Street and went up to her office to file her initial report. Moirin had gone home, and the station was eerily quiet, except for somebody downstairs whistling 'The Rising of the Moon'. She went into her toilet and sprayed her trouser suit with perfume to cover the smell of smoke, and then she sat down at her keyboard. In her mind's eye, she kept seeing Nolan Carroll's face as he struck the match that had set him on fire. He had appeared to be triumphant, but why? Was he celebrating the fact that he was about to outsmart the God who had oppressed him all his life?

Katie was still typing when there was a light knock at her open door. Kyna walked in, wearing a navy-blue cape with wide bell sleeves, and skinny black jeans, and ankle boots.

'*Kyna...* what are you doing here? I thought you were going down to see your old school friend what's-her-name in Kenmare.'

'Shayla. I was, but Shayla rang me to say she'd gone down with the flu. I called in to see if you were still here and Sergeant O'Farrell told me what had happened at the Carrolls. My God, you can't understand anybody burning themselves to death like that, can you? Are you all right?'

'Not the happiest Sunday I've ever had, I can tell you. As soon as I've filed my report I'm going back home to change into something that doesn't reek like a bonfire and pour myself a treble vodka.'

Kyna perched herself on the edge of Katie's desk. 'Would you mind very much if I came back to Carrig View with you? If you don't want me to, all you have to do is say so. You must be fierce shocked still – what with yesterday, too. If all you want to do is have a bath and balm out with Barney and Foltchain, I'll totally understand.'

'No, sweetheart. You're more than welcome. Barney and Foltchain always take good care of me, but their conversation is kind of limited, like, do you know? I'd love to have you there to talk to. Give me twenty more minutes to finish this off and then we'll be out the gap.'

***

As Katie drove back to Cobh, she told Kyna how Nolan Carroll had locked himself in his shed and set fire to himself, and how Hilda Carroll still blamed Roisin for all their ill fortune.

'Not for a moment did she think that Roisin was deserving of any support or any sympathy, and that maybe it was the boy who made her pregnant she should have been blaming, not her. I half-wonder if she knew what her husband was planning to do, and approved of it, or even helped him. If there was any chance of proving it, I swear to God I'd haul her in for aiding and abetting, or even conspiracy.'

'The pain that religion has caused in this country,' said Kyna. 'Sometimes I ask myself what we've done to deserve it. Do we not pray hard enough, or often enough? Are we disrespectful to God, without realizing it? Is it because we keep on taking his name in vain?'

They arrived at Carrig View and as soon as Katie opened the front door, Barney and Foltchain went into their usual tail-flapping frenzy of welcome. They could sense the affection between Katie and Kyna, and so they loved Kyna as much as they had been devoted to Conor.

'You're loopers, you two,' said Kyna, stroking Foltchain and tugging at Barney's ears. 'If they had a nuthouse for dogs, you'd both be locked up for life.'

Katie had cleaned the hearth and relaid the fire in the living room that morning, and so all she had to do was light it. She took the matchbox from the mantelpiece, slid it open and picked out a match, but then she hesitated.

'Would *you* do it?' she said, holding out the match and the matchbox to Kyna. 'All of a sudden I'm feeling like I'm going to gawk.'

Kyna knelt down in front of the hearth, struck the match and lit the firelighters. Once the flames were licking up, she got to her feet and held out her arms and gave Katie the closest of hugs, kissing her cheek first, and then her neck.

'You've had too much to put up with, these past few days,' she told her, kissing her neck again. 'You're only human, Katie. Frank Magorian should have granted you compassionate leave for a few weeks after you buried Conor. You're grieving something terrible, and what have you had to put up with? Not just losing Garrett Quinn, and seeing him all burned like that, but that bombing at UCC, and those shitehawk Riordans raiding The Weavers. And on top of that you've had Brendan O'Kane behaving like a pure unmitigated bastard, and all those horrible stories about you in the newspapers. I'm amazed you've kept your sanity.'

'I have to. I don't want to end up in the nuthouse with Barney and Foltchain, do I?'

'Oh, you can make a joke about it, Katie. But you're expecting too much of yourself, and because of that, everybody else expects too much of you, too. And you come back here every night and you have nobody to talk to and nobody to cuddle you and listen to all of your woes.'

'How about a drink?' said Katie.

'Ooh, please. I'll have a glass of that Redbreast if you have any left.'

'I do, yes. It was Conor's favourite. I bought him a bottle to cheer him up after his operation, but he never even opened it.'

'Katie... he was a man in a million, wasn't he?'

'I don't have any luck at all when it comes to men, do I?'

Katie put on some background music, Beau Jarred's 'Arpeggios in High Altitude', and then she poured herself a vodka and tonic and a whiskey with a little splash of water for Kyna. They took off their shoes and sat on the couch together, while Barney and Foltchain flopped themselves down in front of the fire.

'There was something important you wanted to tell me,' said Katie.

'How did you know?'

'Because I'm a detective. And because I know you so well.'

'I'm worried that it's too soon after you losing Conor.'

'Well, tell me anyway. The worst I can do is burst into tears.'

'I hope you won't. But I've been thinking about it and thinking about it and I don't know how to hold it in any longer. It's probably the most crucial decision that I'll ever make in the whole of my life.'

Katie already had an inkling of what Kyna was going to say, and she silently prayed that she was wrong, and that Kyna was going to surprise her with something completely different. She loved Kyna, but she knew that Kyna was looking for a permanent relationship, even marriage; but apart from her career, Katie wanted to have a strong and understanding man in her life, and she also wanted to be a mother again, before it was too late. After all this time, she still hadn't had the heart to get rid of little Seamus's empty cot, or the romper suits that he hadn't lived to wear.

Although it would upset her, she hoped that Kyna was going to tell her that she had found another woman, and that even though she wanted them to remain the closest of friends, they could no longer be lovers.

But she didn't say that. Instead she said what Katie was afraid she would say, almost word for word.

'I've decided to quit the Garda. I'm going to go in to see Brendan tomorrow morning first thing and I'm going to hand in my notice. If I do that, he won't be able to use those pictures to blackmail you any more, and we can be together without you fearing to lose your job.'

'Kyna – you're one of the best officers in my team. I can't afford to lose you. Sweetheart – I appreciate what you're trying to do, and believe me I'm more than grateful. But I don't expect you to give up your career because of me. That would be such a waste of your talents. And think about it – if you quit – what on earth would you do?'

Kyna looked at her steadily, her blue eyes glistening with tears. She was easily one of the most beautiful young women that Katie had ever known. Not traditionally beautiful, but with elfin bone structure that made her look as if she had just appeared out of a *lis*, or a fairy hill.

'I'd find something to do all right. I can cook. I'm good with figures. I can drive. Maybe I could set up one of those roadside chippers.'

'I hope you're codding me. Like, seriously, Kyna, I'll find a way of dealing with Brendan. I have at least as much on him as he has on me. I was going to tell you tomorrow, but I've had his phone calls hacked and I've found out that he's been paying that Owen Dineen to write stories that make me look as if I'm incompetent.'

Kyna's mouth opened. 'For real? That's incredible. But it's terrible, too. But you've had his phone hacked? That'll land you into a whole heap of trouble, surely?'

'It could do, true. It depends how I play it. But I said to myself that if Brendan's going to shoot me down in flames, he's coming down with me. If they give me the sack, I can always join you running that chipper, can't I? Conor always said I did the best fry he'd ever tasted.'

'Talking of that, are you hungry?'

'I'm not at all, after today. I have a pizza in the freezer, though, if you are.'

'I'm starving, for some reason. I could eat the proverbial nun's bum through the bars of a convent gate.'

'Sorry. You'll have to make do with pizza.'

After Kyna had eaten, they sat together on the couch until the fire had died down to ashes. Katie shooed the dogs into the kitchen and then she and Kyna went into the bedroom.

'This time, I'm giving nobody a look-in,' said Katie, and went across to draw the curtains tightly together. Then she came back, and took Kyna's face in both hands, as if she were holding up a prize that she had won, and kissed her.

They kissed deep and long, their tongues tangling together and exploring the insides of each other's mouths. Then Katie said, 'Arms up,' and lifted Kyna's black sweater over her head. She dropped the sweater on to the bed and then she reached around and slid open the catch of Kyna's bra. She loved Kyna's breasts: they were small and perky but she had prominent nipples, as pink as two sugary sweets, and as she rolled them gently between her fingers they stiffened and crinkled.

'Let's have a shower,' said Katie. 'I'm sure I still smell of smoke.'

They both undressed and went into the bathroom. As they waited for the shower to warm up, they stood in front of the mirror, with their arms around each other's waists. They were admiring each other, and at the same time they were acknowledging their closeness, their sisterhood, and how much they shared each other's dreams and fears.

Katie had felt as close as this with Conor, but she knew that Kyna could see right into her heart, to that innermost need that she had always kept secret, even from the men she had loved, a need that only a woman could ever understand.

They stepped into the shower and soaped each other with Coco Chanel shower gel until they were both as slippery as seals. They kissed each other again and again, and Kyna slipped her finger between the waxed lips of Katie's vulva, stroking her clitoris so lightly that Katie could barely feel it, which only made her want it all the more.

They quickly and excitedly dried themselves in big fluffy white towels and then Katie fell back on the bed, opening her legs wide. She was highly aroused, but she needed more than sexual stimulation, she needed oblivion. She needed Kyna to give her so much pleasure that she could think about nothing else. Not about Nolan Carroll blazing like a wicker man; and not about the bloody webs and strings of flesh that were all that remained of the students who had been bombed in the pharmacy lab. Not about Feargal Grífin falling cursing to the floor; and not about Brendan giving her that sly sideways look of his, half lust and half hatred.

She needed an explosive orgasm that blotted out the past few days as if they had never happened.

Kyna climbed on top of Katie on all fours, smiling. She leaned forward and kissed her, and then she cupped her heavy right breast and lifted it so that she could suck her nipple and flick it with the tip of her tongue. She did the same with her left nipple, and then slowly she began to inch her way downwards, kissing Katie's stomach and her navel and her hips, touching the nerves that made her jump.

'Do you know what you are?' Katie murmured, sliding her fingers into Kyna's blonde hair and massaging her scalp. 'You're a *bhrionglóid fíor* – a dream come true.'

Kyna lifted her head and smiled at her. 'And you... I thought you were an *aisling* the first minute I set eyes on you. A dream, and nothing less.'

She lowered her head again and opened Katie's thighs wider so that she could lick her anus. Katie closed her eyes and gripped the patchwork bedspread with both hands. After a while, Kyna poked her tongue inquisitively into her vagina, which was already wet and slippery, and then her urethra. When she started to lick her clitoris, Katie couldn't stop herself from shuddering, and letting out a little whimper. She wanted to say something, she wanted to tell Kyna that she had never felt anything as wonderful as this, but she was concentrating so hard on the rising tension between her legs that she couldn't remember how to speak.

While she was continuing to lick her, Kyna twisted off the silver Celtic knot ring from her right middle finger and dropped it on to the bedspread. Then she pressed all five fingertips of her right hand closely together, so that it formed the shadow-play shape of a duck's head. With her left hand she parted the lips of Katie's vulva as wide as she could, and slowly worked her whole right hand up into her vagina, as far as the silver-link bracelet on her wrist.

Katie went into a spasm that made her hips bounce up and down on the bed. She thought that the whole bedroom had gone dark and was collapsing in on her, from all sides. She saw stars whirling in circles and she felt as if her insides were violently rippling and would never stop.

Gradually, though, the rippling subsided and when she opened her eyes she saw that the room was still lit by the two bedside lamps. She lifted up her head and saw that Kyna was sitting up now, with a look on her face like a mischievous angel. Katie's thighs were still wide apart and Kyna's hand was still buried inside her.

'You fit like a glove,' Kyna whispered. 'I wish I could keep my hand in here for ever.'

Slowly, though, she drew it out, her fingers all shiny. Katie sat up and kissed her.

'Now it's my turn,' Katie told her.

Kyna said, 'No, no, darling – not yet,' and flopped down on to her side. 'You relax first... let me give you a cuddle and soothe away all of that stress. Come here, Katie, you deserve it and you *need* it. You know you do. I can't have you falling apart. You will for sure if you go on like this.'

Katie hesitated, but then she eased herself back down again. Kyna put her arms around her shoulders and drew her close towards her, so that her cheek was pressed against her small soft breast.

'We have the whole night ahead of us, darling,' she said, stroking Katie's forehead. 'You'll have all the time you need, and when you're ready you can do to me whatever takes your fancy.'

45

'That's it,' said Thomas O'Flynn. 'We're going after them Riordans now, the lot of them. No picking and no choosing. If their name's Riordan or they're one of their family or one of their gang, that's it. We'll be opening up the trapdoor to Hell for them and dropping them down it, same like we did with that blithering eejit O'Malley.'

'That was a drain we dropped him down,' said Breaslain.

'I'm talking metamaphorically, for the love of Christ,' Thomas O'Flynn snapped back at him. 'It doesn't matter a multicoloured shite *where* we dispose of their bodies, it's their souls that'll be going down to meet his Satanic Majesty.'

'Kind of drastic, like, hitting all of them,' said Darragh. 'The razzers will be on to us like a ton of wet manure, won't they?'

'You think that's drastic? They was out to murder every one of us on Saturday, old dolls and *gasúns*, too! If it hadn't been for that fecking gas leak, they could have taken us all out. I still want to find out what sneaky snake told them we was holding Maddie's party there at The Weavers. But that gas leak – that was God looking after us there, boy, and no mistake.'

'The razzers topped three of them, though, didn't they, and lifted the rest? And I heard on the grapevine that Feargal Grífin got himself shot, although it wasn't like fatal or nothing.'

'Feargal Grífin? That header? I thought he'd taken himself above to Dublin to join the Malone gang.'

'He did. But he came back down again. I think his ma lives in Carrigaline and she's getting on a bit. And you know him. He'd do a job for anybody. I reckon he'd even do a job for us if we offered him enough grade.'

'I would in my gonkapouch. Jesus. But don't tell me the Riordans won't have another crack at us, as soon as they get the chance. If we can't even hold a family party without them coming after us, we're not never going to be safe, are we? No, Darragh, it's them or us. Them or us, boy, I swear on my mother's grave. And I'll bet you the razzers won't come chasing us nearly as hot as you think, so long as we're doggy wide. They'll be only too delighted to have somebody clear the streets of Riordans for them, I bet you.'

Thomas O'Flynn was sitting on the banquette by the fake fire at the end of Quinlan's Bar in Watercourse Road, and his cohorts were sitting hunched on stools all around him like a gathering of Hobbits. The Weavers had not yet reopened, and it would probably stay closed for another three or four days. Muireann was sitting next to Thomas in a short scarlet dress and black pantyhose and his hand was resting high up on her thigh, squeezing it from time to time as if to remind her who she belonged to. He had taken her that morning before she was awake, roughly and quickly, and she was still hurting, but she was doing her best not to show it. She managed a smile now and again, and a short snort of laughter whenever Thomas said anything funny, but any astute observer of human behaviour would have seen that she was not only unamused but secretly raging, and from the way she was shifting around on the banquette, that she was in acute discomfort, too.

'So – what are we going to do, Tommy?' asked Breaslain. 'Go round to Barry's gaff in the middle of the night and kick in the door? That would be great, wouldn't it? – to pop them all while they're lying in their scratchers! "Good morning, Barry-boy! Bang!"'

'Get real, Brez. He has all the same kind of security around his house as we do. CCTV, motion sensors, alarms, floodlights, you name it. Plus a reinforced front door, I'll guarantee. Plus he probably has more guns than the fecking Army.

'No... what we're going to do is follow his gang one at a time when they leave his house or when they've been drinking at The Cotton Ball. Only one at a time. If they're walking home we'll jump them. If they're driving we'll overtake them and block them off. Then we'll take them up to Boreen Dearg.'

'What's up at Boreen Dearg apart from Sunday lunch on legs?' asked John Mary John.

'There's a farmer I know up there who owes me a mortal favour, Cronan O'Brien. He was the fellow I was trying to ring before we dumped O'Malley, but he was away on his holliers in Lanzarote and he only came back last night. A couple of years ago he built himself a new farmhouse about half a click away from the old one, and knocked the old one down, but of course the old cesspit's still where it always was. That's a perfect place to hide dead bodies that you don't want nobody to find, as any nun from the Tuam mother-and-baby home will tell you.'

'I hope that Feargal Grífin is out and about soon,' put in Milo. 'I owe *him* a mortal favour or two, I can tell you. I was out walking my dog Pooka last St Stephen's Day and he came up with two of his gobshite pals and started giving me all of that. I told him to feck off out of it and he pulled out his gun and he shot Pooka in the head, right in front of me. So what could I do? It was no use calling the guards. But if we're up for putting a bullet in Feargal Grífin, I'll be first in the queue.'

'Right,' said Thomas. 'So soon as you see one of Riordan's gang, no matter where it is, even if he's sitting in McDonald's stuffing his bake with an Egg McMuffin, ring me. I'll tell you what to do next. We're going to extermify them Riordans, every one of them.'

At the same time that Thomas O'Flynn was holding his council of war in Quinlan's, Katie was talking on the phone to Dr Curran, the consultant at the Mercy who had been treating Feargal Grífin for his bullet wounds.

'He's in reasonable shape now. Neither wound caused any lasting damage, although for a while he might experience some stiffness in his hand and find that he's walking with a slight limp. He was experiencing alcoholic withdrawal delirium last night. As far as I could make out he imagined that he was in a monastery and that we were all monks who were plotting to poison him. But this morning he seems to have got over the AWD and I'm told that he's managed some toast.'

'When do you think we'll be able to come in and interview him?'

'He's under sedation and he's asleep now, but I reckon he should be awake and compos mentis by early this evening, say about six o'clock. If and when he's fit enough, I'll have one of the advanced nurse practitioners ring you so.'

'Thanks a million, doctor.'

Katie put down the phone but immediately her iPhone rang. She picked it up and it was Kieran.

'How're you going on, Katie? Feeling better today, hopefully?'

'Oh, loads better, thanks. Still a little tired, but much more sorted in the head, if you know what I mean. Not nearly so stressed.' When she said that, she couldn't stop herself from thinking of herself and Kyna, and how she had woken Kyna up at two o'clock in the morning, and how she had made Kyna moan at such a high pitch that she had almost sounded as if she were singing.

'Are you all tied up at the moment?' Kieran asked her. 'I'll be going into court in about a quarter of an hour to pass sentence on Donal Hagerty. Justice O'Rafferty's here with me now and we're having a last-minute conflab about it. Maybe you'd like to come over to the courthouse and see me handing down the prison term for yourself.'

'Yes, grand, I will. Of course DI Mulliken will be there because he was the officer in charge of the Hagerty case. But it'll be interesting to see who shows up in the public gallery. The O'Flynns never missed one day of the trial. They were always there, at least two or three of them, and always with the death stare on them.'

'They're the bane of your life, aren't they, those two gangs? Same as the Kinahans and the Hutches in Dublin. I don't think *that* feud will come to an end until they're all in the cemetery. Maybe you should have let the O'Flynns hold that birthday party of theirs at The Weavers and gone deaf and blind when the Riordans went in to wreck it. You could have rid this city of quite a few gowls without having to chase after them yourself.'

Kyna came into Katie's office, in a grey check trouser suit and a grey silk headscarf. Apart from quick, noncommittal eye contact, they showed no affection for each other because Moirin was close behind, bringing Katie a file on a recent jewellery-shop robbery in Winthrop Street, which was still unsolved. Two of the stolen watches had turned up at Dooley's auctioneers in Limerick.

Katie stood up. 'Kyna – how do you fancy heading over to the courthouse with me to see Donal Hagerty sent down?'

'Sure, like. Why not? Anything's better than reading through the heap of paperwork I have on my desk about Doireann Greaney. There must be more than thirty reports on her behaviour from Children First, not to mention her school and her GP, too. I'm pure amazed that it was never flagged up before that she could be a risk to other people, as well as herself.'

'You know what the social services are like as well as I do. It's all good intentions but the left hand and the right hand never know what the middle hand is up to, do they? Go and fetch your coat.'

They crossed Anglesea Street from the Garda station to the courthouse. Katie would have loved to hold hands with Kyna, but of course that was out of the question. They didn't mention last night, either, and they tried not to think about it, in case one of their team noticed the obvious magnetism between them. Their team were all detectives, after all, and they were trained to read facial expressions and body language.

They found Kieran and Justice O'Rafferty in Stephen Herlihy's office.

'Ah, so pleased that you could come over, Detective Superintendent,' said Kieran. 'And you, too, Detective—?'

'Detective Sergeant, sir. Detective Sergeant Ní Nuallán.'

Justice O'Rafferty was looking drained and strangely bloodless and she had dark smudges under her eyes, as if she hadn't been sleeping well. Katie went over and said, 'How are you, ma'am? I thought you'd be interested to know that we're making considerable progress in finding out who murdered Justice Quinn.'

'Really? Do you have a suspect?'

'We do, yes, but it's early days yet. He's a member of the Riordan gang, and he was arrested along with the others on Saturday, during that fracas at The Weavers.'

Justice O'Rafferty thought for a while, and then she said, 'Do you have any idea at all *why* Justice Quinn was murdered?'

'I should be interviewing our suspect later today. Maybe I'll get some idea from him then.'

'I can't work it out, do you know? Surely the Riordans wanted Donal Hagerty to be given the maximum sentence possible. I don't think they have any geniuses among them, but even they must have realized from Justice Quinn's summing-up to the jury that we had no intention of letting him off lightly. It was not only Michael Riordan he shot, after all. It was his innocent wife and children, and that was an act of inexcusable evil.'

Justice O'Rafferty suddenly clamped her hand over her mouth and her eyes brimmed with tears. Katie lifted her hand as if to lay it on her shoulder to comfort her, but then decided that she was a justice of the High Court and perhaps she had better not.

All the same, she glanced across the office. Kieran and Kyna appeared to be having an intense conversation and Stephen Herlihy was talking on his mobile phone, so she said quietly to Justice O'Rafferty, 'You'll have to forgive me for asking you this, but you may or may not know that Garrett and I were more than close at one time.'

Justice O'Rafferty took her hand away from her mouth, blinked away her tears and stared at her. '*You?* You mean you were—?'

Katie nodded. 'It was intense, but it didn't last long. That was just how Garrett was. He was passionate, and adoring, and when I was with him I felt like I was the only woman in the world that he had ever wanted. But as it turned out I *wasn't.* He may have been passionate, do you know, but he had a fierce short span of attention when it came to women. It was like he was worried that he was going to grow old without having slept with every available woman in the whole of Ireland.'

'So what is it that you were going to ask me?'

'I think you know that, ma'am. I kind of guessed it the first time I talked to you, and your tears tell it all. But my sincere apologies if I've misread them.'

A court usher appeared at the open door and gave Stephen Herlihy a salute. Stephen Herlihy clapped his hands and said, 'It's time, Your Honours. Detective Superintendent Maguire... Detective Sergeant Ni Nuallán... if you'd like to follow me. DI Mulliken's already in the courtroom.'

Justice O'Rafferty called out, 'One moment, Stephen,' and she beckoned Katie to come closer. She turned her head away, as if she were seeking judicial guidance from the portrait of Chief Justice O'Brien FitzGerald hanging over the fireplace, and then she said, 'We became lovers, yes, during the course of this trial. He told me that I was the woman he'd been looking for all his life. Two weeks ago he promised me that he was going to tell Orla that he was leaving her, and that he would ask her for a divorce.'

Katie waited for Justice O'Rafferty to say more, but all she did was pluck a handkerchief out of her sleeve and wipe her eyes. As far as Katie was concerned, though, she didn't really have to add anything to what she had said already. The agonized expression on her face was far more eloquent than words.

***

Katie and Kyna sat in the body of the courtroom, next to Detective Inspector Mulliken and Detective Cushley, and facing the registrar, a fiftyish woman in a purple dress who looked like a retired schoolteacher. The courtroom was still new, and smelled new, with plain polished wood panelling, and high windows all along the sides.

Behind them, the public benches were crowded, and when she turned around, Katie recognized at least three of Thomas O'Flynn's gang, including his older brother Doran, although she couldn't see Thomas himself. They were all sitting on one of the front benches, so they must have arrived early.

Before Kieran and Justice O'Rafferty appeared, she heard a murmur at the back of the court, and when she turned around again she saw Barry Riordan walking in, accompanied by two hard-looking men in those tight buttoned-up coats known in Cork as farting jackets.

Barry Riordan saw her looking round at him, and made a pistol gesture with his finger and thumb, and grinned. Threatening a garda was an arrestable offence, but she doubted if anybody else had seen it, and this was hardly the moment for her to go to the back of the court and lift him.

At last it was 'All rise!' and the two judges came in to sit down behind the bench. The bailiff signalled to the two uniformed gardaí standing beside the witness box, and they left the courtroom, returning two or three minutes later with Donal Hagerty.

Donal Hagerty was taller than his brother Billy had been, and not so stocky, and unlike Billy he had thick black hair, brushed to the left at a forty-five-degree angle, as if he were standing in a stiff sideways wind. He sat in the witness box staring at nothing at all, and it was noticeable to Katie that he didn't turn around and make eye contact with any of the gang members sitting at the back of the court. He had probably been warned by the O'Flynns what would happen if he gave the slightest suggestion that he knew them.

Donal Hagerty was ordered to stand, and then, in the clearest and most theatrical of voices, Kieran calmly reminded him that he had been found guilty on three charges of murder. Together with Justice O'Rafferty, he had taken into consideration a probation report on Donal's deprived background, a psychiatric report, and pleas of mitigation from his defence barrister because of his alcohol and drug use.

'Notwithstanding these, I hereby sentence you to life imprisonment on all three convictions, to be served concurrently, with the statutory minimum of twelve years before you may be considered for parole. The court is adjourned.'

'All rise!' shouted the bailiff, and with that, Kieran and Justice O'Rafferty stood up and walked towards the door behind the bench.

Before they had reached it, though, Katie heard a scuffling sound from the back of the courtroom. When she looked round, she saw that Barry Riordan was standing on one of the benches and shaking his fist.

'Wrong man!' he screamed out. 'Right sentence but wrong fecking man! It's Tommy O'Flynn should be going to prison for this! *He* paid to have my brother and his family shot – Tommy O'Flynn! This gom you have in the dock here, he's nothing but a puppet! Go and haul in Tommy O'Flynn!'

Doran O'Flynn and Breaslain had already been making their way towards the exit, but now they turned around, pushing aside the people who had been following behind them. They hurried along the aisle behind Barry Riordan's bench, seized his arms and pulled him over the back of the bench on to the floor. Breaslain knelt down beside him and started to punch him, while Doran kicked him repeatedly in the ribs.

Barry shouted out and swore, and his two minders climbed over the bench and dragged Doran and Breaslain away from him. They started struggling and punching each other until one of the minders head-butted Doran, so that he dropped to his knees, stunned, and Breaslain managed to tear himself away and head for the exit, shouldering his way through the frightened and bewildered crowd who had come to see Donal Hagerty sentenced.

The two gardaí and the bailiff managed to struggle their way to the back of the court. Barry Riordan had now been helped up on to his feet by his minders, and the bailiff gave Doran a hand to stand up. Katie and Detective Inspector Mulliken approached them, and one of the gardaí said, 'Arrest them for affray, ma'am? Or violent disorder at least. You can't say we don't have enough witnesses.'

As he brushed down his sleeves, Barry Riordan stared at Katie hard and unblinking, as if he were silently daring her to charge him. Katie took Detective Inspector Mulliken aside and said quietly, 'I'm going to let them go. If we start foostering around with a minor charge like affray it's only going to complicate our investigation into what we really want him for. Besides, I want him to be relaxed and off his guard and thinking he's got one up on us.'

'You're not even going to give these fellers a caution?'

Katie shook her head. 'We're so close now to a possible indictment for conspiracy to multiple murders. I'll be questioning Feargal Grífin later today with any luck. We don't need to be faffing around with paperwork for a bit of a tussle in a public place. Riordan's lawyer will only say that he was distressed when he heard Donal Hagerty's sentence. After all, it was his brother and his sister-in-law and his niece and nephew that Hagerty shot dead. Quite honestly, I think I'd be off my head myself if any of my little nieces and nephews were murdered.'

Detective Inspector Mulliken nodded. 'Okay, ma'am. I have you.'

With that, he went over and spoke to the gardaí, and then to Barry Riordan and his minders and Doran O'Flynn. Katie stayed where she was, saying nothing. The courtroom was empty now, apart from them. After a brief conversation, Barry Riordan turned to Katie, smiled, and gave her a mocking salute.

On their way back across the road to the station, Katie said to Kyna, 'You're quiet.'

'Oh. Am I? I was thinking about Justice Connolly, that's all.'

'Thinking *what* about Justice Connolly? I have to say that I like him.'

'I know you do. And he likes you. In fact, he more than likes you.'

'Really? What did he say?'

'He said he thinks you're beautiful and clever, and it's beyond sad that you should have lost Conor.'

They went up the steps into the station and crossed the reception area towards the lifts.

Katie said, 'Kieran's been pure understanding, I'll say that. He hasn't come on to me, not at all.'

'Biding his time, probably.'

There were four Kynas in the lift, Kyna herself and her three reflections. 'Don't start getting jealous on me, sweetheart,' Katie told them. 'Kieran's a new friend for me, nothing more, and he's been nothing but a comfort.'

There was CCTV in the lift, so Katie could do nothing more than smile and hope that Kyna believed her.

46

Katie was at last beginning to feel as if all the critical risks that she had been taking might be starting to pay off. With Brendan and with Orla Quinn it had been like playing two simultaneous games of poker in which she knew that both of her opponents held strong cards against her, but she was hopeful that she could win if she bided her time.

She had always believed that no matter how plausible a hunch might be, it was evidence that counted, and nothing else. She had seen so many prosecutions collapse because witnesses had proved to be liars or fantasists or out for revenge, and so many cases fall apart because the investigating officers had clumsily signalled their suspicions, allowing the offenders time to disappear or to devise some plausible alibi.

That was why she relied so much on the expertise of Bill Phinner and the Technical Bureau, and it was Bill Phinner who came to her that afternoon and gave her the evidence she needed if she was going to be able to prove who had arranged for the devastating bombing at the School of Pharmacy.

The nurse practitioner at the Mercy had just rung her to tell her that Feargal Grífin was fit to be interviewed, and she made an appointment for 6:30. Five minutes later Bill came in, looking as if he had been told that his grandmother had been struck by lightning and all his pet chickens had died of infectious coryza. He was carrying a large green briefcase.

'I'm off to question Feargal Grífin at half-past six,' she told him. 'I can't wait to hear him explain how his gun was used to shoot both Billy Hagerty and that traveller fellow, what was his name, as well as being used to shoot at me and Justice Connolly.'

'Timbo Coffey, that was the traveller's name,' said Bill. 'Coffey the Conker. There was a piece in the *Examiner* a couple of days ago about his bare-knuckle boxing days. But I have some new forensic results for you here, which I think might brighten up your day a little.'

He opened his briefcase and handed Katie a clear plastic envelope, about A4 size, with two ragged pieces of brown paper in it.

'We found these yesterday afternoon stuck to the ceiling of the pharmacy lab. Almost the entire ceiling was scorched brown and discoloured with smoke, so we didn't see them until we used the ultraviolet.'

'Where did they come from?' Katie asked him.

'Of course they could have come from anything. There were shreds of paper all over the lab, thousands of them, like a snowstorm. And these two pieces – they have no identifying words or numbers on them. But, hallelujah, on one side of them they *do* have fingerprints. We whizzed them off to AFIS as a rush job, and they came back this morning and told us who they belonged to.'

'And?'

'They belong to a feen called Breaslain Hoobin. One of the O'Flynn gang, forty-three years old, with an address in Fair Hill and a record of assault, theft, criminal damage, drug possession and threatening behaviour. The box containing the bomb was covered in brown paper, and this tells us beyond any doubt that it was Breaslain Hoobin who carried it into the lab.'

'So in all probability it *was* Thomas O'Flynn who set it up – as we pretty much guessed. But Mother of God – all he had to do was *threaten* them, those High Five. They were only kids. He didn't have to blow them all to pieces. It was tragic.'

'Unfortunately, we still don't have sufficient forensic evidence to connect O'Flynn himself directly to the bomb. Of course there's not a chance in hell that some thick violent eejit like Breaslain Hoobin could have thought of blowing up the pharmacy lab, or had the grade to pay James MacGreevy to put the bomb together for him. But we have no fingerprints or DNA that link O'Flynn either to its making or to its deployment.'

'We have nothing either,' said Katie. 'No recorded phone conversations, no CCTV. We were hoping that we could track down whoever bought the pressure cooker, but Kitchen Magic at Ballycurreen has no record of selling one for more than nine months, and they're the only outlet in Munster that stocks them. Our best chance is for James MacGreevy or this Hoobin fellow to come out and finger O'Flynn for being the brains behind it – although we know why they're too scared to. If they did that, they'd have to leave the country and never come back, and maybe even that wouldn't be far enough or long enough. You remember Mikey Lynch? He hid himself in Slovakia and they still found him and put a bullet through his head, although we could never prove it was them.'

'Ah, I might have the magic key to that,' said Bill. 'Here's some more evidence for you.'

He opened his briefcase again and took out a large kitchen knife, also contained in a large transparent evidence bag.

'This is the knife that was retrieved from the drain in the men's toilets at the Zombie Lounge. Between the handle and the blade we found microscopic traces of blood, which we were able to match with blood samples from Tadhg Kimmons, the young fellow who was stabbed there. So this is the weapon that killed him. The handle itself was unfinished wood with no patent prints on it but we were able to fume it with iodine and detect several reasonable latents. Some matched Kimmons, but superimposed on top of them were a thumb and three fingerprints which – surprise, surprise – match the AFIS sample for Breaslain Hoobin.'

'Perfect,' said Katie. 'Or as near perfect as we can expect, under the circumstances. Now we can haul in Hoobin on the charge of murdering Tadhg Kimmons, without putting Muireann in any danger. But we won't mention the bombing, not to begin with. First let's see how much pressure we can put on him to incriminate O'Flynn.'

Bill Phinner sat back, and now he looked as if at least some of his imaginary chickens were beginning to convalesce. 'I thought you'd see it that way, ma'am.'

'Oh – one more thing, Bill. How's it coming on with Eamonn O'Malley? Have you worked out yet how his head was crushed?'

'We have a couple of ideas we're still working on, ma'am. We thought at first that a heavy sash window could have been slammed down on his head a few times, because of the indentations on both sides of his skull. But a sash window would have had to be banged down fierce hard to have caused that kind of damage, and it would have caused parallel indentations, and these are definitely at an angle to each other, like his head was squeezed in a giant nutcracker, like we said before, or some tool resembling a huge pair of pincers. So we're looking at a whole range of possibilities. There's an industrial compression machine that they use for testing the strength of toys, among other things, and that machine can be adjusted to apply huge pressure at all kinds of different angles. There's at least a couple in use on the Togher industrial estate and we'll be checking them out. We'll find out what did it, don't you worry.'

'Thanks, Bill. Once we know *what* we'll have a good chance at finding out *who*.'

A uniformed garda was posted outside Feargal Grífin's room at the Mercy, and he jumped up like a jack-in-the-box when Katie and Kyna came along the corridor.

'Afternoon, ma'am,' he said briskly.

Katie nodded towards Feargal's door. 'Any trouble at all?'

'Your man was a bit shouty earlier on. He didn't like the fish they gave him for his lunch, something like that. He's been quiet ever since, though. His solicitor's in there with him.'

Katie and Kyna went into Feargal's room. He was sitting in a chair by the window, wearing a hospital dressing-gown, his right hand wrapped in a thick white gauze dressing and his arm in a sling. He was staring mournfully out at the car park like a child whose mother is late picking him up from school, and he didn't even look around when Katie and Kyna came in. Katie knew his solicitor: Sheenagh Finegan, a chubby young woman from Keenan & Doyle, with hair like a cottage loaf and a way of tutting and smacking her lips between every sentence as if she disagreed even with herself.

'Don't get up,' said Katie, although Sheenagh gave no indication that she was going to, and Feargal couldn't, with his wounded knee. Sheenagh had her laptop open and earplugs in her ears and she lifted her hand as if she were telling Katie and Kyna to wait until she had finished what she was working on.

Katie and Kyna pulled over chairs and sat on either side

of Feargal. He looked from one to the other and then said, '*What?*'

'We've come to ask you one or two questions, that's all,' said Katie. 'As you know, you've been arrested and formally charged, and so the caution that you were given then still applies. Anything you *do* say, and all that.'

Sheenagh pulled the earplugs out of her ears and said, 'That means you don't have to say anything, Feargal. Not unless you want to.'

'As if I fecking didn't know that. I've heard it enough times in me life.'

'Feargal—' said Katie. 'You don't mind if I call you Feargal?'

'You can call me Billy the Bullseye if you want to. You seem to get your rocks off taking potshots at me, after all.'

'Feargal, you were arrested for threatening behaviour and for illegally carrying a firearm. But I'm afraid there's more that you have to answer for, because our ballistics experts have examined the Glock pistol that was taken from you at the time. They've conclusively proved that it was the same pistol that was used to shoot and kill Billy Hagerty outside The Weavers, and the same pistol that was used to shoot and kill Timbo Coffey. Not only that, you used it to shoot at myself and Mr Justice Connolly, which you've admitted, and all I can say is thank the Lord your aim was off and you missed us.'

Sheenagh said, 'Feargal – you don't have to respond to that. That's not even a question. DS Maguire – do you have a copy of that ballistics report for me to peruse?'

'I'll send you a PDF, Sheenagh. But we can prove beyond any doubt at all that Feargal was responsible for murdering Billy Hagerty and Timbo Coffey, as well as attempting to murder me and Justice Connolly. There are no other prints or traces of DNA on the murder weapon apart from Feargal's. Nobody has ever touched that gun except for him.'

'I thought you came here to interview my client,' said Sheenagh, with a tut. 'So far you haven't asked him even one question. Not that I would advise him to answer.'

'Oh, I'm going to ask him one now, Sheenagh, no bother at all. Feargal – do you understand that we have sufficient evidence to have you locked away for the rest of your natural days? That's two murders we can prove that you've committed, plus attempted murder.'

'There's no need to answer that, Feargal,' said Sheenagh. 'If they have the evidence, like they say, let them formally charge you and take you to court and prove in front of a judge and jury. You're under no obligation at all to make their life any easier by committing yourself.'

Katie persisted. 'You do understand, don't you, Feargal, that if you confess to those two murders and that attempted murder, the judge will reduce your sentence by a fair few years? I mean, that's the law. But if you plead not guilty... well, your view of the world will still have steel bars across it when you're a white-haired old man.'

'I'm saying nothing, *cailleach*, nothing at all.'

'Feargal, you won't help your case by being derogatory,' Sheenagh clucked at him. Then she closed her laptop and said, 'Is there anything else you wanted to ask, DS Maguire?'

'Yes, as a matter of fact. Who put you up to shooting Billy Hagerty, Feargal? If you tell us that, you could be looking at an even greater reduction in your sentence. Was it Billy Hagerty you were after, or was it Thomas O'Flynn? Or both of them?'

Feargal took off his glasses and looked over at Sheenagh in what appeared to Katie to be the first sign that he was panicking. He might be gang-hardened, he might be close to psychopathic, but she could see that the desperate quandary he was facing had started to sink in.

Sheenagh shook her head, as if she were telling him to say nothing, but Kyna leaned over to him and said, 'It's all very well to tell us to eff off, Feargal. I don't blame you. The guards have never done you any favours, not once in your life, have they?'

'Well, *you're* not, either, are you, girl?'

'Don't be so sure. If you can tell us who told you to take out Billy Hagerty, then we may be able to help you. I mean, think about all those years and years in prison. You'll have to do twelve. That's the minimum. But supposing it's twenty? Supposing they never parole you at all before you die? Whatever you've done, do you really want to pass away in a prison cell? Do you never want to see the sea again, or stroll down Pana, or drink with your pals in a pub?'

'Don't listen to her, Feargal,' said Sheenagh. 'I know this one. She's the honey-talker.'

Feargal lifted his bandaged hand up and down like a fretful child with a fat white teddy bear. 'I don't know,' he said. 'She's telling the truth, isn't she? They *do* knock years off your sentence if you tell them what they want to know. I spent three years in fecking Wheatfield and two fecking years in Limerick so I know what it's like inside. You think you can stick it out but some days you just feel like hanging yourself or cutting your fecking throat to get it over with.'

Katie said, 'It's up to you, Feargal. It doesn't matter to me one way or the other, except that you'll save me a whole rake of boring paperwork. If you choose to spend the rest of your days in a cell, good luck to you, that's all I can say.'

'Come on, Feargal,' Kyna coaxed him. 'Whoever told you to do these jobs, they've kept their hands clean, haven't they, while you've been hauled in? Sure, we can understand that you might have owed them a favour, or felt some loyalty towards them – all gang members together-like – and maybe you were a touch afraid of them, too. But think ahead to ten years from now. Unless you give us a clue to who they are, *they're* going to be jetting off to holidays in Majorca and drinking champagne at the races at Mallow while *you're* sitting on your bunk in Rathmore Road counting off the years.'

'Feargal, for your own good, I strongly advise you not to name any names,' said Sheenagh. 'The legal ramifications... they'd be enormous. And you'd be laying yourself open to mortal danger, there's no question about that.'

Feargal was gnawing at his lip. Katie was sure that he wouldn't be concerned at all about any legal complications, even if he could understand what they were. But he must know without a doubt that if he betrayed them, whoever had put him up to killing Billy Hagerty and Timbo Coffey would come looking for him, and it was likely that they would take their sweet sadistic time in exacting their revenge.

'We can give you witness protection,' said Kyna. 'You'd still have to serve some time, but you could do it in Cloverhill, which is medium-security, or even Loughan House, and we'd give you a new identity, so none of the other inmates would know who you were.'

Feargal still looked uncertain, and when he looked across at Sheenagh she shook her head yet again. But it was then that Katie said, 'Justice Quinn.'

'Justice Quinn?' Sheenagh asked her. 'What exactly do you mean by that, DS Maguire?'

'We wanted to see how Feargal would respond if we offered our help in reducing his likely sentence for murdering Billy Hagerty and Timbo Coffey. All we wanted to know is *why* they were murdered and who wanted them dead, because it obviously wasn't Feargal himself. He was just the hit man. But – since he seems to have rejected our offer, for whatever reason, I'll have to ask him about the much more serious charge of murdering a justice of the High Court, Mr Justice Garrett Quinn.'

'You're not suggesting that Feargal murdered *him*, are you?'

'I am, yes, and what's more we have the evidence to prove it. I've come here this evening prepared to charge Feargal with his murder and caution him accordingly.'

Katie turned to Feargal and said, 'If you'd murdered any law officer before nineteen-sixty-four, Feargal – a prison warden, or a garda in the course of his duty, or a justice of the High Court – you'd have been hanged. Now we're more merciful, and you'll only be given a mandatory life sentence. No parole, though. You'll never be coming out.'

'What evidence do you have?' Sheenagh demanded.

'CCTV and forensic. We have footage of Feargal driving away from Justice Quinn's house in Justice Quinn's car on the morning that His Honour was murdered, with Justice Quinn in the passenger seat. And apart from that, Feargal not only has the careless habit of leaving his spent cartridge casings scattered about, he forgets that boots leave footprints in mud, and even in grassy verges.'

'I'll need to have sight of *this* evidence, too, of course,' said Sheenagh, although she was much less confrontational now, and the *tut* at the end of her sentence was barely audible. 'You should have given me prior notice.'

THE LAST DROP OF BLOOD

But Feargal waved his bandaged hand again and shouted out, 'Forget it! Fecking forget it! I did it, yes, I admit it! But you're right! It wasn't me!'

'Feargal, no!' said Sheenagh. 'Don't say another word!'

'I'm not going to be banged up for the rest of me life because of her!' Feargal roared at her. 'I didn't even know he was a fecking judge until I saw it on the telly! It was her! His wife! She rang me and she met me at Henchys up at St Luke's Cross and she said she'd pay me two thousand yoyos if I got rid of him for her.'

Sheenagh said, 'Feargal – I'm begging you. Please don't say any more.'

'She said she'd have him all doped up and all I had to do was help her to carry him out to his car. Then she said, do whatever you want with him. Drive the car into Tivoli docks so it'll look like he had an accident and got drownded.'

'To be absolutely clear about this, you're talking about Justice Quinn's wife, Orla Quinn?' said Katie.

'Like I said, I had no idea at all that he was a judge. She gave me the two thousand in cash and off I went. But I'd already decided not to drive his car into the Lee. I'd left me own car up on the Ballincollie Road so that I could get away after. Then I went to the petrol station and rung for a taxi to take me down to Tivoli.'

'When was this? We couldn't see you arriving at the Quinns house on CCTV.'

'I had the driver drop me off on Lover's Walk, that's why, so he wouldn't know where I was going, and Mrs Quinn let me in by the side door so the neighbours wouldn't clock me.'

'But you didn't tell her that you weren't going to drive the judge's car into the dock?'

'I'm not thick, like. If I'd done that, I knew there'd be too much evidence left in his car once the guards had fished it out of the docks. I know what you lot can do these days. You would have found the dope in his body and my DNA on the door handles and fibres from my kecks and all that kind of shite. I mean, that's why we always torch cars when we're through with them.'

'Pity you forgot about footprints,' said Katie.

'I had too much on my mind, like. It was a hell of a job dragging your man out of the passenger seat and sitting him down behind the wheel, because he was so fecking floppy. But as soon as I'd done that, this run-down pick-up truck came past, didn't it, with this old knacker at the wheel. He even give me a wave and "how're ye?" I'd seen him around a few times before, this old feller, and I think he knew me, too. So as soon as I'd lit up the second petrol tank and the Jag was well alight I went after him. I guessed that he was on his way back to the halting site at Water Lane.'

'What was your intention when you went after him?' asked Katie.

'Feargal—' said Sheenagh, but Feargal ignored her.

'I don't know. I suppose I was meaning to have a word with him, like, and tell him that he never saw me.'

'And what if he'd said that he *had* seen you, and wasn't going to deny it, if anybody asked him? Like the guards, for instance?'

'It didn't turn out that way.'

'So how did it turn out?'

Feargal now began speaking in a monotone, as if he were describing a film that he had seen. 'I turned on to the Ballyhooly Road by The Bridle and I saw his pick-up truck in the car park there. I was going to go into the pub myself and talk to him there, you know – maybe buy him a couple of gatts and tell him to catch a dose of amnesia. But then I saw that there was a two-bulb parked there, too, and he was standing outside, and a couple of guards were giving him down the banks by the look of it. I waited on the opposite side of the cross, by the petrol station, like, to see what was going to happen next.

'I think the guards must've heard the Jag's tanks blowing up, and then seen the smoke, because they suddenly shot off like the divil was after them. The knacker started walking down the road, and I could tell by the gatch on him that he was totally langered. I guessed the guards had warned him that he couldn't drive.'

Sheenagh had given up trying to silence him now, and she was furiously texting her office.

'Go on,' said Kyna gently.

'I passed him by,' said Feargal. 'I passed him by and then I parked a bit up ahead of him, and then I walked back. He asked me if I was going to give him a lift. He was bolloxed, I tell you, so that he could hardly stand up, with gawk all down the front of his shirt. I said that I'd give him a lift if he forgot that he'd ever seen me.'

'And?'

'And I know he was halfway out of his head, but he cursed me and said that he'd never been a liar in the whole of his life and he wasn't going to start lying now. He lifted up his fists as if he was a boxer, you know, and he came at me, screaming like a fecking banshee. So what could I do?'

'You could have driven off and left him. And he *was* a boxer, once. Coffey the Conker.'

'I couldn't leave him, could I? He'd seen me next to the Jag. He was a witness.'

Katie was silent for a few moments. Then she said, 'Are you willing to testify in court that you were paid by Mrs Orla Quinn to murder her husband, Mr Justice Quinn?'

'No. It was herself that doped him. Me – I was only supposed to dispoge of him. Like I say, it was her suggestion that I drove his car into the docks.'

'But if you had done that, he would have drowned, and that would have meant that you *did* murder him. As it was, you set fire to his car instead, with him in it.'

'Yes. But it wasn't me who doped him.'

'What I'm getting at, Feargal, is whether he was alive when you set his car alight, or not.'

'He was doped. But, yes. I suppose he was.'

It was then that Katie said, 'Excuse me,' stood up, and quickly left the room. The garda outside said, 'Ma'am?' but she didn't answer him. She walked along the corridor until she reached the door that led to the car park, and went outside.

She stood beside a wall and let out a howl of grief, her eyes bursting with tears. She could hear him, she could hear Garrett inside her head, turning over in bed and stroking her hair and saying, 'My red-haired merrow. You caught me in your net, didn't you, and now I'm yours, trapped for ever and a day.'

As they drove back to Anglesea Street, Kyna said, 'He admits that Orla Quinn told him to get rid of Garrett, but he totally refuses to say who told him to shoot Billy Hagerty.'

'Yes, but think about it. Would you, if you were him? There's nothing much that Orla Quinn can do to him, is there? But I'm pretty sure that it was Barry Riordan who ordered him to hit Billy Hagerty, for whatever reason, and if he ratted on *him*, his life wouldn't be worth living, even in jail. Especially in jail. There are more of Riordan's gang in jail than there are out of it.'

They crossed over the Christy Ring Bridge, and a full moon was reflected in the river. 'You didn't tell me about the footprints,' said Kyna.

'No? Well, of course not.'

'Why not?'

'Because there weren't any.'

'What? You're codding me, aren't you?'

'How else was I going to get him to confess? We have no conclusive forensic evidence that it was Feargal who set fire to Garrett's car. Okay, we have the CCTV footage of him driving away with Garrett from Tivoli Park, but that's purely circumstantial. A lawyer could argue that anything could have happened between there and White's Cross, and the only witness who saw him on the Ballincollie Road that morning is dead. But he believed we have footprints and now we have a confession. We don't even have to borrow his boots while he's in hospital and photograph a few false impressions.'

'Do you know something?' said Kyna. 'You're a whole lot wilier than I ever thought. Sometimes I wonder who you are.'

47

Gavin Garvey came out of The Poor Relation pub on Parnell Place, trying to shrug on his coat and light a cigarette at the same time. He had his lighter in his left hand and his right arm up in the air, still tangled in his sleeve, when Darragh and Milo came briskly up behind him, seized his arms, and started to drag him up towards Oliver Plunkett Street.

'Lay off me, you fecking gorillas!' Gavin swore at them, and tried to wrench himself free, but Darragh jabbed a pistol hard into his ribs. Parnell Place was busy at that time of the evening, but no passer-by was going to interfere with three hard-looking men who were obviously having a scrap.

'Keep the peace, Gavin, or I'll do for you here and now.'

They had nearly reached the corner of Oliver Plunkett Street when there was a piercing two-fingered whistle from behind them and a loud voice shouted out, 'Hey! Stop! What the hell's going on there? Gavin?'

Gavin twisted his head around. Big Rory Madden had just emerged from The Poor Relation, buttoning up his coat. Big Rory was one of Barry Riordan's hardest enforcers. He spent most of his evenings around the clubs in the city centre, making sure that the Riordan drug-dealers weren't harassed by gardaí or other gangs. He was well over six feet five inches tall, with shoulders as wide as a beam engine, a Neanderthal jaw, and jet-black hair that was brushed straight up and made him look even taller.

He started to stride towards Milo and Gavin and Darragh,

but Gavin croaked out, 'Rory! Stall it, will you, boy! He's a nine on me!'

Big Rory didn't hesitate. He pulled an automatic out of his inside pocket and fired at Milo from less than five metres away. Milo's right ear was blasted off in a spray of blood and he pitched sideways on to the pavement.

Darragh swung Gavin around so that he would shield him, but for all of his bulk Big Rory was quick on his feet, and he feinted to the right like a rugby player and shot him in the shoulder. Darragh shot Gavin in the side at point-blank range and the bullet burst inside his liver. Blood spouted out of his mouth and he dropped on to his knees, clinging at Darragh's coat.

Big Rory fired again, twice. The banging of gunshots echoed all the way around Parnell Place and had people stopping in the middle of the street to see what was happening, or ducking into shop doorways. Darragh toppled backwards, but as soon as he struck the pavement he fired back at Big Rory.

Big Rory stood utterly still. Darragh fired at him once more before his head fell back and his fingers slowly opened up like a dying crab so that his pistol clattered on to the concrete.

There was a strange silence. Four or five cars had stopped and several drinkers had come out of The Poor Relation, but when they had seen the bodies lying on the ground, nobody had dared to come any closer.

Big Rory turned slowly around and started to walk back towards the pub. After only three steps, though, he started to sway. He managed three more steps and then he stumbled forward and crashed face down on to one of the benches outside the entrance.

A few minutes later, the night air was screaming with the sound of sirens, first of all from the south, as three Garda squad cars crossed over Parnell Bridge with their blue lights flashing, and then from the west, as two ambulances that had been waiting outside the Mercy Hospital came speeding along South Mall.

Katie was opening her front door at Carrig View when her iPhone rang. She shooed Barney and Foltchain into the kitchen and then said, 'DS Maguire.'

'It's Robert, ma'am. There's been a shooting on Parnell Place. Four men down. Two Riordans and two O'Flynns.'

'All dead?'

'I'm there now. They're all extinct, yes, and we know all of them. Rory Madden and Gavin Garvey, both of them Barry Riordan's men. Darragh Colfer and Milo Milligan, the one they call "Milo the Minder". Both of them O'Flynns.'

'No civilians hurt? No collateral damage?'

'No, thank God. A broken window at The Welcome Inn, but that's all. Fortunately there was nobody sitting behind it.'

'Have you retrieved the weapons?'

'One Glock 17 and one Sig-Sauer P226.'

'Mother of God, this has been coming for a long time, hasn't it? It's open war. Keep me posted, Robert. We'll have an emergency meeting first thing tomorrow. I'm determined to crush those O'Flynns and Riordans once and for all.'

Davey Horgan said, 'I have to drain da snake, lads, and then get back to the auld doll. She was cooking me something special tonight, drisheen I'll bet, and she'll be after giving me the seven shows of Cork for coming home late.'

He stood up from the table where he was sitting with Barry

Riordan and three other members of Riordan's gang. He staggered a little but managed to hold on to the back of his chair to regain his balance. All five of them had been drinking here at The Cotton Ball since lunchtime, drowning their grief at the loss of three of their number at The Weavers and the arrest of eight more. They hadn't yet heard the news about Big Rory Madden and Gavin Garvey.

Seven pints of Murphy's and some melancholy songs from Sally O'Dare and the Cider Boys had only made them sadder and angrier and increasingly incoherent. Barry couldn't stop threatening to cleave the tripes out of all the O'Flynns and every garda he came across, but the reality was that his gang had been seriously depleted and he was fearful that he would no longer be able to exert the same control over the city's drugs business, especially in Blackpool and Ardpatrick and Farranree. It wasn't only the O'Flynns who concerned him: there were plenty of other violent gangs who would jump in and try to take over if they caught the slightest hint that the Riordans no longer had the strength to hit back at them.

Davey weaved his way past the bar to the men's toilets. He pushed the door open with his shoulder and went inside, already unzipping his fly before he had reached the urinals. Another drinker was just finishing off, giving himself a shake and wiping his hands on his trousers before shuffling back to the bar.

Davey stood in front of one of the urinals and closed his eyes in relief. He heard the toilet door swing shut behind him as the other drinker left, but he didn't realize that somebody else had entered at the same time. It was Breaslain Hoobin, who had been sitting for the past hour and a half on the opposite side of The Cotton Ball, watching the Riordans becoming steadily drunker, and waiting for his moment.

Davey heard his footsteps on the tiled floor, and became aware that he was there, but he still didn't open his eyes.

'Jesus,' he said. 'I didn't realize one man could have so much piss in him. Eat your heart out, River Lee!'

Breaslain said nothing, but drew a large carbon-steel carving knife out of the inside pocket of his coat. He stepped up close behind Davey, so close that he was almost touching him. For a split second, Davey sensed how close he was, and that something was badly wrong, but before he could turn around, Breaslain reached over his left shoulder and gripped his ginger-bearded chin like a vice.

'*Gaaah!*' Davey choked out. That was all he could manage to say before Breaslain sliced his throat from side to side, cutting open his carotid artery and halving his Adam's apple.

Davey collapsed in a spray of blood and urine, hitting his head on the urinal as he fell. He lay sideways on the toilet floor, his legs trembling like a slaughtered pony, while Breaslain wiped his knife on the back of his coat and then quickly walked out. Unlike the time that he had stabbed Tadhg Kimmons, he had been prepared for this killing, and he was wearing blue rubber gloves.

He left The Cotton Ball and crossed the Old Youghal Road to where his Datsun was parked in Glenamoy Lawn. He climbed in, snapped off his gloves finger by finger, and started the engine. Before he drove off, though, he took out his phone and rang Doran.

'It's done, boy. One of them any road. I don't know his name but I seen him around a fair few times with Barry before.'

'Okay, good man yourself. I'll tell Tommy. That's one for Darragh, God rest his soul. What we need now is one for Milo.'

As Breaslain prepared to pull out of Glenamoy Lawn and head back towards Blackpool, a Garda squad car came driving slowly along the Old Youghal Road. He sat with his head bent down, his heart beating hard, until it had passed The Cotton Ball and disappeared from sight. Praise God nobody could have yet paid a visit to the men's toilet.

His heart would have beaten even harder if he had known that he had already been identified as Tadhg Kimmons' murderer and that he had carried in the bomb that had killed so many young students at the UCC School of Pharmacy.

Two unmarked Garda cars were parked outside his mother's house in Farranferris Avenue, and four plain-clothes officers were listening to music and yawning from time to time and patiently waiting for him to return home.

At ten to midnight, Katie's phone rang again. She had been expecting a call from Kieran, but it was Robert again.

'Sorry to disturb you, ma'am, but I thought you'd want to hear this.'

'Good news or bad news?'

'Both. One of Barry Riordan's gang had his throat cut at The Cotton Ball about two hours ago. A fellow called Davey Horgan. A minor thug with two convictions for assault and another for stealing a motorbike.'

'Dead?'

'Oh, stone. He nearly had the head taken off him.'

'Any witnesses?'

'Ah, this is the good news. Nobody at the Ball saw Horgan being killed, but we've arrested Breaslain Hoobin. We lifted him at his ma's house in Farranree. He must be the thickest man in Cork, and that's saying something. He couldn't believe that we had any evidence against him, but of course we have his prints on the knife that he used to kill Tadhg Kimmons and the wrapping paper from the bomb at UCC. On top of that... Sean Begley recognized him as soon as we fetched him into the station, because of his chin, and the gatch on him. We matched him with the CCTV from the bombing at UCC, and there's no question that it's him all right. Like you advised us, though, we still haven't mentioned the bombing to him or charged him for it.'

'That's fantastic news... but what does that have to do with the fellow who was killed at The Cotton Ball?'

'Everything. When Hoobin was searched, we found a carving knife in his coat pocket, still with smears of dried blood on it. When I questioned him about it, he admitted that he'd cut Davey Horgan's throat. He said it was in self-defence. Davey Horgan had tried to attack him in the toilets at The Cotton Ball, that's what he said, simply because he was one of Tommy O'Flynn's men, and he'd had no choice.'

'Were any weapons found next to Horgan's body?'

'He had a Swiss army knife in his jacket pocket, unopened.'

'You're right. Hoobin must be the thickest man in the county. But you've made my day, Robert. We're really starting to cut the ground from under them, those two gangs. Give us a few more days and weeks and we'll have them all arrested... Barry Riordan and Thomas O'Flynn, too. The fiercer they fight each other, the more they lay themselves open to us catching them.'

'I wonder what the *Sun* will be saying when we haul those two in?' said Robert. 'No more of that "top cop flopping", I'll guarantee it.'

He spoke in his usual deadpan voice, but Katie could tell that he was proud of the progress that their detectives had been making against the Riordans and the O'Flynns, and that he was proud of her, too.

48

The next day, half an hour before it grew light, Katie drove to Tivoli Park with Detective Sergeant Begley, Detective Scanlan and Garda Neasa O'Connor. It was a bone-cold morning and the finest of soft rains was falling.

Normally, Katie wouldn't have gone along with her detectives to carry out an arrest like this. Detective Sergeant Begley and Detective Scanlan had a District Court warrant, which was all they needed to charge Orla Quinn and take her into custody. But this was personal. Orla had arranged for the murder of a man she had once loved. Not only that, she was anxious to find out if Orla was really prepared to carry out her threat to reveal that she and Garrett had been having an affair during the trial of Phinean Joyce.

They parked outside the Quinn house. There were no lights at any of the windows, and the upstairs curtains were still drawn. Detective Scanlan rang the doorbell and they waited for Orla to answer, chafing their hands together to keep warm.

At last the front door opened and Orla appeared, barefooted, in her dressing gown.

'Kathleen,' she said, looking directly at Katie and ignoring the other officers. 'Have you any idea what time it is?'

'Are you going to invite us in, Orla, or do we have to do this on the doorstep?'

'I suppose you'd better come in.'

They all went into the living room and this time they left their shoes on. It was symbolic, in a way. They were saying that it doesn't matter if we leave wet footprints on your carpet, because you won't be coming back here for twelve years at least, and possibly not for the rest of your life.

'Orla Maoiliosa Quinn, I am arresting you for soliciting the murder of His Honour Mr Justice Garrett Quinn. You are not obliged to say anything unless you wish to do so, but anything you say will be taken down in writing and may be given in evidence.'

Orla stared at Katie intently. 'Are you serious?'

'Do I look like I'm joking?'

'I can never tell with you, Kathleen. But I have nothing to say. Not now, anyway.'

'In that case, perhaps you'd like to get yourself dressed so that you can accompany us to Anglesea Street. You'll be able to contact your solicitor, of course, once you're there.'

'I'm perfectly well aware of my rights, thank you.'

'I have to advise you that we'll be carrying out a search of this house for any evidence that implicates you in the death of Justice Quinn. Garda O'Connor here will accompany you upstairs while you dress in order to make sure that you make no attempt to conceal or destroy such evidence should it exist.'

Orla didn't answer that, but stayed completely still for a moment as if she were trying to remember where she had left her car keys. Then she walked stiffly out of the living room with Garda O'Connor following close behind her.

'She doesn't seem too bothered about it, does she?' remarked Detective Sergeant Begley. 'Myself, I think I'd be filling my pants if I was charged with killing a judge.'

'She doesn't yet know that Feargal Grífin has shopped her,' said Katie. 'And she's a lawyer herself, remember. It wouldn't surprise me if she's already made sure that she's disposed of anything that could lead to her conviction – like whatever sedative it was that she used to put Justice Quinn to sleep. I'd guess Rohypnol or something similar. But if we can trace Justice Quinn's phone calls and texts, we may very well find some personal messages between him and Justice O'Rafferty, and if we can prove that Mrs Quinn found out about their affair – well, that will go to motive at the very least.'

After about a quarter of an hour, Orla came downstairs, dressed in a plain black suit and a grey silk scarf. She put on a long green raincoat and then Garda O'Connor led her out to her car. The day was growing lighter now, although the clouds were low and grey and ragged, and it was still persistently raining.

Before she got into Garda O'Connor's car, Orla turned around and called out, 'Kathleen,' just loud enough for Katie to hear her. Katie went over and waited for her to speak. She said nothing to Orla herself. She wondered if it had occurred to Orla that Garrett may still have been alive when Feargal had cremated him, even if he was unconscious.

Orla turned to Garda O'Connor and said sharply, 'This is personal, if you don't mind.'

Katie nodded to Garda O'Connor and she stepped away, out of earshot.

'I've only one thing to say to you, Kathleen. You made the mistake of your life when you slept with my husband. Now you're going to pay for it, and even if I'm convicted, you'll still be paying for it long after I'm paroled. You'll be paying for it till the day you die.'

Katie stared back at her. The rain was prickling her face and she blinked raindrops from her eyelashes.

'May God forgive you,' she said, 'because I never will.' With that, she walked off to join Detective Sergeant Begley and Detective Scanlan.

***

At 3:30 p.m., Katie held a media briefing so that she could tell the press that Feargal Grífin had been charged with the murder of Justice Quinn and that Orla Quinn had been arrested for instigating it. She also told them that Feargal was being held for the killing of Timbo Coffey.

On top of that, she announced the arrest of Breaslain Hoobin for the murder of Tadhg Kimmons and Davey Horgan, although she said nothing about him being identified as the man who had carried the bomb into the School of Pharmacy at UCC.

'It sounds like you've been outdoing yourself, Detective Superintendent,' said Dan Keane from the *Examiner*, with his usual cigarette behind his ear. 'What happened to the floppy top cop?'

'You'll have to ask your colleague Owen Dineen about that,' Katie replied, and at the back of the room, Owen Dineen grunted in amusement.

'There's always ups and downs when it comes to keeping law and order,' Katie continued. 'It's a game of catch-up. All of a sudden we'll have some gang smuggling in girls for sex from some country we've never even heard of, or another gang peddling a party drug that's only just been invented. Then for no reason at all we'll have a fashion among the young gangs for stabbing each other, or for buzzing around the city centre on mopeds grabbing people's mobile phones. I fully admit that it takes us some time to identify what's going on, but once we have, I believe that my team of detectives here in Cork is the most effective in the country, and the announcements that I've been able to make this afternoon are solid proof of that.'

Owen Dineen raised his hand. 'So how's it coming on with the bombing at the pharmacy lab? You've said nothing at all on that, have you, even though that was the biggest loss of life that we've ever had in Cork in one single criminal outrage.'

Katie looked down to Brendan, who was sitting beside her. Technically, he was supposed to be chairing this briefing, but he had little choice except to allow Katie to take it over, since she knew all the relevant facts about the arrests that she had made. Besides that, the press were eager to know how she was fighting back against the accusations of incompetence that had been made against her in the *Sun*. That was a story in itself.

As a matter of protocol, she had informed Brendan that it was Breaslain Hoobin who had carried the bomb into the laboratory, and of course he knew that James MacGreevy was still in custody for having built it. But she had also insisted that he should make no public statements about the bombing until she could establish beyond any doubt that it was Thomas O'Flynn who had ordered it and paid for it. He wasn't to give the press any optimistic hints, either, nor leaks of any kind.

'Our investigation is ongoing, Owen. That's all I can tell you at the moment.'

'Are you any closer to making an arrest than, say, you were yesterday? Or the day before?'

'Our investigation is ongoing, Owen. I've nothing more to say on the subject.'

She could tell from his edginess that Brendan was itching to stand up and announce that they had already identified the bomber and the bomb-maker. If *he* were to say it, the media would quote him instead of her, and it would give the impression that he was leading the investigation, rather than her. The bombing had not only attracted attention in all of the Irish media, but in the UK, too, and even worldwide, so it would do a great deal to burnish his reputation, both in Ireland and abroad.

Katie gave him that hard green-eyed stare that she reserved for those officers in An Garda Síochána who made no secret that they disapproved of a woman being promoted to detective superintendent. *You may patronize me because I'm a woman but I'm a professional first and I know exactly what I'm doing. If you say one word and mess up my investigation into Thomas O'Flynn, I'll make you wish that you had been pushed into the River Lee, too.*

Brendan gave a complicated smile of acceptance that wasn't really a smile, and said nothing. She could sense, though, that he was preparing himself to pull the rug from under her. She was beginning to have too much success, and if she managed to bring down both Thomas O'Flynn and Barry Riordan, she would be unassailable. Even Frank Magorian would have to admit that she had cleaned up some of the worst crime in Cork. If it came out that she had been having a relationship with Kyna – even if Brendan had kept the pictures – it would do little to threaten her career.

It was time for her to start playing her own cards, such as they were.

49

She caught up with Owen Dineen halfway down the steps in front of the station. He had paused to light a cigarette and when she called out, 'Owen – a quick word with you so, if you have a minute!', he blew out smoke as if he were exploding.

'DS Maguire... how can I be of service? I'm afraid I don't have any handy clues that could help you.'

'No, you're grand altogether. I have plenty of clues of my own, thanks. Not that I always share them with you and all the rest of the newshounds. Look, it's stopped raining... why don't we go across to The Hub and I'll treat you to one of those fancy craft beers.'

Owen raised one eyebrow suspiciously. 'After all I've written about you, you're offering to buy me a drink?'

'Why not, Owen? I've a thick skin, do you know? In this job, you have to. And besides, I'm not one to bear grudges.'

They crossed over the intersection with Copley Street and went into The Hub. It was an old pub with a yellow-and-blue frontage that had been given a new breath of life by bringing in a variety of local Irish beers and strong European lagers. It was still an 'auld fella' pub inside, with dark wooden panelling and walls crowded with framed pictures and a worn-out carpet that looked as if it had been rescued from an episode of *Minder*. Katie bought Owen a pint of Wicklow Wolf Pale Ale and a diet tonic water for herself and they sat down at a small circular table by the window.

'I'm not going to beat around the bush, Owen,' said Katie. 'I don't object to criticism if it's fair, and some of what you wrote was justified, I'll admit. Like I said back at the briefing, the gangs will always try to stay one step ahead of us, and we can't always predict what they're going to be up to next. But we're catching up with them fast, and most of what you've written in the *Sun* has been biased and pure unfair, especially against me personally.'

Owen sipped his beer and wiped his mouth with the back of his hand. Then he lifted up the glass and said, 'This is a powerful pint, this is. Fruity, do you know, like citrus and blueberries, with a hint of malt.'

Katie said, 'Were you really so broke that you needed to take money from Chief Superintendent O'Kane to write pieces about me like that, bringing me down?'

Owen gave her a quick, furtive look and then looked away again.

'You're not going to try and deny it, are you?' Katie asked him. 'Come on, Owen, we need to talk about this. Even if you've been calling me an incompetent detective, I'm still a detective, and I have proof.'

Owen stared at his beer. 'How did you find out?'

'Oh, listen to yourself. Do you think I'm going to tell you that? But I'll tell you something that I *will* do, and that's inform your editors at the *Sun* that you've been accepting bribes to write derogatory and malicious articles about a senior Garda officer. I don't think they'll be overjoyed about that, do you?'

Owen was silent for over a minute. Then at last he said, 'What do you want? I can't go back and unwrite those stories, and I can't see the *Sun* publishing any kind of correction. They were slanted, those stories, okay, but they weren't factually inaccurate.'

'I want a letter from you admitting that you accepted payment from Chief Superintendent O'Kane to write stories that deliberately cast me in a bad light. I want you to list how much money he paid you, and when, and I want you to sign it.'

'If I do that for you, will you hold off from telling my editor about it?'

'I don't know. But I'll consider it. It depends what kind of a response I get from Chief Superintendent O'Kane.'

'He's going to be having some kind of a seizure, isn't he?'

'More than likely. I hope so. He's been working away at undermining me ever since he arrived at Anglesea Street.'

Owen was silent for another minute. He sipped more of his beer and Katie could see that he was thinking hard.

Eventually, he said, 'If I give you that letter, how are you going to use that against him? Are you going to get him the sack? Or are you just going to hold it over him, like, so that he stops trying to discredit you?'

Katie was quite impressed with him when he said that. It showed how astutely he had assessed the situation between Katie and Brendan, and how he was trying to work out a way to protect himself from losing his job.

'Again,' she said, 'it depends.'

He leaned closer, so that she could smell the beer and cigarettes on his breath. 'If you undertake only to use my letter as a threat, and you promise not to disclose it to anybody else, like the Assistant Commissioner, say, or the Garda Ombudsman, or the *Sun*—'

'Then what?'

'Then I could give you some information that could help you to convict Barry Riordan of murder. Or conspiracy to murder, anyhow.'

'Serious?'

'Dead serious. But you'll have to swear on at least sixty-seven Bibles that you'll never let anybody know where you heard it from. If you do, I might as well put on my best suit and go round to Jerh O'Connor's funeral home and lie in a coffin all ready for my wake.'

'Fair play. If you absolutely guarantee that you'll give me that letter, I'll guarantee that nobody will ever know that it was you who told me whatever it is you're about to tell me.'

Owen looked around the bar, and when he was sure that none of the other customers could hear him, or were even in his line of sight, so that they could lip-read, he said, 'Barry Riordan it was who ordered Billy Hagerty to be shot.'

'Well, I guessed that. After all, it was Feargal Grífin who actually shot him, and Feargal's been working for Barry Riordan on and off lately, hasn't he? Do you have any proof?'

'I do, yes. I have a recording of an interview that Billy Hagerty gave me three days before he was hit.'

'Billy Hagerty gave you an interview? What about?'

'He needed money to pay for an appeal against his brother's sentence for murdering Michael Riordan. The *Sun* pays for stories, as you know, and my editor was prepared to pay him two and a half thousand for this one. Even more, if there were any follow-up stories, like Barry Riordan getting himself arrested.'

'To be honest with you, Owen, I don't think there would have been much of a chance of Donal Hagerty having his sentence reduced, even if he had appealed. It wasn't only Michael Riordan he shot, remember – he shot his wife and his two little children.'

'Sure, like. I don't think we'll ever know what happened exactly because Donal was halfway out of his head, but things went badly wrong. The point is, he wouldn't have taken the job at all if he hadn't owed Thomas O'Flynn a rake of money for drugs. Thomas O'Flynn gave him the choice: either you shoot Michael Riordan or else I'll have you and your family kicked out of your house and you can go and live in a homeless shelter, or Dunnes' doorway.'

'So is that the story that Billy Hagerty wanted to sell to the *Sun*?'

'None of that came out in court, because Donal didn't dare to rat on Thomas O'Flynn. But that was only part of the story. The real sensational story was that Billy Hagerty used to be Neala Hagerty, his sister. Billy Hagerty was transgender.'

'I knew that, Owen. I saw his body at the morgue.'

Again, Owen looked around the bar, just to make sure that nobody had come to sit any closer. 'But did you know that Neala Hagerty used to be Barry Riordan's girlfriend, and that they lived together for over two years?'

'No, I didn't. My God. Is that really true?'

Owen swallowed some more Wicklow Wolf, and nodded. 'You wouldn't have thought it, looking at him when he was Billy, but he was not bad-looking when he was a girl. He showed me photographs of him and Barry together and there's even one of Barry shifting her. I mean, she wasn't a *beour* by any stretch of the human imagination, and she was on the chubby side, but I've seen a lot worse struggling to try on a size twenty-two sweater in Penneys.'

'But what do you think Barry's motive was, for having Billy shot?'

'I reckon it was my story… or rather my story that never was. Barry knew that after Neala had become Billy, he started to hang around with Tommy O'Flynn and his boys, but that had never seemed to bother him. Somehow, though, he found out that Billy had been talking to me, and that I was planning to write a story about their time together as lovers, and I'm sure that did it.'

'Do you know how he found out?'

Owen shrugged. 'It could be that one of his gang had seen us together, although we'd been careful only to meet in pubs where we knew that the Riordans never drank, like An Fear Dubh up at Ballincrokig. But Billy had taken all of their photos into Budget Print in Washington Street to be copied, and it could be that one of the staff recognized Barry in the pictures and tipped him off. Who knows?

'As it was, Billy was warned off by one of Barry's gang – as he says in my interview – and the day after that interview I had a phone call myself at about two o'clock in the morning. It was some Norrie telling me in no uncertain terms that if I wrote a story for the *Sun* about Barry's former lover turning herself into a man, that would be the last story that I ever wrote. Barry Riordan the hard gang leader was not going to be the butt of every transgender joke that ever was.'

Katie said, 'That makes sense. I've only run into Barry Riordan once or twice, and he's always struck me as prickly, and extra-prickly with women.'

'You're bang on there. He has about as much sense of humour as a bed of nettles. But come here, DS Maguire – do we have a deal? I'll give you the letter that you want, and a copy of Billy's interview, so long as you promise that my name is never made public in connection with either of them. There's nothing in the interview to identify me... it's like Billy talking in a monologue. The letter... I know you may have to show it to Chief Superintendent O'Kane, but hopefully he'll believe that you have it and you won't have to. But it can't be seen by anybody else.'

'Very well, Owen. If you stick to your side of the bargain, I'll stick to mine. But I have to warn you that I have no idea how Chief Superintendent O'Kane is going to react. He's fierce unpredictable and he may tell me to do my worst. In which case I'll get back to you. We're both taking a desperate risk by agreeing to this arrangement. Both of our jobs are on the line. But it's the only way forward.'

Owen finished his beer. 'My mouth says have another one, but I have a deadline to meet. I trust you, DS Maguire. Actually, I always did. Please accept my apologies for all those malicious stories. I was in the height of loberty and it seemed like a way to get back into the black without doing too much harm. I promise you that every story I write about you from here on in will praise you up to the heavens.'

When Katie returned to her office she found Kieran there, talking to Moirin.

'Kieran… how was your day?'

'Long – and tedious – and procedural. We were hearing applications in that Gallagher Finance fraud case. How about you?'

'Fraught, to say the least. But at last I'm beginning to feel that I'm getting my ducks in a row. This last week has been a pig's dinner from beginning to end.'

'So long as it hasn't been a dog's breakfast. Listen – I guessed you'd be after having a hard day so I thought you might like to join me for a quiet dinner somewhere, or maybe just a drink.'

Katie could see Moirin smiling. She smiled back at her and then said, 'Yes. I was planning to head straight home but it would be great to chill out and have a talk. Moirin? Is there anything that needs my immediate attention? Any phone calls?'

'Mathew McElvey rang you because he had a question about Mrs Quinn's arrest, but he said it could wait until the morning.'

'Grand. Let's go then.'

They were about to leave when Kyna came in, with her coat on.

'Oh,' she said, when she saw Kieran. 'I was going to ask you if you fancied a Chinese at Yuan Ming Yuan.'

'Sorry. Justice Connolly has already asked me out. Maybe tomorrow?'

'Okay. Maybe. I'm not too sure what I'm doing tomorrow.'

With that, Kyna turned around and walked off.

Kieran gave Katie a questioning look, as if he was aware that Kyna was upset but wasn't at all sure why she should be. As far as he knew, Katie was her boss, and that was all.

'Come on,' said Katie. 'I could really use a drink.'

50

Kieran took her to the Cornstore restaurant on Cornmarket Street where they sat together at a tiny table and shared a seafood platter and a bottle of Chardonnay. They talked for over three hours, but not about crime or legal proceedings. Katie told Kieran nothing about Barry Riordan and Billy Hagerty, nor about Owen Dineen and the bribes that he had taken from Brendan to ruin her reputation.

Kieran talked about books and films that he enjoyed, and his favourite holidays in Portugal, and told her jokes. He was sensitive to Katie's grief, and he was careful not to intrude on it. By the end of the evening, when he arranged for a taxi to take her home, she felt relaxed and cheered up and more than ready to face up to all of her problems again. Very slightly drunk, too.

He opened the taxi door for her, and kissed her on the cheek. As he closed the door, though, he caught his fingers in it, and said, 'Shite! Oh – excuse my language! I nearly lost half of my effing hand there!'

'Jesus, are you okay there?' Katie asked him.

He flapped his hand and gave her a rueful smile. 'Don't worry! The Good Lord was looking after me! He knows that I need my hand for handing down sentences to the wicked in this world! Listen, Katie – if you're not up the walls later this week, maybe we can meet up again.'

'I'd like that. In fact, I think you know I would.'

On the way home, Katie closed her eyes and thought about everything she and Kieran had talked about. Then, as they were passing Fota Wildlife Park, she suddenly pictured him trapping his fingers in the taxi door. She pictured it again and again like a flicker-book and then she opened her eyes and took out her phone. Although the taxi was jolting and she was less than sober, she managed to prod out a text to Bill Phinner.

'O'Malley's head... how about a car door?'

Katie spent the next morning at home, catching up with her laundry and tidying up, and then taking Barney and Foltchain for a long breezy walk around the tennis club.

She was nearly home when her phone rang. Barney and Foltchain immediately stopped and waited for her.

'Kathleen, it's Muireann. I'll have to be quick so. Tommy and Barry Riordan are planning to meet up this afternoon. What it is, there's been too many of them shot on both sides, like, and they're talking about calling a kind of a truce.'

'I suppose that's good news.'

'Well, yeah, but from what I heard Tommy saying, it's more than that. They're planning to share out the drugs business between them and break up all the other gangs. They're starting with the O'Neill brothers, but that's the only name I heard Tommy mention.'

'Where are they meeting, Muireann, and when? Do you know?'

'It's three o'clock, at—'

Muireann was abruptly cut off. Katie said, 'Hello? Hello? Muireann?' but there was no answer and she knew better than to ring her back.

She looked at her watch. It was ten past twelve already. She jogged back to the house with Barney and Foltchain trotting beside her, and then she phoned Conall at the Technical Bureau.

'Conall? It's DS Maguire. This is urgent. I'm sending you a smartphone number and I need you to track it and keep on tracking it. It belongs to Muireann Nic Riada, Thomas O'Flynn's girlfriend. Apparently Thomas O'Flynn and Barry Riordan are meeting at some location at three this afternoon but I don't know where. O'Flynn almost always takes Muireann along with him, so there's a good chance that you'll be able to find out where they're getting together.'

'Not a problem, ma'am. I'll get back to you.'

'Thanks, Conall. You're a star.'

Katie rang for an A-Cab. Then she shook out two dishes of Irish Rover kibbles for Barney and Foltchain and filled up their water bowls. She was hungry herself so she took an apple from the fridge before she went through to the bedroom and quickly changed into her navy blue trouser suit. She checked her pistol, slipped it into her hip holster, and then she tugged on her overcoat. When she opened the front door, Anthony was already waiting for her in his taxi.

She felt tense as she was driven into the city. She had reckoned on bringing down the O'Flynns and the Riordans, but mostly by exploiting their intense hatred for each other. If they were going to form an alliance, no matter how shaky it was, it would be much more difficult for her to break them up.

Anthony said, 'A pet day today, for a change. Windy, like, but good to see some sunshine.'

All Katie could manage to say was, 'Yes.'

She called Detective Inspector Fitzpatrick and Detectives Caffrey and O'Sullivan. When they came up to her office she briefed them about Muireann's phone call.

'Oh, Christ,' said Robert. 'Those two joining up isn't going to make our life any easier, and that's for sure.'

'We can't let it happen,' Katie told them. 'It's as simple as that. They're dangerous enough when they're fighting each other, but if we allow them to form an alliance and run the whole of the city's drug trade together, they'll be a total menace. They'll have more money, more influence, and they'll be able to put the squeeze on many more nightclubs and restaurants and other businesses.'

'So what do you have in mind?'

'One of Bill Phinner's communications experts is trying to trace Muireann's phone for me. If we can find out where O'Flynn and Riordan are meeting, then we can haul them both in for questioning. We don't yet have all the evidence we need to make one hundred per cent sure that they'll be convicted of conspiracy to murder and setting up an illegal drugs consortium – but we have enough to arrest them on suspicion of both charges.

'I didn't want to lift them so soon, but I don't think we have much of a choice now. Once we have them here in the station, we can question them separately, and we can give each of them the impression that the other one was responsible for ratting on them.'

'Do you think they'll fall for that?'

'I have no idea. But there's no harm in planting the seed of suspicion in their minds, is there? They've been sworn enemies for years, and they're not getting together because they trust each other. It's because they don't.'

'Well, it's worth giving it a shot,' said Robert. 'We're so close to gathering enough evidence to take them to court, the both of them. If we can only persuade that Breaslain Hoobin to admit that O'Flynn sent him to bomb those students, and if

Feargal Grífin can find the nerve to say that Riordan ordered him to shoot Billy Hagerty—'

He was interrupted by Katie's iPhone playing *Mo Ghille Mear.*

'Ma'am? It's Conall, from the lab. I've been able to track that mobile. It was in Quinlan's Bar on Watercourse Road to begin with, but now it's been taken to Clery's office building on the Old Mallow Road.'

'Clery's the electrical company? They closed down about six months ago, didn't they?'

'Yes. I just googled it. The building's still empty as far as I can make out.'

'How long has that phone been there now?'

'Over ten minutes, without moving. There's been no calls on it, in or out, not since I started to track it. I waited for a while before ringing you in case it was taken off somewhere else. But it's a quarter to three now, and if O'Flynn and Riordan are meeting at three, I'd say that's the likeliest location.'

'Thanks, Conall,' said Katie. 'We'll head up there straight away. Let me know if there's any change, won't you?'

'I will of course.'

Katie and Robert and Detectives Caffrey and O'Sullivan hurried downstairs and out to the car park. They climbed into their unmarked Toyota, with Detective Caffrey driving, and sped out on to Old Station Road with their tyres squealing. Katie called Inspector O'Rourke as they crossed over the river and asked him to send at least two squad cars to back them up, but not to switch on their sirens and to stay well out of sight of the Clery building until she gave them the signal to move in.

Traffic up to the Old Mallow Road was slow, but Detective Caffrey weaved in and out of it, and ran through two red lights, and it took them less than ten minutes to reach the Clery building. It was set back from the road behind unkempt hedges, a five-storey concrete building streaked by years of rain and pollution. They parked outside and made their way cautiously towards the entrance. Four cars were lined up in the yard at the back of the building, a Toyota Land Cruiser, a Range Rover, an Audi and a large black Mercedes saloon.

Through the grimy windows of the reception area, Katie could dimly see at least five men standing around smoking. They must be Thomas O'Flynn's and Barry Riordan's bodyguards, hard chaws who usually spat at each other and shouted obscene insults and gave each other V-signs. Now they were so engaged in conversation that they failed to notice Katie and her three detectives until they ran quickly and quietly up each side of the front steps and swung open the wide glass door.

All four detectives were armed, and they fanned out and levelled their pistols at the bodyguards while Robert shouted, 'Hands on your heads! All of you! *Now!*'

The five men slowly raised their hands, looking bewildered rather than aggressive. One of them started to lower his right hand so that he could take a drag at his cigarette, but Robert said, 'Drop that fag! Don't even think about it!'

Katie went up to the tallest of the five men. He had a shaved head and white scars on either side of his mouth where he had obviously been given a Croppy Boy smile with a razor. She recognized him as one of Barry Riordan's gang who had occasionally sat beside him in court during the trial of Donal Hagerty.

'Where are they?' she asked him.

He didn't answer, so she looked away for a moment and then looked back at him.

'What if I arrest you for obstructing a Garda inquiry? You know the penalty for that, do you? A three thousand euro fine or six months in prison. Or both.'

While she was confronting him, Detectives Caffrey and O'Sullivan were going from one man to the other, patting the pockets of their coats. They lifted out two automatics, a Browning and a Sig-Sauer, and four knives, including a machete.

'Where are they?' Katie repeated.

'Who d'ye mean?'

'Are you thick or what? You know full well who I mean. Your boss Barry Riordan and Thomas O'Flynn.'

'Upstairs,' one of the other men told her, a short, skinny Afro-Irish fellow with frizzy hair. 'Second floor. It's the only room in the building with chairs and a table.'

'Well, thanks a million for that,' Katie told him. 'Ronan – Jamie – would you check if our backup's turned up yet? If they have, tell them to come in and arrest these clowns, would you?'

'Hey, we've done nothing,' protested one of the men. 'We only came in here for a smoke, like.'

'Trespassing on private property carrying loaded firearms and knives is hardly what I'd call "nothing",' Katie told him. 'You're going to be lucky if you end up in Rathmore Road for less than a year.'

She saw that the staircase was over on the left-hand side of the reception area. It was unlikely that the lift was working, and even if it were, the sound of it would give Thomas O'Flynn and Barry Riordan an early warning that somebody was coming.

She said, 'DI Fitzpatrick?'

If the two gangsters were upstairs by themselves, she didn't think that she and Robert would have any trouble in arresting them. She knew that Thomas O'Flynn never carried a gun, any more than he ever carried a phone.

They climbed the stairs as quietly as they could, even though the treads were covered in crunchy grit. When they reached the second-storey landing they saw that one of the office doors was wide open, and they could hear voices.

Katie paused, her pistol raised in her right hand, and listened. Then she turned to Robert and frowned and silently mouthed the words, *Who's that talking?*

They weren't men's voices. They were women's, and they were sharp and angry. Katie could hear one of them saying, 'You don't think you deserve this? Really? You never thought you'd die all peaceful in your sleep and go to Heaven, did you? You pathetic shitehawk!'

'Come on,' said Katie. She and Robert stepped into the office with their pistols gripped in both hands and Katie shouted, *'Freeze!'*

She could hardly believe the sight that met them. The office was bare except for a dusty boardroom table and six chairs. It was gloomy in there, because the windows were covered with broken venetian blinds, but a crucifix of sunshine lay across the middle of the table, which gave it the appearance of an altar.

Thomas O'Flynn was sitting on the left of the table and Barry Riordan was sitting on the right. Barry Riordan was holding a cigarette, although it had burned almost all the way down to the filter and left a caterpillar of grey ash on the tabletop, so he clearly hadn't been smoking it.

Standing behind Barry was Megan, still with a plaster across the bridge of her nose. Close behind Thomas was Muireann, all dressed in black – black roll-neck sweater and black jeans and boots. Both of them were holding Glock automatics, pointed at the heads of their respective partners.

Muireann glanced quickly at Katie, but neither she nor Megan lowered their pistols. The muzzles were less than seven centimetres away from the back of the men's heads. Thomas and Barry were staring at each other and Katie had never seen expressions like theirs on anybody's faces before. It was an extraordinary mixture of fatalism and contempt.

'Muireann, Megan, come on now... put the guns down,' Katie coaxed them.

Muireann vigorously shook her head. 'There's no way, Kathleen. No way at all. This is what I've been building up to for months. If I'd been able to lay my hands on a gun sooner I would have done it sooner, believe me. You know why I got myself involved with this bastard... why I put up with his putrid smell and the disgusting taste of him and let him have his way with me when he wasn't so polluted that he couldn't stand up, let alone get his langer up.'

There were tears in her eyes but she continued to speak firmly and angrily. 'God alone knows what my poor young sister Bryanna saw in him when she first met him. Whatever it was, it wasn't enough to make her stay with him long. She tried to get away from him but he dragged her back and got her addicted to the crack so that she'd never leave him again. And within three months she was dead of an overdose.'

'That was her own stupid fault,' put in Thomas. 'I wasn't even home at the time. You can't fecking blame me for it.'

'What do you mean, you toad? Who got her on to the stuff in the first place?'

'It was her that wanted to try it out, like, and you can't say that she wasn't old enough to make up her own mind. So curiosity killed the fecking cat. But don't you go pointing the finger at me.'

'Holy Mary, Tommy,' said Muireann. 'This world is going

to be a far better place to live in once you're gone. I thank Megan here for fetching me this gun because I'm going to have sweet dreams for the rest of my life about blowing your head off.'

'Muireann—' said Katie.

'No, Kathleen, I'm not putting down the gun and the only way you can stop me is to kill me. My Bryanna is standing here right beside me now, or at least the ghost of her is, and she would never forgive me if I didn't give Tommy the punishment that he should have been given before he was even born. He should have been aborted. I'm only doing what his mother should have done, even if it is forty years too late.'

'Megan, put down the gun,' Katie told her.

Megan shook her head, too. 'The day that your husband smashes your face into your kitchen sink, then you can tell me that I'm wrong to do this. And you know as well as I do that he's had other people killed himself. Poor Billy Hagerty – he had *him* done for, for one, and what harm did Billy Hagerty ever do to anybody?'

Katie could faintly hear the echoes of shouting from the reception area downstairs. The uniformed backup must have arrived to take away the bodyguards.

'I'm going to give you one last warning, Muireann. You too, Megan. Put down the guns, put up your hands, and step away from the table.'

'Are you deaf, or some kind of mongo?' said Barry, turning his head around. 'You heard what Mrs Maguire told you, and she's the law.'

There was a moment of extreme tension. Megan shifted from one foot to the other, and nervously licked her lips. Muireann pointed her pistol even closer to the back of Thomas's head. Beside her, Katie could see out of the corner of her eye that Robert was lifting his pistol and aiming it at Megan.

'No, Robert,' she said very quietly, and she reached out with her left hand to lower his pistol down again.

Megan fired. Even though Katie had been prepared for it, the bang still made her jump. Half of Barry's face was blasted away in a shower of blood and jawbone. His tongue lolloped out of the side of his mouth and one eye was left dangling on a string of optic nerve.

A split second later, Muireann fired. The top of Thomas's skull flapped up like a pelican's beak and his brains were splattered in bloody beige lumps all across the table. Some of them clung to the front of Barry's coat.

Both men's heads dropped forward, surrounded by acrid whorls of gun smoke.

'Holy Christ in Heaven,' said Robert, lifting up his pistol again. But both Muireann and Megan laid their guns on the table and raised their hands. They were trembling, and their faces were as white as if they had been dusted in flour, and it was obvious to Katie that they were deeply shocked.

'Muireann – Megan – I'm arresting you both for murder,' she said. 'You are not obliged to say anything unless you wish to do so, but anything you say will be taken down in writing and may be given in evidence.'

'That was for Bryanna,' said Muireann. 'Now my poor darling sister can rest in peace.'

Megan raised her chin as if she were proud of what she had done.

'That was for me,' she said.

As soon as she spoke, Barry's body slid sideways off his chair and thumped on to the floor.

***

They stepped outside the building to get some fresh air and wait for the ambulance and the technical team. The bodyguards had all been driven away in two Garda vans and would be up in front of the court tomorrow morning. Muireann and Megan had been taken away in separate squad cars. The media had already got wind of what had happened and were gathering on the opposite side of the Old Mallow Road.

Katie was sitting on the front steps when her phone rang.

'Bill Phinner, ma'am. There's a team of six technicians just left.'

'Thanks, Bill.'

'I also thought you'd like to know that your idea about Eamonn O'Malley was bang on, to coin a phrase. Me and the team were overthinking it, checking out all those fancy compressing machines. His head *was* crushed in a car door, and what's more we've even been able to identify which car. A Toyota Land Cruiser, such as was registered to Thomas O'Flynn. There's even the indentation of lettering on the side of his skull.'

'I think the same Land Cruiser is up here now at Clery's. You'll be able to check it for sure now.'

'It's a pure shame you won't be able to arrest him. I would have liked to have seen his face when we told him that we'd not only found O'Malley's body but worked out how he was killed.'

'There's no chance of that, Bill. He doesn't have a face any more.'

51

Katie's meeting with Assistant Commissioner Frank Magorian the following afternoon was so low-key that it was more like a quiet discussion about what arrangements they should be making for an unloved relative's funeral.

Frank stood by his office window, looking out, as if he were talking to somebody who was standing on the window ledge outside. Katie sat in the tub-like leather chair in front of his desk, her head slightly bowed. She hadn't slept all night and she was feeling frayed and exhausted.

'Your decision not to open fire on those two women and thereby prevent them from shooting Thomas O'Flynn and Barry Riordan was perfectly understandable,' Frank intoned. 'However, your judgement will have to be evaluated by the National Bureau of Crime Investigation and even as high up as the ministry. In the meantime, I will have to suspend you from duty.'

'Yes, sir. I understand that. But of course I wasn't about to shoot two women in cold blood when they were threatening to kill two of the most serious gangsters that Cork has ever known. And as I've told you, I have evidence that Barry Riordan was guilty of conspiracy to murder and I expect shortly to have evidence that Thomas O'Flynn was guilty of murder.'

'Well, that's good. If your evidence against them is accepted in court, it's likely that your action will be considered to have been justified. What's your evidence against Barry Riordan?'

'This can come out now, since Riordan is no longer a threat to my informant. But you'll see that it implicates a fellow officer.'

Katie opened the envelope on her lap and took out a copy of the letter that Owen Dineen had given her, only that morning. She held it up and Frank came away from the window and took it. He stood reading it for a long time before he spoke.

'This is a very serious allegation indeed. I shall have to raise this with Chief Superintendent O'Kane immediately.'

'Owen Dineen didn't give me permission to show that letter to anybody else except for Chief Superintendent O'Kane. But now it's a question of my career or his, and I'm afraid my career as a senior Garda officer has to take precedence over his career as a reporter of sensational news stories.'

Again, Frank was silent. Then he said, 'What was his motive? I mean, *why* did Chief Superintendent O'Kane want you to be given such critical write-ups in the press?'

'You'll have to ask him that, sir. He has several personal reasons for feeling such enmity towards me, but I wouldn't wish to discuss them unless he brought them up, and in any event only in front of a proper Ombudsman hearing.'

'Very well, Kathleen. I'll take it from there. Meanwhile, I have to ask you to leave the station promptly. I'll be in touch with you when a decision has been made about your actions in regard to Thomas O'Flynn and Barry Riordan. Whatever the outcome of this, your performance during your time here as detective superintendent has been superlative. I've probably failed to compliment you as often as I should have done – but then, well, you know me. In any case, I'm offering you my praise and my appreciation right now, and I hope that'll go some way to make up for it.'

Katie went back to her own office to collect her purse and her coat.

'What's happening?' asked Moirin. 'Where are you going? I thought you were holding a media conference this afternoon.'

'I'm suspended, Moirin. Not for ever, with any luck. But thanks for everything, and most especially that never-ending supply of cappuccinos.'

She drove home to Carrig View. When she arrived there, she rang Kieran. He was still in court, but she left a message for him. She sat down in her living room next to the ashes of last night's fire, feeling as if the whole world had suddenly come to a dead stop, and the clock would stay at 3:37 for ever. She wondered what it would be like if it never grew dark.

She took Barney and Foltchain all the way down to Whitepoint Moorings, where there was a path that ran alongside the harbour. The wind was ruffling the wide stretch of silvery-grey water but it also made her feel refreshed.

She was still standing by the railings with the two dogs sitting beside her when her phone rang. It was Kyna, and she sounded as if she were crying.

'Frank Magorian's told me that I'm suspended and that even if they decide that I can stay on, I'll have to be transferred.'

'Oh, no. Oh, Jesus. It's that Brendan. He's been talking to Brendan and I'll bet you anything you like that Brendan showed him those pictures of you and me. He swore *blind* that he'd deleted them, but I never believed him.'

Kyna found it difficult to speak for a moment, but then she said, 'Anyhow, Katie, you know I'm not the one for you.'

'How can you say that? You know how much I love you.'

469

'I know you do. I know. But it's a man you need in your life. You need someone like Kieran. Someone who can look after you properly. Someone who can give you another baby, like Seamus, God bless his little soul. I can't do anything but mess up your career. I just hope I haven't messed it up now.'

'Kyna, please. Don't be upset. Kyna, please don't cry. Why don't you come down here to Cobh tomorrow and we can spend the day together.'

'It's no use, Katie. You need a husband. I'm no good for you at all.'

'Kyna—'

But Kyna had gone, and Katie was left by the harbour with the wind blowing and only the dogs for company.

She tried ringing Kyna several times during the evening, but Kyna didn't pick up. Katie hoped she'd feel better when the shock and dismay of being suspended had worn off.

The lead story on *Ireland News* the following morning was the shooting of Thomas O'Flynn and Barry Riordan. It was also reported that both Chief Superintendent O'Kane and Detective Superintendent Maguire had been suspended 'as a matter of procedure'. No further details were given about either of them.

Katie had always imagined that she would feel a surge of vengeful satisfaction if she managed to get Brendan sacked from his job. There was no doubt in her mind that he would be permanently dismissed for the offence of bribing a news reporter, especially to libel a fellow officer. Somehow, though, it only made her feel empty and slightly depressed. It had all been so mean and pointless.

She rang Kieran. Maybe they would be able to meet for dinner again tonight and he would put a smile on her face. But again, he didn't answer.

She decided to drive down to the centre of Cobh for lunch at The Quays. She didn't like eating on her own but she could text all her friends during the meal, and she loved their seafood chowder.

When she opened the front door, she was surprised to see Kieran climbing out of the passenger seat of a taxi.

'Kieran! Aren't you in court today?'

He came up the steps of her porch. 'No,' he said. 'The Gallagher Finance case was adjourned until next week.'

'You should have told me you were coming. But never mind. I was about to head off to lunch. Now I'll have someone to talk to.'

'Katie—'

'Ah, right. You got my message about my being suspended. But you don't have to look so grim about it. I'm sure it'll all be sorted out. Those were two of the worst villains ever that were shot. I don't know what you think, being a judge, but it wouldn't surprise me if Muireann and Megan were only given suspended sentences.'

'This is nothing to do with your suspension, Katie. DI Fitzpatrick knows that we're friendly and so he rang me and asked me if I'd tell you this in person.'

Katie suddenly felt icy cold.

'What is it?' she asked him. 'What's happened?'

'It's bad news, I'm afraid. It's Detective Ní Nuallán. It's Kyna.'

At that moment, a ship leaving the harbour let out a loud, mournful moan, like a mother whale who has lost her young. It echoed across the estuary and echoed again from Monkstown, where Katie's late father used to live.

Katie said, 'You'd best come inside, Kieran.'

Kieran stepped into the hallway.

'Do you want me to take off my shoes?' he asked her.

'No. Yes. It doesn't matter,' she said, and closed the door.